THE HANDS OF LYR

ANDRE NORTON

THE HANDS OF LYR

An AvoNova Book

William Morrow and Company, Inc.
New York

AVON BOOKS
A division of
The Hearst Corporation
1350 Avenue of the Americas
New York, New York 10019

Copyright © 1994 by Andre Norton
Published by arrangement with the author
Library of Congress Catalog Card Number: 93-45829
ISBN: 0-688-13417-3

Library of Congress Cataloging in Publication Data:

Norton, Andre.
  The hands of Lyr / Andre Norton.
    p.   cm.
  I. Title.
PS3527.O632H36   1994   93-45829
813'.52—dc20   CIP

First Morrow/AvoNova Printing: June 1994

AVONOVA TRADEMARK REG. U.S. PAT. OFF. AND IN OTHER COUNTRIES, MARCA REGISTRADA, HECHO EN U.S.A.

Printed in the U.S.A.

ARC   10   9   8   7   6   5   4   3   2   1

THE HANDS OF LYR

Chapter 1

THE RYFT WAS DESOLATION, A SEARED scar rendered so by the brute force of men and the curse of Black power. Above, grey clouds roiled endlessly; any trace of sun, winning through by chance, brought neither warmth nor healing to barren earth long lost to life. The river which divided the Ryft into nearly equal parts was a sullen, twisting stream, its shores entangled now and then with skeletons of short-lived reeds.

There remained still marks of what had existed here—tumbled foundation stones of once snug garths, small but prosperous manors. Dark splotches created memories of former orchards, the trees now only charred butts, long burned.

To the north loomed the Heights of Askad, that pass cutting them showing like the slice left by a great war sword. Once the Great Highway had run there, but during the last frantic struggle between defender and invader the cliffs themselves had been summoned by shadowy and forbidden means to choke that passage, burying men and animals alike in rubble to close the way.

Westward was a snarl of cliffs, clefts, caves, peaks—a

wild and haunted country upon which man might never have set seal of ownership. To the east was another stretch of Heights, not so forbidding once on a time, but now displaying the stolidness of a keep wall—imprisoning the Ryft. Southward—yes, the remains of the old Highway wound there but the river was gulped down by a chasm and what lay beyond was desert without the water that had once meant sustenance for travelers.

She had been waiting since before dawn, that bone thin woman in a much-mended robe as grey now with age and the grime, which not even the most strenuous attempts to cleanse it loosened, as the rocks among which she half sheltered.

Wind crossed the Ryft, not bringing any scent of growing things, rather a faint taint of old death and forgotten fires. It stirred the flap of the hood which lay back across the watcher's shoulders, pulled at the ragged wisps of grey hair which had been knife hacked short but which fringed in her grey-brown face until she lifted an impatient hand to push them away.

No beauty in that face—the nose was the beak of a winged hunter, the eyes were deep set, the mouth a slit narrowed sternly to repress. Yet here was life alone in the Ryft—life and an impeccable purpose housed in one skeleton stick of a body.

She faced north as she had been doing since the first lightening of dawn, searching with eyes still keen, also with that inner sense which perhaps was rusty from lack of use for so many years. Her mouth tightened even more. Yes! There could be no denying what was coming—after so long—so very long!

Movement afar, some small dots of figures were emerging onto the black stretch of the Highway where it left the Pass of Askad behind. Not soldiers . . .

She who had once been named Dreen, when there were those still living to call her so, twisted her hands

in the braided rope which formed her girdle. Her pale
tongue showed between her lips, moistening them.
Ready . . .

But, once that stumbling procession advanced farther
down the Highway, she edged swiftly back into a crevice
between two upstanding rocks. Having drawn up her
hood and pressed herself against the stone which was
the same color as her robe, she stood completely motionless, so was lost to any but the keenest and most
searching sight.

Nosh wavered forward step by stumbling step. Soon,
she thought dimly, she was going to fall. And today there
was no Ilda to urge her up. She gulped but she was too
worn and wrung to cry. Her eyes were fixed, not upon
the pair of children plodding hopelessly ahead, rather
she saw what had broken her at their dawn rising—the
blood, the dusty, matted strip of hair.

Ilda must have crawled out of Nosh's sleep-loosened
embrace, slid from beneath the scrap of blanket they
shared, venturing out of the campsite to relieve herself,
for she had been ailing with cramps for the day. Then,
when Nosh aroused at the sounds of sighs and moans of
the awakening camp, to go a-hunting . . . The wakwolves had found this pitiful band of refugees easy prey,
picking off a night's rations at their desires.

They were children, all of them, stumbling in that
lagging hopeless march. Once, Nosh could not remember now how long ago, they had been gathered together,
given shelter of a sort, food—her stomach ached when
she thought of food . . . She had met Ilda there and they
had bonded, as did all the children sooner or later.

Then the soldiers had come. There had been spears
and swords and those who had striven to save the children were cut down. Like a herd of small animals their
charges had been driven out, followed, killed if they

lagged. She and Ilda had wondered often why they had not been slain at once like Haggeen and Farker and the rest of those who had tried to shelter them. But for some reason, known only to these who rode bony horses and wore rusted armor, they had been merely set in motion, sent marching south.

For some reason, as unknown as that which started them on this cruel journey, their herders provided them with a small measure of meal, and they had caught rock lizards, torn lichens free from rocks to eat. Though some of those killed rather than assuaged the ever-present hunger.

Three days ago they had reached a blockage of the Highway where a wall of fallen rock provided barrier. There their guard had halted but urged them on and because they had no other place to go, they did.

Few of them were left; Nosh could not count the survivors. She did not even care. Ilda was gone and soon she, also, would feel teeth at her throat and know the death which comes to helpless prey.

She became aware that there was no longer any struggle up and over rocks. Instead the Highway was clear and open and reached downward at a gentle slope. She had straggled even farther behind but that meant nothing to her now. She did not even know why she kept on, yet something in her gave her a whisper of strength and set her forward.

Then she stepped upon a sharp edge of stone. Her ragged sandals had long since worn away and the sudden pain of that jerked her back into the here and now. There was water—a river ahead. The foremost of their small company had reached its banks. She dropped into the dust and rubbed her foot. Looking along the downslope to that curl of water. She was thirsty.

"Alnosha!"

The child's head jerked about. Had she heard that

low call, or had she only thought it? No one had given
her that name for a long, long time—how long she could
not remember.

"Alnosha!"

Surely that call came from the rocks beside the Highway. But no one, not even Ilda, had known her as anything but Nosh.

"I am"—some instinct of wariness made her answer—"Nosh."

The tall rock moved. No, it was a person, a woman
in a long robe the same color as the stones.

"You are Alnosha," the woman said and knelt beside
her; taking from a pouch at her belt a small greenish
cake, she forced it into Nosh's half-reluctant hand.

"Eat, child."

The cake had an odd smell but Nosh crunched it between her teeth, tearing off a great mouthful as if she
feared this treasure might be snatched from her. The
woman had taken up the child's foot and was touching
with care the bruise rising from the stone.

"No skin break, that is good. This land is poisoned;
sometimes even the dust can bring death. But we do not
need to linger here, Alnosha. There is already a place
prepared for you."

Before the small girl could move, the woman, with
strength one might have thought beyond her spare figure, swept her up and was carrying her.

"They—the others—help for them?" Some dim
memory, near leached out of her by the death march,
made her remember the rest.

"There are many fates spun by Lyr, little one. I have
only knowledge of one; I can only offer aid at Her command. Those others must finish out their own life weaving as She has set it. For you, Alnosha, there is here a
new pattern."

She wove a way among standing rocks until she came

to a site where there had once been walls set and these had remained largely in place though they were stained by fire marks. There were still two stout rooms, remaining walled and roofed.

Faint traces of paint could be seen in the curves of complicated carvings on those walls. There was a pallet made of woven reed mats against that wall which bore a curve of crystal, part of the rock itself. The woman placed Nosh on the pallet.

She moved with her quick stride to a corner where there was a stone chest, shoving with her hand until its lid slid along and gave her an opening through which she brought out a packet of dried leaves.

Nosh finished the cake, licking the last of the crumbs carefully from her dirty fingers. She did not ask for more—there had never been a second helping of any rations given her in the past.

The woman crumbled one of the leaves from her bundle, rubbing it carefully between the palms of her hands as if those were millstones and she were grinding meal. Then she took the dusty fragments in one palm and reached for a gourd from which she dribbled water onto what she held to form a paste. Having mixed this to her satisfaction, she came back to Nosh.

"Let us tend this, child." Her fingers patted the paste over the bruise. Once done she sat back on her heels to meet the girl eye to eye.

"I am Dreen," she said. "In these years that is all the name I claim."

"You live here?" Nosh's curiosity had awakened from the stupor of the early morning.

"Here and abouts," Dreen returned somewhat evasively. "And now you shall also, little one. For She has so decreed it."

"She?" questioned Nosh.

Dreen's stern mouth quirked as if she would smile and yet could not remember the way of it.

"Our Lady Lyr, little Alnosha. But you will learn all about that in future. For now it is one thing at a time. Such as a good dollop of faxchon stew."

There was a fire burning in one corner of the room set on a well-built hearth and from a kettle slung over the low flame there came a smell which made Nosh swallow. Dreen used a ladle to fill a bowl carved from stone, but so well that its sides appeared no thicker than might those of an earthenware pot. Its rim gleamed with a ring of silver and there were more of the worn carvings over its outside.

Nosh took it carefully in both hands. The heat of it felt comforting. She could guess it was still too hot to mouth but she turned it around and around, striving so to cool it until she dared attempt to try the contents.

Like the warmth on her hands, so did the thick substance in her mouth, sliding down her throat, bring a new feeling she could not yet put name to and which was like a blanket about her shoulders against the chill thrust of the wind.

She gulped it all, for the portion was small, and then, without any manners, polished the interior with her tongue, striving not to miss the last possible taste.

Dreen had left her eating and was moving about. She had returned the bundle of soothing herb leaves to the chest, closed it, and now she had gone to the opposite side of the room. Here a ledgelike slab, apparently hewn also of stone, jutted out of the wall, supported on the outer corners by pillar legs of rock. Arranged along the back of this table were a number of thick books, their outer covers much worn, so that the leather that covered the thin sections of protecting wood was scuffed and torn in places.

Books—Nosh knew what they were. Once—yes, once she had seen some like those. They were—they were being thrown into a great fire. And there were soldiers there and—and one in red and black. . . .

Her breath caught as that memory stirred. Books—many soldiers came and others—and they—killed.

First the books and then the round-faced man in the ink-splattered green robe. His features made for gentleness and laughter, now a mask of terror. They had . . . thrown him also. She had tried to scream and a hand had closed over her mouth, cruelly gagging her as she was wrenched away into darkness.

When that darkness had lifted she had been in the half-roofed hut with Ilda and she had fought memory, living only for the hour that was now, looking no day ahead and no day back.

"They burn books," she said. Dreen should be warned; the woman had been good to her. Maybe she did not know what horrors followed possessing books.

Dreen, standing by the table, her hand outstretched to take one of those volumes, looked over her shoulder at Nosh.

"Yes. Books are knowledge, child, the distilling of knowledge from many minds and times. If they can be destroyed, then much that should be known is lost. Yes, those with whom you have been burn books."

"They can come here . . . " Nosh tried to make her warning clearer.

"They will have no reason. All who dwelt here are now dead. I do not think we shall see invaders again. He who sent them has done the worst that his power would allow him to accomplish. These books remain and you, Alnosha, shall learn of them—for it cannot be otherwise. I dreamed the reaching dream, and you came even as I saw you would do."

And thus it was that Nosh began indeed a new weaving and there came a second life into the Ryft. Hard as their existence was, she grew and learned—and not the least—discovered her gift.

Chapter 2

IN SPITE OF ALL THE LAMPS IN THE WALL brackets, the torch standards, the great hall below was murky and the coils of throat-drying incense smoke gathered in a fog-cloud. Kryn kept the moistened cloth tight in his left hand, using it at closer and closer intervals to mask his mouth and nose, his only weapon against some whooping sneeze which might or might not catch the attention of someone in that crowd around the altar below.

He had inched out on this beam two hours since, using the one chance when the priests were at their evening meal and so the guardianship of the inner shrine was but a formality. After all, who dared the wrath of the Voice of Zellon to invade the sanctuary in such a heretical fashion?

The weight of the novice's robe, which he had used all his cunning born of the teaching of woodcraft hunting to snag from a hook, wrapped him too snugly—it was hot here but he dared not make any move to relieve the ache of joints. His perch already made his head swim and he fought to keep under the sour sickness which surged upward from his belly into the back of his raw throat.

Sick—yes, he was sick—ill from more than just the heavy taint of the incense, the heat, the height from which he must look down at the shame of his House. His House—on his lean boy's face his lips drew back to show teeth as might those of a threatened wakwolf cub.

Would they never be done with that harsh chant which punished the ears? Yes, they were giving this occasion all the ceremony they could think to summon. It was not every day that the Voice could bring down one of the remaining High Houses. This was a triumph for Valcur indeed, one he would want to draw out to the fullest extent. Back, row on row, in the hall, their attention all for the altar, were those he would bend to his will.

Kryn blinked as he noted the blue tabbards of Zine, the black and green of Goran, the rust red of Jaspar. Let them watch—were they too blind to understand that what was to happen to Qunion now would not long be withheld from encompassing them in turn?

There—there—he forced his eyes to center on that fourth patch of color—rich brown of his own wearing. He swallowed quickly and wiped the cloth across his smarting eyes as well as his tingling nose. Kryn had no wish to see *THOSE* any better.

The chanting halted on a sharp upward note. That miter-crowned and awesomely robed figure moved out to stand before the altar. He turned, with great ceremony, to salute the altar itself—there was no embodiment of statue or symbol here—the All Knowing and All Being was not to be so reduced in the eyes of His servants.

Then Valcur swept about once more to face the congregation gathered there. To his left was a figure wear-

ing the dull grey of the land slaves, a red cord across
one shoulder giving him the rank of overseer; to his right
was one of the Temple guard, an officer whose over-
shadowing helm made him unrecognizable to the young
spy overhead.

A sullen roar sounded, emitted by the trumpet fashioned from the curled horn of a field varge—such a summons as brought slaves to their labor. There came a
moment of silence, as if everyone under the high curve
of that roof held their breath.

Then out of that knot of brown came a man in fighting mail, though unhelmed, carrying that head covering
in one arm, his other touching the hilt of his sheathed
sword.

Again Kryn swiped his hand across his eyes. Hot
words were on his lips; he forced them back. His mouth
worked, his tongue gathered saliva, he spat.

Valcur waited as the warlord came forward. There was
no uncertainty about *his* stance; he had no fears that this
prey well within the nets he and his had spread would
be hard to handle now—no, it was as it had been three
times in the past four years—another House was to be
erased from the Rolls of the High Born.

The warrior stood at the foot of the steps leading up
to the altar. His head was tilted up, his eyes fast on the
Voice. There was still that silence as he dropped the
helmet which rang as it struck the pavement, bounced
and spun back toward the congregation. Unseeing, his
eyes still on the priest, the warrior unfastened his sword
belt, allowed that honored weapon to fall. . . .

Kryn sucked in a breath. His teeth closed upon his
wrist and he bit down upon his own flesh that the pain
might, in some way, keep him from shouting out his
despair and shame.

Now the man below was fumbling, still without looking to see what he was doing, at his mail shirt. That fell

in turn. He stood reft of armor, or house cape; now he wore the coarse grey of the slave.

Valcur reached out a hand toward the overseer on the one step below him, not looking to his servant, with the simple knowledge that he was there and ready to move at his gesture. Into the priest's grasp the man passed a noosed rope. With expert ease, Valcur, having taken one step forward, tossed the loop of that about the head of the once warrior. As it fell on his shoulders the man went to his knees. There was a moan from those behind him—those who had been coerced into following him.

"Hafner, in penitence for your many sins against the One and those who are His servants, you have come to swear bondage of body, of mind, of soul, not only for your own wicked self but for all of those of your shared blood—even unto the end of this world. Is this not your free wish?"

Kryn hid his eyes but he did not stop his ears. That voice now answering—something had gone out of it—it was toneless, the voice of one whose spirit was already dead.

"I do so swear, that my many sins may be forgiven in the labor which I and all of my House and blood will give—through my life and theirs, and their children's—even unto the end of the world."

"Call forth your blood, bondsman," commanded Valcur. "They must come at your call. . . . "

The kneeling man hunched a little around on the surface where he now knelt. His head had sunk forward until his square chin rested against his broad chest.

"Charessa," his voice was still toneless but it had not lost its clarity. "Ylla, Ranor, Sonon—"

There was a cry from that small grouping of brown coats and then a woman came forth, carrying against her breast a small child. Behind her came two boys, their faces set with a kind of horror. One of them held hand to the hilt of a long hunting knife. As he came forward to stand behind his father the guard's officer deftly jerked that out of his reach.

The overseer came forward with the bustle of one about his business holding ready a handful of the noosed ropes. He twirled them out and about, until each of those waiting there had been so symbolically bound. But Valcur, surveying the handful of the degraded, frowned.

"There is another of your blood, bondsman," and there was a snap of anger in his voice. "Where is he?"

"He has betrayed his House, thus he is not," Hafner answered heavily. "He spoke so to his lord that he would have been struck down had he not drawn steel and fought his way out. That one has not been named among us for five days, nor will he ever be again."

"Such a one is outlawed," Valcur said and there was a satisfaction in that. "The Blessing of the One will fall upon anyone who will have his blood. Let it so be proclaimed. Now, bondsman, be sure that your grievous sins will be forgiven and those of your blood will buy peace for you after your ending. . . . "

The officer had picked up the sword Hafner had discarded. Kryn saw him pass it to one of the lesser guard, who bent to also retrieve the helmet and the mail. The overseer caught up the end of the noose about Hafner's neck and gave it a slight jerk as if to arouse the man's attention to the duties of his newly chosen life, and others wearing the grey came forward to so lead his family behind him.

Valcur summoned the guard's officer with a lift of finger and bent his head to confer with him in a low voice. Slowly Kryn's jaws released their hold upon his wrist. He tasted blood. Now, he would have to move. Had he been wise, he would have been well away from here two days ago.

But there was Honor to argue against such wisdom.

The sword Bringhope, which these lorshogs had just borne out of sight. He could not leave that . . . Up to the last he had hoped that this strange stubbornness which had taken possession of his father would be broken. Hafner in the past ten-day had become as another person.

He had had the normal failings of any man but he had never prated before of mortal sin and the need to cleanse his House blood. Kryn had come home from a visit to the hill pasturage to be greeted with such a turn-around in the speech he heard in the great hall that at first he could almost believe that he had indeed wandered into another keephold. And the others—his step-mother—though her eyes had held the shadow of fear—had upheld his father's wild bewailing of his sinning. His half brothers—they seemed cowed and he could get nothing of sense out of them. But the contagion of fear, if fear it was, had not spread to him. He could guess what would happen in the end—this very disgraceful scene he had just watched in sick horror. So he had done what he could to make plans.

The House of Qunion would continue—even if in outlawry. To that he was bound even though his father, in this wild frenzy, had thrown him out. To continue to exist he would need all the wits, training, and luck he could draw upon. However—first there was the sword.

With the ceremony being over, the congregation was filing out. He trusted that those of the other three remaining Houses had taken the lesson to heart. Though Valcur and his invisible god might be so firmly in control now that they would march willing victims to him even as Hafner had done.

Kryn edged backward inch by anxious inch on the beam where he had lain. He believed—or hoped—that the Voice would think him already on the run, certainly not in the very heart of the enemy's territory. Reaching the crawlway from which this beam sprouted, he arose to his hands and knees.

He had never been a fervent follower of the One and the Temple was largely unknown territory. That he had found this secret way in was a piece of fortune he could not count on continuing. But his goal now was the armory of the guard. House swords carried legends—they were not to be used by anyone not of the Blood—every warrior knew that it called down the wrath of Those Gone Before were that to happen. No, he was sure that he could find Bringhope hanging with the other swords of the Houses Valcur had brought down in the past few years—if and when he could reach that storage place.

The twilight had fallen before he managed to extract himself from those upper ways only used by repairmen on whom the upkeep of the temple depended. He pulled the novice's robe tightly about him and wound a way downward by ladder, then by narrow inner wall steps, until he came upon that door which gave upon the courtyard.

Kryn eased that open to a slit through which he could gain some sight of what now lay ahead. The armory of the guards lay to his right beyond his line of sight, and between him and there was a wide stretch of pavement. The guard was coming off patrol—he heard their voices and the clang of a carelessly held spear before he caught sight of the men themselves.

That Valcur had gotten the countryside to accept the fact that he—and the One—maintained a private army was another puzzle. Supposedly the One ruled beneficently. Kryn's lips again shaped a snarl. Why then would His own place need to be so guarded? But it was these guards who, under the oversight of one of the priests, collected the temple tax every fourth month—and they were undoubted useful in controlling such large congregations as had gathered here this day.

Kryn waited. The twilight deepened, broken here and there by just a flare of bracket-mounted torch. There was a thickening of shadows into which his robe might well melt.

He knew nothing of the duties of a novice. Could he be apprehended by being in the wrong place? Messages—could the lesser ones of the temple serve as messengers when there was a need? That could be his only excuse if he were trapped.

There had been very little coming and going before the door when he finally decided to make the attempt. To linger here certainly availed him nothing and time was now an enemy. He must be out of the temple, out of the city, and away from any main road as soon as he could.

Kryn slipped out of the door and stood in the open air, for the first time in hours drawing in breaths which were not scented or dust clogged. There was no moon tonight and the air had a feel that, as a hunter by choice, he recognized as promising rain. So much would he be favored.

He wanted to dart across the courtyard, be as swift about his task as he could. But he held firmly to prudence. Clasping his hands together within the cover of his wide sleeves, having pulled his cowl over his head, he stepped out with the purposefully unhurried tread of one going about a task but not a too-demanding one.

Twice his breath caught a little as he passed others— first a couple of guardsmen plainly off-duty and bound for the delights of the town—and then a true priest. However, the latter did not look in his direction at all, all his attention being directed to the fan of inscribed book leaves he was holding in his hand, in spite of the fact that the dark must have well hid what was written there. Saying some office, Kryn decided.

The armory was to the side of the guardroom, walled

on the other side by the barracks. There were lights within both of those and the sounds of voice but no one moved in either doorway. Then Kryn was at the armory; there was a faint light within which shone through a slit window above his head. He could not be sure there was no one there.

He dared wait no longer. There were tricks even an unarmed man could use for offense and defense. Among the guards of his House there had been men well versed in several outré methods of such. Though he was only a clumsy beginner, he had practiced faithfully and had been able to take on the hulking brute of a poacher he had faced just two ten-days ago when the other had tried to pull steel on him.

Heartened by that memory he tried the door. If it were locked, he knew a couple of other tricks; his acquaintanceship with the guards of merchant travelers was wider than his father had ever guessed. His father— he had no father!

The door yielded and he slipped in. There was someone before him—that officer who had supervised the disposal of his father's dishonored weapons and gear. And, just as Kryn had supposed, he had looped the belt latch of the sword scabbard over a hook on the far wall.

There was a large stand of spears, not unlike a tree's trunk, to his left. Kryn dodged behind that. The officer picked up the hand lamp he had brought and came back toward the door. Kryn waited. No matter how much he hated the man and all he stood for, this was no time to start revenge. If he could come unseen and unhunted out of this place, the better for him now.

The door opened; the officer and his light were gone. Kryn was left in the darkness. Cautiously he began to edge forward, trying to remember what he had sighted in the glow of the now-vanished lamp.

Then his outstretched hand met the wall with some

force and he felt along it for the sword. He did not try to twist the scabbard loose. No, cover his tracks here as the poachers of the Heights did. Instead he caught at the hilt and worked the blade free. Then he felt along that surface until he touched the rack he had remembered. It took only a moment to slide out one of the common blades there and then return to wedge that into Bringhope's place.

Hugging the bared sword against his body, he regained the door. It was locked as he thought it would be but the only weapon he had dared to bring into the temple, a needle thin bootknife, solved the secret of that and once more he was free in the night.

The gates were danger but he already had an answer to those—to win over the wall in the same place where he had earlier entered, and that way he went. Once on the dim-lit street below he took off the robe, wadded it into a ball, and thrust it into one of the sewer openings. Then he strode, with still enough caution to keep to the shadows, back to the small inn where a sign bearing the arms of his own House creaked in the rising wind. Smarle had better repaint that sign as soon as he could—there would be danger in showing the Crown barred sinister now.

The door was shut; there was only the faintest glow in the window. Kryn wrapped softly the agreed upon pattern.

A small gap showed and a voice urged him in.

"It was done then?" the man who bore a disfiguring scar across his cheek asked harshly.

"It was done." Kryn showed him the naked sword.

The other eyed him up and down. "You are young, too young..." he said slowly. "How many summers now?"

"Fifteen," Kryn returned. "But I am no youth tonight."

Smarle leaned forward and looked into his eyes. "No," he agreed flatly, "you are not, my lord."

"Until the betrayed is restored, I am what they have named me, outlaw. I will take to the hills—of those and their ways I have learned somewhat. It was very well that I followed such rough running these past years. I go tonight if the way is open."

"It is open," the innkeeper nodded. "There may be others to follow you. These temple snakes seek to devour or enslave us all."

"Change your sign quickly, Smarle." Kryn was already shrugging his way into the coat the other had ready. There was an empty scabbard too, as if the innkeeper had been very sure of his success. He fitted Bringhope into scuffed leather and picked up the pack on the table. Smarle had already shoved aside a cask of ale and now he was feeling about the floor. His fingers caught in the concealed hollow he sought and he pulled up a trapdoor.

"Good fortune, House Hope," he rasped as the boy swung down into a dark which had been carefully mapped for him.

"Guard yourself, Smarle," he got out as the door fell back into place and he was left to face what time might bring.

Chapter 3

IT WAS DIFFICULT TO MARK THE PASS-
ing of seasons under this never-changing cloud-filled sky
when there were no new leaves to herald the spring,
ripening grain to proclaim summer. There was indeed a
period of chill when the zarks and the other rock creatures disappeared for a time and that might mark winter,
though no snow fell nor did the river ice over.

Nosh knew that she was growing older, for there
were changes in even a body as lean as hers and now
she was near as tall as Dreen. She had become skillful—more so even than Dreen—in several small things
which made their life a little less hard. She had
grubbed in the blasted orchards around those stumps of
trees which now seemed as hard to crack as stone. But
patient rubbing with rough chunks of river gravel
smoothed the pieces she loosened, and, padded with
reed fiber and given thongs of twisted snakeskin, after
several efforts, she turned out sandals. More snakeskin
could be braided into belts and pouches for the carrying
of small objects.

Her weathered hands seemed sometimes strangely
aware before the rest of her as to what could be done

with odd scraps which she saved jealously. And it was her hands which, one morning when she was collecting gravel for one of her scraping chores, at last answered to her gift.

For as she picked out the best bits for her purpose, her fingers seemed of themselves to cup around one piece. There was no sun to see it by but the fingers which pinched it now tingled with a new warmth. Nosh laid the find to one side and then selected what looked to her to be another small chunk twin to the first. But there came no tingling, no feeling that she held something which was more than the rough piece that it looked. Once more she tested that first selection and could not deny the answer in her fingers.

She knew that of old there were indeed things of power. But the devastation of war and the passing of years had turned such into near legends. Had this bit of gravel once been perhaps a part of what men had once treasured as a focus for power? Dreen would know. Spilling the rest of the gravel she had gathered, Nosh hurried back to the rock-hidden house. Breathless in her haste she spun the stone across the table, where the woman sat patiently weaving on a small handloom a section of reed thread cloth into what might be stitched in length into a garment.

"This—it is alive in my hand!" Nosh flexed her fingers. "It is from the river. None else made my hand feel so."

Dreen stared from the excited girl to the bit of gravel and then back to Nosh. Then she reached eagerly for the stone and sat weighing it in her own hand before she turned it over and over, holding it close to her eyes. Finally she reached for her knife—it was very precious, that knife, for it was worked metal and its like could no longer be found in the Ryft.

Recklessly, first holding the stone close to her eyes,

the woman pecked at one spot on the surface of the piece. She worked with infinite care for her precious tool but somehow she managed to chip away a fingernail length of the covering. What lay beneath was smooth, and, even in the limited light, Nosh could see the color—not blood red, not the brazen of the desert sun— but some hue between those.

"Eye of sun." Dreen let it fall to the tabletop. Then swiftly she arose and went to one of those stone storage chests, one she had never opened in Nosh's presence. She brought out a bag of aged hide, dusty and flaking. And from it she poured a number of pieces of stone, some showing flecks of color, some as dull as the rock walls about them.

"Take them up," she ordered Nosh. "Name what is here!"

Wonderingly the girl obeyed. And from somewhere she did not understand she named names—named them with the surety as if she actually saw what she examined:

"Sun eye, moon tear, sky skin." One by one she set them in a row. "Another sky skin, two night drops, a moon tear, but it is flawed." (What made her say that?)

"Sun eye of the day, another of the evening hour." She had indeed named them all.

Dreen was staring at her and, without dropping that gaze, raised her right hand to the neck of the robe she wore. She drew out a thong of skin to which was attached a small woven net imprisoning something which gleamed and blinked even under this dull light.

The woman hesitated for a long moment and then she pulled the thong over her head and, cradling the net and contents in her hand, she held out her treasure to Nosh.

"Touch!" Her voice was a whisper.

Nosh obeyed. Then she gave a small cry. There was flame in that netted gem, enough to make her put her finger to her mouth as if she would lick-soothe a burn.

"I . . . there is no name . . . "

Dreen nodded. "Not easily found in this world now, child. You might deal in gems all life long and not handle such as this. This is star-bright, akin to something greater which has been long lost. But it is enough that you have the Hand gift. It will serve you well. For it has many sides—and you will come to learn them. You can tell false stones from the true, flawed from the flawless, and perhaps even it will be given to you to read the past of those of great note, which is a power in itself."

"What—how can it serve us here and now?" asked Nosh slowly. She was no longer afraid, but rather beginning to wonder how any such gift might aid in some way to better their harsh life.

"For here and now you must use it for searching. Even as you have trained your eyes for the reading and your hands for writing, your tongue for speaking, so must you now make familiar to you this gift."

Thus Nosh did search the gravel from time to time, for some short period each day, and the little pile of rough gems began to plump out a reed bag of her own. She especially occupied herself so during Dreen's absences from their shelter.

Life in the Ryft followed a harsh pattern but Nosh had known little else for a long time and what she found here now was far better than what lay behind. She learned the trick of turning over the flat stones lapped by the dusky river water and clapping hand expertly over the wriggling creatures so exposed.

Certain of the dull dark reeds could be twisted out of the mud, washed, dried out by spreading thinly over the nearest level rock. Then their roots could be sawed off with a stone-bladed knife supplied by Dreen. Such roots, ground between stones, formed a coarse powder near enough to meal to be made into cakes and baked. While the stems, pounded against rocks, twisted and turned, split into ragged fiber threads for weaving.

There were plants to be found also. Dreen had showed her on the second day of her coming into the Ryft a patch of black soil which appeared to still hold some use for growing things and pointed out to her the sprouting leaves straggling there, herbs to be treasured.

Lizards and snakes were to be found among the crags but of these Dreen made careful choice. One could stone and skin, for example, a fat-bodied, many-legged thing which wore a sprinkling of yellow spots across its scaled skin. But the slender silver-scaled snake making its home within one of the rocky pockets was not to be disturbed.

One could seek out the horny-backed, rusty toad, but the frill-necked lizards which ran when disturbed on hind feet like a miniature person—those were to be spared.

At first Nosh thought that these taboos were born from the belief that the flesh of snake or lizard contained some poison. However, she came to realize quickly that there was another and perhaps greater reason for the immunity. The first time she saw Dreen, seated beside a rock, one of the silver snakes swaying before her, Nosh had grabbed at the weapon of her own devising, a leaf-shaped stone she had managed with much effort to secure with reed cords to a long dead branch pulled out of the sour soil. The branch she had tested for sturdiness and she was proud of her weapon-tool.

"Not so," Dreen's voice cut through the girl's fear. "This one is not any threat to us. Behold!" She held out her hand and the snake, swaying yet closer, appeared to caress her hard flesh with its flicking tongue.

"So also is the zark—" The woman gestured to her right and there were three of the lizard things, standing upright but leaning a little back, so that their tails were supports to hold them erect. They might have drawn near in desire to confront Dreen for some reason.

The woman hissed, and in Nosh's ears the sound was close to that made by the snake before her. Then, turning her head a little, she made somehow a clicking sound. At last she spoke in a very low voice:

"Sit still, child, let these learn you, for you will find times when they may be for you both weapon and guide."

In spite of her inner shrinking Nosh slowly put the crude axe-club down and sat watching the snake. It had slewed around and was now facing in her direction, its pupilless eyes full upon her. Like a stream of clear water it uncoiled and flowed until it was before her even as it had been with Dreen.

"Put out your hand, Nosh." Though the woman's voice remained low, there was the snap of a command in it.

Nosh made herself obey. The snake had recoiled and began again the swaying of its head. She could mark the strong fangs in its mouth and she doubted that those were there for appearance only. Then—she felt the lightest of touch from the forked tongue.

"So," Dreen's words came almost as a croon, "now you are known and you must learn what this tie will mean for you, but that learning comes from within you."

She looked again to the waiting lizards and clicked. The foremost of the three leaped from its stand. As the snake flowed away to make room the frilled one had squatted before the girl.

"Again—your hand—" Dreen ordered.

She did not feel quite the same shrinking this time. There was something about this zark (as Dreen had named it) which interested her, but did not raise her fear. She held out her hand and watched in something close to awe as that head bent so that the creature seemed to sniff at her knuckles.

Dreen appeared to relax a fraction, and nodded as if she answered some question which had not been voiced. She might have been giving a signal for the snake; the lizards were gone with flashing suddenness.

Thereafter during the days when she went hunting Nosh was often aware that she was under observation and would look up to see one of those scaled heads peeping over a rock or around some time-hardened chunk of half-burned wood.

But it was not only the seeking of food—though that was of first importance—which occupied Dreen and Nosh during those days. Though the land about them was so definitely dead, there were storms at intervals which whirled the dust of the long-uncultivated fields into fogs and kept them both under cover. And when that happened Dreen would light one of the bowl lamps—striking flint to the worn knife blade to induce a spark onto the reed fiber wick floating in a cupful of fish oil.

Then the books were brought out and lesson time began. At first Nosh could see no reason for this—and her old fears returned that the ability to read might bring her to death were it known. But at length a long-sleeping part of her mind stirred and she began to look forward to the acquiring of these new skills. For she not only learned to read, but also to write. And not only in one language, for Dreen insisted that it was well to be able upon occasion to greet strangers in their own tongues—though what strangers might come here she never made clear.

From time to time ever since Nosh's coming the woman had taken a ration cake and had gone off for the day, making it plain that she was about some business which did not concern the girl. At first at each of these disappearances Nosh had known fear, feeling that perhaps Dreen had deserted her and the small safety she had known here would be lost. But when the woman returned on the morning of the day after she had left each time, Nosh relaxed and accepted these departures and returns as a part of Ryft life.

Each time she had returned Dreen had brought supplies (sometimes she had also a small pouch of salt) with her, and always a reed basket filled with rich black earth, and they had spent the next few days enlarging and enriching the garden of herbs. All the time they so worked together the woman had played instructress, drilling Nosh thoroughly in the use of each plant they so carefully tended until the girl could recite from memory much herbal lore. That this patch would and did grow plants which withered in the rest of the Ryft was just one of the many puzzles Nosh could find no answer for and gave up seeking.

Each time Dreen left she headed to the west and that mingling of jaggered rocks which repelled all thought of journeying there, though it would seem that she knew well where she would go and what she was to do there.

Nosh spent those days alone in ways of her own. It was her pride to be able to greet Dreen on her return with some surprise—such as a new supply of dried fish, some pages of one of the books mastered, a piece of knotless weaving. They had sparse garments. Dreen's robe was patched with both pieces of reed cloth and even bits of toad skin. Nosh, whose single garment when she came here was already too small, had fashioned a kilt of reed cloth and a cape of strips of snakeskin, both of which gave her body the freedom of movement she needed for all her tasks.

Now when Dreen left, the girl put in time at the riverbank, not only harvesting reeds when in season but in sifting the gravel, testing her gift over and over again. Sometimes when she held a find between her palms pressed close together and closed her eyes to concentrate upon that which she held, she felt that it was not the crude and dull lifeless thing she had found, rather she saw a mental picture of the stone cut, polished, and in all its glory. She made a few attempts to rough-polish some of her finds, but without success.

Meanwhile she wondered now and then what was happening in the world beyond the barriers containing the Ryft. She never tried to force memory upon herself. But sometimes she speculated that perhaps all the world without knew only death and that she and Dreen were the last of their race yet living.

When that dark thought entered her mind she went to the rocks and gave the clicking call Dreen had taught her. It was difficult to know one zark from another but over the change of seasons she had come to distinguish two—and they appeared to be always the first to answer her summons. One was a shade taller than its fellow and there was a small pucker in its frill as if it had once suffered some hurt which had healed awry. The other always clicked to her loudly as if glad at her summons. She named them—the large Tarm, and other Wasin. The memory she had so long suppressed supplied those names as if once they had had meaning for her. And Nosh was sure that the creatures knew their names when she uttered them.

It was at such a meeting that life changed for the second time for Nosh. Tarm was on the top of a tall pinnacle of rock and now he appeared to be staring north along the pan of the forgotten highway. He clicked loudly and emphatically and Nosh got to her feet, only to dodge down again at once.

There was movement along the same pass trail the

children had followed that time seasons past. More refugees? But wariness was deep set in Nosh. She slipped
between the rocks, keeping well to cover and moving to
a point from which she could see more clearly.

Chapter 4

THE WIND HAD A CUT TO IT, A PROMISE of the stark cold season to come. Kryn drew tighter the cumbersome hide coat, a size or so too large for him, which he kept on by an arrangement of strings and his sword belt. It smelled vilely of the lorshog pens where its previous owner must have spent some lengthy time in those days before Kryn had lifted it from a hook in the empty stable.

Empty stable—he had been too late—by how much—an hour or so? A day? The guards and the priests had swept the small manor bare. He had hoped that it, being the farthest out of the House holdings, and a meager one compared with the riches of several keeps and manors, would be the last to be visited by Temple greed and he would find there both a mount trained to mountain roving and supplies.

Now Kryn still chewed on a half-rotted apple gleaned from the orchard, grimacing at its taste. But the fruit was something with which to fill his aching belly. He had eaten the last of the food Smarle had given him a day ago.

He had crept upon this small hold of High Skies, refusing to drop any of his wariness, as might one of the outlaw raiders. Well, was that not what he had become— an outlaw and a raider—if he would keep life in his body?

No villager, no landkeeper, would give him aid or shelter. The fact that High Skies was deserted was proof enough that the message of the downfall of his House had spread nearly to the borders of this land. Before him were only the Heights and those were fabled sources of death and destruction—and had been ever since High King Trustan had fallen in the Battle of Twin Forks and left his weak-willed son slave to the Temple, whether he wore their collar or not, to claim the throne.

Masterless men—armsbearers whose lords had been slain or given in tamely to Valcur's sort—landsmen who had seen their fields put to the torch at harvest season, their sturdy garths plundered and wrecked, yes, and those others also who had blood on their hands from murderous crimes of the private sort—those were to be found above and beyond.

Kryn had had the garth under survey for near half a day and had not seen even a course-hound move, a fowl flutter in the muddied courtyard. Surely there was no one left and he could see no reason that there would be any guard in hiding. Or did Valcur suspect that he would head hither? His choice of life was well-known—there had been many sneers about one who willingly followed the ways of the hills in preference to that of the arms court and the banquet hall.

Trap—no trap? Kryn brought from his belt pouch a copper targuin, a third of his non-inheritance. He gave it a short spin and marked the features of High King Bancus staring up at him. So, there was no reason why he should not try his fate. To take the upper trails with as little as he carried now was little better than choosing

to set his bootknife to his throat and being done with
all of it.

But he had waited until the sun was down behind the
mountains and he slipped from shadow to shadow with
all the expertise he could summon. The silence of the
garth was daunting. This was a place he had left only
little more than a ten-day ago alive and ready to welcome any traveler. Of course those he left here were
now swept away—slaves even as their former lord. The
recently garnered harvest would have been transferred
to the stores of the Temple, as would all the animals.
Everything of value would have been claimed and
would be carefully audited.

He had reached the lane which led to the foredoor.
As he expected the lane was deeply rutted by the
wheels of wagons. Still he halted to listen with a hunter's
trained ear for any sound from the cluster of buildings.

Wind in the trees that framed the ground before the
house was bringing down already some of the leaves
slain by the chill. Kryn flitted on and then saw that the
door was barred with broad bands of red cloth set crosswise and centered with a large gob of wax imprinted
with the Temple insignia. Such a warnoff would send
any casual comer on his way careful of no intrusion.

To break that would only be a betrayal of the presence of one who did not bow to Valcur. But also that
marking meant that the Temple's forces had not made
a clean sweep of what the house contained.

Kryn moved around the side. The window slits were
likewise so barred. But there were secrets at every garth
since the days of the Blancanter raiding forces, and perhaps the Templers had not thought of that.

Kryn dropped to his hands and knees and felt along
the stones set to form the foundation. He counted,
pushed, and faced a dark cavity into which he swung,
dropping to the cellar hole beneath. He smelled the

heavy fumes of new wine and of ale, enough that one might become drunk on them alone, and his feet splashed in a pool which spread from one cask to the next. They had beaten in the heads of those . . .

Not a Templer trick, they would have wanted to save this. But old Harkvan—he was of a temper to destroy what he could manage, to save it from the robed thieves.

Kryn swished through the riverlets of drink and found the crude ladder leading up to the house. There was light here for the trapdoor was wedged partly open— wedged by a . . .

For a moment Kryn clung tightly to the ladder and swallowed.

A limp hand dangled down toward him. And he thought he could put name to the face pinned in the crack of the door in spite of bloodstains now veiling it.

Harkvan himself.

Kryn climbed, somehow pushing the body away, to stand in the flag-paved kitchen. There was more blood by the door and a second crumpled body. Kryn made himself cross the big room. Wasver, Harkvan's trusted horse trainer, a great slash across his middle letting out a twist of guts. Above the smell of the spilled wine and ale from below arose the stench of death.

Somehow Kryn found himself able to do what was to be done. Harkvan lay at rest, his servant beside him. But nothing could erase the pain and rage which death had set on their features.

Harkvan—he had not been ready to kneel with a slave rope about his throat—not he! Kryn rubbed his hand across his eyes and wished for a raw moment that it was Harkvan's blood in his own veins.

Searching, Kryn found what was to him a treasure. Knowing the old garthmaster's habits, he looked about in a certain cupboard craftily concealed, and discovered what he had hardly dared to hope for—a bow well sea-

soned and with a packet of strings, a quiver of arrows
fletched by Harkvan's own patient and knowing fingers.
There was a blade, also, set in a plain scabbard. Not as
long nor heavy as Bringhope, closer to an oversized
knife.

Further rummaging turned up a backpack stronger
and larger than that Smarle had found for him, and in
the wall-set bed of the great room there were still folded
blankets, one undersewn with nar fur as soft and warming as the robe of any High King in winter.

There was food also—put down in crocks in the store-
room. Those must have been overlooked—perhaps the
death of the garthmaster and his man had somewhat limited the looting.

The nature of that stored in the crocks Kryn knew
well—lean meat smoked, sliced thin, then covered with
dried fruit which was pounded well into it. Rations for
those who in the winter must cover the outer range of
this holding to make sure that there were no intruders,
animal or man.

He discarded his stinking coat and from another blanket fashioned a rough answer to it—cutting a circle in
its middle for his head and pulling it into belt after hacking off two sides for freedom for his arms.

In his crossing and recrossing of the kitchen he had
kept his head away from the dead. Now that he had all
which might mean the difference between survival and
defeat for him there was a last respect for him to accord
Harkvan and the groom.

From the big room Kryn dragged what was left of the
bedding to to cover the bodies. Then he hunted up two
of the lamps, splashing their contents over that mound,
heaping at its sides what was left of the firewood in its
pile beside the wide hearth.

It had grown dark in the room and he could barely
distinguish the improvised bier by the time he had fin-

ished. He stood several steps down the ladder and then
threw upon the oil-soaked cloth a small torch he had lit
from the snap-spark Smarle had provided.

There was an upward whoosh of flame and Kryn
jumped from the ladder. He shouldered the pack he had
earlier slung down, with the weapons snug in its lashing,
and was out into the night with all the speed he could
summon.

Nor did he turn until he had reached the first of the
smaller hillocks which dotted the pasturage. The night
was alight behind him, flames showing from each of the
sealed windows he could sight. He stood for a long moment to watch until he was sure that it was well alight.
Let Valcur try to wring any more from that!

Burdened by the pack, Kryn trotted on into the night
as the light behind him increased and threw his own
shadow hurrying ahead of him.

This was familiar territory for him but only as far as
the Falls of Umbra. And the terrain was such that any
tracker could pick up his trail. He believed that he had
no time to try tricks of concealment—not now with the
garth blaze as defiance which would sting the Templers
into a hunt. Valcur was no fool and he was not served
by fools; they would guess the tie between the outlawed
son of the disgraced House and the destruction of the
farthest west holding of that House. And the Temple
did not forget any more than it forgave.

So he pushed on, covering the way he knew, at the
best speed he could summon as the ground ahead became more broken and arose steadily hill by hill. Toward
morning he realized that he must rest; his legs shook a
little when he paused to pant heavily at the crown of
one such rise. Now he looked ahead and around for
some shelter he dared hole up in.

There was a small ruffle of fir trees on the downside
ahead and those seemed to offer the only cover he could

sight. Wearily Kryn wove a way down, his wine-soaked, muddied boots stirring the thick blanket of fallen needles.

Dawn was already lightening the sky and he saw that the copse was centered by a tree taller and thicker trunked than those about it. Fastening a twist of rope to his pack, he left it on the ground, climbing until he was able to wedge himself into a limited space between trunk and branch. The raising of his pack was almost more than he could do, he was so shaken with fatigue. But there was nothing else which promised even a shred of safety if trackers were already on their way.

It took Kryn two days more to work past the Falls of Umbra into the unknown country. He had the luck to knock over one of the pacer hens, fat from the fall crop of nuts. Not daring the use of fire, he made himself choke down strips of raw flesh, fighting his queasiness with grim determination.

On the trail it was hard to keep track of time. He was no longer sure how long it had been since he had left the garth. This was country rich for the hunter and trapper. He lay in the sun on a rock and watched a herd of laster-deer, led proudly by a buck with antlers which stretched near the length of a man's height. They moved with the confidence of those who knew no enemies. It was true that even the rock cats prudently gave way to a laster buck when it wore its full armament.

Kryn was careful to refrain from using his arrows, even when some good target presented itself. In the first place he must be ever on the move and he could not deal with a carcass of an animal too large to be eaten in more than two meals. So he kept to the smaller game, of which there was plenty.

In these last days before the coming of winter in the Heights, the animals were preparing for that season, avidly seeking to fill their bellies before hibernation as

most of them—save the large browsers and predators—
slept away the season of snow and ice.

He, himself, must hunt some base he could use for a
permanent shelter during the cold. Thus he prowled the
upper ways, sometimes using the convenience of game
trails, to try and discover a cave.

The few he had found were too shallow and one had
a carpeting of bones in the rear studded by the dried
dung of one of the cats. He had no desire to dispute
ownership of that refuge.

At length he crossed two mountain meadows and
worked his way arduously over the Heights which
framed them. The cliffs ahead looked promising and he
could hear the sound of a fast mountain stream. Perhaps
it was that which masked the attacker.

Kryn sprawled forward, gasping for air. He had been
struck such a blow on his now much leaner pack as to
drive the air from his lungs. Then another body crashed
down on him, pinning his outflung arms tightly to the
earth. He tried to heave himself up, when into his line
of vision there flashed a naked blade edge to his throat.

"Move and you die." The voice spoke with the tone
of one engaging in an ordinary conversation—which
somehow made the words it shaped that much more
deadly. The spurt of fear was echoed by his anger
against himself for being taken so easily. He had become
careless in the days when roaming this territory apparently free of his kind.

Templers? Valcur must indeed have had his rage
aroused to carry any pursuit this far.

"What have we here?" Another voice.

"Turn him over, Jaspron, and let us see," ordered the
first speaker.

The weight on him switched and the hands on his
wrists, there must be two of them keeping that, tight-

ened and pulled. Kryn rolled over, his pack holding him
somewhat free of the ground.

There were four of them—but not uniformed Temple
guards. Instead they wore leather oddly splotched with
dull colors as if intended to blend with leaves and brush.
Two were middle-aged and had about them an air he
knew—these were or had been armsmen, trained fight-
ers in some lord's colors. The other two were younger
and kind recognized kind—these were hall born.

"Who are you, youngling, who dares the Heights?"
The elder of the two touched Kryn's side with the toe
of his thick foot covering as if to remind the captive of
his status.

"What hall gives post to your banner?" Kryn found
his voice.

"A spy, put knife to him," one of the armsmen urged.

The younger of the two noble born dropped to balance on his heels as he stared intently at Kryn. Then he
spoke:

"So the Crown Sinister is your banner, youngling?"

"How . . . " began Kryn.

"How? Two warm seasons back. Qunion guested
Garn in friendship. What chances now in the lowlands?"

Garn—he did not remember this young man but then,
like all unnamed warriors, Kryn had kept much to the
background and his place at the feasting board had been
afar from the high table.

Garn—Garn had been one of the first to feel the
clawed paw of the Temple. But that was rumor only—
a story of the Head dying of poison given by his cousin
who wished to heir. The cousin had died in quick Temple justice and Garn's claim forfeited because of the
stain upon its new lord.

"Qunion is gone," Kryn said. "They used their devil
arts to make the Head swear the slave oath—"

He heard a whistling of indrawn breath from all of them.

"Valcur goes far," the elder of the nobles said. "So Qunion . . . " He reached down and before Kryn could move, his wrists still prisoned by the armsmen, the stranger laid two fingers on the hilt of Bringhope. "I think Qunion still lives, even as Garn. Well met, kin by misfortune."

And thus Kryn passed into the fellowship of the highlands.

Chapter 5

Nosh tensed as she watched that troop of horsemen advance into clear sight—soldiers! Her slender body quivered in a first shudder. The books—Dreen—Fire . . . Memories bit at her, making her hands shake, her feet stumble as she wriggled back from her spy post.

These could not follow a trail across bare stone. And they were not riding at more than an amble, as if winning through that stoppered pass had worn energy out of them. Nosh forced memory away, concentrated on the present. The books . . .

She reached their refuge and set to frantic labor. The books she swept from their safe alignment on the table, pulling out strips of twisted snake hide to anchor them into a heavy pile but one she could deal with. Then— supplies . . . She got out the woven reed bags, poured into them the ground root meal, the strips of dried fish and amphibian flesh.

There were other things—but those she could not hope to save. Perhaps if the searchers came upon a deserted house, they would not believe any chase worth their while.

Nosh made two trips back into the forest of rock spires into which Dreen had always disappeared on her mysterious journeying. The books she took first, then shouldered the bags of food. Now, she must be alert against Dreen's return. The woman must not be allowed to walk into open danger.

She had never followed Dreen. There had been something oddly forbidding in the woman's attitude when she had withdrawn on those trips. But Nosh knew the general direction in which the other always disappeared.

First she hunted a hiding place for all she had brought from the house. There were crevices aplenty among these rough pinnacles which seemed almost, the farther she won into their circling, to be like the trunks of ravished trees frozen forever into immobility. But she must get farther in.

A clicking caught her attention. Wasin, surely it was Wasin, had flicked into full sight. It was almost as if he were calling to her. A moment later Tarm appeared at the level of her own feet. His frill was expanded to its farthest extent and he flashed back and forth, going and returning in a blink of the eye.

How much did these understand? Their excitement was manifest. Were the zarks attempting in some way to guide her?

Nosh hurried on, her back bent a little under the weight of the books. There was a crevice ahead, larger, darker as if it ran deeper. By the gap of that Tarm was standing, still now, his head cocked to one side as if he were watching her steadily to make sure she was coming. Nosh dropped her first burden into the dark cavern mouth and hurried back for the second.

She could hear something else, echoed, perhaps even magnified, by the wilderness of spires about her. Her hand went to her mouth and helped to stifle the sound her fears raised.

Above the sounds of hooves on rock and the jangle of war gear, there was something else. She shivered even more. Chant—a One chant. She did not have to get a fair look to substantiate her guess this half troop was a-prowl, but that riding with them was one of black and red robes—the burners of books—the choosers of victims to be slain.

She gave what was almost a leap into the mouth of that dark wedge, stumbling over the book package and falling painfully, to scrape knees on the rock. It was dark—so very dark that she was sure the hidden space before her was large.

Her hand, outstretched to lever herself up as fast as she could rise, slipped on a smooth glob. Into the dark about her arose scent—the scent of fish oil. Someone who had borne either a lamp or a well-soaked torch had come this way—Dreen—it could only be Dreen!

Nosh's eyes had adjusted somewhat to the gloom which the daylight from outside cut the deeper interior dark. She was not in a cave as she had first thought, at least not one which was small enough to end within her present range of sight. Instead the blackness reached ahead and she had the drops of the oil slippage to guide her on.

The book bag she pulled well to one side. She could not bear a double burden and their future might now depend more on food than those remnants of old knowledge.

Using her left hand against a wall Nosh could not see, the other steadying the carrying thongs of the bags slung over her shoulder, the girl ventured on. She heard no more clicking—the zarks perhaps had not followed her here.

In spite of her slow advance and her attempting to

feel her way, she twice struck against a wall as the passage took another turn. Then at the third such happening she saw a thinning of the gloom before her. Dreen returning with a torch to light her way?

No, this did not have the comforting ruddiness of fire—rather it was grey even as the land lay under the weight of the outer sky. She perhaps had won through what was not a cave at all but a tunnel leading once more into the open.

At another curve of the wall Nosh uttered a small sound of astonishment. The light was brighter, clearer. She stumbled out into such a place as might have greeted a wanderer in one of the old chronicles which Dreen had taught her to read.

For a long moment she could not see the source from which that blaze about her sprang—somewhere over her head. But it was what was embedded in the walls, lying in pieces before her feet, which parlayed the brilliance of light. Crystals—clear with rainbows of light, crystals ruby-hearted with inner fires, crystals of the cool green of the fabled sea, blue, gold . . .

Nosh rubbed her eyes and allowed her food bag to drop. Now that she could center her sight on one portion of wall she could see that those colors were not scattered heedlessly but that they wove patterns. The girl stretched her head well back to look aloft. There the fire was ruddier. She could make out, in spite of the smart that the flashing of the crystal brought, a ball suspended there.

This gave out light—murky and smoke-tinged in itself but enough to awaken the glory of the crystals. Yet looking at that ball brought a quick shaft of fear, though not a fear out of memory, to trouble her.

The globe had no place here; that she knew from the moment she sighted it. It was alien in spite of the fact that its tainted light fed the radiance which was true and right.

Its suspending chains supported it directly over a pedestal in what appeared the center of that chamber. On the pedestal was . . .

Nosh somehow lost fear, was drawn closer, closer step by eager step until she could reach up and—no, she could not quite lay hand on what was planted there—some buried will was stronger than hers.

However, she could see it well, almost as if the brilliance of the flashes around her were subdued for a moment to aid her in that. It was—her own hands drew back just before her breast and came together, wrist pressed to wrist, palms slanting back as if her curved fingers now caressed and held some cup or vessel.

There were the wrists before her eyes, the palms acurve, all fashioned from rainbow-coated crystal as if some being of an alien blood had left so a sign of once-life.

But the fingers—they had been snapped away, leaving only shattered stumps. Needle-pointed slivers here and there marked the places where they had been rooted.

Her lips parted and she gave a sigh. Just as fear had struck earlier, so now did a shattering sense of loss grip her. She wavered to and fro as she fell to her knees, and the tears which she had thought long ago exhausted came once more to wet her cheeks, the hands she held to her dusty face.

There was worse than sorrow to be faced here, Nosh discovered, as she continued to kneel. There was evil—stemming not from the shattered crystal—no—it came from that ball which hung aloft. Old evil, crafty evil. If she could have laid hand on a spear to give her reach room, she would have struck that thing from its support chains, dashed it to bits on the floor even as the fragments of crystal lay in mounds like miniature desert dunes.

She had no spear—but perhaps a fragment of crystal could be thrown. Nosh had developed a strong pitching arm to help her for a hunt when straightness of an aim might mean the difference between going fed or hungry for a day.

Hitching around, she scrabbled in the nearest drift of crystals, hunting one of the proper size and weight. Blood spotted her discards as her flesh was scored by sharp edges, but she was beyond pain at the moment. Only one thought filled her—to destroy that hanging above.

Her fingers closed. She nearly dropped what she held—though she had not been aware of the tingling which had followed her delving, insensible to the messages sent by her gift, this surge of power, fire-hot, could not be denied. She was holding a length of the pure rainbow-shadowed crystal, turning it around to see it the better. Its form . . . ! Nosh got hastily to her feet and once more studied the broken fingerless hands. She did indeed hold a finger! Fingers—let her find the fingers . . . She laid that first one with care on the pedestal and turned to search even more madly for the other shards which must lie hidden among all the glitter on the floor.

"Not here. . . ."

Speech in this place was a shock. Nosh swung around, absently licking her bleeding hands. Dreen stood there. The woman moved to her side.

"That to be sought is not here, my child. Yes,"—she had followed Nosh's gaze as it went to the fragment she had placed aloft—"one has come into your hands. Alnosha, left as a guide—a measure. Just as the others will and must do in their time and place. Lyr has chosen, your gift is Goddess-given, thus it must Goddess serve."

"What . . . ?" began Nosh in a shaken voice.

"You look upon the desolation of Razkan." That last word appeared to twist upon her lips as if she spat it.

"The Ryft was the garden of Lyr and Her goodness covered it. Fruitful was all life, for when the sun's warmth touched Lyr's tower it was drawn and brought down through a channel of the rock hither, to be caught and cupped in the Hands of Lyr, directed up again so that all healing and fruitfulness could be spread. So it was once."

Dreen raised her head to look upward at that murky ball which seemed now to be casting forth a mist, a thickness which one could not really see but only sense—the smearing of all that was vile across the beauty of the crystals.

"To everything its season," Dreen began again. "The High King in those days was a man of ambition, but not one, at first, who would war to obtain what he could have. No, he sought other means—through ways which hosted cruelty and death not only of the body but of the essence which is its indweller. What strange learning he could gain for himself he drew upon diligently. But there is this, child, which is the rule of all such delving— dark calls to dark even as light to light.

"When there comes a troubling caused by a new power stirring in the world, to that power inclines such people as won to dominance before it. Thus there came to the High King, in the guise of a seeker in the same ways, a stranger.

"A stranger and a thief, for he had already stolen from rightful Guardians knowledge that they would keep from troubling the world. First this Razkan played the part of a student sitting at the High King's feet. He had patience, for he wanted to gain much but he did not want to betray himself in the learning. Little by little he let forth, as if he had recently discovered such, bits of the forbidden knowledge he nursed in memory, and the High King was delighted.

"Already the king had driven from him those who had begun to suspect what he did in secret. And in their places of authority he put weak men already under Razkan's control.

"Too late those of goodwill learned what was being done. Then began the revolts—and when those were put down bloodily, the High King had found a love for battle and so looked about him for a world to bring under his heel.

"Just as dark looks for dark to increase its power, so does it look for light to destroy as a potential enemy. Razkan learned quickly of Lyr and he performed such a piece of magic as was daring even for him. Out of his own thoughts he evoked—that. . . . "

Dreen pointed to the globe. "It appeared without warning on a high feast day. Under a great burst of malignant force the Hands were shattered so that those who served Her were stricken. But also they knew that Lyr could not be forever broken. Here goodwill would rest, draw to it knowledge large and small, and they knew that the battle had not ended the conflict.

"Thus those left who had served her—many had died in the attack—each took up one of the fingers and they spoke together for the last time, saying that they would bear their fragments afar—separately—until there would come a talent which would find each in turn and bring them hither again. Once more the Hands would catch the bounty of the sun and return life to the Ryft.

"But Razkan knew well that his opponents might have been beaten in that first attack but their way was not yet finished. He sent fire and sword into the Ryft and Lyr's fair land ceased to be. And in all the seasons since—and they can be numbered as many more than you are alive, Alnosha, there has been a waiting. I am the last of the blood of those who were Lyr's birth-named servants. I waited for you, Alnosha, you and the gift of the Goddess. Now comes the time of faring forth, and the way will not be easy, nor the path straight and smooth. Take that again, child."

She gestured to the broken finger. Warily Nosh obeyed. There was a warmth in it. All at once it seemed right that it should touch her flesh, as if it were a part of her.

"It would seem that Razkan stirs also. The High King who became his puppet is long dead, but he left two sons—one born by law, one by outlawry. His own line prospered, his son by shame founded a House in a border town. And Razkan, he arose to being a God that all must serve—thus keeping the people in thrall through the priests and their guards. . . . "

"Those of black and red," Nosh said in a half whisper.

"Those slayers of men, burners of books, makers of slaves, faithful sons of a false God." Dreen's voice had taken on a sharp note as if she might be pronouncing some fate from which there would be no escape.

"He is now old beyond the reckoning of men. Now—able to prolong his life as the seasons pass. The time came, Alnosha, when the dying winds of red war brought you hither—even as She had promised. Search for Finger upon Finger, child. Your gift will lead you true. And when you hold all within your grasp return to the Ryft and what is to be done will be."

"There are soldiers in the Ryft now," Nosh said. "I came to warn you. . . . "

"A thought must have crossed Razkan's mind. Or, perhaps,"—she looked up to the globe—"he has left certain safeguards? So we must be away, Alnosha."

"Out of the Ryft—?" The dead valley had become such a refuge to her, hard though the life was, that she shrank from leaving. In her hand the Finger of crystal was warm, almost like a cover of protection.

"Out of the Ryft, yes, and into the western broken lands. It may be that we shall find there some as will give us aid in our going."

So began another life for Nosh, the one only of her partial choosing.

Chapter 6

IT WAS A HARSH LIFE THE HEIGHTS HELD for men. The band led by the once heir of Garn had done what they could to survive. There was just such a cave as Kryn in his flight had hoped to find, where there was room not only for the handful of men but six of the surefooted, small, and stocky, hill mounts—though as usual those were not for the taming and must be mastered every time they were put to rider or burden.

Before the snows sheathed them in they made two raids on Templers, slipping down from the hills by ways the maps of which lay only in outlawed heads.

Once they added a smith and carpenter to their band, snagging them out of slave chains. And so Kryn got his blooding in the way of outlawry and he agreed that the only good Templer was a dead one.

They kept well aloof from any garth or fieldman's hut, having no wish to draw the hatred of the Temple on the innocent, attacking only armed convoys which they could take from the clever ambushes Jarth of Garn planned.

When snow blanketed them one of the armsmen from the north set about the fashioning of queer footgear

51

made as if they were to walk on stiff netting fastened
in wide ovals to their feet. And there was some hot language used before they were able to shuffle on the surface of the drifts. But this gave them a freedom the
enemy could not hope to obtain—unless in the Templer
forces there was also some man from Varsland.

They had stationed a permanent watch—to be
changed each day—at a point which overlooked a curve
the highway must take because of the nudge of the
river. Yet there were but slim pickings after the first
snow. Apparently the Templer crews had brought in all
the rest of the harvest, the dregs of their looting of sequestered garths. Those who took the trail now were
huddles of people, dazed, adrift, ones who had dared to
flee the slave rope.

It was Kryn on duty there with Rolf, the very man
who had put the snow webs to their use, who sighted
that single rider one morning. It was obvious to the
watchers the stranger could barely hold himself in the
saddle, and his mount plodded as if it were near the end
of its strength. The pair reached the point just below
where the two were crouched in hiding before the
mount came to a stop, spraddled its legs wide as if to
hold its body erect and then, with a wailing sound which
might have come from the throat of a man, fell, the rider
caught with one leg under the kicking animal.

His cloak was torn away in his feeble struggles to free
himself and when its hood jerked to show his face,
Kryn's hand shot out to grasp Rolf as the latter rose to
his knees ready to launch a bolt at that now hardly moving rider.

"No Templer!"

"He rides—and he wears no House tabard."

"He wears it on his face," Kryn returned. He made
his move before the other could stop him, swinging
down to the roadway. The mount stirred again, kicking

out, and then screamed as only an animal meeting death can as its head flopped back, an arrow protruding from one eye.

Kryn was at the side of the fallen man. Now that the cloak had been pulled away during its owner's struggles he could see clearly that brown splotch at the breast, welling blood again centering it. Then Rolf was with him and together they pulled the man free.

His eyelids fluttered, he gave a small groan, and then he was looking up at the youth his gaze one of recognition.

"House Heir . . . "

"Yes, Ewen—so they did not get you either!" Kryn, having settled the man as comfortably as he could, reached to explore the wound . . .

"No matter, Heir Hope . . . " One of the other's hands closed on his wrist. "I am death called. They caught me outside. . . . " he frowned a little as if memory was fleeting—"do . . . not remember now. They had a sniffer . . . sniffer Bozi . . . " Now his features twisted with hate. "Remember, Heir Hope—it—was—Bozi as sniffed me for them!"

Rolf had, with more gentleness than his clumsy-seeming hands suggested, unlatched the stranger's tunic. The welling pool of blood had become a steady flow. He looked to Kryn and shook his head.

"Heir." The man on the ground might have seen and understood that gesture of sentence. His eyes were fixed on Kryn and it was plain that he was making a great effort. "Lord—Hafern was magicked—mind magicked! Stand to arms—for him—for your House. But—there is evil behind evil. . . . "

Blood bubbled in the corner of his mouth, straggled in a thin line down his chin.

"Gromize . . . said . . . ride . . . warn . . . "

"Gromize! But he is dead!"

"Not . . . so . . . he has power . . . small power. He sent a searching dream for you. Then . . . me . . . this . . ." His hand slipped from that tight grip he had been keeping on Kryn's wrist, wavered to his belt pouch. "For . . . you . . . get Bozi for me, Heir . . . I am your man."

Kryn met his gaze steadily. "You are Qunion House Kin, Ewen. Armsmaster, Banner bearer." The old titles came easily somehow. "Yes,—there will be a reckoning with Bozi. . . ."

Ewen's head rolled, turned on Kryn's shoulder. He gave a shudder and then was quiet. The young man looked to Rolf over that limp body.

"There is now another among the shades to cry me on."

Rolf nodded and then spoke with a practicality which drove any emotion into heart-hiding. "Best we get him off the road, Kryn. Listen!"

Loud and sharp, as if fate had been running mute and only now gave tongue, came that savage cry—and more than one. Wakwolves—the scent of blood reached far for such as them.

Perhaps the dead mount would delay them for a few helpful moments. Together Kryn and Rolf slung the body between them up into that crevice of their spy hole. And then beyond that to where there was the rubble of a last season's land slip. They worked fast, covering what they had carried with the largest and heaviest stones they could find, hearing already the snarling battle going on over the dead beast. Taking up bows they returned to their perch. The twilight of the cold season was advancing, but not so much that it veiled the feast below. They could pick their marks with ease and, fortune favored, the pack was a small one—perhaps a single family of dam and sire and this season's cubs.

With the precision of long-practised marksmen they

shot and wakwolves died, several snapping at the arrows which brought them down.

"They've hunted far into the lower lands," Rolf commented.

"There is stock gone wild in the upper garths—perhaps the Templers did not sweep as clear as they would like. Such are easy hunting—better than facing the horns of the laster."

Kryn left the battle station and went to stand once more beside that grave. It was already beginning to snow and the white flakes would soon drape here a pall.

"He was a man—to ride with such a wound," Rolf commented in a harsh voice.

"He taught me the sword, the bow. He was closer to me often than my father." His father—what Ewen had said now echoed—"Magicked . . . " he repeated softly. "So—someone plays with other power than steel and muscle."

"Magick," repeated Rolf and then he spat. "It is of the Dark One." He drew back a pace or so from the grave as if he feared some taint could issue forth to touch him.

Kryn transferred the small rolled purse Ewen had brought to the second pouch at his own belt.

"This Gromize he spoke of . . . ?" Rolf made a question of that.

"A learned man—for that reason hated, for he would not be one with the Temple. He claimed guest right in our hall from time to time. My—my father in those days was at one mind with him against all Valcur stood forth. A season ago he left, saying he was going on a seeking journey—and the news came by merchant caravan that they found him dead. . . . "

"Dead or not, he seems to have spoken with this armsmaster," Rolf observed. "I do not altogether like such hearing. The dead should stay safely dead."

"It may have been only a story—his death," Kryn commented. "Ewen was no spirit seeker."

"Do not speak of unchancy things, and come! The snow grows and there will be none to exchange watches with this night."

They put on their snowshoes and backtrailed, but memory rode on Kryn's shoulder and whispered in his ears as he went. He saw much of other times and what he saw fed that never-dying fire of anger he kept guarded within.

Back at the cave, which was now the only shelter he knew, Kryn shared the news with Jarth, the Garn lord, and his young brother Hasper. The three hunched close at the fireside which provided their only light as Kryn unfastened the pouch.

What it carried was such a surprise that he sat dumb for a moment or so. There had been no roll for the reading there, nor anything save a palmful of stones, flat discs as if they mimicked the coins any traveler would carry.

"Pattern stones!" Hasper made identification first. "Give!" He held out his hand and Kryn mechanically dropped the discs into it. "Heat!" With his other hand the young Garn lord seized upon what had become a handy fire tool—a section of steel mount from a shield. He now set out the stones in a row on that and thrust it into the reaching flames.

Those strands of fire might have been a scribe's ink, for there appeared on each stone markings which grew the more visible the longer they were held to the heat. Then Hasper brought back the length of metal, careful not to allow any of its burden to slide into the fire.

The symbols on the stones now revealed were clear enough but Kryn could only pick out one or two in translation.

That one held the scarlet of the Temple but there

was a marking slashed across the clear circle—a marking of black. And the next stone to that carried the sign of a sword unsheathed—war. . . .

"That is the High King's mark,"—the Garn lord pointed to a third stone—"and look what lies across it." The same black mark seemed to threaten the clearly inscribed two-tiered crown.

"Temple threatened?" hazarded Kryn. "The High King also? A revolt?"

House Lord Jarth was studying the last two of the stones. One of those had sparks of light such as might mark tiny crystals urged into life by the heat and they were also set in a line, while edging that faint line was a soft green, somehow pleasing to the eyes.

"That—that . . ." Jarth's scowl grew knottier. "Old— Nurse Onna!" He ended in triumph as one who brought to the surface some long-buried memory.

"Onna—but she died years ago," his brother objected, "and never did she meddle in great affairs. What has a nurse of fieldman blood to do with matters here and now?"

"Onna was more than a nurse—you cannot truly remember, being so small the season she died. She had once been something else—no fieldwoman—but a priestess."

"Priestess!" Kryn was entirely at a loss now. It was very well-known that the Temple allowed no woman within the ranks of its servers. Valcur was one to fashion more and more restraints for his church to place upon all women.

"Not of the Temple. From another place and time. She had many skills and she was heart-friend to our mother, although there were many years between them. When our mother came by bride right Onna was already at the High Keep and no one spoke against her. When she was dying she called upon one of the maids, for our

mother had perished a few days earlier—the coughing
death took them both. And she gave her a thing and
sent her away. This much I know for I had hidden myself in the wall hangings, wanting to go to Onna with
our mother no longer there. I do not know what she gave
the maid who was from the borders of the high country
save it was something shaped like this and it shone in
Onna's hand but, when the maid took it, it turned dull
and seeming of no worth. And Onna in her dying called
upon a power I had heard my mother speak to when she
thought herself private . . . LYR. . . . This power was unknown in temple land. Unless we were spied upon.
They did send a priest who had the stench of a sniffer
about him at Onna's death but she had left nothing for
the Temple to claim."

"Lyr—the symbol of another power to rise?" mused
Kryn. "And the last—what have you to say for that, Lord
Jarth?"

The last stone was dully grey save in its heart there
was a spot which seemed less opaque, almost as if this
bit of rock had sprouted an eye. And that was the first
to fade.

"No," Jarth said, as stone by stone the pattern faded
while they cooled. "I do not think revolt. Perhaps something else—an addition to our troubles, not a diminution
of them. Power over Valcur, power over the High King.
But in neither place Temple power—if I read this
aright. I wish your Gromize's warning, if warning this
collection is meant to be, was plainer. There has been
talk for some time of war. . . . It is a pastime for the High
King in his Hearth Keep to sit before a table the top of
which is fashioned to copy our own hills and valleys.
Through this they say he moves the small figures of an
army, trying out this strategy and that—for he believes
that he was born to be a commander of armies and he
chafes against the Temple-held peace."

Kryn shifted his weight a little. "But if there is power against the Temple, against the king, is that what he fears?" He had never been one to linger in the halls and listen to the gossip concerning high personages, rather he had wanted the open about him and not the buzzing of such as always had much to say behind their hands.

"No. The king looks southward—or at least he reads many of the old chronicles. He does not realize that what he covets is already dead and gone. But his ambition rides him and perhaps there will come one who will feed him into war. It may be that Valcur wishes him to play out his dreams in such games but—remember Razkan?"

"But that one is long gone," protested Hasper. "He withdrew overseas and no man has seen him. So they prate wildly about him as if he could blow mountains about with his very breath and stamp a city into dust."

"In his time he did both," answered Lord Jarth quietly.

Kryn was nodding. The very man he had buried this eve had been the first to really talk about Razkan and rather than vagueness of legend his stories had held the ring of truth. Ewen's own grandfather had been one to see such a display of power in the last of the long war when Fire had descended from the sky to char the enemy into nothingness. A servant of Razkan had done that; and if a servant could perform such wonders—what of the master?

"Still—you read war in these," he said to Jarth. The stones were yet warm but he could pick them up now to restore them to hiding.

"I think so. But the message remains unclear. What we can do is prepare to take any advantage offered us."

And with that Kryn could agree.

Chapter 7

THERE WAS MUCH TO BE DONE BEFORE
the two left the forsaken shrine of Lyr. The books Nosh
had dragged with her were hidden in a cranny of the
wall just before the entrance to the crystal cavern, while
the supplies she had also brought were divided into two
smaller packs. They ate of the root powder cakes and
each sipped sparingly at the water in the scaled pouches.

When they were done Dreen moved forward once
more to stand before the pedestal of the shattered
Hands. She began a chant, the words of which were beyond Nosh's understanding—something very old from
the morning hours of time itself.

To the girl the sullen gleam of the threatening globe
above them was somehow forced back into its source
and the glory of the crystals flared into higher and braver
life. Then Dreen beckoned to her and, when she went
obediently to the woman's side, she saw ready in her
hand that much-used blade which was the only steel she
had seen in the Ryft.

Dreen caught at one of Nosh's braids, loosing it from
its cording, and sawed off a length of the girl's dark hair.
Her blunt, callused fingers, used to the small loom of

weaving, to the plaiting of reed stems, were quick at work and soon she held a bag.

"This will hold what you carry and in a measure, as long as you wear it against your body, will keep that safe. Hide it well."

Nosh slid the sliver of crystal into that silky bag and hung it between her small breasts by a length of hair she herself pulled from her own head. Once done she looked to Dreen for further orders.

The woman made a circle with her hand which indicated the floor about them and those drifts of crystal heaped and scattered there.

"Seek, Alnosha. In the old days much treasure was brought here to adorn the shrine. Not all which lies here is crystal—some of it is more."

Nosh flexed her fingers. In the Ryft their sustenance depended upon their own physical efforts; in another place perhaps such finds as she could make might well mean success or failure, life or death.

She knelt to seek and she found. These were not the dull, unworked gems such as she had discovered among the river gravel. However, in their way they were as hidden, for their glory was masked by the crystals among which they lay. In the end she held out to Dreen a double handful, ranging in size from those a reed tip could cover to some as large as a fingernail. The woman shook them into a piece of her robe she had worried loose by the knife, and tucked the harvest into the slight blousing above her rope girdle.

"Well enough. But remember this, child: men—yes—and women, too, will kill for such a treasure. We must use it carefully, and, should you be left alone—"

"Where are you going then?" Nosh knew a flutter of fear.

"We do not choose our fates, save when we first set foot along chosen roads. I have seen many seasons, Al-

nosha, and you are young. It may be that I shall not be
with you to the ending of this quest. If that be so—
make sure you take this." She patted her body where
that hidden bag made a small lump. "But use what it
holds with care. Now,"—she stooped and picked up the
rope about her pack—"we make our start. If dreams are
aright, those who have come seeking will not be satisfied
in a hurry concerning our absence. Their master,"—she
nodded to the globe overhead—"must indeed be astir."

There was a second exit to the crystal chamber and
through that Nosh followed Dreen. The way was narrow
and a rough one, twice the woman needed to turn sideways to inch through a tight squeeze, and Nosh suffered
scrapes on her arms which tore the stuff of her snakeskin, lizard hide, reed-woven clothing to leave smarting
furrows on her flesh.

Then there was once again a dull light ahead and
Dreen slowed.

"Here for the night," she said. "There is a spring
beyond and we can fill our water bags, for the march
ahead will be a dry one. I know the way—for two days
perhaps. Beyond that I have not ventured, and we must
take our chances."

There was a patch of green about the spring where
water bubbled in a worn basin hardly bigger than the
pot which had hung over Dreen's house fire. Nosh with
a quick, skilled hand, caught two of the legged fish.
They might not offer more than a good bite apiece but
every such addition to their supplies was to be prized.
Nor did she shrink from eating her catch uncooked.
There could be no fire here with the sky still light
enough to show smoke against the clouds and be a signal
to bring any watcher in.

They lay that night in the very small opening to the
passage from the place of Lyr. Dreen had sat for a long
time as full darkness closed in, her two hands clasped

tightly at her breast enfolding the stone she wore there in its reed bag, her eyes closed. Yet Nosh was sure that she did not sleep.

Much the girl had learned from the onetime priestess, but not all Dreen knew or remembered. The woman might even now be rousing power which would aid them in their flight and Nosh drew away as far as she could from the other lest she disturb what might be a seeing trance.

Instead she felt for her own talisman and the warmth of it was a comfort, somehow soothing and finally banishing fear. She felt a growing desire to be away—out of the desolation of the Ryft—into a world where there were still growing things, and people. Though, memory warned her, the latter were to be feared more than any countryside.

There were streamers of pale dawn across the sky when she awoke from a sleep wherein she might have dreamed but if she had, she did not remember. Dreen's hand lay on her shoulder.

"It is well that we go. . . . "

Nosh sat up. "They come?"

"Not as yet. But they seek and they have one among them who is no common armsman. What power that one may evoke I cannot tell. However, last night he was mind searching and only Our Lady kept that threat from us." Her hand went again to the stone she wore.

They ate very sparingly and, having drunk their fill, filled their water bags as full as they could. Dreen turned south along the thread of stream which runneled from the spring. It was colder here, and under the flint grey sky they moved closely together as if the very land was a threat they must face.

Only too soon their water guide was swallowed by a crevice. Now they faced a climb and Dreen moved along the base of that, studying the face of the barrier until she pointed to a rough space on the wall.

Nosh made certain her pack was well placed, even as Dreen was doing, and then she followed the woman's example and climbed. To her surprise it was not quite the ordeal it had seemed from below—there were niches in the rock as if they had been purposely cut there for the convenience of travelers. Then they reached a ledge which sloped upward to the left and offered the best footing they had seen that day.

Nosh took the opportunity for a quick look back over the path which they had come. She was not sure of the ability of the one Dreen had spoken of in warning. Could such a searcher indeed pluck out of the very air some trace of scent as might a wakwolf, or look upon a bare rock and know that a foot had trod there?

When they had reached the top of the height to which the ledge took them, they faced a different kind of country. There were broken rock spires aplenty immediately before, even as there had been in the Ryft, but beyond those there was a stretch of level land where she could sight moving dots, not keeping in a purposeful line as might a troop, but rather scattered and slow in their going.

"Armsmen?"

"No—those are laster-deer at graze. And to see them thus is a sign that there are no intruders near. They are careful as to sentry duty—the does have their outer beats along the edge of the herd. And they are not to be surprised when so in the open."

Beyond that mountain meadow where the lasters fed was a dark tangle of trees reaching up and up along the side of a height taller than any Nosh remembered seeing. The dark green of that growth cast a shadow of color and reminded one that the Ryft's fate had not been suffered elsewhere.

They descended cautiously among the outcrops of rock, knowing only too well how easy it was to take a misstep where small stones slid if weight was pressed on them. And beyond that grey wilderness there was a tangle of brush. For the first time there was sound. For busy at their harvesting of near-dried berries were flocks of birds, so unheeding of the travelers in their greediness that they did not take wing until Nosh plucked a taste from one of the thorned branches, and then they only scolded harshly.

Live birds were strange to Nosh. She had only seen their like pictured in one of the books which had been written about the life which had once swarmed in the Ryft. The colors of some of these busy feasters were dull for the most part but there were others which displayed bright splotches of hues from red through orange to yellow, through green to blue.

Dreen herself was busy pulling the fruit from the branches, thrusting handsful of it into their ration bags as well as into her own mouth. And Nosh quickly followed her example. But the bushes here were so matted that she could not win through them and they did their harvesting along the edge, still moving south.

Above the bird cries sounded a bellow, which came, Nosh was sure, from beyond the barrier of the growth.

"The laster have picked up our scent," Dreen answered her unspoken question tranquilly. "And—since they move—they have some reason to be wary—as if hunted in their time."

They came at last to the end of the berry patch and into the beginning of tree growth. Nosh breathed deeply of the fresh scent the breeze brought her. This was indeed like coming into another world.

Dreen halted not far into the woodland and stooped to pick up a length of young sapling brought down when one of the larger trees had crashed to earth ahead of them. It was a straight length, though knotted near one end with the stubs of branches. Dreen thudded the thicker end against the ground, then swung it up to balance as if she held an armsman's spear.

For the first time since she had seen this strange alive land Nosh thought of perils other than those offered by the hunters of her own kind. Wakwolves—she swallowed. Against a wakwolf what good would that crude pole be? But the wolves were known to hunt mostly at night and, perhaps by nightfall, they themselves would have found shelter. She herself started looking at the downed branches which lay half-buried in the thick carpet of other seasons' needles, but found none which suggested the possibility of being converted into a weapon, no matter how rough.

They won through the small wood and were now on the verge of the meadow. Nosh looked for the lasters but there were none to be seen. The valley was narrow at this end and the open space had assumed almost the sharpness of a sword point. However, southward it widened steadily and she thought that the heights which walled the level land there were some distance on—they even seemed to be masked in haze.

Dreen stepped boldly into the open, her sapling pole in her hand. There was a weaving of the autumn-browned grass, a scuttling and a squeaking which brought Nosh to a wary halt. Dreen regarded the girl over her shoulder with one of her faint smiles.

"There are dwellers in the grass, child. They mean us no harm even as we offer none to them."

The nature of most of those dwellers Nosh did not know but there were two birds who arose almost clumsily from the waves of growth, to fly a short space north, and subside, hidden by the meadow's cover once again.

Overhead there were flyers also—one which sailed close on wide wings. Another of the grass-dwelling birds arose and that hunter from the skies swooped and made a clean catch, carrying its prey aloft as it winged directly to the heights.

The ease of that hunt was so swift and quick that Nosh stared wide-eyed.

"A rathhawk," Dreen identified the hunter. "They seldom miss their strikes. That was a female, her young may still be a-nest though it is late for them to linger so."

Nosh dared now to bring her earlier fear into the open. To see that one skillful hunter about her business was enough to remind the girl unpleasantly of another.

"Wakwolves . . . " She did not quite make a question of that.

"Perhaps. But in a land as rich in prey as this one we need not fear them to sniff our trail. They turn upon our kind only in times of starvation. Those which hunted along your path into the Ryft were caught in a country where there was very little left save the rock snakes and the zark—neither of which could make more than a mouthful."

Which was a little heartening, Nosh found. They came to a grazed spot where the lasters had taken their fill and insects buzzed up from piles of fresh dung which the travelers avoided. Thus they came to that other massing of trees which marched from the meadow skyway upslope.

There they found a stream flowing so clear that Nosh was able to see the scuttling of the rock hiders at its bottom. And she went to work speedily to entrap as many of those that she could while Dreen, having shed her pack to lie beside the girl's, started back into the meadow, making slow sweeps of her hand to part the grass, now and then plucking up a small plant which she added to a growing bundle.

When she returned Nosh had a goodly catch laid out on a rock surface. There was sun here—it had just won from behind a cloud which might be the ragged fringe of those cloaking the Ryft—and the warmth of that on her shoulders felt good and soothing.

Dreen took out her knife and sawed free the roots of the plants she had garnered. Then setting some stones together and bringing a handful of driftwood to be broken into small bits, she lit a handsbreadth of fire. Nosh strung her catch on a piece of the drift and set it within the heat of the fire while Dreen washed the soil from the plant roots which were thick and bulbous, and pushed them into the full grasp of the flame, which she proceeded to feed into higher force.

There was little smoke, for the wood was very dry and the heat was comforting. Still Nosh was wary. Where they had taken their place was on the stream bank and there were trees and brush about. In fact the tree branches reached out to break into near invisible ribbons the smoke which did arise. Yet she was still uneasy. Dreen's early speech concerning that hunter on their trail who had certain powers was not one to make one content in a strange country.

However, the answer to their fire when it came was not what she expected. She had been eating hungrily of one of the tubers which roasting had reduced to a sweetish mealy state when Dreen's head went up, and, to the girl's surprise, the woman's lips shaped a sound Nosh had never heard before—a whistle almost birdlike in its trills. At the same time her hand fell on Nosh's arm as if to restrain and reassure the girl.

Out of the trees across the stream there advanced men. Nosh's hand flew to the talisman of Lyr, though at that moment she was certain it could bring them little aid. Dreen made no move to pick up her spear club. Instead she remained sitting calmly where she was, as the leader of those who had come out of hiding splashed across the shallow stream to join them.

Chapter 8

THE OUTLAWS WENT ON SHORT RATIONS during the fourth of the cold months. For all their struggles to amass supplies there were limits as to what they could garner. Also those trains of the Templers largely vanished when the last of the harvest had been plundered from the forfeited estates near the Heights. But lean bellies were not new to those of the band—and neither was hard labor, as Kryn discovered during the months when spring first touched the mountain uplands.

There was no division now between lord and armsman as to labor. Kryn drove a pair of field varges, taken the season before from a deserted fief and carefully tended during the cold, to plow a field as if he had been born to the soil, and then took his turn to break up the muddy clods of soil for the sowing of upland millet.

It was backbreaking, exhausting labor, but as Jarth had made clear to them all, if they were to continue to exist, they must be able to depend upon more than raiding plunder or the hunt for their supplies. The snows had shut off the scraps of news gained during scouting, so they could only guess what might be happening in the lowlands—and their speculations were usually on the dark side.

Yet there were none among them, hall born or commoner, who were ready to argue that they move out away from the headquarters they had established on the fringe of what had once been their homeland. If any of the speculation which had been aroused by the only half-read warning of Gromize's stones was being answered by action to the east, they had no way of knowing. Though there was often talk around the fire at night of what the High King might or might not do, whether the Voice might be urging a crusade of sorts. The shadow which might dwell behind both king and priest they did not discuss; their knowledge was too limited.

With the coming of the spring they alternated field work with scouting, taking it turn about. The scouting being a venture to be desired. At first it would seem that the whole of the country immediately below the Heights had been deserted.

Cautious exploration of deserted garths and manors proved that certainly no one else had ventured there during this season so far. They gathered what they could in the way of tools which could be reshaped into arms of a sort and twice drove back lean-flanked varges that had been left to winter.

They came across more signs of wakwolves and wild things than any had seen that far into the lowlands before. The watch on the highway was reestablished. But this silent land in itself made any man wary and restless.

It had been fully expected that with the coming of better weather the Temple slaves would be sent to the upper lands and they laid plans for the possible taking of such convoys and freeing their people. Yet none such appeared.

Three times Jarth called council and each time they had once more heated the message stones but they could learn nothing more.

"They are not asleep," the young Lord of Garn commented. "One can feel it. . . . " He was silent a moment and Kryn knew that prickle of excitement which roughened his skin momentarily as if he had stepped into one of the icy mountain pools. "If we but had a Dreamer!" Jarth brought his fist down on his knee.

Kryn tensed. A Dreamer—did not the Voice proclaim that all dreams came from his One? To deal even marginally with such craft was to risk being drawn into some net of the priests.

Hasper must have noted his reaction. "You think a Dreamer would serve us ill?"

"I believe that a Dreamer would be a key—to open the door to the hell that One is supposed to keep for us. Unchancy things are for the dark and the priests!"

"Not all are of the dark," Jarth returned. "In the days before Valcur made his One the center of all worship, Dreamers were welcome and honored. Lives were saved by dreams. But—in this much you are right, younger brother, such knowledge is tainted in our land. Perhaps it is not so however, elsewhere . . . " He stared musingly into the fire. And then he spoke more abruptly.

"We have salt, the seeds from the Rosclare garth. I think it is time we seek some news elsewhere."

He did not explain, nor did any one comment when the next morning, Jarth and Rolf were missing from the cave, their trail packs with them. Kryn's curiosity was tinged with wariness—what had salt or seed to do with their present quest for what was happening on the lower lands? Had the Lord of Garn gone to the shrine of some other power, which perhaps was supposed to favor his bloodline after such a mixed offering? But Kryn refused to give in to that curiosity and ask questions when there had been none from the others.

Jarth and Rolf were away for four days and slipped back into their quarters at nightfall as if they had never been gone. They ate heartily of the deer which had been luckily brought down that day and then became the center of a circle of listening men.

On a square of worked hide Jarth had stretched smooth on the rock floor before him, the young lord shook out four packets from the pouch he had carried in the front of his jerkin.

"Fever seal . . . " He pushed one of those packets to the side.

An herb Kryn recognized, having picked up something of the lore of what the growing things could do to alleviate the ills of men earlier from the foresters and, within the past few seasons, from these new comrades.

"Mold hold." The second packet joined the first. "Tongue leaf." The third packet was given a name. But Jarth sat for a moment holding the fourth.

His fingers loosed its cord fastening and he spilled out the contents freely on the hide. The message stones— but they had tried those over and over with no better results any time. However, with them this time there was a flake of glittering crystal, a thin sliver which was half a finger long and hardly more than a needle thick. And the stones appeared to have fallen naturally in a circle about that pointer. Had he not seen it with his own eyes, Kryn would not have believed what followed.

Jarth had set his hands back on his knees. No one else was in touching distance of the hide. But that glitter of tiny rod was moving of itself—it must be of itself. And in its going it touched each of the stones with its tip.

There was no fire needed this time to bring the symbols to life. Temple stone flared and it appeared to Kryn that the black mark across the One's hated symbol thickened and pulsed almost as if it were a vile worm, as did the brand across the king stone. But the stone with the sprinkling of crystal blazed high, almost as if it were afire. On swept the point and came almost to the final stone—that which had the sullen, ugly heart spot. That stone it did not touch, but it wavered back and forth before it as might an armsman seeking the best way to attack a well-armed foe.

"So it is," Jarth said slowly. "Temple—king—both driven by that greater than either. We stand on the brink of a dark struggle, comrades, and one which we defeat or die—no, worse than death awaits us when we face—that!" He pointed to the heart stone.

The sliver had ceased its twitching and lay quiescent, the emblems had faded from the stones. They were all dead and dull again.

"What else?" asked Hasper. "She dreams—what has she dreamed then?"

"She dare not seek the dreams—she swears that there is that awakening—that which felled all good before and would move again if it is threatened, and she thinks it might sense any use of the power now. We must wait and judge for ourselves. However, that which she has sought for years has been with her for some seasons now—new power—different and so perhaps more equal for the battle."

"What manner of power?" Hasper asked.

Who was this "she," Kryn wondered. A Dreamer? But apparently Jarth and the rest were ready to accept her as untainted by the Temple. Another outlaw—such as themselves? But power-tainted—all this talk of power was playing into the hands of the Temple. The priests sought out any who had the old knowledge and disposed of them quickly. They said that a sniffer could detect the taint of power for far distances. Such a sniffer as Bozi . . .

Kryn knew Bozi well enough. He had been of the family line—distant—of Qunion. When a youth younger than Kryn at his outlawing, he had entered Temple training. He was not a priest—but rather one of the hunters—those determined, vicious ones who turned their own kind over to Temple slavery—or the fires. He had never doubted that Bozi in some manner had brought down the House of Qunion—for Bozi had hated and envied and planned far ahead—that much Kryn was sure of.

But who was "she"? The medical herbs must have come from her—thus she at least was a healer. In that small way she could be a help and not a hindrance. But at that moment Kryn was glad she had not dreamed at Jarth's asking—they wanted no such beacon set to bring disaster on them.

As the warm season advanced the upper farms remained unworked. There were two slave convoys on the highway, heading to the mines. One was too well guarded to be taken by their force. The other they ambushed by night and found their number increased by near twice. Since they could not sustain such a number, they sent them westward, Kryn learning that beyond the broken lands were wide prairies where the cancer of war had not struck. Once there, he heard, those they had rescued had joined a traders' caravan headed for the main trade city of Kasgar.

Then their scouting parties, daring to range even farther eastward, reported the signs of large companies on the march as if an army were assembling.

"We are not their intended prey," Jarth said. "A large force sent into these hills, where we can make good use of every crevice and trail, would be speedily at a disadvantage. And they are moving south. Perhaps King

and Voice have decided at last to seek the empire both
have dreamed of. Yet they will pass through the Ryft,
and beyond that lies desert these days, for the river is
swallowed at the end of the valley and continues underground, no longer watering the plains beyond. They
needs must prepare a supply train such as will take them
some time to assemble, perhaps even until next spring.
Meanwhile what we can do to delay them, we must."
Thus the Outlaws of the Heights split into small bands
and ventured on expeditions into the plains lands, farther and farther. Now they did come on land under cul-
tivation—all Temple owned, slave worked. What small
loot they could carry on captured stock they did—fields
just beginning to ripen were put to the torch. The garths
and manors were often too well guarded to be attacked
by small parties, but before they learned caution Templers and overseers were cut off and killed and the slaves
urged to make themselves free of whatever they wished.

Those of the Temple could never be sure where they
would hit next, and twice bodies of well-trained cavalry
with some knowledge of such kind of warfare were sent
out to bait traps—one of which nearly caught the squad
of which Kryn was a member.

He had gained man's height in the mountains and the
hardness of his life had made him as lean and dangerous
to deal with as the wakwolves whose hide made his winter cloak. But he did not carry Bringhope. Much practice
with the veteran armsmen of the band had made him
sword sure and swift but he would not risk that badge
of his House in such combat—the heavy blade being
made more for the smashing attack of full battle than
this quick skirmishing and retreat.

They were cut off from a clear path back to the
Heights, having had to elude pursuers with a round-
about circling. And they had two men with bandaged
wounds; only dogged determination was keeping them

on their feet and going. The command of their small party lay with an armsman who had served well in the north, and coming south had been the key to freedom for Jarth and Hasper when they had had to flee before the Temple hunters.

Lars was a dour man, quick to light upon the smallest mistake, sour of speech and sullen of visage. But even Kryn had come to know that underneath this unattractive packaging there was a man who, had he been hall born, might have led an army with honor and ease. He was now one of the two who wore an improvised bandage, his arm tight trussed to his own bow stave to hold it immovable.

Kryn dropped to rearguard as they went. He was quick enough of eye and he had learned caution early. Now he would select some vantage of copse or rock and lie up while the others made their way along, all his attention for their back trail.

So it was that he first sighted the rathhawk. It circled on wide-spread wings—but this was not its land—and Kryn was wary enough for anything out of the ordinary to note that circling. The more he watched it the more he became convinced that this was no common predator from the outer wilds new-come to the lowlands.

Though it appeared to be at hunt, yet it did not make any strike, only continued to circle, each round it made tacking more and more out over the country through which their own party passed now. Circle, glide, but never strike. Yet that was uncanny for Kryn's own moves, wilderness trained as he was, had stirred up two fat ground pigs before he had reached his present cover. Surely hawk sight could pick up such easily—for the rathhawk was noted for its far-sight.

Now the bird hung so above him that he had to look up at an awkward angle to keep it in sight. And having come that close, it gave him sight of something else.

Rathhawk plumage was uniformly dull grey, though dark edging on some of the larger wing pinions gave it at times a curious mottled appearance. Its head bore a crest which did not rise except when it attacked, a beak could tear the hide in strips from the back of a colt, its claws could clasp the life out of small prey with one grasp of talons.

This circling thing now above him showed something else. Against the feathers of its broad breast sparked a glint of red. Then, as it made another turn, that swung out and away from the body for an instant. Long enough for Kryn to be sure that the bird wore about its neck some object suspended on a thong.

Any departure from the norm here was to be instantly distrusted. He had never heard of rathhawks being tamed to the will of man, but those of the Temple were ever about a search for new ways to spy, and new servants to do so. If this was Templer launched, then indeed it was the worst threat which his own kind had yet faced.

The copse in which he sheltered had several trees of good girth and height. Kryn worked his way around the base of the nearest, taking good effort to keep leaves and lace of branch as coverage against hunter eyes from above. He shucked off his war pack, stripped himself of sword and all else which might impede his climb, and hitched his way up the tree.

Though the movements of leaves and branches might now indeed alert the winged spy, for such he believed the rathhawk to be, still the bird could not get a good look at him—yet.

Kryn worked his way a little out along the first branch which offered some support. He steadied himself, shoulders against the bole of the tree trunk and loosed the grip of his hands. What he would do was chancy and it had little chance of succeeding perhaps but he could try.

With his left hand he reached out to another small branch and began to pull at it, using what strength he could to send it swaying. Rathhawks were hunters of the open country but they had one prey they would follow even into the woods. How good might he be in counterfeiting that?

Pursing his lips, Kryn gave voice to a call—hoarse enough from the strain of what he would do, but also akin to the proper pitch of sound. His right hand was ready with the knife he had carried up in the front of his jerkin.

There was a scream from overhead—much closer. Kryn cried an answer to that challenge. He jerked sharply at the bough and cleared a space for sight. Against the tree in which he sat there came a sharp blow. Leaves fluttered down. There was a tearing . . . the rathhawk was acting according to his kind and after the female he believed was hiding from him.

There was a heaving, a swaying in the boughs above. The hunter had landed, was working his way into denser foliage savagely aroused now. Kryn waited until he saw a segment of grey-feathered body, and, with all the patiently learned skill he had acquired during the past seasons, he threw.

A hoarse squawking, then a weight came bouncing down from branch to branch until the rathhawk fronted him. The knife still hung from one dropping wing but the darting head with its cruelly curved beak, the upheld and flexed talons of one foot were not to be lightly dismissed, even with the difference in size.

Kryn kicked, felt a sharp pain as claw and beak scored through his hide boot, but his attack, as quickly decided upon as it had been, won. The rathhawk vanished with widely beating wings, screaming as it fell, enmeshed in boughs and torn leaves.

Near as quickly Kryn dropped after it. There was a

moment to seize sword, to strike at the creature beating on the ground and then he stood panting, looking down at the enemy lying with its head nearly shorn away.

He rolled it over with the toe of his boot to discover that his eyes had not deceived him. There was a light cord about that twisted neck and on the ground lay a disc of gleaming red. Kryn stooped, reached, and then jerked back.

Instead he picked up an edge of branch and with it worked that cord free from the body of the bird, brought it free to dangle the disc in the air. A tracking device? A control for the hawk itself, to send it into attack? He could not be sure of either—only that it was something better left alone. The unknown in this country was suspect.

He draped the thong over a branch of sapling and left it awhirl in the breeze and turned to follow, at the distance-eating lope, the rest of his squad.

However, by nightfall they had made sure of something else: That the force which had nearly taken them was pushing on, heading determinedly south toward the Ryft, and it was moving at such pace as to suggest that not only a strike at them had brought it here but that it had business in the broken lands to the south.

When they had skulked along enough to make sure of that, and that the force would not turn again to hunt them down, they withdrew back to their own headquarters. Kryn told his tale of the bird which had searched through the sky and no one had any answer to that.

Once more Jarth consulted the stones, and this time the sliver of light he had brought back from his trip turned to the stone with its sprinkling of crystal dust and blazed high, the small particles embedded in the stone itself answering with sharp sparks as if flint had met with steel.

"So," Jarth said. "There is a new way before us. She calls and that call will be answered."

Thus at daybreak their band split. Lord Jarth, with Rolf and Kryn and three of the most experienced and woodwise of the outlaws, were the trailers again. It was midday when they came down into a new country where no hunt nor enemy had drawn Kryn before. A stream curled over a gravelly bottom, thickets of brush masking part of the banks.

Kryn scented the thin trace of smoke though he saw no fire, but on the other side of that river there were certainly two who waited—their dull clothing half disguising them except when they came closer to growing greenery. The taller stood in quiet waiting, her companion crouched by her side, and Jarth splashed into the stream toward her, the others following him.

Chapter 9

THOSE APPROACHING DID NOT WEAR THE
hated color of scarves or helmet quills Nosh remembered. Armed—yes—they had arms, although the
swords remained in their scabbards and they came to
shore before Dreen with bared hands. It was plain that
the woman had no fear of these, in fact had perhaps
sought them out.

He who now swung up on the low riverbank to confront Dreen was young, and unlike most of those who
were at his back he was clean-shaven; also the bow he
made to the waiting woman was that of lord. How did
Nosh know that? one small part of her mind asked. What
did she know of lords save what she had heard of those
beings who dwelt apart and looked upon such as won
their living with their hands as less than the blooded
animals tended in Keepmounts. There was another like
the firstcomer in carriage—younger and with a bitter
twist to his mouth, a heat in his eyes as he looked from
Dreen to her as might a wakwolf choosing prey.

This was no friend certainly. Still the leader's hand
fell familiarly on his shoulder and drew him forward.

"Heir to Qunion, Dreamer," the first man introduced

his fellow. The others, who plainly were trained and tested armsmen, splashed ashore but gathered a little away from the four on the bank as if they hesitated to intrude.

Dreen inclined her head. For a long moment the younger man stared stolidly back at her as if this meeting was none of his wishing. Then abruptly he ducked his head in a short gesture which had none of the grace of his companion's greeting.

"This is Alnosha." Dreen turned her head a fraction in summons and the girl reluctantly drew closer. There was that in the attitude of the second man which made her as wary as if he *were* wearing the black and red of those who had played hunter in her world.

"Alnosha," the elder of the two repeated and gave her a smile and bow. Again the other moved slowly as if loath to follow the formalities of an older and more gracious life.

"They enter the Ryft, they hunt," Dreen said. "That, which was the thinnest of shadows, moves again."

"We have seen. But those we spied upon would not have had time to reach your sighting," he answered her.

"Then they had forerunners, Lord Jarth. I cannot foresee because I dare not dream. It appears to me that we cannot choose our time now, we must move in answer to that which is thrust upon us. But we cannot remain any longer, and our own quest waits."

"We can give you cover on your way, Dreamer," Jarth replied quickly. "Are you thinking of trying the westward ways?"

She smiled a little. "It would appear now also that we have no other choice, Lord Jarth." But her eyes went beyond him to the other waiting there.

"You have hate in you." She made that both a statement and a question.

The younger man's mouth twisted as if on words

which were sour. "I like nothing of priests—and gods—"
he spat out and Jarth rounded on him with a frown, but
before he could speak Dreen made an answer.

"That is a matter for you alone," she said. "If you
think me akin to the Voice, why"—she shrugged—"you
are mistaken. But I do not force that belief upon
you. We serve no Temple, listen to no Voice . . ." Her
hands came up before her breast, wrist to wrist the palms
slanted back, the fingers separated as if hers were the
broken Hands of Lyr.

Nosh saw two of the armsmen duck their heads, and
heard a faint mumble as if words once often repeated
had found voice again.

Dreen had spoken calmly, almost as if she rebuked a
small child who did not understand. Nosh saw the
younger lord flush but his hot eyes did not leave Dreen's
serene, age-worn face.

"The Temple took my House," he said in a rough
rush of words. "They destroyed that warrior, my father,
and brought him to the slave noose—for they so poisoned his mind that he came to their bidding as does a
pack varge when one jerks the reins. I do not know how
they work their dark will—but that they can turn a
strong man into a slave with words alone—that I have
seen done."

"They did not take you also," Dreen said. Her hands
had dropped once more to her sides.

"No—nor shall they! I am Kryn and while I remain
Kryn and no slave, the heart of Qunion is not lost."

"You have nothing to fear of shadowy whispers from
my Lady," Dreen returned. "That which besets you is
also enemy to her."

Lord Jarth moved, putting himself a little between
Kryn and the woman. "This is no time for argument
concerning powers, Dreamer. You have asked our aid,
there has always been light between us, so thus we serve

as we can. Let us return to our own place."

"Well enough." Dreen bent and picked up her pack but Lord Jarth straightway took it and thrust his own shoulder through the carry loop. Nosh had reached for her burden also only to find that Kryn was following the lead of his companion and taking it up.

Dreen kilted up her robe skirts to face the river, Jarth putting out a hand to steady her as she went. But Nosh avoided aid—if Kryn had thought to offer any—and splashed into the chill water, cold enough to send a chill up her body.

They became a line of travelers, each following in the footsteps of the one before—two of the armsmen scouting ahead, then Kryn at the fore, Nosh quick after him having no mind to be separated from what poor belongings she had managed to assemble. Jarth was behind and close to him Dreen, then the others bringing up as a rear guard.

It was plain they were following a game trail, there were the printing of laster hooves in the earth, but the size of those beasts had opened a fairly wide passage for men.

Now began a rise in the ground and there they filtered into brush, losing sight of each other. Nosh moved up to tread nearly on Kryn's heels, disliking the thought of being perhaps left behind in this place. He never looked around and she thought perhaps he was not even aware of her. Then she tripped over a protruding root and would have fallen had his hand not shot out to grasp her arm and steady her.

"You are a Dreamer too?" He addressed her then abruptly.

Nosh shook her head. "I have not the powers. Dreen says that even she dares not use them now—we are watched—she thinks."

"By what—men, shadows—birds?" He half snapped those questions as he might loose arrows.

"Birds?" she repeated, totally at a loss. How did one watch with birds?

He might almost have read her thought, perhaps he did a little from her expression. "Rathhawks..." he continued, his voice a murmur which suited the closing of the brush around them.

"Rathhawks." Again she merely repeated his word without any understanding.

"Yes, rathhawks above!" He made a gesture toward the sky now hidden by the heavy growth around them.

When she did not answer at once he muttered impatiently. Then in a sharp voice continued:

"There was a rathhawk scouting—perhaps scouting for the very men who were hunting you out of the Ryft. It sighted me.... But if it was to report, it did not." He gave a little sound which had nothing of laughter in it. In a few sentences he drew a stark picture for her of hunted turned hunter and what had come of that.

"This thing that it wore." Her mind fastened upon that—perhaps because it sounded to her like one of those stones from which she could read. Maybe if she had it here between her two hands, she could have discovered the nature of the rathhawk and who seemed to control its flight.

"What was it like?"

Kryn's long-legged stride shortened and she was carried on to become level with him as he turned to face her.

"What do you know of stone power?" he demanded, and there was that hostility back in his eyes as he stared sharply at her.

"Only," she kept to caution, "what there is to be read in the old books. Dreen had such—we could not bring them with us—so they are hidden now." Was he one who could see only good in the destruction of old learning? He might be at odds with this Ruler priest he seemed to hate, but that did not mean that he was ready to accept other forms of learning.

But the mention of books seemed to lighten his scowl rather than deepen it. "Did any such tell of a rathhawk amulet tied to some seeker?"

Nosh shook her head. They had paused for a moment in their struggle with the brush. She could hear elsewhere the sounds of the rest of their party. But she was glad of this chance to catch her breath. Kryn was man tall, though she was sure now that his years were not many more than her own, and he had made no allowances for her shorter pace in this scramble.

"It was red,"—his fingers measured off a space for her—"and this size. I did not want to touch it—who knows what power might be loosed by the unknowing. It looked like any common stone, save that it was centered with a hole through which a cord was threaded and it was dark red such as no rock I have ever seen—unless colored so for some purpose."

"There are no birds left in the Ryft," Nosh said slowly. "But I have heard that there are coursers like to wakwolves which they turn upon slaves who try to flee. And those are obedient to the will of those who use them so. Dreen can summon the loop snakes, though she has never seemed to use them for any purpose. And the zarks—they are curious and they will come if one does not make a sudden movement and gives the click call." She thought of Tarm and Wasin. "It was they who first warned me of the coming of the soldiers—Tarm must have sighted the troop from his perch on the spire. Yes, in that they served well. But it was by their will, not mine."

Kryn shrugged and started forward. "There is no way to know that we can learn. We can only watch."

It took them two days of traveling to reach the stronghold of the outlaws. Though, after the first morning when they hurried to put the river behind them, Jarth had held them all to a slower pace. He spoke much with Dreen, taking his place beside her at intervals, their voices only a murmur since there was no room in this rough country to journey in a group.

That the woman of the Ryft and the outlawed lord were old friends Nosh was certain. The rest of their company kept their distance from Dreen as if they held her in some awe and Kryn markedly avoided her. Though he gave a kind of grudging companionship to Nosh. By the first evening her sandals, water-soaked in the stream, scraped by stones and roots, were frayed into strips swinging loose from her feet and ankles. It was Kryn who produced from his own pack a second pair of the same double-hided boots that he and the rest wore.

These were slippery to the touch from the grease rubbed in to keep them supple, and the smell was unpleasant. They did not fit—Nosh had to ball what was left of her own footgear and pack the toes before she could lace the boots tightly. But they were kinder to her bruised feet than any covering those had known in her memory. He shrugged aside her thanks even as he heaped up fallen needles from the mountain trees to make her a bed beside Dreen's. And he swiftly withdrew to the other side of their improvised camp.

However, when they gained that chain of caves the band called their home there was even more comfort. Nosh, used for years to short rations, eyed in wonder a whole haunch of laster turning, to loose rich drips of grease, on an improvised spit in what had been fashioned as a hearth many times the size of that which had held Dreen's small household fires.

There were tasks Nosh noted that even such as she who had no skill in woodscraft could do—the grinding of nuts, as she had ground the reed roots, into a coarse crumble from which she could fashion cakes glued together with that same dripping grease caught in a charred length of wood and stone below. She watched one of the armsmen fletching arrows with the same delicate skill one might use in weaving and set about copying his art until Lord Jarth himself swore he could not tell her work from that of a man who had known it all his days.

Dreen had been forced to give up her long-worn robe as Nosh had had to discard her woven and pieced clothing. They took on garments of deer hide, the lacing of which again Nosh could do with the same skill she had used for the braiding of snake skins. She moved freely in the breeches and found the jerkin snugly warm in the chill evenings.

There were the growing fields to be tended. Nosh spiked up some root vegetables—for their present eating—and for storage in one of the far-in caves which held the chill of midwinter even when it was full summer without.

Secretly she marveled at this world—rugged and mountainous as it was—for its difference from the ever-grey death of the Ryft. At times she wanted to sing aloud with sheer pleasure of the color and life around her—though that she kept to herself. But she was shadowed by a new worry.

Dreen, who had always been so impervious to every ill about them, as enduring as the devastated Ryft, grew slow of step, and stooped of back. She drew Nosh often into companionship while she spoke with emphasis of herbs, of healers' potions, even breaking at times into the cadence of the old power spells which she urged upon the girl until Nosh had them right, word for word, but was sure she would never attempt to use. Sometimes Dreen would halt in mid word and frown—rubbing two fingers across her furrowed forehead as if she were trying to remember. Her thin-lipped mouth would work as if she chewed upon the word but could not free it for speech. She would sigh and her shoulders would sag. Nosh was always quick then to lean forward and set her hand gently on that one, rubbing Dreen's head, stroking it smoothly and saying in a half whisper:

"Do not fret yourself—everyone forgets for the moment. It will come. Remember the tale of the Dreamer with three far eyes?" And then she would launch herself into one of those accounts she had read in the books. Hoping thus to prove to Dreen that she was indeed still the eager student and that Dreen's knowledge was what she must have.

She was well aware of the uneasiness which was growing with them all. Though they were laying in supplies for the coming winter, yet more and more scouting parties would go eastward and Nosh knew that there was now a steady stream of bodies of men headed south into the Ryft. It was, she knew well, the constant thing they were all waiting for—when that stream of forces would swing westward—for the death of the Ryft would not offer anything to those marchers and beyond lay only desert. They could not continue to head blindly south.

There came a night when Lord Jarth and his brother, plus one of the armsmen of much experience—Rolf— with Kryn lagging behind, came to that small side cave which had been made private for Dreen and Nosh.

Lord Jarth was plainly ill at ease but what showed on his brother's face was eagerness which Rolf also displayed. Only Kryn's scowl seemed to set him entirely against whatever his leader wanted.

From within his jerkin Lord Jarth brought out a small hide bag and stood, rolling it about in his fingers as he spoke:

"Lady, matters are moving and we do not know

where, how, or why. Yesterday Groff found sign of a scouting party here in the west. We have sighted two sniffers within a score of days—and one might have been a part of such a party. We do not ask you to dream since you say that that is a danger to us all. But can you read these for us? They came as a warning from one who had some power but there are none of us who know the right code.

"Once before I showed you these and you gave me another telltale to put with them. Only that tells us no more."

Dreen looked up at him, her face without emotion, and then she made a gesture and the four dropped cross-legged before her. Lord Jarth seemed to take that welcome as another order and he spilled out on the rock before her bundle of sleeping furs the contents of the pouch, which clicked down to the cave rock but did not roll.

Nosh edged forward until she could see them clearly from beyond Dreen's hunched shoulder.

"As I told you, Jarth,"—there was a tired note in Dreen's voice—"the code is not one of our devising. The Ryft had its own ways and knowledge and that held by ones beyond its borders were not like. But . . ." Her eyes had fallen to the one in which were answering sparks of light. "Child." She did not turn to look at Nosh, but her voice was that which had for so many seasons summoned the girl to tasks. "Use Lyr's gift—it may be all that we have."

As Lord Jarth stared in astonishment, Nosh put forth a reluctant hand and picked up the closest of those stones—the one on which was incised the Temple symbol with that black slash across it.

She cupped it in one hand, closed the other above it. There was warmth which flared. Not such as came from the gems her fingers discovered, rather something harsher. Involuntarily she closed her eyes.

Still she saw! Saw a great hall crowded with people and one who stood on a dais above that throng. Under a great mitered headdress his face was pinched, fined to skin over bone. And his eyes . . . his eyes were those of a trapped creature who sights certain death on the way.

Nosh found the words—describing what was before her—the heat of the stone was too much; she gave a small cry of pain and dropped it. But there was another will overriding hers—Dreen's—or something beyond even the priestess? Nosh picked up the king stone and looked from closed eyes.

Again a man with a haunted face, one who sat and gave orders with feverish speed to those passing before him—as haunted as had been the first.

"Priest—King . . . " Jarth said wonderingly as she allowed the second stone to roll out of her grasp. "Yet you say—reader of puzzles—that they are haunted men."

"They fear greatly," returned Nosh simply and then leaning far forward so she could reach it, she picked up a third stone. Not that of the crystal speckling but rather the one with the sullen fire in its heart.

Straightway she would have flung it from her again but she could not. There was darkness but not the darkness of night or even of a curtain—it was a-writhe as might curl a snake in death throes. Then in the heart of it came a nodule of light which seemed to grow like some noxious plant.

It was a sickly red as if blood from some deadly wound were mixed with poison which fed upon it. There was no man here—only that eye of light.

But . . .

It searched! Nosh screamed. One of those gathered there struck out at her cupped hands, the force of the blow sending the stone spinning out of her grasp.

Dreen's head was up—she was staring at the wall of the cave beyond the men; Nosh nursed her hands against her breast. Tears of pain squeezed from her now open eyes. But...

It searched!

She was aware dimly that Kryn had moved—it must have been his blow which had loosened her from that bondage. For that thing would have held her until its questing fastened directly upon her—that she knew. And she cowered, folding down in near a ball.

"It seeks!" Her voice shrilled into a shriek.

She heard Dreen's voice now, unshaken, holding firm, and from the woman's lips came words Nosh only dimly recognized. Power against power.... She wanted to put her painful hands over her ears to shut out that rhythm.

Then...

There was a roar which drowned out Dreen's spell. Nosh shook now, not because of terror, though that held her tight, but because the very rock about her was shaken as one might shake a robe to free it from dust.

Chapter 10

AS THE WORLD CRASHED IN UPON THEM Kryn had a flash of bitter thought. This was what came of dealing with powers. He heard a scream—blotted out by a crash. Their dim light was gone and the dark world around him now was one of madness where even the stone beneath him was heaving like a sea wave.

His head hurt and when, lying as he did now, he raised a hand to it his fingers met wetness and he smelled the unmistakable scent of blood. There was a brilliant flash—not over where he lay but to the left, searing eyes so that one could not see anything revealed by it.

More screams and cries. Cautiously Kryn moved his legs. There was weight on them but his actions freed him. More light—from which he cowered away, his face buried in the crook of his elbow as he lay.

Then—there was silence—complete and somehow deadly—until through it came cries, groans, oaths . . . The rock under him now seemed stable enough for him to lever himself up and he did.

There was no cave darkness about him, rather the grey of twilight. He blinked to clear his tearing eyes and peered out into that. Where the main cave of their mountain fortress had been there were piles of jaggered rock and the open sky of the coming night. By that most subdued of light he could see some movement.

Many must have been fatally trapped in that assault out of nowhere, but there were men getting dazedly to their hands and knees, swaying, then turning to try to aid their less free comrades. Kryn sat up and the whole of that which was about him whirled in a dizzy dance until he gritted teeth and willed himself into a measure of strength. It was his turn to look at those who had shared this inner portion of the cave with him.

"Jarth—Jarth!" a voice shrilled up at his side and he saw a shadow figure digging frenziedly at a pile of rocks—sending those flying in all directions, with no heed as to where they might thud home. Kryn dared not try to stand but he could crawl, and that he did, to where Hasper worked to free his brother.

As Kryn reached out his hands to aid in that labor he found himself looking down into the lighter splotch of a face, but that was a ruin and Rolf, he was sure, would never answer any war call again.

"Help—ME! Dreen . . . " A small hand caught at his arm, dragged him a little around. It was the cursed young priestess—she who had pulled this all down on them, for that what had happened was not of nature he had been sure from the beginning.

She was using full strength to urge him away from the brothers, farther on to another mound of stones. From the edge of that projected a thin, long-fingered hand raised as if to beckon them on. The other one—death summoner. Well, death had come and let her make the most of it—if she still lived, which he doubted.

There was a flash through the air and a stinging blow on his cheek rocked him back to sprawl painfully among the scattered rocks.

"You—help!" There was a fierce determination in

that order and in spite of himself Kryn obeyed.

Someone out in the main cavern had been able to kindle a torch and the light reached them as its bearer wavered in their direction.

"Lord Jarth?" a call delivered in a voice hoarsened by rock dust.

"Here . . . " Hasper replied and his one word was emphasized by the roll of the rocks he was feverishly tossing.

Kryn saw the girl clearly now. She was scrabbling at the fallen debris, her dust-coated face patterned with thread thin trickles of blood, her eyes only for the prone body beside which she crouched.

In spite of his hate for what she and that other had done, even though it had been at Jarth's own bidding, Kryn hunched closer and began to give her aid.

There was no movement in the body they worked jerkily to uncover. As soon as the face, turned to one side, was free Nosh's hand went out seeking the pulse at the jawline. He had seen fear before on many a face but what he read on Nosh's now set Kryn to work faster until the whole lank length of the woman's body was free.

"Dreen!" Nosh's was near lying on the priestess now, her mouth to the other's mouth, her hands pressing on the older woman's ribs. She was striving to bring back air to those lungs but it was a battle already lost. When Kryn tried to tell her so she fended him off with an arm and continued her struggle. Kryn shrugged and looked now to where Jarth lay.

They had freed the commander and Hasper was holding his brother's head on his knee. Jarth groaned and tried to rise but Hasper restrained him. He looked across that limp body to Kryn.

"Layon—get Layon!"

The one of their company who had a rough knowledge for the tending of sick and wounded, men and animals both. Somehow Kryn got to his feet and remained there by gripping the shoulder of the man with the torch who was now in their midst.

By some chance of fortune—and any sign of fortune was to be treasured now—it was Layon himself who had come to light the scene. He thrust the torch into Kryn's hold and knelt beside Jarth, his hands moving across the other's body slowly, as if he forced himself to keep that touch as light as he could.

"Broken ribs," he reported, "and the leg. If there be internal hurts, we cannot tell."

He was blunt but Kryn tensed. It was far better perhaps that Jarth had perished at once than he drag out dying when they could do so little to abate the pain.

"Dreen . . . ?" it was a quavering cry which paid no attention to the cluster of men.

Kryn involuntarily held the torch higher. Nosh sat now with the priestess's head cradled against her breast. She was not crying, but there was such a desolation on her face as to make it one of the mask of the damned such as the priests of One used to overawe their worshipers.

"Dreen?" she called but there was no answer. Layon paused in his work over Jarth. He peered closely to where Nosh supported the priestess and then shook his head and went back to his attentions to Jarth.

Nosh settled the heavy head of the priestess on her knees and with both hands brought out of her jerkin something she wore on a cord about her neck. She plucked at it frantically, until there fell out into her hand something which caught the torch glow and became a thing of living fire. Nosh pressed it against that unresponsive head she supported and he saw her lips moving as if, in less than a whisper, she was repeating again some magical formula.

No! She was not going to again draw in upon them another stroke of that power! He swooped to catch at her wrist, jerk her hand up and out, trying to shake free from her grasp what she held that he might grind it into harmless dust.

Nosh's head darted down, her mouth opened, and her teeth closed on his fingers, breaking flesh and bringing blood, so that instinctively he loosed his hold and pulled away. She stared up at him through the tangled loops of her dust-laden hair, and her eyes seemed to hold the glint he had seen in those of the she wakwolf he had slain at the time of Ewen's death.

"Dare—!" she spat at him. "Dare, Killer, you who own no god nor goddess! This is of Lyr and it could well be your end, man of blood and death!"

He could see now that what she held was a length of gleaming crystal a little longer than one of her own fingers but of a similar shape. Again she touched it gently to Dreen's forehead.

To Kryn's astonishment—for he had been sure the woman was dead—her eyes opened and Nosh stooped lower so that their gazes met.

"Dear...daughter...in...the...the light," though the words were only a whisper, yet for some reason Kryn caught them clearly also. "Go...go forth—the search..." She paused as there was a bubble of blood at the corner of her mouth. Nosh gently wiped it away with her finger. "The time—it is very short—do what must be done." From somewhere she had drawn the strength to speak the last few words in a strong voice. And then her eyelids fluttered but she still seemed to hold to life by a strong will, for she added:

"Dear...daughter *SHE* sent me...grieve not... *HER* hands await..." The blood burst more strongly from her mouth and she gave a last great sigh.

Nosh bent to kiss that bloody mouth. Her features

were set, mask hard. Carefully she rebagged the crystal and stowed it out of sight again. With care, as if she still tended the living, she stretched the priestess out on the rock, folding the woman's gaunt hands across her breast, before she looked up to Kryn.

"She must be given to the fire..." she stated with the firmness of one in authority. "Honored—for she was the last..." Her voice quivered and then she quickly gained control of it. "She will be honored!" Her chin came up, and, small and young as she was, he understood that she intended that her wishes be carried out.

As at length they were. But Dreen's body was not the only one given to the flames that day. Nearly a third of their force died in that encounter. And those who had been outside the caves when the power blow struck had had worse deaths, for the whole side of the mountain was charred and fire stained. Such a force was beyond the understanding of any of them, Kryn thought.

Now—they must salvage what they could from the caves which could no longer be trusted. Most of their mounts had died in the mountain flame. And exploration to the storage caves had to be taken as a perilous job, slowly and with all care, for rocks still fell within.

Jarth lay in an improvised tent outside. He had not yet recovered consciousness, for which Kryn and his brother were thankful, for the rough usage they had had to use to unite his bones would have brought a hell of pain. There were five others sharing his shelter and in as bad if not worse state—one died before the falling of the next night.

Nosh, once she had left Dreen, came to aid in their care. Dreen had taught her much and well and she brewed draughts which brought sleep and held away pain, and seemed to know without being instructed just how to help Layon reset broken bones and bandage wounds.

Fearing that the stroke which had broken their rock fortress might only be the beginning of an assault and that there could be some force now marching in upon them, those who were whole, or only bruised or slightly wounded, set up a tight guard and the scouting parties went out without orders.

Now and again Kryn's path crossed Nosh's. To his sight the girl showed no sign of grief, certainly none of horror at what had happened from her own act. He longed to accuse her of that but it was Jarth's rule held here and he must wait for the lord to recover enough to take command before he made such an accusation.

However, he tried as best he could to keep an eye on her, make sure that she would not indulge in any more treachery, such as perhaps signaling lurkers below. Though the mountain fire had burned off most of the cover and there was no way any advance upon their position could go unnoted. Unless—startled at a sudden thought—Kryn looked skyward. It had been a grey day—though luckily no rain had fallen—and now it was dusk. He remembered only too clearly that rathhawk with its strange necklet. Such could well hang above them now and be reporting just how hard hit they were.

Rathhawks—and if they circled closer in, the night would give them excellent cover. Those of the camp dared not douse all fires—they needed the light too badly to serve the wounded and those who worked to salvage what they could. He could not hope to find any answer to the birds if or when they came.

They had dragged the carcasses of the dead mounts as far from their present rough camp as they could. The bodies were badly charred but they had no way of burying them and what wood they had they kept for the funeral pyre of their own kind.

Rolf was gone—and his going was a blow. Kryn knew that Jarth depended upon the veteran armsman as he might on a known shield comrade of the old days. Warfare was Rolf's knowledge and he had all the cunning and learning to make him invaluable to any commander. Hasper served his brother well as a left hand, but Rolf had certainly always been his right since they had come into outlawry.

With Jarth unable to frame an order, and Rolf gone, Hasper would be in command. Kryn did not fault the younger lord. He was a worthy son of his house and he had learned to live in and on the wild, but Kryn wondered whether he could take rulership here over many men twice his age and experience. He would stand with Hasper no matter what happened but he hoped with all his heart that Jarth would recover.

The time was bad. They were only a short way from the first thrusts of winter. Their supplies, so carefully stored, might well have been nearly wiped out. And their present place of refuge was known—to someone— or that blow would not have fallen so true and drastically. It had been an ill day when Jarth offered shelter to those two from the Ryft with their strange powers. . . . See what had chanced from the evoking of such?

There came no report from their own scouts as to any movement cross-country but they did not relax any vigilance on that account. And other scouts went out farther westward, seeking another place in which they could hole up before the coming of the winter snows.

Those varges which they had used for heavy field labor and for the transport of burdens had not died with the mounts, for they had been at graze in a field on the western side of this height ridge. Hasper, Layon, and Kryn worked on ideas for some form of transport via the plodding beasts to a new country, if and when they could find such. And all through the days Kryn kept a close eye on the sky for the sight of rathhawk wings.

Unfortunately Jarth developed a fever which took his

counsel out of their decisions. It was very plain they could not remain where they were so exposed. And to burrow into the cave linkage again after what had happened was out of the question. At last Hasper summoned to a meeting all those not engaged in scouting and asked for suggestions.

The most practical one came from one of the men who had often been on westward scouts.

"There is the well at Dast," he spoke up hesitatingly, as if half expecting to be interrupted before he got his offering completely in words. "That is valley land, and did not our Lord Jarth once consider an outpost there before thinking it too far from the borders we watched? The place can be better sheltered than any hereabouts, there is forage for the varges—and our hunters have not combed those hills too often. There is still chance before first snow to build up our supply of smoked meat."

"Dast," Hasper repeated slowly, as if by that word he could summon up a mind picture of the site. Then for the first time his gloom broke a little. "Dast! Yes, that is close to the merchant lane—if need be, and there is chance, we can hope for trade. The southerners have little liking for Templers and have we not often sent others who refuged but could not join with us thereabouts to join caravans? Also if we go by the long cut, the travel will not be too hard for those we must transport." And he glanced at the tent wherein lay those still unable to care for themselves.

Kryn was willing to agree to the idea when Hasper put it swiftly to a vote. Triscor, who had made the suggestion, was designated to scout ahead and mark the best trail they could hope to take; he left before nightfall.

Kryn trailed along behind Hasper as they went to the tent in search of Layon to discover the healer's point of view concerning such a trek. Someone sitting just outside the door flap raised head at their coming. Kryn scowled. For all her heal-aid he thought no more of that half-priestess than he had when she had pulled the strange and awesome wrath upon them.

She had been engaged in lacing together strips of wakwolf skin to fashion a cold weather cloak. And she favored them with that usual blankness of countenance she had worn since she had stood and watched the bier flames take the body of her mistress.

Without a word she slid now to one side to allow Hasper entrance to the shelter. There was no room for Kryn to crowd in also and he must stand without.

It was she who broke the silence: "Where lies this Dast, armsmen?"

He was half-inclined not to answer. Why did she want to know? That she might set on their trail that which she had aroused? If Hasper had the full sense of their troubles, he would see this one remained behind when they marched out. Jarth had openly favored these women; but Kryn had distrusted them from the first sighting.

She continued to look at him as if able to pierce his silence with her will, and at last he spoke.

"Dast is on the western side of the Heights. It is a meeting place for traders on the south trek. But there will be little chance of meeting with such now—the season is past and if any caravan comes, it has been so delayed that it is in some danger. We have not gone there except to visit now and then, for the borders are our concern."

"Those are still your concern, armsmen?" she asked, never stopping in her lacing to give him full attention. "This has been a force to reckon with . . . when it met man to man with Templers . . . is it so now? But that . . . " She hesitated and her hands ceased work, one of them raised to rest on the breast of her jerkin. "If *that* which searched comes again . . . "

"At your summons?" He was goaded by his own worry into demanding.

Once more she was silent. Then he saw the very tip of her tongue touch her nearly closed lips, sweep across as if freeing the words which followed:

"I have the talent Lyr has given, armsmen. That cannot be twisted or misused—for then any power aroused would revert to blast me. That is the nature of power— the power of light. I have had laid on me the will of Dreen and through her the will of LYR Everlasting. There is that I must do. It has nothing to do with you or these men who fight for their freedom and justice. Dreen said with her dying that time itself was moving against us. Thus I must be on my own way—if it leads to the Dast and then perhaps southward—that is where I must go. What raised the rock itself against us used such power that it must be drained—for now. So it is well that we all make use of this time as best we can."

"You speak the truth, Dreen Daughter." Hasper had come out of the tent. "We have little time left. If the first storms find us here, few will last through the winter."

Nosh nodded and turned back to her work but Kryn thought angrily that Hasper was missing the point . . . that if he intended this scrap of a female to accompany them, he was asking for trouble indeed. And he turned away to busy himself with sorting over the pile of equipment they had managed to salvage from the caves.

Chapter 11

IT WAS WELL, NOSH THOUGHT, AS SHE shouldered her pack some days later, that she was already trail tried. Once or twice her thoughts flitted to that other deadly march into the Ryft. But since then there had been the journeying with Dreen and the confidence she had gained from what she had learned—not only from the priestess—but from her own endeavors. She still kept company with the healer, standing ready to aid when he had any need of help. So she was to travel now with the slow-moving train of varge-supported stretchers.

The hill company that was left split into two—one portion to travel with the wounded, the other bringing up the rear. To her satisfaction that dour and unpleasant Kryn was attached to the latter while Hasper commanded the fore. She had not met with such outward suspicion and hate—not since she could remember—though there was that dark time deep buried which she flinched from recalling.

He was right in that her talent must have drawn the attack which had blasted this company. As Dreen had pointed out—power drew power. And if that other was already perhaps seeking, it had quickly made her touch a goal at which to aim that blow. She wondered what had become of the message stones—they were probably well buried—let them remain so for safety's sake.

They were following now a rough trail which had to be cut for the passage of the varge-borne litters leaving a track easy enough to be followed. But there was no way one could take men suffering broken limbs with any stealth. As it was Layon and she were called upon time and again to make sure that the ties holding those bodies in place had not shifted, ready with drinks of herb-thickened water to give as much freedom from pain as they could.

At least one anxiety had been eased—that fever which had threatened to devour Jarth had finally left his broken body. He was very weak but knew them and understood what they were doing, agreeing at once with the decision which had been made.

The weather, which had been cloudy, now turned against them and rain began to fall, a rain which had some of the ice of sleet in it. They piled over and around the injured all the robes and cloaks which could be found, men shivering in that steady falling water without any covering that the others might be given all the comfort possible.

Rain also made the way they followed slippery. Only the pace that the ponderous varges went, at almost less than a man's walking speed, planting each hoof firmly, kept them from a disastrous slip. Lighter-footed, faster mounts would have had to be led by their dismounted riders through this. But for even the varges the pull against the clinging mud was hard and they had to have frequent halts to rest the blowing beasts.

It was during one of these that Nosh, assured her aid was not at need, cut to the edge of their way and found a small hollow beneath a dead tree which had been kept

from measuring its length against the ground because its
branches embraced and laced with those of its nearest
fellow. She allowed herself some mouthfuls of dried
laster flesh, chewing the stringy stuff with vigor to make
sure she extracted the small existing flavor and moistening it enough to swallow. Her hunger had brought her
here but as she chewed she was suddenly aware of
something else.

Cold as the rain had chilled her flesh, Nosh felt a
growing warmth between her breasts. She pulled apart
the lacing of her jerkin far enough to be able to touch
that hair bag in which rode the Finger. Yes, it was
warm—rapidly exuding not only heat but a glow of light.

At first she hunched in upon herself. What would follow? Another blasting out of nowhere? Thinking that
she scuttled away, putting the tree which had sheltered
her, and more and more room, between her and that
sorry procession halted on the trail. She wanted no harm
to come through her again.

As Nosh crawled, fearing to rise to her feet now lest
she be sighted and her danger understood, she suddenly
felt the wet, fern-grown soil give way under the hand
she had put out to steady herself. With a cry she had
not time to check, she tumbled forward down a slope
into a narrow ravine cutting almost hidden through this
land.

Her fall ended with force as she brought up against a
rock and she whimpered. But under her other hand,
through the hair veil which held it, the crystal Finger
flared as might a new-lit torch. And that flare was answered!

Somehow Nosh pulled herself to the other side of the
rock. The hand which helped to draw herself came
down on something hard, which cracked under her
weight, slight as that was. She felt the scrape of a sharp
edge of something across her flesh.

A bone! There was no mistaking what protruded, lying in two pieces now where her weight had broken it. And there were more. She who had been nurtured in the dull death of the Ryft felt no dismay as she stared down to trace the outline, tumbled though the bones were, of a skeleton—sighting at last what was not another smaller rock but the dome of a weather-darkened skull.

But it was what lay within that tangle of bones which made her totally unconscious now of the remains. There lay a twin to what she carried—a second crystal Finger!

Swiftly she caught it up, pried open the drawstring bag, eagerly comparing it to the one she carried. It was a little longer than her first find but no two fingers on a hand were the same length, so that was only the way of nature.

Working with infinite care not to break the bag Dreen had woven, she got both of the Fingers into hiding, now aware of a crashing near the cut edge of the ravine. They must have heard her cry and come in search. But this was a secret of her own and one she was not about to share. She made very sure the two Fingers were completely hidden before she raised her voice and called— to see the last one she wished to find her so—that Kyrn—staring down, his expression one of disgust—or so she deemed it. A moment later he was joined by one of the armsmen and together they dropped a rope by the use of which she was able to reach the top.

That the rear guard had caught up with them was a factor which bothered the whole company. It was so plain that they must match their pace to the slowness of the varges, and also keep touch between the two parties.

Nosh gave no explanation as to what had happened, save that she had thought to see a pacer hen and hoped to add it to their supplies. Kryn had grunted before he left to gather his party and hold them while the varge train got into a floundering move once more.

Her good fortune in finding the Finger led to memories she had tried to wall out—as she had earlier ones. She did not want to think of Dreen as she had last seen her, resting in death on the bier the torches were already setting a-smolder. It seemed to her bleakly as she kept to the slow pace beside one of the varges, where she could watch the man swung in the litter between the two animals, that whenever she had found a stable friend in this dreary world, the end was that she was left alone again.

Now, resolutely, she pushed her thoughts into another channel. How had this Finger come among the bones she had stumbled upon? Dreen had said that those who served Lyr and had remained alive after the fragmentation of the Hands had taken the Fingers and scattered that they might preserve those precious pieces for the future. Had one of those priestesses—or priests—come this way, been slain, and left without burial? If the Finger had been carried in any bag, that had long since rotted away. But now she knew this much—that what she carried would eventually lead her to another—and in time—if she herself was not lost to the quest—to all of them.

It took them nearly twenty days of marching along that rude trail before they found their way down a last slope and could see the edge of the western plains lands. The last few nights in the Heights had been perilously chilly, and they had lost another of the injured during that painful trek.

Lord Jarth still lived, but in the last two days he had lapsed into something which was not a normal sleep, nor even unconsciousness. For his eyes were open at times, though if anyone strove to get his attention, he remained unanswering, blank of expression. Layon called upon all his skills and Nosh was able to supply some bits of lore from Dreen's teaching. At least they had kept the lord and the other three injured men still alive.

It was near to sunset when they were joined by a guide from the advance party, who had already marked the best way down the slope, and so they came to Dast.

There were crude buildings there—their walls largely formed of rocks fitted roughly together with a banding of dried mud rounding outward from around the stones it was meant to anchor. The roofs were saplings cut and then fitted together with an overmasking of what was a mixture of mud and the long prairie grass. But this was better than they had dared to hope for.

Jarth and the other injured men were settled in the largest of these shelters, which had been cleaned by the advance guard, of the debris left by the various merchant caravans of the past season. There had been four of those, according to markings left on one wall block, and the last two had spoken of trouble from raiders.

"Outlaws . . . " Hasper was considering those abbreviated messages. "But who? We found no sign of such. And certainly we do not prey on the caravans and never have."

"We are overmountain from the movements of the Templers and the king's forces. What we saw of them were heading south not west." Kryn had brought in the rear guard with the welcome news that none of their back trail scouting had turned up any evidence that they were being followed.

"Look here . . . " Hasper traced some last scratched signs with a fingertip. "Warning—and it lies under the listing of the last caravan. Note how each added in their own fashion from the reports of general travel, water, forage for animals and the like—running down to this. This last one speaks mainly of trouble. Two guards shot

from an ambush and a try at a night raid, beaten off by
the caravan.

"We made contact earlier in the season with Balisas—
his sign is by this second record. All was well then. But
after that last, another warning. It is late in the season
and no trailwise merchant would willingly linger, even
if the bargains were greater than he expected. These
deal mainly with the Zandu of the northwest—furs—
some jade rock—once in a while tusks of a Qerna bull.
Light stuff—but worth enough to make the trip pay,
long and hard as it is. They are more heavily laden going
in than out—for they carry weapons, cloth, salt to trade.
If there was a fifth caravan—what has become of it? The
mountain passes into Zandu country must already be
snowed in."

However, the fate of unknown merchants was not
their present concern—rather work on the shelters to
make that housing as secure as they could before the
first snowfall. The varge ate steadily, welcoming the
prairie grass, brown-dried as it was. After the nature of
their kind they were building up as speedily as they
could those rolls of fat which would keep them going
over the lean times when fodder might be sparse.

Six of the men were told to hack at that same grass,
bring it to thicken the thatch of the roofs. Water drawn
from the great well which centered their settlement was
mixed with earth into thick mud to be tramped and
pounded down over that grass. Kern took two of the
varges and two men and headed back up the way they
had come, returning with mountains of dried wood
lashed on the complaining beasts—and they made such
a trip there often, taking each time different animals.

They had lost so much, but there were hunters out
too. Fresh hides were pegged down, to be scraped clean
and softened as best as possible. Nosh, having inspected
with a critical eye the tufts of grass, began to sort over

each bundle brought in and laid aside certain lengths. Her serpent skin cloak, near long worn to nothing, was her pattern and she essayed now to copy that weaving after a fashion.

She took her full share of the cooking, the nursing, even of mixing the mud. There was no division here between the labor of man and woman—men scraped at the hides and, in spare moments, turned scraps into footgear. She gave a hand where it was most needed.

However, in those moments free of general duty she set doggedly to weaving with her grass, one layer, another, until she had a strange-looking garment—like an oblong with a hole in the middle. That slipped over the head and then the narrowing of each side left free enough the arms, but the long fore and back panels could be belted in. Once on, the garment could be stuffed breast and back with loose grass. She found it warmer almost than the hide clothing she had been wearing and Layon, seeing her in it, immediately wanted one for himself. So Nosh found herself excused from all else so that she could weave for them all.

In search of longer and tougher grass she would venture farther from the pocket of settlement and discovered then that the prairie was not as smooth a land as it looked to be—there were gullies, and once she found a dried stream course.

Squatting down there she wiped her sweaty, earth-stained hands with a tuft of the grass and looked to the gravel of that long-dried bed. Her hands were scraped and raw, cut in places by tough grass edges. But . . . her talent was still with her. She had no warning from the crystals she carried but her fingers closed unerringly on a piece of water-worn stone that showed, as she turned it around, a green glow. Jade . . . her studies with Dreen made her sure of that.

How far it might have been borne along by the van-

ished floods she could not tell—she had never heard of
the stone being found anywhere but in the northwest.
But where there was one piece there might be another.
Her grass gathering forgotten for the moment, she swept
her hands slowly across the drifts of gravel.

In the end Nosh harvested four pieces, the other three
smaller than the first water-worked pebble but worth,
she was sure, the labor of her hunt. She was about to go
farther upstream when she heard that cry . . .

It was more moan than call and she had some time
locating its source but at last she found a dead mount,
arrows in its flanks, and beside it a woman—or rather a
girl, she saw as she turned her over. There was a wound
in the rider's shoulder, the shaft of another arrow,
though broken, still protruding from the flesh. And the
stranger's whole upper garment was sticky with blood.

As Nosh tried to examine that wound the girl's eyes
opened; she stared in terror at the other and tried to jerk
away.

"Vor—Vor—" her voice shrilled.

"I give help," Nosh tried awkwardly to reassure her
find. "You lose blood—I must bind as I can until you
are at Dast . . . "

She loosened her belt and pulled off the grass garment. Somehow she must get that on the stranger as a
binding against that blood flow. She had nothing else
here to serve.

The girl screamed as she worked, threw out an arm
to beat her off. Then she fainted and Nosh finished her
hasty binding. She had no way of getting her to Dast
without help and that she must get as soon as possible.
Starting on a dead run, she headed for the refuge. Soon
enough she was back, Layon on her heels, his arm
crooked about some hastily caught up lengths which
could be used for bandaging.

The girl still lay as Nosh had left her and Layon went

about his business with dispatch while she gave him what aid she could. Three of the others had come pounding out to see what had happened and Layon dispatched two of them back to Dast for one of the litters on which their own injured had been transported.

"She is of a caravan," the healer reported as he worked. "Hers is city clothing from the south. Ah, may she remain still unknowing while we get this out." He was touching the stub of arrow gingerly. "This is fresh. . . . "

"Hunted?" asked Nosh and got quickly to her feet. The gully walls were high here; there might be those even now on the trail of the stranger and close enough to bring danger not only to the prey who had escaped them but also to those who would succor her.

However, it seemed that the third man who had come up must have already been aware of that possibility, for he put a call whistle to his lips and blew a sharp, high note well understood in the code the outlaws had set for themselves.

The tall grass, Nosh thought swiftly, might cover the advance of any who were canny enough to crawl. It grew in places as high as a varge's thick shoulder. But certainly the weaving of the grass stems if any so advanced, would give them away to men as keen-eyed as those who would answer that call.

If there had been any follower close on the heels of the wounded girl, he held off and lay in hiding now. Nosh saw the well-armed men of the day guard scatter outward in a fan behind which they carried the caravan girl back to the shelter. If she had regained consciousness, she gave no sign of it. Nosh glanced around once to see one of the armsmen behind them shouldering the saddle and equipment of the dead mount.

As they settled their discovery on one of the pallets within the shelter Hasper came hurriedly in. The girl's

white face was turned aside as Layon had settled her as
best he could to work on her wounded shoulder. Hasper
squatted down on the other side, looking from her to
Layon and back again and at last turning his head in
Nosh's direction.

"Where did you find her?" he demanded.

Nosh spoke of the gully of the dried stream. And
added:

"She was greatly afraid and when she saw me she
called out 'Vor.' "

"Vor . . . " he repeated. "But that cannot be so. There
are no Vor this far north—unless there is much going
wrong about which we do not know. And Vor are no
enemies to the traders. . . . They are not a friendly people save with the Mimians—but that they would attack
a caravan . . . How long?" He shot that question at
Layon.

"It could not have been long—she could not have
ridden far and her mount was badly shot—it would not
have kept going for long."

Hasper's face tightened grimly. "So. If there are those
who are preying on a caravan near here, then they are
such as are no friends to us either."

He was gone and a moment later Nosh heard again
the code whistle, this time sounding assembly. But that
had hardly died away before there was a shouting. She
saw Lord Jarth jerk on the pallet across the hut, try to
lift himself, and she was instantly beside him in re-
straint.

"No, Lord Jarth. You must not move. . . . "

For the first time in many days he looked up and she
saw recognition in his eyes as if the din had drawn him
back from that far place where he had been hovering.

"What chances . . . ?" His voice sounded weak but it
was plain she must answer him.

Nosh reported the finding of the stranger, that Layon

thought she was from a caravan. But she had to raise her voice as that distant din grew ever louder. Now she could distinguish in it the bellows of varges being goaded past their usual pace, and once there was a scream which surely came from a human throat.

Lord Jarth caught her arm and there was surprising strength in that hold.

"See . . . see what is happening!"

She obeyed, gaining the door of the hut just in time to see a large, varge-drawn wagon careen in toward the well. She would not have believed those heavy animals could move at such a pace. Behind it was another, and then a third.

Beyond there was a swirling of dust where the prairie earth, grazed nearly bare by their own animals, was being cut by the sharper hooves of mounts. Some of those were ridden by men in green robes, but the rest were wearing the mail of guards—though there was no sign of either red or black as she had first feared.

The whole scene was so cloaked by dust, and those within it moved so fast, that she could not be sure of just what was happening. But at length those who made up the incoming party drew closer and here and there Nosh could see some of the armsmen drawing bows and shooting with their deadly precision. Not at the newcomers but back along the route those had traveled.

Thus the merchant Danus of the fate-ridden last caravan made it into Dast.

Chapter 12

"THIS IS NO VOR." TUVER, WHO HAD taken Rolf's place as Hasper's right hand and under officer, used a hearty nudge from his foot against a limp body, rolling it over on its back.

"He's wearing face paint," protested one of the few caravan guards who had survived the trail battle to Dast.

"Maybe others beside the Vor go in for such," Tuver returned. "But he's a head taller than any Vor I've ever seen and I made the south trail twice in past seasons. Also where is his warrior band—and whoever saw a Vor with hair the color of dried prairie grass? When did they jump you?"

The guard drew his hand across his forehead as if trying to remember something which the attack had driven from his mind.

Kryn looked down at the dead man. He certainly was not wearing any Templer trappings, nor the colors of the High King. As the guard had pointed out, his slack face was overlaid with an intricate pattern of color which was heaviest about his now staring eyes as if it were meant to provide a mask of sorts. His hair was a dusty brown and those open eyes a faded blue which was nearly grey.

He was as tall as the two men now standing over him and his clothing, which included a jerkin oversewn with dull metal rings, was nearly as shabby as that of the outlaws.

"Must have been three days back," the guard began slowly. "Yes, Garmper had just shot a rathhawk. . . . "

Kryn stiffened, and glanced hastily skyward. A rathhawk!

"It had this thing on a string around its neck," the guard was continuing. "Garmper turned it in to the Master—never saw anything like it before, none of us had. Then, we'd gotten the carts lined out to forward and Garmper went down—an arrow through his gullet. I don't know why they didn't just stay their distance and pick us off. But instead they came for us, yelling their heads off, shouting some gibberish about meat—suppose they meant us.

"Master Danus knows all the tricks and we entrained as fast as we could—most of us fighting off the buggers while Danus enforted with the wagons.

"We beat them but good. Didn't see any of them get away—it was as if they were crazed in their minds, taking stupid chances just to try and kill us without trying to protect themselves. It was just plain slaughter, like a wakwolf in a salzon corral. Only we weren't no salzons—and they weren't no wakwolves either. They went down right easy when the boys got into action.

"There were about twenty in that gang—at least we counted that many bodies. We lost two men besides Garmper—one of them Master Danus's sister's son. And he doesn't take kindly to that.

"We sat there entrained but we were in the open and if they came at us all fired high again, we could not hold too long. The Master—he said try to make it to Dast. Oathar volunteered to do a bit of scouting and came back saying he couldn't see no trace of any and perhaps we had gotten them all. So at last Master Danus decided to risk it for a dash here—those trail varges can be pushed to more speed than you believe when a man really uses the prod—makes them crazy mad and they push fast to get at anybody riding ahead.

"Well, they hit us again. Seemed to come right out of the ground, cut off the last wagon—Rayan says how he saw two of them go at the varges, one got trampled but the other brought down the nigh leader. Master Danus's new wife from the north was in that. But she is no city woman—she got to one of the mounts and rode—but away from the train and we could not go after her—must have been dazed like. They say she was found by your people."

"She was arrow wounded," Tuver answered. "Your master is with her now. It looks as if we must fort up ourselves—if these,"—again his toe touched the body,—"are going to come down on us again. You say this new wife is from the north . . . ?"

The guard nodded. "He wedded her three ten-days ago. Made a good treaty with her people and her father turned her over to seal the bargain."

"Might it be that her people were all not in favor of that?" For the first time Kryn took part in the conversation. "The fact that she was shot might have been a mistake—and when she left she was trying to reach these raiders."

"They're not like any of the Kolossians; that's her tribe. At least not like any I've seen. Kolossians don't paint and they wear their hair in a top braid. . . . Makes a handle, they say, for their war god to pick up his own after a battle. Also she didn't seem to be unhappy about the wedding—looked to us all that she might have urged it her own self. She was always asking questions about the city and how we lived there, as if she wanted to see it all for her own self and was very happy to be on her way to do so."

Tuver looked across the torn and trampled ground. They had already removed three dead caravan guards and two of their own and there were new wounded awaiting Layon's ministrations. "I make it about twenty some down here," he said. "Sentries are out and we've done what we could to fort up here."

The three remaining wagons of the caravan had been wedged in between the huts. Kryn knew there were archers on the roofs, lying flat now but ready to rise at any sign of trouble. Three of the outlaws and two of the guards were busied about each downed body of the enemy, stripping it of any weapon, hunting also, Kryn knew, for any clue to the identity of the raiders.

"Might have expected it north of the far range," the guide continued. "But usually there's no trouble near Dast—the treaty has held a good long time. We don't know what made this bunch go for us."

"The rathhawk," Kryn said and turned swiftly to seek out the crude fort they had set. Did this Master Danus still have that rathhawk pendant? Was it like the one he had been too cautious to touch himself? If he had taken it back to the refuge, would that have brought a similar furious attack? But he would swear these were no countrymen of his and was equally sure that they were not mercenaries somehow enlisted in the High King's service—the Temple did not hire such, making sure that all their forces were faithful followers of the One.

The need to know drove him to that hut claimed for the injured and he pushed aside the hide curtain used to form a door, finding the interior dusky and hard for the eyes to see anything.

What he made out first was Jarth, his back braced by a heavy twist of the grass they used for bedding. And Kryn felt suddenly lightened of a burden when he saw

that the Garn lord's eyes were clear and he was plainly
alert again to what was going on around him. Though
another mission had brought him here, he went first to
Jarth.

"They are Vor?" Jarth demanded of him. "The Master swears they are?"

"Tuver says not. They are not like the Vor in either
looks or equipment. Also the guard with him says they
are not Kolossians," he added for good measure. "They
are painted though—"

"Any face can be painted," Jarth snapped. His frustration at being tied to his bed was now plain to be seen.

"There is something else," Kryn said quickly, "something this caravan master may be able to help with. One
of his guards shot a rathhawk. It was wearing something
around its neck—and he took it to his master. Afterward
he was the first man to be killed."

"Rathhawk?" Jarth's gaze narrowed. "Yes, I remember. You, too, had a meeting with such but you survived."

"I did not touch the thing it had worn."

"Sssoo . . . " Jarth drew out that word. "This guard
who also killed did—and took what he had found to his
master. The attacks came afterward."

Then he turned his head and raised his voice a little,
"Dreen Daughter, I think we have need of you."

As she came away from one of the other pallets Kryn
had words of disagreement on his tongue but Jarth's expression stilled them. They certainly wanted no more
experiments which might bring back that fury which had
blasted them and the refuge. To let this girl meddle
with such things was a risk they were fools to take. But
here Jarth commanded and he himself had nothing but
suspicions on which to base his distrust and aversion for
her and all her talents.

Now Jarth spoke to Kryn. "Ask the Master to come

hither, this thing must be made as clear for him as it is for us."

Kryn crossed to the other side of the hut, where they had rigged a curtain of sorts to give the wounded woman at least an illusion of privacy.

"Master Danus?" Kryn hesitated to touch that hanging.

"Yes?" The man who looped aside the curtain with one hand was of middle years, his face browned by the many suns of much travel. Unlike the men Kryn had always seen, he wore a neatly trimmed beard and the dark of that hair was threaded with silver. Thin of body and rather slight of build he still gave the appearance of one who had long wielded authority.

"Lord Jarth wishes to speak with you, Master." Kryn had been too long from the manners of the keephalls to make that any more than a bald statement.

But it was seen that Master Danus took no offense and was perfectly willing to go to Jarth's pallet, dropping beside it to sit cross-legged so that it was not difficult for them to meet eye to eye. A little apart Nosh was also seated. Her face wore that mask which seemed to grow harsher with the days. For the first time Kryn was obliged to remember that the dying priestess had named her daughter, which meant a deep tie between them. Though he did not believe they were true blood kin. What had it meant to this girl—and he admitted to himself that she was very young—to be left among men with whom she had no common cause? Yet—she had power—and look what that power had drawn upon them!

Lord Jarth leaned forward a fraction and it was Nosh who swiftly moved to tuck in that roll which supported him so it served to the best advantage.

"Master Danus, Heirkeep Kryn heard a strange tale from one of your men—that this guard shot a rathhawk and found about its neck a pendant stone—this is true?"

For a moment the merchant eyed him and then seemed to come to a decision.

"It is true." His hand went to his belt pouch and he pulled out a small bundle wrapped in a bit of cloth. This he flicked open and then held his hand toward Jarth so that he might see the round of what looked like dull red stone, pierced at its centermost point—unmistakably so able to be strung on a cord.

"Dreen's Daughter,"—Jarth did not touch the stone, but looked to Nosh—"what does he hold?"

The merchant stared at the girl in open surprise. She had raised her hand as if to take the offering and then jerked away. A grimace distorted that mask she wore.

"Lord, remember!" she said.

"This may be a matter of saving lives..." he answered her.

"Or of losing them," she returned with some heat.

The merchant stared from girl to man and back again, plainly entirely puzzled. Then Jarth made explanation:

"This is Alnosha, chosen daughter to a priestess of Lyr. She has reading hands—Lyr's gift."

Danus sucked in a breath and stared at Nosh wide-eyed.

"Lady." He gave a quick nod of the head as if in tribute. "Such I have heard tales of but never have I met one. Can you read this?"

He moved his hand, cupped the cloth-enwrapped stone closer to her. "Can it be true that this in some way brought about all our troubles?"

The girl bit her lip, looked to Jarth as if in protest.

"Dreen's Daughter," he said slowly now. "If this thing is truly a danger, let us know. We ask for no full reading—only a warning."

Kryn wanted to send that stone flying out of reach and yet he also realized the importance of really knowing what power might be locked within it.

Then quickly, as if she would lose her courage if she lingered, Nosh took the stone, gathering it up by its wrapping. Holding it in her left hand she gingerly touched the tip of her other forefinger to the stone, closing her eyes, tense, near holding her breath.

There was . . .

It was as if she were looking through a window into a strange room in which shadows appeared to take on tangible weight. In the midst of that chamber, of which she could see clearly so very little, there were a series of perches. On some were rathhawks preening, or sitting with their heads oddly drawn back into their shoulders, their fierce eyes closed as if they slept.

Before those birds was a standard of dark metal, which upheld a globe of sullen grey shade, under the surface of which crawled lines of blood red, and night black, twisting and turning as if snakes were so imprisoned.

Nosh knew that globe—or its fellow! She broke contact immediately. To hold that was to attract such attention as had blasted them before.

"This is evil," she said. "Part of an old evil—Dreen would have known more, for she held sentry against that for many seasons. The rathhawks serve the same power that the eye stone summoned. Yes, it might well be true that this is a linkage with that power and it could so bring down death on those who carried it without being attuned to it as the birds must be."

Again the merchant sucked in his breath. He reached out and grabbed the stone from Nosh's hold, taking care, Kryn saw, not to allow it to touch his flesh. Getting to his feet he gained the door of the hut in two strides and whistled, bringing to him one of his servants.

"Take this and grind it to powder—do it here and now!"

Kryn nearly flinched and then looked to Nosh to see

whether she would raise a denial. Would such destruction arouse the power she believed was linked with it?
But she said nothing, only sat frowning, as if in her own
mind she was weighing one need against another.

Stones were easily found, fallen from the rough-set
walls. They watched the servant set one firm on the
ground and place the wrapped stone at its middle. He
looked about him, passing out of their line of sight for
a moment, and then was back with another rock, which
had a rough point on one side. Going to his knees, he
raised that crude tool and brought it down, with unmistakably his full force of arm, on the small bundle. When
he raised the stone a second time they could see that
the cloth was spread wider and there was no visible
lump in it. He looked to Danus who nodded sharply—
clearly an order for a second blow.

When that had been delivered Danus himself
twitched away one corner of the wrapping.

"Dust," he reported.

Kryn relaxed a little. He had been so sure that this
destruction would call forth a bitter answer—perhaps
they had yet to wait for that.

Nosh spoke first: "It is well to have that out of Dast;
give it to the earth."

"Retaliation?" Jarth asked.

She shook her head. "I do not know. This is what I
saw." Quickly she reported the sight of that strange
mews which she had spied upon.

"No one keeps rathhawks so!" The merchant had
nodded to his servant, who had withdrawn with the
packet which, from his expression, he carried most un-
willingly and was eager to get rid of.

"None that we know," countered Jarth. "But this land
is wide and I have never met any who can tell me the
full length and breadth of it—have you, Master merchant?"

"No," Danus returned. "But why would any seek to spy on us by such means? For rathhawks are few over the mountains and this was plainly on some mission. When my guard brought it down it had been winging over our party for some time and we offered no true prey as such hunt."

Suddenly Nosh turned her head, looking away from the men to where was that curtained corner behind which lay the merchant's new wife. Danus's quick eye had caught that and now he scowled.

"Sofina's people—she—is not a part of this!" His hand went to the knife in his girdle.

But Nosh was on her feet, one hand pressed tight to her breast, the other outheld as if to pluck something out of the very air. No, she knew now it was not the woman—and why she had not felt the pull before she could not tell when twice it had come so clearly. Perhaps it was the hawk stone which had dimmed this in some way. Danus was after her; it was Kryn who stepped between, doing so at a gesture from Jarth.

Nosh went to her knees before one of the packs the merchant had brought in so that things might be taken from it for the comfort of his lady. She dropped her hold against the Fingers and with both hands tore swiftly at the knotted pack cord. It opened far enough for her hand to get in and she groped about, the rising warmth guiding her, until her hand closed on what she sought though it seemed to be caught in something like a setting of metal.

Out into what full light the hut offered Nosh brought a circlet of pure gold, soft enough so that her tight grip dented it a little, and pointing upward from that band was another of the Fingers, as if it were a feather.

"What does she do? That is Sofina's bride crown!" Now she heard a scuffle behind her as if someone was holding Danus back.

Nosh paid no attention, she twisted with full strength and freed the crystal from the now bent circlet. In her hold it was blazing nearly torch bright, while against her breast she could feel the answering warmth of the other two she had found.

"What . . . " Danus sounded astounded.

Nosh dropped the circlet. It had not been in her mind to reveal her own quest, nor could she now. She thought hurriedly of some excuse and answered as best she could.

"This, too, is a thing of power, Master merchant. Though the power is not evil, for this is an amulet of Lyr. But,"—a sudden thought came swiftly—"perhaps it is this that the rathhawk came seeking—why it followed the trail of your wagons. There is this—power calls power—white can summon black whether it will or not. This is of Lyr and I am pledged to Lyr—for fortune's sake, Master Danus, leave this within my hands."

"It is no real gem," he said, rubbing his jawline with one hand. "A crystal only. But Sofina's crown is dear to her. Yet you found and brought her to safety . . . "

Holding the Finger in one hand, Nosh felt in her belt bag and brought out the largest of those jade pebbles she had found in the dried streambed. She showed it to the merchant.

"Jade . . . ! How came you with such a fortune, Lady?"

"Will not your Sofina take this for her headdress? It needs but a bit of polish and the color is fine. As for where I got it . . . streambeds hold many pebbles and some of them are gems."

"And you have the knowing fingers!" He looked at her as if he could not quite believe in it. "Well enough, Lady—the crystal for the jade, and if the crystal draws such as the hawks, we are better off without it."

But were they, wondered Kryn, and continued to so

wonder through the days which followed. There were no more attacks from the raiders—perhaps the destruction of the hawk stone had forestalled that. But there was the future to be considered.

Danus was eager to be on his way again but he had to overhaul his wagons and his loss of guards was a grim matter to him. Those from the refuge had their own problems and in the end Danus, Jarth, and Hasper, with Tuver to represent the men, talked it out.

It was plain that though they had made good strides toward health, those who had broken limbs at the refuge could not go journeying again. Were they to join with Danus as he first suggested, openly eager for the protection of those able to bear arms, the progress of the caravan would be greatly slowed.

At last they gained a compromise. Danus turned over to the outlaws several bales of furs, and some of his provisions—also the arms of those of his guards who had been killed. In turn, Kryn, with two of Jarth's men, was to go with the caravan, be paid off once they reached Kasgar with funds enough to be able to buy what the outlaws would need. Though the cold season was on the way, the prairies were seldom struck by the worst of the storms and, in the meantime, those remaining would continue to rebuild and fortify Dast, establish again a headquarters.

When this decision was announced Nosh came to Jarth.

"Lord Jarth, you have dealt very fairly with me, though I have, unwittingly, brought upon you danger and even death. Now the time comes when I must be about the task Dreen set me, and so I go with the caravan that I may do so."

Kryn was present when she said that and was in two minds himself. But perhaps if any ill followed them now, it would be better to have it strike the caravan than visit upon Dast the fate of the refuge. He hoped once the city was gained he would see no more of her and her uncanny hands.

Danus agreed eagerly. Over the days he had asked Nosh to examine and grade the rough stones he had bargained for in the north, and her expertise continued to amaze him. She had served as a judge willingly, wanting to make sure that the Master of the caravan would consider her journey favorably.

So at last came the morning when the great wagons creaked out of Dast at a much slower speed than they had entered. Sofina had regained her health enough to be able to ride in the lead one. She seemed wary of Nosh, making no overtures to the girl, and Nosh was content to have it so. At least Sofina had made no complaint about losing the crystal, which was now with its fellows in a new, neatly woven hair bag, safely bestowed against Nosh's skin beneath layers of clothing.

Chapter 13

SINCE THE NUMBER OF MOUNTS REMAIN-
ing for the caravan was limited, Nosh had thought to
tramp the march even as she had during the journey
across the Ryft and the one from the refuge to Dast.
The varges which pulled these wagons were of a different breed than those ponderous animals used for burden
bearing and field work. Nor had they been allowed to
graze freely. They kept to a much brisker pace than
those she had known.

Those mounts remaining were used for the scouts,
who rode out on either side of the rutted wagon road,
taking turns at a sweep of the territory. Though there
was no more indication of any raiders gathering.

Nosh was keeping up with the men who formed the
center guard about the train itself, though she had given
her pack to be added to the load of the wagon Danus
used now for his headquarters. However, it was the Master merchant himself who leaned down from the driver's
perch and called to her:

"Lady, mount up—would you be sore footed by
nightfall? There is no need to travel so."

Sofina sheltered in that wagon and Nosh hesitated.

The woman's attitude had been so reserved and off-putting during the days at Dast while the caravan was refitting that Nosh did not want to intrude upon her—even though Sofina had suffered her help while her wound healed. However, Danus had pulled up the double-varge team and she decided that this was not a matter for argument.

She had expected him to wave her into the covered back of the vehicle where his wife sheltered but instead he moved over on his own seat and motioned for her to join him.

During their grading of his gemstones they had at least become less than strangers. Nosh knew that Danus still found it difficult to believe in her talent, but she was indifferent to his continued skepticism. Though he had asked many questions, she had put him off with few answers—saying nothing of Lyr's crystal storehouse—rather placing credit for her talent to the training of Dreen.

She had not even shown him that packet of stones which she had found in her roaming in the Ryft. But she listened carefully to all he had to say in return about the markets for his own finds. And the idea grew in her mind that the best way to start her hunt—if any of the Fingers existed in Kasgar—might well be to find a place with some dealer in gems and learn all the sources for the trade.

However, that was not going to be easy, according to what she had learned from Danus. The gem traders of Kasgar were a tightly organized guild that admitted no newcomers easily—the trade being largely confined to several families who had carried it on generation after generation.

The present head of this guild was a woman, Lathia D'Arcit, whose clan had several generations ago fought their way to the head offices of the guild.

"There was talk," Danus was speaking now since a question from her brought him back to the satisfaction of revealing just how much he himself knew of the internal affairs of the guild—though as a mere outland buyer of gems he had but a very small standing—not even a vote in the general body. "There was talk that a woman was not fitted for such a post—but Lathia is not one to be overlooked and she had double interest, for she inherited from her clan father his shares in the general holdings and also from her husband, who was a cousin by birth, and who never came back from a venture westward about which he was very tight-mouthed before he left and concerning which nothing was to be later learned.

"Thus she came to the headmastership of the guild, calling in the votes of all beholden to her, her father, and her husband—and they were many. But within four seasons she had proved that, woman or not, she was a true guild master. Her household is a fortress—she is the only one who has never lost to the creepers—"

"The creepers?" Nosh interrupted.

Danus appeared disturbed. "Lady, wherever there is wealth there are those who want it without extending themselves in labor. The creepers are those that flit by night, none seeing them to know, preying cunningly on any who have storage of rich goods. It is said that they are also banded together and have a master to set their ploys for them. But of that we do not talk in Kasgar. It is better not to meddle in matters concerning those who are fast and clever with the knife."

"There is no guard then?" Nosh was puzzled. That a city might be so burdened with thieves puzzled her. Though she could not remember any city for herself, she had heard enough reminiscences in the refuge to know something of the life within the walls of the High King's holdings and the like. And one of the outlaws had served as a city guard there before he was framed by an enemy and hunted to the hills.

"There are guards, yes," Danus admitted. "And those who can afford such employ their own, always for travel as I do. But the creepers are sly and clever—they are said to be able to so loot a man's possessions that he is not even aware until they are long gone. Also," he hesitated and then added, "they are said to pay tax even as do honest merchants and the Governing Three. . . . " He shook his head. "That is no matter to be talked about, Lady. All kinds live within city walls and one is never sure of any except a bond friend or a clan kin. To be without such in Kasgar is dangerous. . . . "

"I am without such," Nosh said.

"Just so, thus I am warning you, Lady. Those of the gate will take note of your coming, there will be inquiry as to your business and where you will stay as you conduct that. You have a gift of which I can make use— take service with me and there will be no question."

Nosh considered his offer. What did she truly know of this man save as he had revealed himself during the days at Dast? In a way he was beholden to her in the matter of the hawk stone—for if that had continued in his possession, she now believed he would certainly still be in danger. A city for her would be worse than any wilderness—there she would feel at home as she had been in the Ryft and in the Heights—but with strangers living strange lives, packed house to house within walls—that was a different matter and one she could not yet picture for herself. Still she was somehow sure that she had made the right choice in coming with Danus. To remain in Dast would not have furthered her quest and she could not expect what she sought to seek her out.

"How long would such service last?" she asked now. Again from the talk of the band she had heard something of apprenticeships intended to last for a number of seasons and she had no intention of tying herself by a bond of that kind.

"For as long as you desire, Lady. I have stock in my keeping which I wish to offer at the winter fair—if you could grade and sort for me, it would be worth a fair percentage of the sales take. You are welcome to live under my roof—and,"—he raised his head a fraction, there was a note of pride in his voice—"that is not the least of the merchant halls. Sofina is also new to life in cities—you might well explore together when she wishes to go to the market, the temple, or the Center Garden."

"This sounds a fair bargain, Master Danus," Nosh agreed. "You speak of a temple—is then the worship of the One established also in Kasgar?"

Danus shook his head vigorously. "Not so, Lady. We have heard aplenty of the suffering under that service. Our city protectors are the Three Gifted Ones—there is Armish the thinker, Coshon, the warrior, and the Lady Paulla who loves, and heals, and wishes all well. A man or a woman will call upon the one of the Three who will best forward what is desired. There were other gods in the past—even,"—he gave Nosh a sidewise look—"they tell of one who came to preach of Lyr, a power unknown. Some listened and there was a temple built—but the priest vanished and there was none to follow him. So the temple was left to decay—until Varlard took a portion of it for a storehouse for his hides. Your pardon, Lady, if I seem to speak disrespectfully of what you hold as a power, but that is the way it is."

"The truth is always best, Master Danus," she replied quickly but her thoughts were busy. So a forsaken temple to Lyr stood somewhere in Kasgar—and where better might one hope to find what she now sought? Dreen had said that those who served closely in the great shrine had scattered—taking with them to far places the separate Fingers. Let her discover the shrine of which Danus spoke and she might be advanced another Finger on the path she must follow.

"Will you be one to speak again for this goddess?" he asked now.

"No. I am no priestess full pledged to her, though I was taught by such. What I have learned of Lyr gives me warmth and soothing of spirit, but that is for me—I do not seek to push my belief upon others."

He gave a grunt of relief. "Our Three are not jealous, mind you—not as the One who would make all subservient to His Voices—yet they serve us and we do not go seeking elsewhere. To tamper with gods and goddesses is sometimes a perilous thing."

"Danus!" The call from behind arose over the creaking of the great cart wheels. Sofina had raised her voice high, and there was a peremptory ring in her call.

The merchant planted the long goad in its socket at the edge of his seat. He nodded toward the varges. . . .

"They will follow the wagon ahead. If they balk, call."

Nosh nodded as the man climbed over the bench into the covered part of the wagon. He had given her a lot to think about, though she could not make any firm plans until she saw Kasgar, learned more of the city. Now she became aware of raised voices: however, they were speaking in a strange tongue and she could not understand the words, only the timbre of sound. Sofina's must be the higher one soaring up, a note of anger plain to distinguish. Danus offered a low rumble and to Nosh it sounded very much as if he were trying to soothe his wife, to lighten that anger.

She watched, as the discussion continued, carefully keeping her face toward the front, attempting to make it clear that she was no eavesdropper, watching the changing of the scouts. Two were caravan guards and the third, who had drawn in from before the wagon train, was Kryn.

He swung down from his mount, accepted a sparse drink from the skin offered him by the driver in the wagon ahead. They exchanged words with the outlaw ready to take his place while he, at the gesture of the wagoner, climbed up to join him, so vanishing from view. She was glad that his duties kept him busy and away from the train much of the time.

He had made it so plain that he considered her a danger and that he was relieved when she had announced her wish to join Danus and so pass out of the life of the outlaws. Though Jarth, who had suffered far more from her unhappy act, had been sorry to see her go, pressing on her a choice of weapons, so that the knife at her belt was not thinned with age, and urging her to take care. Yet he had also seemed to understand that this was a thing she must do.

She had heard Kryn's story—of the blotting out of his Hall clan and his outlawry due to the Voice. So she did not resent his contempt for all to do with gods, and his hatred of their power. Once she had reached Kasgar she would probably never see him again, not that that would greatly matter.

Yet she found herself continuing to think of him. Among the outlaws he was closest in age to herself— although his life had roughened him into a semblance of mature manhood. He had known disaster even as she. It was a pity, she found herself thinking suddenly, that his bitterness had warped him so.

Her thoughts flowed to her memory of Dreen and their long companionship. She had learned to trust the priestess, to look upon her as a wall between the ills of the world and her own self. Dreen had given her so much since that morning when she had stepped from among the rocks to welcome her into the Ryft. There was an emptiness in her, but Nosh quickly overlaid those memories with thoughts of the city and of what she might accomplish there.

She did not regret her bargain with Danus. It seemed to her to be a fair one. She would be exchanging service for service, and his stories of the guild and its tight grip upon the whole of the gem trade would suggest that a newcomer such as herself, especially one who looked like a road beggar, would have short shrift if she were to approach even the smallest of the clans. This Lathia D'Arcit—there was very little chance of approaching such as that one.

There was to be a fair wherein all the caravan merchants would show their gleanings for the season. Yes, she could do the grading for Danus and make sure that he knew the value of every stone. Several times during his testing of her she had been able to confound him that a showy piece had not the value of a duller stone. Also—there was the hawk stone—were there other dangers such as that afloat?

She knew from her studies with Dreen that there did exist gems which were the focus of ill fortune and that those through whose hands they passed would suffer. Whether her gift could pinpoint such stones Nosh had no idea. But she was coming to believe more and more in her talent and to attempt to use it in other directions.

Dreen had told her that in the past there had been those who could read whole histories in stones—"seeing" each owner, being able to tell if a gem were stolen or acquired honestly. Perhaps if she had the run of Danus's fair collection, she could do some experimenting in that way. There was also his story of Lyr's shrine—she must learn the way to that. Her hand went to the bundle of the Fingers—she had had to shear a long lock and weave the bag larger—following Dreen's pattern. If she came near one of those she hunted these, she was sure, would prove a believable guide.

There was a stir and Danus climbed back beside her. The merchant's face was flushed and his mouth straight set. He spoke without glancing in her direction:

"Lady, you have freely consented to join this household and lend your talent to its aid. Sofina . . . " he paused as if he could not easily find the words he wanted now, "Sofina has seen very little of the world outside the boundaries of the land held by her people. She is not used to many of the customs of the outer world. I would ask of you that you take nothing she may say in the heat of ignorance as meant to truly belittle you. . . . " Again he paused.

"Would you have me seek her out, speak with her?" asked Nosh, though she was not inwardly welcoming such action. "Perhaps she still thinks of me as one who caused her pain, though it was meant for her aid and not her peril."

"True—truth true!" For a long moment Danus held silent as the wagon trundled forward, shaking them near from their seats since here the trace road they followed was cross marked with deep furrows. "Yes, Lady—perhaps if Sofina knew you better . . . " He did not enlarge upon that but Nosh was alert enough to guess that his northern bride might indeed resent her new husband's interest in another woman.

Nosh herself had no remembrance of any attachments between man and woman, how such were made, and how much they were guarded by formal custom. The fact that Danus had spent time with her alone when they fingered his collection of stones might indeed have been an error.

Now she needed Danus—the more she thought of being adrift in Kasgar the more she saw the folly of trying to establish herself in a city life of which she knew nothing. But if there was to be conflict in his household, Danus could well change his mind and she would be the loser. Even her companionship with her own sex had been limited. She remembered Ilda from her childhood, and after her there was only Dreen.

True enough the priestess had, at her coming to womanhood, made plain to her the needs and changes of her own body. She knew what happened when man lay with woman—but Dreen had treated that all as dry facts such as might be culled from books. In the refuge none of the outlaws had seemed to consider her any more than they would some lad who had joined their forces—not strong enough to become a full armsmen but with her own uses. After the destruction at the caves most of them, save Layon and the men she had helped to tend, avoided her and she had been left much to herself.

She suspected that Danus had a certain awe of her after the affair of the hawk stone and she knew he respected her talent. Perhaps he had spoken of her to his new wife in a manner which had led Sofina to believe that there was more than awe and respect in the way he regarded her.

No time like the present—things which were put off only grew the harder to face with time's passing. She twisted about on the seat to face the interior of the wagon.

"I am friend to your lady, whatever she thinks," Nosh said. "Perhaps if I have speech with her, she will believe that."

She pulled aside the flap of hide which sheltered the interior from the outer world and dropped down from the seat into that snug, swinging room, for Danus did not protest.

There was light enough. The back curtain of the wagon was looped up a little and the daylight had en-

trance. Though boxes were stored along the two sides
of the wagon bed, there was ample space in the middle.
Furs tanned to make coverings formed a soft flooring
and there were cushions of cloth, their sides patterned
with intricate scrollings of thread in brilliant colors, some
of which carried the glint of gold or copper to enhance
the thread. It offered such luxury as made Nosh aware
of her cobbled clothing, her scratched hands, callused
from grass weaving, her weather-browned skin. She had
managed to keep her mop of hair in order by fastening
it in braids, but looking at Sofina she could guess what
a wild thing she must seem.

Though Sofina still rested her arm in a sling to save
any pressure on her shoulder wound, she had somehow
gotten into a robe—which was far from the drab one
Dreen had worn.

This was of a brilliant blue—fashioned from cloth
which glistened when the light fell full upon it. In addition it was lavishly patterned on the shoulders and
about the hem with the same kinds of thread as showed
on the pillows which supported Danus's wife. The robe
was not ankle length as Dreen's had been but came to
the knee, flaring outward in a wide skirt. Beneath that
legs and thighs were covered with trousers made full
until fastened at the ankles with bands of a green shade
which complemented the hue of the robe. Around Sofina's slender ankles also were wide bands of silver wire,
from which dangled bells that tinkled at her every
movement. Her sun-fair hair was twined around a green
scarf and the whole knotted into a round mound of head
covering.

Nosh had not seen Sofina in such clothing before.
While she was being treated for her wound she had body
covering of a coarser cloth and her hair had matted across
her pallet until Nosh had combed and braided it.

Even as Nosh was eyeing the other's splendor in real

astonishment Sofina was surveying her with narrowed eyes, the lids of which appeared too heavy to fully lift. Or perhaps that seeming was brought about by the fact there was a heavy banding of black on their lids to match the black of the narrow, upcurved brows above.

Sofina's features were strongly marked. Her nose was broad and her mouth large, her cheeks now each bore a round red spot, obviously painted. Nosh found this new facade somewhat disconcerting.

"Lady,"—because she was so ill at ease she spoke first—"it is good to see you so recovered and safe again."

Sofina's somewhat thick lips were pursed and now she answered, the trade tongue having with her use a strange accent.

"I have to thank you—priestess." Somehow she made that sound almost contemptuous as if Nosh claimed what she had no right to. "It was you who found me, they have said—many times"—again that same unpleasant note—"also you tended me well. My lord tells me that you have been an aid to him with this strangeness of the hands. Such I have never heard of before. Is it common in this barbarous country?"

"I am not a priestess," Nosh answered, keeping her voice level though she could not put any warmth into it, "and I have been told my Lyr-given talent is seldom known. That I could give you aid, and assist Master Danus in his stock sorting, I am glad. For Lyr is one who wishes peace to all, and we who serve Her do likewise."

Again those black-lidded eyes swept over her. There was a faint curl of what might almost be disgust about the wide, painted lips.

"Peace is always necessary in a well-organized household," Sofina returned. "I am pleased that you agree with me. If you are not to be reckoned a priestess, then how should we address you while you are one with our clan?"

Nosh noted that Sofina did not use the courtesy "lady," by which Danus always addressed her. But she had no intention of suggesting that. "My name is Alnosha," she spoke that one with which Dreen had greeted her so long ago. "Use it as you wish."

"Alnosha"—Sofina repeated. "Well enough. So—as my lord tells me you will be working with him and living among us, I offer you welcome."

But she did not; Nosh knew it as if those words had been twisted into the truth. There was no welcome from Sofina.

Chapter 14

As THE LAST NORTHERN CARAVAN OF THE season, they had not seen many wayfarers, even the closer they came to Kasgar. Kryn's knowledge of that city was hazy for, since the breakup of the Great Kingdom after the death of High King Trustan, the remaining center state of that empire had been in a fashion walled off from what had once been a well-known world. He busied himself with questioning the remaining guards and even the drivers of the wagons, learning all that he could about their destination.

At least it was not dominated by a Temple and Templers did not police it. As best he could discover the local religion was a peaceful one. Any difficulties within Kasgar's ancient walls came from disputes between various guilds—which were mainly legal matters handled by the courts—and the sly attacks of those thieves they called creepers. The latter, he learned, were exceedingly well organized and in the past few seasons had dared to institute a taxation of their own on those who were wealthy.

Many of the guild leaders, those who dealt in more expensive products, turned their headquarters—usually situated in their own houses—into small fortresses, and there were rumors that they even dealt with some Dreamers and small mages for the greater security of power shields.

It was necessary for those entering Kasgar to come with proper identity, to be able to prove they were not vagabonds or rovers. But the fact that he and the two from the refuge would enter as employed by a well-known merchant would cover that. What he needed most were the supplies and weapons for those at Dast. Too much had been lost at the refuge. Three men, with perhaps three pack beasts, ought to be able to return there at much better speed than the caravan kept.

Kryn did not want to linger in the city—the change of seasons was too close. And, though he had never wintered west of the mountains, he wanted to take no chances on being storm stayed—what he would carry was far too important.

Questioning of the guard gave him the names of those dealers best able to answer his demands—and impatience grew within him as he kept to their schedule of alternating as scouts and guards—though there had been no sign of any of the strange raiders.

Now they came into well-watered country, having twice to ford rivers. There were good-sized garths which he surveyed with bleak envy, remembering those of his own past. The harvests were long since in but there were plows already in the fields, breaking up the earth for another planting, perhaps one meant to withstand the winter.

So at length they wound their way through a straggle of villages which served the outer garths and manors. None of them slept in the inns, though twice, when they were nighted near a village, those off-duty went in to taste the sourish ale which seemed the principal drink of the countryside. Kryn was one of the party the second time—not because he had any wish for drinking; privately he thought the stuff offered by these hedge taverns was such that a single sip or two sufficed and one could then nurse the leather mug in which that liquid sloshed for the rest of the evening. Once more he went for the talk. There was too much unexplained in the immediate past.

The attacks of the raiders, that girl's suggestion that the rathhawk had been set on Danus's caravan because of the crystal in his wife's bridal crown, and then the worst coming upon them because of the taking of that stone from a dead bird. He had no trust in the powers nor in those who dealt with them. And certainly he would be very glad to be riding out of Kasgar again, leaving this Nosh behind.

However, his mind kept turning on questions he did not know who or how to ask. Who kept the rathhawks? Such use of the large predators was totally unknown to any of the Hall lords of his own land. And he could not believe that they were part of the Temple's program of coercion and control. Had they been so, there would have been no hiding it—too many eyes and ears were always focused on Temple business.

The High King? Again reports of such training would have long ago been common knowledge. And that blasting of the refuge had certainly not been within Valcur's power. Had he been able to call on such a weapon, the Temple would long since have dominated the whole of the eastern lands.

No, there had to be something behind the Temple, the High King. Was that what was now urging the king's forces south—for what purpose? By all accounts an army might have to march endlessly to reach territory which had not been blasted into nothingness. There was this story of Razkan—the mage who had pushed the world into chaos. But his time was long past. He must have long since died—even if he had disappeared as legend declared.

But—Kryn's hand went to the hilt of Bringhope— what if there was one who picked up Razkan's power to follow even as he, Kryn, had taken up his father's sword—to wreak vengeance when the time came? There was logic in that. Only, the weapon . . . no sword had blasted the refuge. Whatever weapon Razkan might have left to his successor was beyond the bonds of Kryn's imagination here and now.

"It's a chancy thing . . . " The words cut through his thoughts, almost as if the speaker had read them. One of the guards leaned forward to reach for one of the salty rolls the tavern keeper had dumped down before them.

"She has a temper, that one!" his command agreed. "She thinks to be a great lady in the city and Danus is the weapon who makes her so. No, she does not take kindly to his offering service bond to this other. I would not like to get to the left side with any Kolossian woman. Did we not see enough of how they hold the household rule?"

"But the other is a priestess. Sofina would not dare meddle with such."

Kryn realized they were talking of Nosh. So there was trouble between her and Danus's new wife? Well, that was a household matter and of no concern to him—let them settle it as best they could.

"You will sign again?" The first guard changed the subject.

"Danus has dealt fair with us. Yes, I think I will take bond for another season," said the other. "What of you, Hold Heir?" He looked to Kryn, who shook his head promptly.

"Back to my lord at Dast, " he answered shortly.

"Outlaws—it is a hard life," the first guard commented.

"We live it as we can. The Temple knows well how we live—since we make Valcur's men pay for it."

"This Valcur—it is him they call the Voice?" half questioned the other guard. "I heard tell of him last season in Kasgar. There were men of his came to the Three. But if he thought to make some trade with them, it came to nothing. They went out of Kasgar like hounds whipped back to the kennel." He grinned.

"Not all of them, Salser," countered his fellow. "Just before Master Danus headed out in the spring I set eyes on one of them. In the market he was, like any city man—he had up a table and was selling luck charms . . . "

Kryn stiffened. "What kind of charms?" he demanded in such a voice as to bring both men staring at him in surprise.

"Didn't look too close. Me—I carry Cochon's Arrow." He plucked out a thong on which was threaded a silver arrow badly tarnished. "Cochon—I burn a pinch of few-flower to him each time I make it back to Kasgar. He's one to favor a fighting man. No—there weren't no arrows, nor any knowledge rolls which are Armish's sign—and none of the Lady's blue flowers. Odd when you come to think about it. All he had were plain red stones with a spot in the middle which I could not see clearly."

"Red," Kryn followed that at once, "like that rath-hawk stone?"

The man pursed his lips as if he were considering the matter carefully. "Now that you put it that way, Hold Heir, that thing did have the same sort of coloring. Nobody was buying any—least not when I was passing. And he didn't do any calling out, just stood there behind his table waiting, as if he didn't really care whether he sold or not. But I'd take court oath he was one of them as came with the Voice's people."

A man of Valcur's selling luck stones—red ones! Kryn

turned that over in his mind. There was a need for warning, but to whom should it be given? Perhaps he could tell Danus of his suspicions and the merchant would pass that along to someone with the authority to look into matters in Kasgar.

The next day's journey on a road which was now crowded brought them to the city gates. There had been no need to ride scout any more, so the guards and Kryn's trio matched the pace of the wagons. At the gates there appeared to be something of a bottleneck—a line of waiting, and mostly fuming, travelers had built up. Danus himself mounted one of the riding beasts and went forward to see what was holding up their passage.

It was some time before he returned. The guards who had been lounging about began to gather, their boredom now overshadowed by a questioning wariness. Kryn saw Nosh, perched on the wide seat of Danus's own wagon, her raffish garments, like his, looking out of place when compared with the clothing of the travelers who were gathering more and more into a crowd.

What would she do here? Kryn wondered. That she had a marketable talent no one could deny, and she had already made a firm connection with Danus for service. But what would she think of Kasgar? He had never carried on any real conversation with her—he had been too wary of what she was. However, he was certain that she did not come from any city. The skills she and Dreen had shown after they joined the band had been those of people accustomed to living off the land. To set such one in a city, which in Kryn's mind was firmly coupled with intrigue and various undercover dangers, was like flushing a pacer hen with a rathhawk overhead.

Also—there was this tale of the amulet seller. What had he heard both Dreen and Nosh say? Power attracts power—she might be sniffed out as if Bozi or one of his kind had been set on her trail. Out of impulse Kryn left the guards and went to her. At least he owed her a warning.

"Dreamer," he used the common term of the eastern hills.

She looked around, startled, a slight frown lined between her level black brows. She was a thin wisp, with little about her to suggest the woman at all.

"Hold Heir," she acknowledged him with the old title to which he no longer had any claim.

Might as well give it to her swiftly and as baldly as he could.

"There was one here at the season's beginning who came with messengers from Valcur. The guard Ruan said that, though those were sent away, this one remained. He was seen in the marketplace selling amulets—red stones with odd centers."

Her eyes widened and her left hand rose swiftly to press against her breast.

"Red stones . . ." Her voice was hardly above a whisper. "Thank you, Hold Heir, for your warning. Indeed it may serve me well."

He shrugged. "We perhaps fight the same enemy . . ." he returned (but, he said to himself then, not in the same way).

"An enemy unknown, for I do not believe that your Valcur moves entirely by his own will," she echoed the thoughts he himself held. "But I shall watch well there." She nodded toward the city walls marching for a lengthy distance to either side of that apparently blocked gate.

Danus returned, using his mount to shoulder a way through the ever-increasing crowd. His head guard Ruan hurried to where the Master merchant was dismounting by his own wagon.

"I do not know what they are seeking for." The irritation in Danus's voice was very plain. "But the entire gate guard is on duty and they question fully everyone to enter. Something has happened. . . . " He was frowning. "Janner," he raised his voice in a call and one of the gearmen came running. "Janner, do you get among those waiting, try to find out what is amiss in Kasgar that they guard it like a guild master's house!"

The man nodded and was gone. Danus fussed with a pouch thonged to the driver's seat of the wagon and brought out several scraps of dressed hide patterned with writing. He sorted through these, giving each a lingering survey.

"All in order," he said when he had done. "What do they wish?"

Kryn's own curiosity was now fully aroused. Since this treatment of travelers was apparently new, it was a matter for concern. Outlaws? However, his own band were from over mountain, they had made no raids here in the west, and their fight had been with the Temple and its armsmen, not with either the High King's guard or the common people. These visitors sent by Valcur—stirrers up of trouble they must be, but what trouble and how well stirred? Ruan had been sure they had been sent out of Kasgar, not welcomed.

"Master Danus. . . . "

The merchant gave him attention as he packed away his travel permits.

"We have not troubled this land—we of the east."

"That I know—would I have otherwise made the pact with your lord? I have heard of no quarrel with the east— Ha, Janner! What have you heard?" For his gearman had pushed through the crowd to join them.

"Strange things, Master Danus. They say that there have been deaths in the city which cannot be explained and it is believed that perhaps one of the earlier caravans brought a plague with them—"

"Plague!" Danus's hand flew to his mouth as if to stop that ominous word. "Yet they are letting in any people wishing to go—these are not fleeing Kasgar as a plague, rather they would enter."

"That is but one tale, Master. There are others—it is said that the deaths come only to certain people—those given Three Given Powers—those of the shrine—others who are devout and visit there often. The Priest of Armish has a watcher here, those of the following of the Lady Paulla have sent a healer. So far there has nothing been detected but they are to make certain."

Kryn saw Nosh move again, both hands now back at her breast. Those crystals which seemed to mean so much to her—was she fearing that they be detected—perhaps taken from her?

The waiting line moved up. Kryn, walking beside the merchant's wagon, looked up at the girl. Her face was set in that masklike countenance he had seen before— the one with which she faced the world when she scented danger ahead.

"You fear... " On impulse he said that, seeing no one else near enough to hear, for Danus had clambered back into the wagon to answer questions being shrilled out by his wife and Janner had once more pushed ahead.

"I carry nothing of the dark." Her chin rose a fraction. "Even though I seem to you to be one who deals with evil. But this is not the land of Lyr and I am alone— nor am I one familiar with the mysteries as was Dreen. I only know that what I carry must be guarded with my life, and secondly that my life must not be fruitlessly spent, for I still have much to do. The Three Danus told me of—they who hold dominion over Kasgar—are not akin to the One. It may be that any guards they raise will pass without question that which is of Lyr."

Something kept him walking beside her. Perched on that wagon seat she seemed so small, so huddled in, as if she would bow her body around what she carried. Her eyes were closed now. Power... he wanted to plunge away from any manifestation of that, yet at this moment he could not, for a reason he did not understand.

They were finally at the gate and Danus was at the head of their party, waving his documents in the face of the guard. There were a number of fully armed men set to form the borders of a lane down which the travelers were to pass. The city men were well armed, Kryn noted with envy, and wondered if he could take back to Dast such weapons and mail as he saw on common display here.

A man who wore a plumed helm—plainly the commander of this contingent—was flanked on one side by a shorter figure wearing a grey robe, the borders of which were patterned with a tangle of running lines in several shades of green. The priest's head was bare, exposing a nearly bald scalp, but over his eyes extended a thatching of very thick brows.

Both his hands were held before him, clasping a plate of metal very like a narrow mirror, the length of one of his arms, which caught the sun in flashes and showed those who passed as oddly small figures as they went.

To the officer's right hand was a woman, tall, angular of body, her silver hair tightly coiffed and netted, but her expression one of concern. She too held a mirrorlike object, but hers had the orb of the full moon and her robe was a blue which, at any small movement of her body, showed small spots of silver light like the sparks of some cold fire.

The first of Danus's wagons pulled through and those guardians beside the officer were watching intently. Danus himself stood beside the officer who had accepted and was now sifting through his documents. A number of the merchant's gearmen and guards followed, and the second wagon moved into place. Kryn still walked beside that, glancing now and then to Nosh. He thought that she was holding control with all her force of will as

the wagon moved on and those mirrors reflected both
Kryn and the girl perched above him.

Kryn himself was tense. Surely the power Nosh
wielded could be detected. What would happen then?
She might be dragged off to imprisonment in some
shrine, unable to prove she meant no harm.

However—there was no flash of light such as he had
fully expected to see and the wagon creaked on, it and
its inhabitant plainly signaled to be harmless. Kryn
found himself near panting, his hand crooked tightly
about sword hilt. Though why should he care about
what happened to this girl? So far she had meant little
but trouble for those he did value.

Beyond the gate there were three ways to go. A broad
avenue stretched ahead, then they were crossing a street
which ran both right and left, along the inner side of the
wall. However, Danus's caravan took the avenue into
the heart of Kasgar, not turning off that until they were
some distance into the city.

Kasgar was indeed a visible show of the wealth and
might of its inhabitants. Buildings on either hand arose
some three and four stories from street level and had
balconies on which there were tubs planted with
brightly blossoming flowers. The lowest floors of many
of these structures were shops, open to view from the
street, with shelves stocked with colorful goods and
gearmen on duty to sell.

The roadway itself was clean and the gutters, running
on either side, dipped down into holes to drain off any
moisture and refuse which might be left at the passing
of animals and men. Many and powerful smells teased
the nostrils—here a hint of spice, there a rankness—and
the way was crowded with the guards pushing ahead to
clear a path.

They made a turn to the right into a sideway which
quickly narrowed so that the wagons had slim passage

and the men had to fall back between them or behind. This alley ended in a wall in which there was an archway large enough to admit those same wagons and it was held wide open, with a crowd of gearmen and servants waiting to bid Danus and his people welcome.

Kryn and his men were at a loss for a moment until Ruan hailed them and led the way to what was very clearly an armory and barracks combined. The gates were not closed, however, until the varges cleared of their harnesses were led out—to pass again beyond the city wall into the common pasturage until they would be needed.

Danus's house might not be as tall and imposing as some they had passed on the main avenue but it was fully equal, Kryn thought, to any holdhall, doubtless with some comforts few of those could own. He was impressed in spite of himself and for the first time shaken out of his preoccupation with what must be done, knowing instead a strong desire to explore this city which could even dim that which housed the High King's court.

Interlude

THE ROOM WAS DUSKY-DARK. ITS OC-cupant had deliberately jerked the curtains across the long narrow tower windows. Now he hunched in his chair staring, with a rage boiling within him, at the mirror facing his tall thronelike chair. Not the usual mirror, reflecting what was about it—this slick and polished surface had other and sometimes sinister properties. But now it was defaced with a blotch of sickly green-yellow, a thickish blot which was slowly putting down threads to web in the surface below.

He reached out a hand for a goblet sitting on a small stand to his left and gulped down a good gullet full of the stuff—smooth to the tongue, fiery and sustaining in the stomach. Though long ago he had become most abstentious, putting aside the vices of one world for certain titillating pleasures of another.

Still his eyes were on the mirror though there was no reflection there any more. Now he held up his right hand between him and that clouded surface, studying the flesh, the fingers, as if they might be part of another's body.

Age—age striking at HIM! Those Fingers freed from

long loss and pulled out of hiding—ready to push him back into the life of common mankind again!

No!

He straightened. The goblet, put down without care, missed the table and hit the carpeted floor, spilling out what was left of its contents. No. . . .

There were several things he must do but the shock he had just endured kept him for the moment anchored where he was. He had felt a certain fatigue when he had awakened from his reaching trance—enough to stir a vague uneasiness in him. Which had led him here and to this ominous discovery.

Passing years—those governed the powerless ones. They were born, they flourished like field harvest—then the reapers garnered them in—to what? For a moment his thought shifted a fraction. What DID lie beyond death? Not that it was going to suit his lifelong purpose to find out.

They bowed to god and goddess, those seedlings of the world's fields, seeking favors from what did not exist. It was easy to create a god. Now he smiled, a quirk of lip which disfigured what might be the handsome face of a man of middle years, one rich in all talents and desires.

Oh, yes, it was easy to raise a god from the dust— there was the One. That had been a very fruitful and satisfying creation. It had speedily brought under his control such as he could use as tools—some of them fine tuned—such as Valcur. . . .

Valcur . . . the mage's dark eyes narrowed. Tools could turn in one's hand, lose their sharp edging. The attempt on Kasgar—the first of Valcur's failures—though he had, of course, left a legacy which was going to trouble that city for some time.

Those Three who were enshrined there . . . Now he flexed his fingers as if about to close them around some object. Men dream things—because men must have that which is beyond human reckoning to satisfy the need for comfort and a hedge against fear.

He now considered the Three of Kasgar, turning his mind firmly away from the spattered mirror. At the arising of their worship he had tested to see if any stir of true power lay behind their coming. There was a meager portion, too small to unseat his future plans. He had made the decision then to let Kasgar respect the Three, depend upon them until there was a need for a true reckoning.

There was only one—now he snarled and that handsome countenance held what was close to a wakwolf's grim foreface. But that one was powerless—powerless unless . . .

The satisfaction he had known moments earlier was gone. His fingers formed a fist, with which he struck his knee with such force as to feel a response of actual pain.

Now he arose from his chair, turning his back on the mirror, grunting suddenly, and putting his hand to his back as if he felt pain there also. The curse he uttered was as loud as an incantation.

He could not wait any longer—he must set somehow a sentinel for a warning. And, in the meantime, prepare for what could be done were the worst to happen and the Hands returned to Lyr.

He was placed, he thought with a wry twist of angry amusement, as if he were a cook facing the need for tending a number of different pots and spits at one and the same time. He had been so sure . . .

However, there was no surety with power. He should have realized that, kept the thought in mind with each day's rising. Well—what would be his next move?

Two strides brought him to a table on which had been laid a series of patterns which, when one stared at them with intent eyes, took on the appearance of a map—one which would have been recognized by any officer of the High King.

The royal city and that dominated by the Temple were represented by coinlike dots of gold. And there were dotted lines, not as deeply incised as those marking roads and rivers, though some of them followed the course of both—those from Tomanu of the High Court were well marked and led south.

This impression of the countryside was much wider than just the present holdings of the High King and to the south were patches marked in dull grey and black. Beyond the mountains were other markings, and most of those centered on Kasgar. The mage touched a finger to one of the grey patches beyond the Heights of Askad. Dead land, blasted out of any being. He had believed he was finished with what had abode there.

Again his fist balled and he smashed it down on that grey spot. Then he deliberately controlled his anger—and—but he would not admit to the fear which had sparked in him when he had looked in the Mirror of All Seeing this morning. He had no reason to fear—his power had endured for more seasons than any living man could count—and it grew ever stronger. . . .

Unless—he spat as might an enraged cat—unless they discovered the inner secret. But that meddling female was dead—blasted by an attempt to withstand what he had sent. Who stood in her place—a child, a child ridden by night fears and unknowing of the world into which she had pushed her way. Yes, she could be taken, what she carried crushed into such dust that no one might ever aspire to unite the Hands again.

He was nodding in echo to his thoughts. Now he turned swiftly, his cloak flaring out about him, its rich stuff soft in the light. There was a door to this tower chamber and he went out, down a curl of stairway around the wall into another room as dusky as the one he had left.

A figure moved stiffly toward him. As tall as the mage, this newcomer was bare of body except for an apron of hide. The flesh so revealed was a sickly white and very sparse, stretched tightly over bones, if it were true bone alone which formed this creature. The head was elongated, large ears set near the top of the bald dome, and the features were unpleasantly animal-like—the jaw jutting forward as part of a muzzle, the yellow eyes, oddly pupilless and like stones set on either side of a nose which echoed the point of the jaw.

The mage clicked his fingers and the creature fell in a step or two behind him as he neared the center of the room. There was a carrion odor in this place and as the mage advanced there was a rustling. A moment later he was beside a globe set on a high standard.

Before it was a line of perches on which several rathhawks mantled in threat, their red eyes agleam. Again the mage clicked his fingers and the one whom he had met here scooped from the floor a bowl and started along the line of the restless birds, offering to each in turn a fragment of blood-dripping flesh.

But the mage was no longer watching. Instead he had turned fully to face the globe and now stood staring intently into the swirling depths below its cloudy surface, his hands outstretched so that one was, fingers spread wide, on either side of the globe, though he did not touch its surface. A frown of concentration furrowed his forehead.

Within the globe the colors grew faster in their movement; almost one could think they were alternately shaping and dissipating runes.

One of the rathhawks screamed, such a cry as it might

have given upon sighting a foe. The mage's hands drew in, to be clasped together, the long sleeves of his state robe nearly concealing them.

So far he was safe, and he had those who served him well. Some of them never to be suspected. They believed him long dead, vanished overseas. He had taken seasons to construct this hideout and set about it the waver spells so that anyone striving to travel in this direction would be confused without any knowledge of what was happening.

Yes, he was safe, his refuge intact; he had only one stupid child to handle now and that he could do, with ease. The first move was at hand.

Turning away from the globe, he clicked again to his alien servant and the creature unfastened the foot chain of the rathhawk which had challenged. The bird hopped from perch to the servant's shoulder and the mage led the way to the far side of the room. Once there he struck his hands, palms flat, against the stones and there was a grating as two of the blocks swung inward to open a window on the brightness of a clear, chill day.

The rathhawk screamed again. From its throat swung the red disc which linked it to its master's will. It sidled along the arm its carrier held out protruding through that window, mantled and then soared out and away. The window closed and the mage, without another sign to his servant, went back to that upper room.

Now he took up a wad of cloth and swirled it over the mirror, working to clean it as might the most painstaking of maidservants. Having finally got it bright again, he tossed what he held into a metal bowl and it burst into flames, gone in an instant.

He seated himself once more and stared at his reflection. Those faint signs of age which he had detected before certainly had not vanished, but he must make sure that they did not grow any plainer. He would re-main Razkan in his prime, not be eaten up by time. Time was for the stupid, the unlearned. And he was neither.

Chapter 15

Even after several days of living within these walls and being guided through the building in part, Nosh found life strange and difficult. She had been used to the most bare of sustenance and surroundings, but here she was surrounded by what seemed to her near royal luxury.

Danus's house was square, built about a wide court into which wagons could be driven, those same vehicles put into storage in that section of building to the right of the main gate. The gate itself was never opened in entirety except for the wagons, a small portal cutting the middle of the larger for daily use. There was a well near the block which housed the kitchen and beside it a pump and a trough to catch the runoff water.

At the back of this court the building fronted on a street, not as wide as the avenue but in good use, and there Danus had his showrooms on the street floor, before a parlor in which he saw customers of higher caste, above the living quarters of the family.

Left side of the courtyard was a house section which held on the upper floor a dormitory for the maidservants; below, a laundry, and various storerooms. While over the

162

wagon barns were the quarters of the male servants. Flanking the barns themselves at ground level was the armory-cum-guardhouse.

Though Danus might hire extra caravan guards, he maintained a nucleus of men employed by season bond who were responsible for the safety of the house and its contents.

Danus's wares were stored in the household portion of the structure, a strong room which fronted on the shop section but was warded by both human—and nonhuman—methods. The latter came as a surprise to Nosh.

She had shown the merchant a portion of the stones she had found in the Ryft and he had agreed to exchange them for the clothing and whatever else she might need, apart from the food and shelter he was bound to provide for her by their agreement. At the time she did not doubt that the merchant was getting the best of the bargain—but she could not venture forth from the house in the strange attire which had served her at the refuge and during her travels. And she was willing enough to allow him a profit.

Venture forth sooner or later she must if she were to locate the forgotten Shrine of Lyr which lay somewhere within Kasgar. By asking questions of gearmen and maids and building up a map within her mind, she was learning all she could of the city so that she might not be lost in its mazes.

As any settlement of size, it had slowly divided into zones. Because Kasgar was largely dependent from the first on trade, being at the meeting point of the north–south caravan routes, as well as those running east and west, the semi-fortresslike dwellings of the major merchants soon dominated. Danus did not aspire to such palaces as existed along the main avenues of Kasgar. It was not from among men of his standing that the elected rulers, who served ten seasons and sometimes more if those under them prospered, were drawn.

There were some twelve families of such dominance and the Judges (as they were termed) were provided from among their ranks. Nosh gathered from the gossip of those around her that the Judges were limited by their own jealousy, that various combinations existed among them only to be broken and new ones formed. Among these great houses was that of Lathia D'Arcit, though as prosperous and competent as that guild mistress was, she had never achieved election herself.

The second class of citizen included such as Danus, and there existed about fifty clan families which ranked with his household. He himself employed what appeared to Nosh an unusually large number of people, all of whom were bond sworn to him for various terms of seasons. There were the gearmen and women who served in the warehouse and shops. Then there were those by whose care the house was maintained, and the guard. It seemed to Nosh she was always meeting new faces.

The quarters to which she had been shown were not with the maids as she had thought they would be. Instead she was ushered into a small room in the household block and left to explore. There was such a bed as she had never seen—a boxlike affair heaped with woven blankets. Against one wall was a small table on which stood a tall jug of water beside a waiting basin, a rank of towels on the side of the table and some jars which, when she gingerly investigated, gave off a strong fragrance and which appeared to contain a soft soap and some skin oils such as she had seen Sofina make use of.

There was another archway, uncurtained, and she slipped into a second chamber which was hardly bigger than an alcove. Here was a much sturdier-looking table, a plain chair, a shelf bearing piles of scraped skins, so thin she could nearly see through them. In this she thought she recognized a workplace. On the table was a tray divided into a number of small compartments which rested on a flat surface covered with a soft black cloth. She was sure that this was intended for the judging and grading of stones.

Back once more in the sleeping chamber she noted a chest, very old she thought from the rubbed edges of the wood, which she opened to find folded garments of a cut strange to her but manifestly intended for her use.

She laid them out on the bed, washed vigorously with the water (which was delightfully warm and far from the cold of the country streams) and then shed her traveling clothes in a heap on the floor. Save for her snakeskin belt there was little, she thought critically, which could be salvaged from that pile.

Then she puzzled out the new garments. They were of a pleasant color, a silvery grey for the leg-fitting trousers which was not cold but rather had an almost faint rose glow. Over that went a tunic dress such as she had seen Sofina wear. This had a formfitting bodice which laced with rose cords from belt to throat, but below the waist the skirt was wide cut, coming to just above the knee. There were bootlike foot covers, ankle high to cover the hems of the trousers. The upper dress was far deeper into the rose tint, being almost completely that color. But she was so thin, her breasts so meager that she could still hide the bag of Fingers well out of sight without any betraying bulge. When she redonned the snake belt with that knife Jarth had given her there sheathed, she felt strange and unlike her usual self.

There was a mirror in the room but it was small, and in it she could see no more than her head and shoulders. By unhooking it from the wall—and with a great deal of twisting and turning—Nosh did get a faint idea of what she looked like; and that broken series of reflections was totally foreign to anything she had ever known.

At the refuge her hair had reached far more than shoulder length before she had sawed off the ends raggedly, as too long braids were a hindrance in the wilderness life she led. Now she held the glass up with both hands and intently surveyed her own face. All of that she had ever seen before was once when it had been mirrored in a pool.

The ragged locks of hair were as brown as tree twigs, yet in spite of being fine, they were also thick. Framed by them her face was a thin, dark-skinned wedge— broad forehead, sharp spurt of chin. The brows which overshadowed her eyes were uptilted in a fashion quite different from those of Dreen and Sofina and were darker than her hair. The lashes about her eyes were thick and her eyes were also odd compared to those she had seen in other faces, being a blue-green almost the shade of a prime jade stone.

For the rest she thought her mouth looked almost pinched, certainly very thin of lips, and her skin tight and weatherworn. No, she was certainly far from anything fair to look at, but that did not matter.

Picking up the bone comb beside the basin, she set about vigorously to order her hair, making sure the resulting braids were sleek. Well enough she would face Danus's household now no longer in beggar's guise.

She had been brought trays of food daily in her stay but on the third morning there came a knock at the door—she had been pleased that there was a door with a latch on its inner side. Living in among strangers as she must do now, she wanted her own privacy. Now she looked out at a maidservant.

"The noontide food is waiting, Lady. I am to show you where."

Nosh fully expected to be led downstairs again but instead the maid took an upward way and Nosh came out on what she certainly had not expected to find here—a roof garden in which jars of flowering vines flanked those holding what appeared to be near small trees in height. Swung among these were cages of thin-barred metal in which fluttered not only bright birds but, she noted, a jewel-scaled lizard that watched her with eyes which reminded her strongly of Tarm. In fact she paused by that one cage and clicked out a greeting as she might have done to that rock dweller.

The lizard rose to its hind feet, its forepaws, so like hands, grasping the wire bars of its cage, a brilliant scarlet frill expanding behind its head. Nosh extended a finger and the forked tongue flicked forth to touch her flesh in the lightest of contacts.

"Lady!" The maid caught at her hand, jerked it back. "The creature is poison—do not let it near you."

"It wishes to be friends." Nosh was sure of that but she obediently left the vicinity of the cage, the occupant of which was now clicking madly, and followed her guide deeper into this sky-set garden.

Unlike the one inn she had ventured into during their journeying, there was no large table. Instead three low, heavily cushioned chairs were each fronted by a small one, hardly large enough to accommodate the various bowls and plates which servants bearing trays presented. Danus half arose from his seat and sketched a bow in her direction while Sofina gave a very stiff nod. There was certainly about her the air of one being forced to an action she resented.

Nosh was not used to such an array of food, and felt guilty when she saw some plates presented and being waved away, either by the master of the house, or Sofina. Her own portions were purposefully small and she consumed them all—hoping that the rejected food was shared elsewhere—or perhaps the servants of the household dined on what was disdained.

"Now," Danus said at last, leaning back in his chair and wiping a grease smear from his chin, "you have been shown through our ware hold—do you believe you can find your way around?"

Nosh nodded, even though she was not quite sure— that survey of the dwelling had been a hurried one, most of it viewed from the courtyard with only that block containing the place of business displayed room by room.

"You are satisfied with your quarters, Lady?" This time her nod held the full truth.

"Then let us to business. I have been away near a full half season and I am not the only buyer for this ware hold. Also you must meet with my sister's son Gunther, who is our other expert and has made purchases during my absence. If you will excuse us, Sofina?"

Sofina's inclination of the head suggested to Nosh that she was only too pleased at their going, at least at Nosh's.

They found their way down in the block of the store-living quarters building again and Danus led her by a narrow back hallway to that warded room where he stored his gem stock.

He held a square object in his hand from which came a click, releasing the lock, Nosh knew, as a narrow door opened. She followed close behind him only to have the merchant once within that quartered chamber turn and stare at her wide eyes:

"But—I did not yet release the persona wards!"

Nosh was puzzled. "The door opened . . ." she began and then he said abruptly, "Of your goodness, Lady, step back and then within again—if you can?"

She saw no reason to doubt that she could do just that and she was right. When she was once more within the room she saw him slap his fist against the wall and heard the distant clang of a brazen-toned bell. It was only a second before a man came hurrying down the hall. He reached the open door, made to step within, and was repelled as if he had come up against a solid surface so that he stumbled back, his face a mask of complete bewilderment.

Danus held the hand box toward that door and clicked it twice this time. Then the other came charging in, his astonishment becoming angry.

"What tricks are being played, Kinblood?" he demanded hotly. He was several years older than Kryn, Nosh thought, closer to Jarth's age. As well clad as he was, he lacked that inborn air which distinguished the leader of the outlaws.

"No tricks," countered Danus swiftly and shot a glance at Nosh. She was quick enough to guess that her own entrance without difficulty was something to be kept private now between her and the Master merchant. Apparently the ward which one could not see had not deterred her from entering though she had been carefully informed earlier that it was mage set and invulnerable.

"Gunther, it has been my good fortune to find one with seeing hands and get her to accept service for half a season—past the winter fair."

With his hands on his hips, his chin jutting forward in visible challenge, the younger man confronted Nosh. "A legend—Kin lord—you have been deceived by a legend."

Danus laughed. "So? Bring out your garnerings since I have been gone—and let us see proof of legends."

The walls of the room were covered with alternate panels and layers of small compartments, all tightly closed with twisted screw locks. There was no daylight but a bar overhead came into blaze which slowly increased in power a light which it was plain Danus also controlled with the hand box. In the center of the room were four stools spaced at the four sides of a table which, like the one in the small chamber off Nosh's sitting room, was divided into sections around a square of soft black.

At Danus's gesture Nosh took one of the stools. Danus settled on the one to her right. Gunther, his expression not in the least lightened, went to the nearest section of wall compartments and worked with the lock of one, being careful to station his body between his busy hands to shield what he was doing from Nosh.

He returned with a narrow tray which held a flashing assortment of stones, most of them small—only few of good size.

Putting the tray down on the table with a force which was nearly a slam, he said to Danus, his head carefully turned away from the girl, "Part of what Hamel brought in from the south. Some of the better stones are still being cut."

Danus moved the stones around with a fingertip and urging the larger ones out on the square directly below the light before he spoke to Nosh.

"Well, my Lady?"

With her own forefinger Nosh separated the first of the stones from its companions. "Sun stone—nearly first grade—the flaw lies in that the sun is not quite centered."

Gunther stirred but Danus had already picked up the stone and had screwed into an eye a round of crystal through which he viewed the gem.

"Just so," he agreed. "However, the flaw can be corrected with proper setting and will bring a good price."

The dealings of merchant slyness were none of her concern, only the truth of the gem itself mattered.

Nosh leaned closer to the display. There was one— the color was new to her—dark, very dark, and yet with an oversheen as if black had somehow been burnished

to dull silver on its surfaces. She was intrigued enough
to pick it up, not sure she could even give it a name as
she did not remember having ever seen its like before.
Picked it up—only to drop it hurriedly.

"What is it?" Danus asked, already reaching for it to
be viewed more closely. On impulse she caught his wrist
before his fingers could close about it.

"That," she said with all the certainty her talent gave
her, "is of death!" Now she looked up to Gunther..."Who brought this to you?"

His lips did not entirely lose the sneer they had
shaped.

"It is from the south—Hamel..."

Nosh's head moved slowly from left to right and back
again denying his words.

"Blood and death have followed where this went.
Long ago it was a part of great power—dark power—
and the stain of that lies still on it. To handle such,"—
she looked now to Danus—"is like holding a noxious
sweet cake, the poison of which clings. Do not, if you
value your trade, offer this one for sale."

"It is all stupidity!" Gunther's voice rose near a shout.
"The stone is unique—Lord Markus would pay dearly
to add it to his collection. I tell you it will bring this
house such a sum as all these others,"—his hands swept
over the other stones—"will not equal."

Danus had not touched the disputed gem. He looked
from Nosh to his nephew and back again, plainly un-
decided. When he spoke it was to Nosh:

"Of this ill you are certain, Lady? Can you 'read' it?"

She knew he referred to her dealing with the rathhawk amulet. "No, Master merchant. It is very old, it
has passed through many hands..." Now she spoke to
Gunther. "This came to you as it was, already shaped
and polished, is that not so?"

He nodded reluctantly.

"Did this Hamel tell you where he got it?"

"He said something of trading with a stranger from overseas. Hamel knows stones, he could see it was different from most. . . ."

"You say it came from the south," the girl persisted, "but it is of northern work—and wrought so very long ago. I repeat, Master Danus, this you would sell only to bring ill to the buyer."

Danus picked up the stone, almost as if he, too, feared that the evil it carried could taint him.

"Do you believe this?" Gunther pushed away from the table.

Danus did not even look at him. "I have seen this talent at work. It is true—and it can harm or save. What of the rest, Lady?"

She was glad enough to see that black stone pushed to one side and read the others with care. They were prime stones and Danus smiled with satisfaction, complimenting Gunther on his purchases. Though Nosh did not believe that the younger man held her in any greater esteem for the fact that she had verified his own estimates of value.

Danus said no more of the fact that she had been able to enter the strong room in spite of the ward and she had half forgotten about that until they were done with their sorting. But she decided to let the Master merchant bring the matter forward.

What she wanted was a chance somehow to locate that forgotten Shrine of Lyr. She must in no way be tempted out of her own quest.

Chapter 16

"THAT IS THE WAY IT IS, HOLD HEIR."
Danus had flattened both palms on the table in his shop
and was leaning forward, an unhappy look on his usually
placid face.

"Master merchant, Lord Jarth swore a bond with
you—also remember that you sit here now because his
men fought to save you and yours." Kryn had had some
need for control of his sense of justice in the past but
that was being harshly strained now.

"Lord Kryn, what was true last season when I set forth
for the north was one thing, what exists now is another—
and not one of my doing or foreseeing. There is trouble
in Kasgar—at the guild assembly last night there was
much talk of it. Five ten-days ago the Council made this
rule when there were three strangers taken in arms in
the Great Shrine. One of them cut down a priest.
Though they were slain at once, it was proven that they
were not of Kasgar—though none could swear as to
whence they came. Each merchant arms now those of
his own household who are trained. To sell arms to an
outsider, robbing our own people of what may be
needed—that I cannot do.

"I am well aware of the debt which I owe to Lord Jarth, to you, to the rest of his company, but I would straightaway find myself in prison were it even to be suspected that I had provided you with what your lord wants!"

It was plain to Kryn that Danus meant exactly what he said. He had been long enough in the company of the Master merchant to know that Danus was an honest man and the rumors which the guards had gathered bore him out in part. Only this morning Ruan had warned Kryn that he had little hopes of renewing their arms supplies here.

"What I owe I pay," Danus pulled from the baggy sleeve of his robe a purse bag. "Herein is what is equal to all I promised in my bond." He set it firmly on the table before Kryn. The younger man made no attempt to touch it.

"What good," he flared with that small spurt of anger he dare loose from control, "is such? We cannot wear your largess on our backs for mail, draw it to the cord at our bows, swing it as swords! If I cannot gain what my lord needs in this benighted hole, then wherefore I go, merchant?"

Danus sighed. "Were it the year's second season, I would say to Wayport. But that is many days' travel away and at this season the higher pass is certainly closed. With all honesty, Hold Heir, I can give you no helpful answer."

"Provisions, clothing for the cold season?" Kryn fell back on his second need.

"Yes, on such there is no ban. Those I will gladly gather for you—even spare mounts, for with all the caravans returned and the pasturage limited, men will be willing to sell trail-seasoned ones."

Kryn's eyes dropped from the hawk gaze he had held on the merchant to that pouch. To say that no one could

buy arms in Kasgar—if this was like the northern soci-
ety, he knew there might be ways and means—lawful
or not. There were always some willing to weigh gain
against law and have the scales tilt in the favor of gain.
But it would take time—and at present he had no leads
to such a market. He needed knowing a man like Smarle
and here was no Smarle.

"Lord Kryn, you and your men are welcome to this
roof and to employment here—temporary if you wish it
so."

Kryn's eyes flashed back to meet Danus's.

"You expect some trouble, Master merchant?" he demanded.

"There are rumors and always behind such lie the
seeds of truth. In the past three ten-days five have
died—three men, two women. The priests talk of
plague. But what kind of a plague seeks out not the
poor, as heretofore, but rather picks and chooses its victims among those of property and rank? We are ruled
by Judges who in turn appoint three overseers, as perhaps you have heard. This is not a country of many lord-
lings and a king such as you knew.

"It is none of the three who have been sought out by
this strange death, rather those who were their strongest
supporters in the Council."

"Plague—or assassination!" Kryn shot at him. This
smacked of the intrigue which had blasted his own
life—turning seemingly sworn friends into secret enemies.

Danus drew a deep breath. "Be careful in your
speech, lord." He shot glances to right and left as if to
be sure there were no others within hearing. This was
his own office place opening on to salesroom in which
gearmen and buyers came and went. "No, this is indeed
a plague, even though it strikes only a few. So far those
who shared quarters with the dead show no signs of it—

though they are kept pent inside lest they spread the contagion."

"Still," Kryn observed, "your guildmen who are reasonable and quick of wit suspect something more than a freak illness." He was guessing but he believed he was right.

Danus's hands moved back and forth on the table. He had dropped his head so that the younger man could no longer meet his eyes. "Last night Popher, Master weaver, who before all the world was on good terms with all, had three bolts of thrice-threaded glass cloth taken, and his watchman was found dead. Yet he had paid creeper tax. . . . "

"Creeper tax?" Kryn was now lost.

"Lord, it is true in every community there are those who have, sometimes, a great deal of goods, and those who do not. Among the have-nots there are bold and sometimes violent rascals who would prey upon the others. Seasons ago this was true in Kasgar until each of these houses of ours was manned by guards who cost small fortunes to feed, arm, and maintain. Many of the smaller merchants could not afford it and lived to see their livelihood vanish overnight.

"There then appeared a man—as is often the case when there is a heavy problem to be solved. Some say he was not of Kasgar—yet he knew the city and its people as one knows the lines in one's own palm. He somehow drew together those who would prey and formed them into a company not unlike our guilds. They even, I have heard tell, had their degrees of apprentice, journeymen, and masters. . . .

"And they were loyal to this leader—those who might have challenged him were apt to disappear. Having made sure of his backing, he dared to approach the Council itself, not openly, of course, to make a suggestion. That being that each merchant open to any raids pay a set fee to this underground guild and thereafter be free of any major loss. . . . "

"If you pay this—still you have guards . . . " Kryn pointed out.

"True, but another problem arose," Danus sighed. "It would seem that nothing can be simple in this life. It is also possible to hire creepers for private projects—even murder—for agreed-upon fees. If such a fee climbs beyond one's rate of tax, one is open to plunder until one can make a new bargain. Thus, even though a merchant has no quarrel with the creepers, he strives to protect himself."

"Your Council has no city guards?" To Kryn this was a mystifying way of life.

"They are for the protection of the people at large. Should a disturbance occur in a public place, the guard will move in at once. But each merchant's own home and warehouse,"—Danus gave a glance around—"is private to him and his clan; none other can enter without permission."

It appeared to Kryn that there were many loopholes of trouble in this particular arrangement. However, it was of Kasgar and accepted there and he was not. It was none of his business.

"Now,"—Danus had come back to his original offer— "I will give you and your men a short-term bond until you are able to decide what is best for Lord Jarth, since this weapons ban is on and is being strictly enforced. Anyone leaving Kasgar now can take only the protection he wears on his body and his usual arms."

Kryn shifted the bag from one hand to the other, frowning down at the pouch. He was sure that Danus had not stinted them but what it contained was of no service to him now. It might be prudent to do just what the merchant suggested, take temporary service here until he was very sure that he could not obtain what they really needed.

Back at the guard quarters he called the two who had ridden with him into the room in the officer's section where he had been housed and quickly outlined what Danus had told him.

"This Barmrum who is five leader here," one of them said, "he has been hintin' of trouble. There's a feelin' goin' 'round that someone up on top is dreamin' dark, as the sayin' goes. They've gotten awful pryin' at the gates."

"Lord Jarth . . . they need help," the other broke in.

Again Kryn weighed the purse. "Danus says we can take out provisions and clothing. He also talks about extra beasts. Suppose you and Ventro here," he spoke now to the elder of the two, "take what they will allow us to pack. Full bellies and warm backs will help somewhat in the cold."

"And you, Hold Heir?"

"Danus had some interesting things to say on another matter . . . " Quickly he outlined what the merchant had told him about the creepers and their organization. "These seem to be outside the Council law—in fact the Council pays tribute to them. Perhaps they can be dealt with as a law-abiding merchant cannot. It will be a matter of listening and seeking and it will take time. Also it may come to nothing, but on the chance that it will I shall stay."

"Sounds like what Lord Jarth would say," commented Ventro. "Me an' Hansel here can take the trail. Too late in the season for raiders and if they give us travel-trained beasts, we can keep a good steady speed."

Danus appeared to heartily endorse that decision. He himself helped them bargain for beasts, well travel-broken, and now at graze in the outer fields. Owners were eager to get rid of extra mounts before they had to contribute other and expensive food for the animals.

Some twenty days after they had entered Kasgar, Ventro and Hansel rode out, Kryn going with them as far as the main gate. He had entrusted Ventro, having him repeat it several times over, with a short report of what was happening here. At the last moment he wondered if he should add the fact of the amulet seller but decided that was nothing which would threaten the men at Dast whom he was trying to serve.

He had made several visits to the marketplace and had seen the man with his small folding table. The array of dull red discs on that was limited and yet Kryn had never seen anyone actually buying one. Nor did that vender shout his wares and attempt to attract notice as the others around him. Kryn himself made sure with all the skill he could summon that he was not seen by the dealer, though he noted that the man's eyes were constantly sweeping the crowd which passed, either because he sought some special person or else that he had some reason to fear—and somehow Kryn was sure it was the former.

It was on his third trip market-side that he actually saw someone approach that table with its unattractive merchandise. The woman was well muffled in one of the huge enveloping cloaks which women of the upper class wore when abroad from their own homes, and she was followed by a half-grown lad with a house badge on his shoulder, plainly sent to carry any purchases. Kryn was too far away to mark the badge and he dared not approach. The dealer and the woman spoke together and then she moved on. Kryn had earlier counted the amulets remaining—ten of them—now there were nine but he had not seen her pick one up or the dealer hand it to her. On impulse he pushed past a very busy food stall and fell in behind her.

His quarry did not make any more stops but threaded

her way through traffic which at first was heavy and then thinned out as she approached a district of larger buildings, the tri-steeple of the major shrine looming above in plain sight. Kryn guessed that this section of Kasgar was that wherein the major clans of the guilds were settled. He saw guards, well equipped—with arms he envied—at the wall doors of several of the houses as if they awaited visitors.

But the woman and her servant made a sudden turn into another way—one of those back streets such as that which Danus had used to bring in his wagons. And Kryn, lurking well behind lest he be noted on a street which was now nearly vacant, saw her enter through the small door in the large wagon one. There was a painted design above the arch of the closed wagon door and he made careful note of it, determined to find out who was master or mistress there. . . .

Though, he thought as he made his way back to the marketplace, what matter was it of his who bought an ominous amulet? The intrigues Danus had half hinted at meant nothing to an outsider who wanted nothing more than to fulfill the orders of his leader and return to his own country—though Dast was certainly not their native land.

He had gotten no farther in his hopes of finding some line to those who might, for a sizable profit, provide what he needed, though he had listened closely to the talk of Danus's guards, gone with them on off-duty hours to various taverns. Unfortunately the men he wanted might be rubbing shoulders with him in any crowd and he would never know it.

But at least he was learning the city—the lower, meaner parts, for somehow he was sure that it was there he could find a clue to these all-powerful creepers. If they had been originally recruited from the criminals and poor, then this would have been, and probably still was, their native ground.

Luckily a number of the guards he had seen, and many he had met, were not of Kasgar by birth but were outland mercenaries. Merchant stock did not produce on the whole natural fighting men—they needed to draw from the nomadic tribes, the mountaineers, and such, for those armsmen who would count in a fight.

Danus had given him the shoulder patch which identified him as a member of the merchant's establishment for the present, and with that displayed he could walk the streets without question even though his war gear was different from the norm. His ragtag clothing had been exchanged for garments from Danus's stock. Only Bringhope might seem strange to the knowing eye in the street but Kryn was not to be separated from that blade. By day he wore it; by night he slept with it under his hand and he would until the day came when he could hang it again in honor in a free keephall.

Now as he threaded the narrower side streets he did so with the same care as if scouting in the Heights, placing in memory each turn and twist, major landmarks. He discovered that his wilderness training held to the good here. Looking for a new landmark as he halted at the end of what was a very narrow alley, his attention was caught by what had been built directly across the end of that short and littered way. Plainly the building was abandoned, or if in use, only by the homeless. It was just one story high but the doorless opening into the interior showed a remnant of workmanship as if once there had been an attempt to enhance its importance.

Over that doorway was set in the stone a grotesque head, neither beast nor human, but somehow combining both. Yet as queer as it was those features did not repel. Rather they intrigued, making Kryn want to see them better.

He tramped down the alley and stood looking up at that strange and outré mask. It was then he was able to see something else, carved very deeply as if to withstand the passage of years, but placed unobtrusively below the mask as if that was meant to draw all attention from it.

What was outlined there was a pair of hands and they were placed in the same position as he had seen Dreen use at meeting with Jarth—wrists tight together, palms and fingers curved outward facing each other. This must be of Lyr!

He mounted the single step which formed a short platform on which the shrine was set and peered within the doorless aperture. The smells of a place long abandoned were plain. And it was so dusky he could not see even the walls of the windowless room beyond.

A shrine to Lyr—he thought of Nosh. Did she know where this was? Might it be a thing to tell her? But it was clearly derelict and she would find no one of her kind or Dreen's here.

It was near the dinner hour as he made his way back to Danus's establishment. Usually he went in by the rear door but today he found it easier to take a route through the shop. He had just stepped within when he was aware that he faced a fierce embroilment. Danus stood at the door of that inner room which Kryn knew was his treasure hold and well warded. His flushed face was so wrathful that Kryn was a little surprised. He had never seen the merchant in such a rage even when they had battled the raiders.

He was facing that overbearing young lout who was his nephew, a surly fellow perhaps a couple of years to the better of Kryn but who paraded the airs of a Master merchant when Danus was not around.

"A good bargain . . . " The lout's voice was raised. "Lord Markus paid well for it. You listen to the mouthings of that slut and lose a sale . . . Evil in a stone! She is crossed in the head, or trying to work you to her own purpose."

"That stone was not for sale. You broke a house order! Get out of my sight, you dealer in trouble! If ill comes of this, you will take the full blame. I do not want to see your face again this day—lest I take measures to have it rearranged!"

Danus actually showed a fist, although the lout was a little taller than he, and took a step forward, such purpose in his own face that Gunther turned and went, nearly slamming his shoulder against Kryn's as he passed. His expression was black and hard.

Danus retreated into his treasure room and the door of that snapped shut behind him. His curiosity fully aroused, Kryn looked to one of the gearwomen who served in the shop.

"What has happened?"

She looked disturbed. "Gunther sold a gem to Lord Markus—it was one that the Lady said was evil and carried evil with it. She found it among the stones Gunther bought while the master was gone. Now if evil does follow it, the guild Council will hold the master responsible . . . This has been a day of ills!" She threw up her hands in a small gesture as if to signify a rain of disasters.

"What else?" Kryn asked though he was thinking mainly of the gem deal. If Nosh had pronounced the stone a source of evil—he remembered the one which had brought disaster on the refuge. What if the misuse of *THIS* one would bring the same fate to Kasgar? Did Danus even know of that earlier strike?

"The zark," the gearwoman was continuing. "They have been hunting it through the house since the tenth hour this morning. They say it can spit poison," she shivered. "Lady Sofina has had most of the household turning out every room. It is not right to cage such creatures—they are a danger to all!"

Zark? A zark was a rock lizard and he had never heard that they were any danger. Though there might be some variety of the creature which differed from those he knew. He could well believe that its escape was a matter of concern, for the things could move with dazzling speed and also hide in places considered too small to hold them. Danus was certainly not having a pleasant day and perhaps some of his anger was going to sift down and make the rest of the household restless and uneasy. Though that Gunther had been rousted was a satisfaction to anyone knowing that young boor.

Chapter 17

THOUGH SHE HAD BEEN TO THE MARKET several times with Danus, checking on the wares others had to offer, Nosh had had no chance to go exploring in Kasgar on her own. Unfortunately, she discovered, local custom decreed that a young woman did not venture out on the streets unescorted. She chafed at this but, for the moment, wanted no trouble with the merchant.

He had not introduced her to any of his fellow guild members, something which puzzled her. Perhaps he wished to keep her talent strictly for his own use until after the winter fair.

She had said goodbye to Hansel and Ventro when they had left with such supplies as they had been able to gather for those at Dast and she understood very well that Kryn must be greatly frustrated at his inability to gain the arms he wanted. She had watched him take off several times into the city and wondered if she dared suggest that they take such exploration together—the Shrine of Lyr continued to lie to the fore of her mind.

This inactivity wore on one. She did not enter the shop without Danus's call, especially with Gunther there, for she was well aware that he resented her. Just as she kept away from the rooftop garden which, on fair days, was the retreat of Sofina and some of the maids.

Finally she could stand the waiting no longer and determined to appeal to Kryn. After all, in spite of his dislike for power and what he thought she represented, he knew that she had not come to Kasgar without a purpose in mind which was as important to her as his quest of arms was to him. And she decided to wait no longer to make her move.

However, she was still munching on bread and cheese for the morning meal which she took with the gearpeople in a separate room—not wanting again to stir Sofina's possible anger by sharing the master's table—when they were all astounded by a series of screams echoing down from the upper story of the house. Hand at knife hilt, Nosh was the first to go into action.

There was fear in those cries and she had lived too long on the edge of danger not to answer to that. She reached the top of the stairs, nearly to be pushed back down them by one of the maids who waited on Sofina, her eyes wide as her mouth, from which continued to resound those screams. Nosh caught the girl by the shoulders and shook her, though the maid was taller and heavier than she.

"What . . . " She strove to raise her voice over those cries.

Before she could gain any possible answer there was a second scream, even more strident, and down the hall pounded Sofina herself, her hair flying, her overdress unlaced as if she had been interrupted in the midst of her morning toilet.

"Poison . . . Kill it—kill it!" she gabbled.

From below came the shouts of men and Nosh heard the pounding of boots on the stair.

Nosh loosed her hold on the maid and turned to the mistress. "Kill what?"

"The zark..." Sofina was regaining some of her usual poise. "This... this piece of muck,"—she turned on the maid by Nosh and slapped her with a vicious force which sent the girl back against the wall and slipping down it—"this brainless piece of offal dropped the cage and let it out! Kill it!" She swung around to face the first of the guards—"Find it and kill it! Why did Danus ever give cage room to it?" she demanded of the company at large.

"But zarks are not poisonous." Nosh remembered the lizard which had greeted her with its excited chatter days earlier. It had not the appearance of the zarks she had known, for those lacked the brilliant scales and crimson neck frill, but otherwise it shared both their size and general body contours.

"Fool!" Sofina spat at her, "Go pluck it out of hiding with your bare hands—if you dare. It is poisonous as we all know well. Search,"—she turned now to the guard—"every nook, every corner, every shadow, search it out and kill it!"

That those of the house believed her estimate of the danger there was no doubt. More of the guards, and with them some of the servants, all armed with clubs or bared blades, pushed their way into the upper quarters of the house.

Nosh stepped within her own room. There was no use joining in that noisy hunt. In the first place if this refugee from the cage WAS like its Ryft kin, it could move faster than any human. She was very doubtful that they were going to have a successful hunt. And she was wondering about the claim that the creature was poisonous. If so—how did it deliver the poison attack, for it had no fangs such as one of the mafsnakes, no visible stinger on its tail tip as did the clawrunners who lurked under rocks and were ready to assault the unwary.

She had seated herself by the window listening to the

clash and clatter of the hunt in the rooms about. It seemed to have been extended again. Nosh caught sight of men gingerly searching the courtyard below. There was one cry and sudden fall of club but the victim was but one of those rat scavengers which were peculiar to cities.

They were apparently moving furniture now from the sounds. She looked inward at her own small chamber. Sooner or later they would burst in here and want to turn out coffers, pull the bedding off the bed, and generally reduce the room to chaos. Perhaps she should do the searching first and save herself the consequences of such an undisciplined action.

If it were kin to the zarks she had known . . . She squatted down on the floor in the middle of the room and clicked as she would to summon Tarm or Wasin. It took her a couple of tries until she got the proper sound and the uproar of the outside searchers nearly drowned her out. However, she persisted. There came a flutter of color, the blur of a dash so fast her eyes could hardly follow it.

The zark stood on hind feet, its small forepaws outreached to close about, with a velvet touch, the finger she had extended. It threw back its head and clicked. Nosh could see beneath that rainbow skin the wild beating of its heart—it was in the depths of fear.

Very slowly she extended her other hand. For a moment its head reared back a trifle as if its wariness had doubled. But she touched, with the most gentle meeting of skin with scales, its head, rubbing back and forth.

It took another of those eye-startling leaps and was crouched now on her bent knee, looking up into her face and chittering.

Poisonous? These city people were afraid of a shadow. And she was not going to turn it over to be sliced or beaten to death for the only reason that it had somehow broken free from captivity. Sooner or later they were going to reach her room, she had to find a hiding place for it.

Nosh held her hand flat and the lizard leaped from her knee to her palm. Steadying it with her other hand she got to her feet and looked first at the window. She was sure that it could descend the house wall if she were to put it out but that might leave it in the full sight of the hunters.

No. It gave a tiny chitter and reached out to her with forefeet again as if in entreaty. The bodice of this Kasgar clothing was too tight to conceal it, especially if it moved. But the wide skirt . . . she flipped up the edge of that as the lizard made another leap to her shoulder.

The skirt was lined so there were two thicknesses of the cloth that gathered in folds or swung loose at walking. Her knife again. She inserted the point and made a slit, which she tore wider. Would the zark realize what she would have it do? She had never been sure of how much they understood. But she hunched her shoulder a little forward and held the slit apart as if it were the mouth of a bag. The creature leaped, caught at the material, and scrambled its way into the crude pocket.

Nosh went to work on the room so that the disorder she created suggested a frenzied search. And she just made it in time, for there was a knock at her door and she pulled it open to face one of the house guards, drawn sword in hand and looking over his shoulder, one of the gearmen from the shop.

"It is not here." She spread out her hands in a gesture which indicated the upset chamber. "And I know the way of zarks, for they come from my own land. Sooner or later it must seek water—and meat—perhaps you can entrap it so."

The guard nodded. "Makes sense, Lady. Don't see as how we're gettin' anywhere with all this runnin' around. I'll speak to the captain." He gave her a nod and backed out of the room, swinging the door shut behind him.

Had she been wise in suggesting that she knew something of the ways of zarks, Nosh wondered now. More than ever she needed to get out of the house, find somewhere in the open where she might loose her new companion.

This very day she would speak to Kryn. She had seen him leave in the morning but he never stayed away the full day and he might be back long before dusk and so play her escort for a small essay into the mysteries of Kasgar.

Now she pulled out that all-enveloping cloak which women wore on the street, though inwardly she balked at so muffling herself. But to go without it was to attract attention at once and she wanted to do her exploring unmarked as a stranger.

The cloak was equipped with a very wide hood. It was the fashion to clip the center of that to one's forehair and then allow the extra material of its making billow out nearly like her small charge's neck frill. This would be better than the pocket burden which might be noted even when there were so many extra folds.

She was interrupted before she had made any exact plans. One of the gearmen from the shop brought a message from Danus and she obediently sought out the merchant in his small treasure room. His round face wrinkled in a worried scowl and he had a number of small bags laid out on the table, quickly slipping out their contents for a look and then pushing it all back again.

"There is a stone missing." He burst into speech the minute she joined him. "That one which you spoke of as ill fortuned. It was my intent to take it in the morning to the Triple shrine and ask that it be perhaps destroyed in the way those who use the power can do. But it is gone!"

"You have searched all." She looked around at the numbers of small drawers.

"Yes—it is not here!"

Suddenly he got to his feet and went into the outer room, summoning to him by gesture the senior of the gearmen.

"Has Gunther been in this morning?"

"Early, yes, Master. He said that you had a special task for him—something to be delivered to the Lord Markus, it would be a most satisfactory sale . . . that's what he said," the gearman repeated as if he privately doubted that fact.

"The fool. . . . !" Danus barked. "So he has done it in spite of my orders." He seemed to be speaking more to himself than either Nosh or his employee. Then once more he swung around to reenter the other room, saying abruptly over his shoulder:

"Your aid, Lady."

Once inside he closed the door before he faced her.

"The other day when you found that stone Gunther spoke of offering it to Lord Markus. The lord is past master of the Goldworkers' guild and a man of great wealth. But his greatest love is the collecting of unusual gems. That one would certainly take his eye. If the deal has been made, we are in trouble, for Lord Markus does not give up what he has added to his collection and"— he hesitated—"I think what you said of this stone would make it all the more precious in his sight, for he is reputed to have several ill-omened things among his treasures which he never shows publicly. How dangerous is this gem?"

Nosh shrugged. "Master Danus, that I cannot tell you. A thing which has been a focus for ill can be used again by one who senses what it is and wishes to employ it so. Perhaps if this lord keeps it only for his collection, it will do no harm. But were it to fall into one of the dark brotherhood's hands—then again, how can we reckon what ill it can be made to serve?"

Master Danus suddenly looked older, subdued and anxious. "There are tales," he began and then stopped. "No, gossip is one thing, truth often another. We shall hope that it can be as you say, sealed away in a collection box where it and its owner will come to no harm. But Gunther,"—now he was flushed with signs of a rage stronger than any Nosh had ever seen before—"Gunther shall answer to me for this!"

Danus was plainly nursing his anger, as he was abrupt and harsh of voice all morning. He had set Nosh to the grading of a new packet of stones which were all of the moon tear kind. Her fingers quickly found those of better value and Danus grunted at her choosing, but accepted her word as to which were best.

There was still an uproar in the house, to be heard dimly where they sat at work. However, Danus did not appear to take the escape of the zark as any peril, or else he believed that the aroused hunters were fully able to handle that problem. Nosh was careful to adjust her skirt and the creature hiding there made no move. It seemed to the girl that the zark had a better understanding of what would keep it safe than was usual with a pet creature. However, she could not continue to carry it about and must soon find some way of loosing it outside the house.

It was close to the hour of nooning when Gunther at last slouched into the shop and Danus caught sight of him. Once more the merchant's face flushed a deep red and he arose from the examination table so abruptly he sent the stones spread out there shifting perilously close to the edge so that Nosh had to spread out her hands to cover them.

"Gunther!" Danus moved between Nosh and the door to face his nephew. "What dealings have you made with Lord Markus?"

There was a sly smile on the other's pockmarked, greasy-skinned face.

"An excellent one for the house, Danus. He had in his tame expert and it passed the tests. Here—look at what I have added to the house coffers with this deal!" He produced a bag and spilled some of its contents into his hand—pushing that forward until it was nearly under Danus's nose. He might have decided that the smell of those rounds of soft gold would be enough to enhance his standing with the Master merchant.

"You sold the dark stone . . . ."

"How else would I have this?" The young man re-pouched the pieces. "More than we have made for ten-days of dealing, Danus."

He was grinning widely and nodding his head as if he needed such action to enforce his words.

"That stone was not for sale, you stupid fool. Do you want to bring guild law upon us? No man deals in what he knows well is damaged goods—"

"Damaged goods!" exploded Gunther. "It was a rarity from far places! Lord Markus will be glad to see what we have to offer from now on. Even Lathia has not dis-played such a find."

"No! She has sense enough not to endanger so her guild oath. That stone is a bringer of evil and it can be easily traced to this house."

"I am not a fool! I made an excellent bargain . . . " Gunther's gaze swept beyond Danus to where Nosh still sat at the table. "Lord Markus paid near a fortune for it. You listen to the mouthings of that slut"—he pointed to Nosh—"and if I had left it so, would have spoiled a major sale. Evil in a stone—she is crossed in the head, or trying to work you to her own purpose."

Danus was sputtering; there were flecks of spittle in the corners of his mouth as if he wanted to spit at the young man facing him.

"That stone was not for sale. You broke a house order. Get out of my sight, you dealer in trouble! If ill comes of this, you will take full blame. I do not want to see your face again this day—lest I take measures to have it rearranged!"

His fists were balled as if he fully intended to take out his rage in an assault on his nephew. The other flung the bag at his uncle and turned on his heel to go out of the shop. Danus snapped shut the door of the safe room and stood there, panting as if he had been running a race. He kicked out with his toe and caught the bag, sending it in a clicking roll across to within Nosh's reach. She bent down and lifted it to the table. It was indeed heavy enough to promise a good sum. Danus returned to his seat and eyed the pouch banefully. Then he grasped it as if it represented something vile and took it to one of the wall drawers, thrusting it within.

"The stupid fool!" he grated out as he returned to the side of the girl. "Now I must make full explanation to the guild Council—and by rights they will find me irresponsible. A mark against the house!"

A moment later he addressed her directly. "Lady, I am in no mood now to continue with this sorting. I must give time rather to what I am to say to my fellows."

She was glad enough to be released and murmured some placating words, which she was sure he did not hear, for he was staring at the wall now as if he saw a most unpleasant sight there. But he released the door lock for her almost absentmindedly and she went on into the shop.

The gearpeople were huddled in a knot, whispering one to the other. Of Gunther there was no sign and

Nosh was glad of that. She had no wish to confront the man who held her so low.

However, there was another one just about to pass out of the shop into the inner quarters and seeing him, Nosh swiftly followed, coming into the hall beyond close enough to touch him if she would.

"Hold Heir?"

Kryn glanced over his shoulder and then turned to face her squarely. She did not know just how to enlist his help in her project but she could only make plain what she needed.

"Hold Heir," she repeated, "you have learned much of the city—I have seen you going out each day."

"What do you want?" he demanded, and there was a defensive note in his voice.

Nosh came directly to the point. "Have you seen the Shrine of Lyr?"

He did not answer at once, it was as if his thoughts followed in a different pattern. Then:

"This day I found what might have been that shrine. It lies in the worst section of town and has long been deserted by the looks of it."

"But it is Lyr's." She needed so much to believe that.

He shrugged. "There was a carving on the portal, hands upturned. I saw your priestess make such a gesture to Lord Jarth upon their meeting."

"Can you take me to this place?" Her one hand guarded the concealed crystals. If what she sought might be hidden there, this would tell her so.

He looked impatient, as if he wished her gone and wanted no part in what she desired.

"Hold Heir," she said deliberately. "You have that which means more to you than your lifeblood." She pointed to his sword. "I seek what may be the same to me and the place to begin the search is in the shrine of the One who has made me *Her* servant. . . . "

"All right. Get your street cloak and we shall go right away." It was plain he had no liking for this expedition. She wondered why he would do her so this service when he held her so low.

It took only a few minutes to mount the stairs. The clamor of the zark hunt was still to be heard—Sofina fiercely urging them on with what approached screams. Back in her chamber Nosh pulled on the cloak, fastening the head clip, then urged the zark out of that skirt pocket. Again the creature appeared to understand what she wanted of it, giving a leap to her shoulder and then burrowing into the puffed back of the hood, where she felt its light weight steady against her shoulders.

So equipped she went below to find Kryn already at the courtyard gate, impatience plain to read in his face and body.

Chapter 18

Nosh found it difficult to match step with her companion. He strode along as if on some errand which he wanted quickly done. They did not head along the way Danus had taken when he had made her familiar with the marketplace but rather into a narrow side street.

There were passersby here but none with personal guards or the colorful outer robes which marked a substantial merchant. She noticed almost at once that Kryn's eyes were never still, that he kept watch while they moved forward as he might had he been on a scout from the refuge. Nor did he talk.

They wound a way which bewildered Nosh and which she believed that she could not retrace by herself. The houses grew smaller, far less imposing than those near the heart of the city, and the few shops which fronted on the street had second-rate merchandise as far as a fleeting glance could tell her.

But . . .

Her hand moved under her cloak to cup over the hidden crystals. No, she was not mistaken. Just as before she had been drawn to the skeleton and its treasure, so now she met another such reaching out.

"There is one following—" Kryn spoke sharply enough to gain her full attention for the moment. He had paused and was looking back in the direction from which they had come. "We may seem easy taking for some ambitious one of these creepers they talk of—"

Nosh glanced around but could see no one except an old woman bent nearly double under a bundle of firewood and beyond her a man, plainly deep in drink, lurching along.

"Who—?" she asked, unable to see any harm in either and pushed by the need of her quest.

Kryn frowned. "He is gone now . . . small—perhaps only a boy—such can run spy errands."

"Spy errands—" she was echoing when he grasped her arm.

"Let us get on with this before we draw more attention," he snapped.

Kryn turned abruptly into the side alley, where their boots slipped on nauseating slime and there were piles of debris to be skirted. So they came to face the deserted, ruinous fore of the shrine.

Within the bag the crystals flared but that was hidden by the folds of the cloak. At Nosh's right ear sounded the sharp chitter of the zark that had ridden motionless and without voice until now. Its scaled body pressed against her cheek as its head shot forward.

Within . . . did what she seek lie within? She was upon the one-step platform, working the bag of crystals out of hiding. Their heat was building; what she sought must be very near. But—not inside . . . Up—up—not forward.

She jerked at the cloak's cowl and looked up. There—from the mouth of that grotesque mask there was a glimmer which could not be mistaken. But how to reach it . . .

"What is it?"

Kryn had stepped a little to one side and now was eyeing her with something close to suspicion.

"What I seek . . . it lies within the mouth of that!" She gestured to the mask.

As if to make sure that he understood that gleam above strengthened. Surely he could see it, and, by his frown, he did. But how could she reach it?

It depended on how firmly it was set within that hold, and the containing factors must be strong that it had remained so carefully hidden for so long. It might have been even plastered within—though she doubted that because of the brightness it displayed now.

She glanced back along the cluttered alley. At first sight she could see nothing which could serve as a ladder. If she could find a pole, prod into that mouth to judge how hard set it was . . .

She felt the scrape of scales against her chin as the zark's head went into the open, turned up as if it knew just what she would do here. Kryn turned swiftly and went back down the alley—he would have nothing to do with a thing of power—that she knew. But she was not going to leave this place until what rested in that mask's mouth found its way into her hand.

However, she had mistaken what Kryn would do; he came tramping back, holding a splintered-end length of pole.

As he joined her the zark freed itself entirely and leaped for the pillar supporting the pediment which held the mask, showing the same speed for climbing as it did in its racing leaps. It clung with one forefoot and both back as, with the other forelimb, it poked into the mouth of the head.

Then it turned its head and looked down to Nosh, its chitter loud and demanding.

"Call it away!" Kryn ordered. "Let's see if what you seek can be loosed by prodding. . . . "

Nosh raised her hand and waved at the zark, one part of her thoughts astounded by the creature's actions. It was proceeding as if it knew exactly what was needed. She had never put Tarm or Wasin to any such test—perhaps the zarks were far more than her species rated them.

Now she sounded the imperative chitter to attract the lizard's full attention and then waved again. To her joy it edged sideways from its hold, but still clung, as Kryn raised the pole and with the shattered tip explored the crevice of the mouth.

He was exerting strength now. And the pole bent a little. Then he gave the butt he held a blow of his right fist. The pole curved, broke. But the zark was already back at its first place, groping within. And then there was a gem-bright flash, seeming, for a moment, to illuminate the whole of that dismal alley, while on her breast the other Fingers answered with a heightening heat.

The zark held it so for only a moment, then it gave a cry as if in pain and let its find fall. It was Kryn who moved with a fighter's speed and caught the trophy out of the air before it could touch the pavement. He held it for a moment, looking at it with an odd expression and then held it out to Nosh.

"Power again. You garner it in but how will you use it?"

"I do not know," she said truthfully. "It is my task to find and guard. For your aid I am truly grateful, the more so as you turn yourself from such things."

"Such things," he snapped with a trace of anger, "are not for men—or women. To hold such power would tempt anyone to use it for gain—and against it there is very little defense. How *WILL* you use it, Dreamer, reader of stones?"

"Not for ill." Her own irritation brought that statement swiftly to her lips. "Lyr is not of the dark." She paused for a moment and then added, "Lord Kryn, you hold such in abhorrence, but the hour will come when you may reach out your hand, even as you did to catch this thing of Lyr's, to draw to you something greater and more dangerous even than your sword, mighty though you hold that to be."

His frown grew darker but he did not answer her. Nosh turned to call the zark, who leaped easily for her shoulder and worked its way quickly into hiding in her hood.

The day had been overcast and here in this alley there was a shadowing close to dusk. There was beginning a fine drizzle of rain, which slicked the pavement even more so that they went at a slower pace, making sure of their footing as they took each step.

They had not quite reached the street beyond when Nosh gave a half-choked cry and wilted to the slimed stone. Kryn's hand fitted to his sword hilt but he did not have time to draw it. The blast of strange, choking particles in the air brought him as quickly down and helpless. Nor could he understand what or who had attacked. And as he went into mind darkness he still struggled to loose his weapon.

Nosh first became aware of a faint noise her mind sluggishly connected with the zark. She breathed, choked again, and then that stinging in her nostrils was gone, instead she was drawing into laboring lungs air which had fresh, clean scent. She tried to move and found out that her own cloak had been used to enwrap her past any chance of freedom. But she could open her eyes.

The zark was patting her face with both forefeet, its chittering clearly a sound of concern—fear. When her eyes met its small ones it braced itself back on its tail as one might sit on a stool, its forefeet fluttering as if it endeavored to convey some message.

She realized that she was not in the open. What or whoever had brought her down had not left her in that alley. Kryn! Was he also trussed nearby, a fellow prisoner?

Nosh looked beyond the zark's head. There was a wall there, and draped across it strips of shining cloth, woven loosely back and forth. When she stared straight up she found herself regarding a ceiling across which were massive beams. Now she looked to the right. Another wall, but on this was a picture painted in glaring colors—weirdly shaped flowers—if those blobs were intended to be flowers.

Wherever she now was it was not the establishment of Master Danus—the little she could see being wholly alien to the conventional fittings of that house. Nosh tried to lift her head and found that the folds of the cape tightened across her throat warningly.

The Fingers! Her hands were too tightly bound for her to reach for them but at her thought there had been a warming. So those had not been taken from her. But why was she prey to any in Kasgar?

"Ah, you have joined us again, Lady." The voice was soft, gentle, and, Nosh instantly felt, deadly. She looked straight up at the man standing over her.

He wore a long-sleeved robe of deep purple, confined at the waist with a girdle set with stones, finely cut to glitter at his every movement. He had a narrow face, framed in a bush of hair which was near to the color of flames. Eyebrows of the same shade jutted out over eyes of a green as brilliant as a sea stone. His nose was long and a little crooked as if it had been broken in the past and not carefully mended. His mouth was curved in what might be a smile, until you saw what was mirrored in those eyes.

Now he stooped a little and reached down, his hand, with its bone thin fingers, closing on the mass of her cloak. And with no appearance of exertion he lifted her up, transferring her swiftly to a chair, but making no move to free her. The zark chittered and streaked up from the floor to its half-hidden perch on her shoulder.

She could see much of the room now. The furniture was very plain, lacking all the carvings which graced those in Danus's home, and it appeared to be made of a material like a well-burnished metal, dull red in color. While the floor was patched with squares of fur—wakwolf hides, she thought.

"You have questions, of course." He had seated himself in another chair facing her. "Always there are questions." One of his hands made a small fluttering motion as if he were waving the unwanted from his path. "You are at liberty to ask them. I shall, of course, answer what is necessary and that is very little."

"Who are you?" She found her tongue. This man was unlike any she had ever met. Was he a mage—he had about him such an air of consequence and power that she could come to believe even that.

"Who am I? Now that is indeed a question. You see, I am different things to different people. To you I intend to be an employer."

"And how will I serve you?" She kept her voice level, feeling that she must show no weakness to this man.

"As you have served others, my Lady, with those very useful hands of yours. Part of my desires are gems—I have a trained eye to shift true from false. However, I understand your gift goes even farther—you can read the past—or even projections of the present with your talent. I have many eyes and ears within Kasgar. I am very well served, as you shall discover. And some of your feats have been reported to me."

He leaned back in his chair and put the fingertips of both hands together, regarding her over them with that subtle, unpleasant smile.

"A man in my particular position has enemies—they stick as fleas to a beggar, if you will excuse such a coarse comparison. Some of these have particular twists of thought; they are not to be dismissed too lightly. Thus I need a guard—you!" That last word came out with the force of a blow.

"And if I do not choose this service?" Nosh asked evenly. She felt the stir of fear as if she were reaching for one of the evil-splotched gems.

"Oh, I think you will. Have you not been serving Danus in the same general fashion? Too well to suit some members of his household. I have them to thank for your presence here and you need have no thought of any rescue from that quarter. After all, what I am asking of you is a matter of the light—not the dark—I merely want to protect myself and my organization. You will find me a generous employer, I assure you. Ask of me anything within reason and it shall be yours."

"Let me go!"

His smile grew broader. "I said within reason, Alnosha. That request is not reasonable for me."

"Kryn—what have you done with Kryn?" She decided to attack on another path.

"Your young guard? Well, he is also under this roof at present, and in not very pleasant quarters. But his situation may depend upon your willingness to do as I wish. Though he interests me—he may yet prove to be a luck stone I can play in my private game."

Kryn had been drawn into this net because of her. Nosh accepted that and at the present it might be very well to agree to what this man wanted, insuring that both she and Kryn have a chance.

"You want a bond swearing?" she asked. "I cannot do so since I am still bond to Danus."

He waved a hand. "My needs outweigh those of that little man. You have already served him and he must be content with that. No, Danus will learn nothing save you and one of his outland guards disappeared—for all he knows you have taken the trail back to that raggle-taggle of outlaws at Dast. If necessary, there will be those ready to swear you departed so. What I will within Kasgar becomes at once so. Now—surely you want to be free of body and brought into company as becomes a talented one. Will you serve me?"

"You say," Nosh observed, "that I have a choice. It seems to me to be a very limited one. Thus I am forced into your path, lord." She gave him the honorific as certainly his presence suggested that he was of high rank—though she knew very little of the castes of Kasgar.

Now he leaned forward a fraction, his gaze holding hers as if that meeting of eye to eye was another bond he laid upon her.

"Swear," he said, "on the Hands of Lyr!"

What did this one know of the Hands? At least she had not been plundered of the Fingers since their warmth had been with her through all this interview.

"By the Hands," she agreed slowly. "But you are no follower of *HER*."

"True. There are many different Powers that be, and each man oaths by the one which he believes in. And since it pleased you to seek out Her forgotten and dishonored shrine this day, it would seem that you believe you owe Her obedience. Though surely all power has departed from that place long since."

The Finger! Then those who had captured them had not seen—surely they must have come too late!

Nosh summoned up all her courage: "By which do you swear, lord? This oath must not stand alone but your word joined to mine."

He gave a little laugh. "Well put indeed, One of Lyr. Very well. I will oath also that you be well received in this house by your bonding. Also, if you wish it, your guard will not be harmed. After all, he is about a task of his own which interests me greatly."

"Now . . . " He stood up and came to her, going around to her back where she could feel a fumbling through her cloak. Those tight swathes which had held her captive loosened and she could move freely.

Her new employer turned to the wall and pulled one of the tags of fabric woven there. In the distance she heard the sound of a bell.

As he returned to his chair he spoke again: "The zark. You bear it free of any caging. It is a thing of poison and if you cannot control it, it must die."

"I can control it," Nosh returned quickly. "It will not attack here."

"Of course, it did not when it awoke," the man conceded, "and I have a liking for the strange. Maybe that can be put to service also, we shall see."

The wall behind him opened to form a narrow doorway and a tall woman came into the room. She bowed her head to the man and then looked at Nosh. There was no surprise in her expression; she might have been any gearwoman or maid waiting for orders.

"Sahsan, this is the Lady Alnosha. She is to be quartered in the inner rooms."

The woman said nothing, only beckoned to Nosh, who arose, feeling giddy for a moment so she had to catch at the tall back of her chair to steady herself.

Once more the man's smile became more pronounced. "I am distressed, Alnosha. The Take-dust often has a lingering effect on those who inhale it. But

Sahsan will see that you have the proper drink to allay such minor discomforts."

Nosh still kept her grip on the chair though that momentary giddiness was now past.

"Since I am to serve in this house, what is the name of the master?"

He nodded. "Yes, I am forgetting the proprieties. I have several names, you see, and which one I use depends upon whom I seek. But you can call me Markus. Ah, you have heard that name before?"

There must have been some small change in her expression which had triggered that question.

"I heard of a Lord Markus who was a collector of gems," she returned.

"You have heard aright. As Markus I am a collector of gems—as you shall very soon see. But there is time for that. Meanwhile you shall be my guest."

The woman reached out and laid her hand on the girl's shoulder. She was tall, taller than many of the men Nosh had seen. And she wore leather as might a trusted bodyguard, with a long, sheathed knife at her belt. Her hair had been cropped to a thickish cap and there were blue lines of a pattern crossing her forehead, swelling down over her cheekbones. She must also be a foreigner in Kasgar, Nosh decided.

She yielded to that touch on her shoulder and followed the woman through the door, which slipped shut with a loud click behind her.

They were in a narrow hall running between two walls in which there were no breaks of doors or windows and which ended in a steep flight of stairs. These they climbed past two doored landings, until at the top Sahsan swung to the right and clapped her hand, palm flat, against the wall—a wall in which Nosh could see no line of doorway. But there was one, low so that her guide had to bend head to go through, though Nosh found it of comfortable height.

Another corridor, but this had doors, all closed yet visible. Sahsan kept on to the very end, where she applied her palm as she had done before to release some locking. The room into which she ushered Nosh was not unlike the girl's quarters in Danus's house—except for the colors. Each wall was splashed and splotched with raw color which made Nosh blink as she glanced at it. For so long her life had been spent with the muted, death colors of the Ryft, with the mingled greens and browns of the Heights, that such a display was enough to make one catch one's breath, blink and blink again.

There was a single window in the wall facing that which held the doorway and through it one could indeed see the sky but it was slotted with bars which shone metallically in spite of the lack of sunlight without.

A narrow bed was against the right wall and it had a pile of coverings which were thick and quilted, each of which was a different hue, but matched one of those used in painting the walls. In addition there was a small table placed beneath the window, a single chair drawn up beside it. Another table to the left was plainly meant for the purposes of body and face care. It was topped by a mirror and, standing in a sentry row along under that, were small bottles and boxes.

Sahsan stalked across the chamber past that and once more smacked the wall. Another sliding panel and Nosh could see into a space hardly larger than a cupboard, which held a shallow bath and a seat for the use of waste purposes. That was something she had not seen at Danus's for there the washing room had been fairly large and used by all members of the household.

"Thank you." Nosh broke that silence which had held since they had left Lord Markus's presence.

Sahsan's reply was a grunt. It was plain that she had

no interest in this new member of the household past her lord's order to see Nosh housed. She turned and went as if she had taken time from a more important task to bring Nosh here and must now return to it.

Nosh freed herself from the imprisoning folds of the cloak—the zark having made one of its flying leaps to the windowsill. It was small and slim enough to slide between those bars and gain its freedom but it made no attempt to do so.

Having washed away the ill-smelling stains left by her collapse in the alley from her hands and brushed down her clothing as best she could, Nosh seated herself by the window, drawing the bag of Fingers out of hiding and staring down at them. Was it by ill luck alone, or by intent that she had been taken by this Markus?

He had hinted of betrayal within Danus's house. And Gunther had sold an evil stone to a Lord Markus—it must be the same one. No matter how he had forced bond on her, she must give him warning of that gem if he showed it to her; Gunther had had no liking for her; Sofina had tolerated her only by the will of her husband—either of them could have passed along the knowledge of her power.

She restored the Fingers to hiding and turned to the window. This house was a story higher than the one next to it. She could see down into just such a roof garden as Danus had established. Though at present there was no one there.

By her own word she was prisoner here—but she was well aware that she would have been so even if she had not given oath. And that imprisonment might have been far worse than assignment to this room. Seating herself again, she began to study the walls. The riot of color was like a blow at first but, somehow, when she put hand to the bag between her breasts images began to emerge out of the general mass of curved or broken lines.

The painter who had worked here had had a pattern in mind and while that was still very far from what Nosh considered of worth, yet it made a strange sense which grew clearer the more she traced certain lines from one place to another. Yet it was too strident, it wore on her the more she tried to understand, and suddenly she swiftly lowered her eyes to the tabletop, groped once more for the bag of Fingers, and took them out of hiding, centering her attention strictly on the glowing crystal. If there was any malign purpose in assigning her room, she would work to defeat that.

And the crystals answered her hardly understood wish, flaring up hotly in her hold, their rainbow light flickering before her eyes and yet not bringing the stain of those violent colors.

She dared to look again at the nearest wall. The pattern was clear, and the color did not strain her eyes. In fact that glare was subdued. And she recognized the design for what it was—for she had seen its like in the books Dreen had guarded.

These walls had been painted by one with dark knowledge, and the purpose was an insidious breaking of the will of anyone entrapped here. But with the crystals that would fail, though she might have to play the hard role of one entirely cowed into submission. Was Kryn fast in some such chamber? He had no crystals to break the spell—could Markus take him over in bond for any use the lord desired?

Chapter 19

KRYN CAME BACK TO CONSCIOUSNESS slowly. He opened his eyes to see, over him, not the sky but stone. The caves? It was hard to force his thoughts into order. No, the caves were long gone. Some sturdily built keephall?

His mouth was dry and when he tried to swallow he could not raise any saliva. But that small act restored memory. They had been coming away from that twice-cursed shrine—why had he been moved to visit it the second time? There was no good ever to be associated with the powers. Some said there were both light and dark, but to him they were all to be avoided.

Coming away from the shrine—then dust—strange dust which clogged the nostrils, ate at the lungs. A weapon he had never faced or heard of before. And now he awoke here with a pounding head and weakness which even his will could not defy.

Though he could not yet raise his head, he could turn it. Wisps of straw stood up and he realized he was lying on a heap of the crackling stuff. Nor was that fresh either. His small movement caused a puff of evil mustiness to bring a coughing spell.

211

Beyond that straw, not too far away, there was the grey of a stone block wall. What light existed here was close to dusk and he had to strain his sight to pick out something else—that mid point on the wall, rusted metal formed a ring bolted fast to the stone. From that hooped a chain, the end of which reached beyond Kryn's field of vision. Yet, as he watched, it swayed a little and it did not reach the floor.

His head settled somewhat and he tried raising it from that foully matted straw. Out of nowhere came a hand, greyish as to skin, nearly skeleton thin. It touched him gently on the forehead.

"Be careful, young man . . . " A voice nearly as rusty as the chain hoop brought his eyes away from the wall to sight the one bending over him. Rags for clothing, a body which was so bony he could mark each rib, and above that a mat of grey beard which masked the lower part of a pallid face, rising on the cheekbones to tangle with head hair of the same hoary shade.

Only the eyes were free of that appearance of general age and misuse. Meeting those seemed to Kryn to infuse strength into his own body. He drew up one arm to help lever himself up, needing to know where he was— though he already guessed he lay in some form of prison.

"Where . . . ?" He forced his dry tongue and mouth into speech.

"Where . . . in the creeper lord's private safekeep for those he may find use for," the other answered. He had turned himself a little where he squatted by Kryn's side and now he held, with hands which shook, a small, chipped lip bowl.

"Drink!" It was more an order than a plain urging.

The water was brackish with a foul taste which nearly made Kryn spit it out again, but at least the liquid allayed some of the dryness of mouth and throat. Having given the bowl back to his strange companion, he was able to sit up, and watched the man cross the cell on hands and knees to place the bowl carefully in a niche of the wall where there was a smear of green slime and a drip of water to spatter down into that container.

It was when he got a full look at his fellow captive that he shuddered. It was plain why the other had crawled. Both feet were gone, scars thick about the site of the amputations. Kryn swiftly looked down the length of his own body.

He had still his booted feet. But all which covered his body now was the leather undershirt and breeches. Gone were his belt, his mail shirt, his . . . sword!

The thought of the loss of Bringhope for the second time jerked him out of the last remains of the lethargy the dust attack had left with him.

He could see the chain now as it swung out, its other end a collar which had fretted the neck of his companion until it left calluses as deep as scars. His hands went to his own throat and touched a band of metal, his head jerked to the right. Yes, he was bound by just such a chain and collar to a similar wall ring.

Why was he here? The creeper lord's safe prison— but he had been trying to meet with that lord, or at least some major underling. The weapon . . . now his hands sought his inner money belt only to find that also was gone.

The old man had crawled back to his side. "They plucked you, boy. They aren't the kind to waste any-thing providence can send them."

Then the other gave a croak which might be laughter. "Oh, you have some profit to be wrung out of you or they would have slit your throat wherever they brought you down and you would not be here. Guard, eh? Per-haps they have a visitation in view—your continued breathing will then depend on how much you can fur-nish them with knowledge of your master's wards and

such. If you value your feet, your hands, you'd best be
quick to answer."

Kryn shivered, but not from the chill of this place,
which had only a window slit well above his reach to
bring in air and limited light. He could not control his
glance at the other's mutilation. And the old man deliberately thrust forward the nearest leg for him to view
that scarred stump.

"You were a guard?" Kryn asked slowly. They must
have left him with this man to provide an object lesson.

"No. I had other knowledge." Again he gave that
cackle of laughter. "Markus might have killed me but
for some reason he keeps me still—though the shrine is
gone and no one in Kasgar raises a voice in Lyr's praise
now."

"Lyr!"

The maimed captive slewed around to face Kryn fully.
In the eyes above that mat of filthy beard there came a
light. Swiftly with his skeletal hands he shaped that
same sign Kryn had seen Dreen use. He waited for a
moment as if expecting some answer from Kryn and
when it did not come, he let his hands fall limply. Yet
there was still an eagerness in his rusty voice as he
asked:

"What know you of Lyr?"

Kryn hesitated in turn. Though he could see no reason for hiding the little he did know.

"I met a priestess of Lyr . . . in the Heights. Her chosen daughter is here in Kasgar set upon some quest. I
was with her at a deserted shrine when I was taken. . . ."

Nosh must have been taken too, yet she was not in
this cell. A stark guess as to what might have happened
to the girl shook him. Where did they hold her and why?

"There was the girl—Nosh—Alnosha—Dreen's chosen. When they brought me here was she also with

them? Where could they have taken her?" And his dark
thought added "*Why?*"

The other's eyes were fully alight as he continued to
stare at Kryn as if so he could search out the depths of
the youth's memory.

"Dreen . . . " he finally repeated, then added: "Where
did you meet with this priestess of the Hands?"

"Well away from here—in the Heights. Those which
border on Askad are a part of them. She and the girl
came to us for shelter because there were searchers in
the Ryft once more."

"The Ryft!" It was like a cry of greeting given force.
"Out of the Ryft! Then . . . " The man was shaking as
if wrapped around by some winter's blast. "Then there
is coming the end. And this Nosh, she was with you
when you were taken. Why had she gone to a deserted
shrine, was it her choice?"

Would it be betraying Nosh perhaps to tell what he
knew? Perhaps this hard-used prisoner had been put
here as a stark lesson, perhaps he had another service—
to trick Kryn into some disclosure which would threaten
or condemn them both, he and Nosh together.

He picked his words carefully. "She is a follower of
Lyr. I sighted the shrine while exploring the city and
she wished to see it. Thus we went—and were taken."

The footless man heard him out and then he once
more crossed the cell on hands and knees thick-callused
by such traveling. There was another pile of rotting
straw there and he scrabbled in it, sweeping back the
foul bedding to the stone underneath.

With his clawlike hands he picked along the edge of
a stone until by pressure of palm he could urge one end
up and it stood instead of lay. Out of the hollow thus
opened he pulled a small roll of rags. Now he turned his
back squarely to Kryn, held what he had freed close to

his chest so the other could not see it or what he would do.

But there was no missing the sudden gasp which the other captive uttered then. He turned to look over his shoulder at Kryn with another of those measuring stares.

"She is of the Hands!"

Once more he was busied with the bundle, returning it to the hidey hole, pressing that down and shifting the straw over it. Now he came closer to Kryn.

"If they guess . . . " It was hard to read expression in a face so deeply beard-matted but there was distress for the first time in those eyes. "Tell me the truth, armsman, does this Nosh have the Talent of the Hands—can she read stones?"

He might as well admit that much, for Nosh had displayed the ability freely in Danus's house and any servant there could have tattled of it to those outside.

"Yes." She could read too well, he thought with some of the old bitterness, remembering the end of the refuge.

"At last . . . " Those words were a whisper so low that Kryn had difficulty in hearing them at all. Now he wanted information himself, though how much he could depend upon this source he did not know.

"You say that they want information from me. Have they tried such a game before—with others?"

"I do not know, save that they tried it with me. Only I had nothing to give—the shrine was a small one and had no wealth. Why they continue to let me live I do not know." The answer was matter-of-fact, words from one who had accepted what had come to him and no longer hoped for anything else.

"But,"—now there was a sharper edge to his words—"if you companied with one having the Talent, they would wish you under their fist. Markus reaches high, and he has gained great power here in Kasgar. The

Council and the Judges are rulers in the light of day, he is supreme in the shadows of night. When a man is ridden by ambition he takes any tool which can be used. Lyr's Hands were known long ago—before Razkan's power broke us of the east. Markus is one ready to make use of any talent he can find. This girl—he will keep her—and . . . " Slowly that bushy head shook from side to side. "She, being what she is, will not prove an easy tool for him."

Kryn stirred. He had, he believed, no real tie with Nosh. In fact he had wanted very much to see the last of her. But now . . . he need only look at those stumps from which the feet had been shorn to realize that he must consider her even as he did Lord Jarth and his comrades of the Heights—one entitled to all the strength he had to offer. But she had power . . . recall only what she had drawn upon the refuge. Surely if she were really threatened she could break her own bonds here also.

There was a grating sound from one side of the cell and Kryn was shaken out of that thought in an instant. A section of the wall blocks moved and opened a door.

Kryn got to his feet. The throat band with its chain hampered him, but he was determined to meet whoever came standing and not on his knees.

The man who did enter was no different in face and gear from any of the guard he had known in Danus's house. Though there was a brutal cast to his features and a certain unkemptness to his equipment and mail which suggested that those who served Markus, at least as gaolers, were not the best of possible armsmen.

He stood for a moment in that doorway, his fingers hooked in his sword belt, surveying Kryn, paying no attention to the other prisoner. Then a wide grin parted his thick lips.

"Thought you was a fighter, eh? Marchin' around in

good link chain an' carryin' a lord's sword. Took you easy, we did, boy. We knows what to do with the likes of you."

"Shut your big mouth, Crawg, we ain't here to exercise our jawbones." A large and meaty hand fell upon the lout's shoulder and he was shoved aside by another, who dropped on the floor a broken basket in which rested two greyish loaves.

Kryn made no move toward the food; in fact he had a suspicion that the chain would not allow him that much distance. Nor did his companion. But it was to the latter that the second man spoke:

"Loosen up your tongue, old one. Lord Markus may have some questions for you. He's been doing some thinkin' an' when Lord Markus thinks we get busy. You better think yourself—how you are goin' to answer him. Still got you a pair of hands, ain't you? How would you like to be rid of one—maybe both of those?"

His fellow guard laughed. Then he kicked the basket so that it whipped across the floor and struck against Kryn's right boot.

"Eat up," he ordered as they both disappeared, the door grinding shut behind them.

Kryn stooped to the battered basket. It was plain that what it contained was near famine fare, but he was ready for it as his empty middle proclaimed.

He took one of the small loaves, its crust nearly stone hard, and tossed the other to his companion. It was nearly toothbreaking and he strove to crack it apart with his hands, hoping to find it softer within.

"Wait." His cellmate crawled to that basin which caught the drip of the greenish water and returned with it in his hand. He planted his own loaf end down in the inch or so of water which had gathered and twisted it around before passing the bowl to Kryn to do likewise.

The smell of the loaf, or else the water it had been

softened in, was gut-twisting. But resolutely Kryn managed to break loose a bit of the moistened crust and
picked eagerly at the inner substance, which was almost
equally hard.

It was a meal which had to be consumed slowly, risk-
ing teeth. And the taste of the stuff was nearly as foul
as the smell. Even in the most hungry days of the refuge
he had never been reduced to dealing with a noisome
mess such as this.

However, the food was not all-important now. It was
that suggestion of the guard, threatening his cellmate,
which was foremost in his mind as he chewed the hard
mouthful he had managed to break off.

He swallowed and spoke: "That was a threat. . . . "

The other was still grinding away at his portion but
he nodded.

"Did you see the death stone?" he asked after he had
swallowed with an effort. "He is the second such to wear
one—in my seeing."

"Death stone?" Kryn tried to remember the appearance of both men in detail. Then he tensed. Yes!
Around the neck of the one who had delivered that
warning had rested a thong and sliding across the breast
of his rusty mail shirt—one of those amulets! The ones
he had seen displayed in the marketplace.

"Out of the old legends." The other had again im-
mersed a fraction of his loaf in the bowl. "It is said that
things such as that—truly serving the dark—were given
to those Razkan had reason to tie to his cause. To touch
one opens a way between the dark power and the one
who wears it, so that the Master can see what happens,
even deliver messages thus. I have not the Hands—but
I have served Lyr and it is given to those of us who
remained loyal to sense even at a distance such devil-
ment."

Kryn found himself believing the old man.

"There was a man in the marketplace selling such amulets," he said. "Though I only saw one pass into other hands. It was a woman who took it."

"A way to breach walls without losing men," stated the other. "So—they are selling them openly in Kasgar. Now I wonder if Markus has a hand in that. Though anyone who plays with such is a fool beyond all bounds."

"They looked like the stones the rathhawks wore." Kryn downed another bite of the stone hard bread.

His companion stopped in the middle of inserting his loaf once more into the bowl.

"What tale is this, young stranger?" There was a force in that demand as if he were a Hold lord in command.

Kryn found no reason not to explain that part of the past. And when he had finished, the other stared straight at that wall which had sprung a door, as if he expected some ill to come through it.

He lifted both his bony hands and rubbed aside the overhang of hair on his forehead, smoothing the grimed skin above his eyes back and forth. It was as if he were trying to bring to the fore some long hid memory.

"It is hard," he said slowly. "Once, if you can believe it when you look upon me now, I was a keeper of ancient knowledge. That is why Markus took me in his net. But what I could tell him was not what he wanted and he believed that it was stubbornness on my part, so . . . " He made a small gesture toward his scarred legs.

"What information did this Markus want?" Kryn worked at the bread, twisting it and striving so to soften it a little.

"Old lore, mostly. What I had to say I did, for there was no reason not to repeat what has been written in many chronicles. I think what he truly sought was a Dreamer."

"Nosh!" If Markus knew that about the girl, he could

twist her, even as Kryn worked this hard bread.

"She dreams?" demanded the other.

"She can lay finger to a stone and see . . ." Kryn answered slowly. "The priestess she followed dreamed—could touch another in a dream. But I know nothing of such powers . . ." Nor wanted to either, he added silently.

"May Lyr cup Hands over her! Markus will use her whether she will or not. His men wear death stones. . . ."

"She knows those," Kryn answered. "She dealt with one, as I told you."

"But not when it was in the possession of an enemy," the other pointed out. "Markus has access to many secrets—and few of these he shares even with those who believe themselves close to him. I fear for this Nosh. . . ." He looked down at the last of the bread in his hand. "Armsman, Markus will lay a blood debt on you—through the girl if she does not serve him. There was one taken with me. . . ." His head dropped toward his chest as if he no longer wanted to exchange glances with Kryn.

"I was no Dreamer but I had something of power—none could serve Lyr from boyhood and not gain that. I was . . ." Again he hesitated. "I was of the Ryft by blood, though we had long lost that land to death. And my House was a proud one—I was Gudelph of Far Garth. And she who shared my exile was of the Inner Circle. Her name—remember it, armsman!" There was a sudden fierce note in his cracked voice. "For some day it must be honored before the Great Hands. When they took us for Markus she was quick, quicker than I, and escaped in her own fashion by the blade of one of those who were minded to ravish a priestess. So Markus lost his Dreamer, and he who let her choose death was himself killed—in a most unpleasant way. But remember her name, for she died with pride—she was Darthia."

Kryn felt anger spark within him. He knew well the fate of women who fell as booty into the hands of arms-men of the dark mold. Nosh—was Nosh to be treated so?

Gudelph might be reading his very thoughts for he answered: "This Nosh need not fear that—her talent means too much to Markus. He will keep her safe as long as he has a use for her."

"And when he believes he has gotten all he can from her?"

"Then . . . wish her a blade even as Darthia had."

Kryn got to his feet and went to the wall wherein was set the ring to which his confining chain was fastened. Had they left him even a bootknife, he might have had a small chance to work at that. There was a crust of rust thick upon the metal but when he grasped the chain in both hands and exerted all his strength he knew that such an effort was hopeless.

Gudelph watched him and when Kryn turned he was shaking his head. "Not even a varge could break free of that."

"Perhaps, but I am no varge which has only the mind of a beast, I am a man."

"To Markus you will be a tool at his pleasure. Death is a better portion. . . ."

Gudelph stopped almost in mid-word. His shaggy head turned a fraction as if he were listening. Then he hunched himself over more closely to Kryn.

"They are coming. If it is me they take—yes, if they have me forth it may be for the last time. Listen, then, armsman. You have seen that block which moved . . ." He pointed with a claw finger to his pile of straw. "If there is a chance for you and I do not return, take that which is hidden there and guard it well. By the grace of Lyr it cannot be detected by those of the dark. And only the dark rules here. So have I managed to keep it. But it must go to one with the talent—your maiden Nosh. Swear to this!"

He caught tight hold on Kryn's wrist, reaching up from his crippled crouch.

"It may be that I shall also be taken," Kryn pointed out.

"But—there is always a chance and you are not maimed. Swear!"

The force of that brought an answer from Kryn, a half-unwilling one. "I swear."

There sounded that grating again and the door opened. The same two guards shouldered through the narrow opening. One held a bared blade and made a circling with its point at Kryn's middle, sending him back a step or two and holding him at a point while the other guard loosened Gudelph's chain and yanked it along, dragging the cripple across the floor.

"Rest easy, boy," said the one holding Kryn at sword point, "your time will come. But Lord Markus wants the old one first."

The first guard, dragging the cripple like a leashed hound behind him, edged back into whatever passage was left beyond. Now the sword wielder backed, his point still threatening, went through the door.

Kryn stood, fighting his growing rage. He was near as helpless here as he had been in the Temple—one against how many? Gudelph was no fighter—and he was weaponless. But—why had the guard held Kryn under a drawn weapon—did they somehow still fear him, un-armed and chained as he was?

Chapter 20

ALMOST NOSH COULD BELIEVE SHE WAS forgotten as the hours passed, night gathered darkness outside her window, and still no one came. Though Sahsan had not provided the restorative Markus had spoken of, her dizziness faded away—mostly because, she came to believe, she had concentrated on the crystals. However, she was hungry and the zark had come to her several times chittering and pulling at her sleeve, doubtless wanting to be fed.

She had early tried the door and discovered that it was locked, but she had expected no different. As time passed boredom caught her. She found herself looking more and more at the wall patterns. As it darkened inside the room some of those lines began to glow with a radiance of their own. Yes, she was more and more aware of some subtle trap.

Finally, aroused by the hungry chittering of the zark, she took the creature to the window from which could still be seen a portion of the roof garden below. Based there were lamps aglow here and there among the potted plants. Pointing in that direction Nosh sought to encourage the zark to go hunting for itself. And again the creature caught the meaning from her thought—at least it squeezed between the bars and vanished.

Whether she would ever see it again she did not know, but at least she had accomplished one thing this day: she had made sure that it had not died under club or sword in Danus's house. Danus—he must be wondering what had become of her. If he followed the pattern Markus had laid out, he would think her bond broke, gone back to the trail with Kryn to return to Dast.

Kryn—Markus had said he was a fellow prisoner—less well situated. The Hold Heir's dislike for her would certainly be fed by this last change in his fortunes. He had been dragged into imprisonment because he had done her a favor. Thus, she was indebted to the somewhat sullen young man who resented her talent so strongly.

She seated herself once more in the window chair. There had been much she had learned from Dreen's books. But there had been gaps in that knowledge which even the priestess had been unable to bridge. Lord Markus had that stone of ill which she had detected for Danus. How great a weapon that might be for one of dark power she could not tell. Did Markus intend to use her talent to find for him other such ominous stones, that he might build an armory of such? She was inclined to believe that to be the truth.

And all she had for defense was a knowledge, faulty because of holes in her learning, and the Fingers. She now had four—there were six more—and they could be scattered afar, even into the plains lands. All which she had to guide her was that one stone would awake at the coming of the others and so reveal its hiding place.

A sound at the door made her turn her head. That portal swung aside and the stolid Sahsan came in, a tray balanced on the flattened palm of one hand, her other hanging loose as if to ward off any attack Nosh might be inclined to make. Though how the woman might believe that she offered any threat, Nosh could not understand. They had taken her knife from her belt while she had been unconscious and she had no other real weapon on her.

Sahsan set down her burden on the bed—which must be meant to serve as a table in this sparsely furnished apartment.

"Eat," she ordered and went to lean her broad back against the wall, standing like a servant waiting to complete some task.

Nosh was willing enough to obey. It seemed that she had to thank Lord Markus for giving her guesting service, as the food she found in the covered dishes was equal to the best Danus had to offer. She ate heartily, long trained by a sparse diet to make the most of a full meal when it was offered.

However, she found it somewhat intimidating to eat with Sahsan staring at her in that fashion. There was that in the woman's attitude which kept Nosh from trying to talk. And now she found herself hurrying, bolting down the contents of the last dish so that she would be free of that surveillance.

"Thank you." She felt as if she must break the lowering silence.

To her surprise Sahsan came away from the wall and stationed herself within touching distance of Nosh. Her right hand swung up, middle fingers and thumb bent under, only fore and little finger pointing outward.

It was a gesture the girl had seen used twice before—by the guards who had come with Danus into Dast, meant to avert the peril of ill power.

Though Sahsan said nothing, she waved that half fist back and forth in front of Nosh's face, nearly touching the girl. There was an expression on her face at last, that of loathing fed by fear.

Having so warned Nosh off, the woman took up the

tray and went back through the doorway, leaving Nosh knowing just how she must be judged by at least one of this household.

There was a chittering cry and a small body squeezed between the bars, took a flying leap, to land on her shoulder. Nosh scratched behind the fluttering frill and the forepaws patted her cheek. At least she had with her one devoted comrade. But she must not forget Kryn.

Deciding that she would not be visited again this night, she readied herself for bed. At the last moment she placed the bag of crystals beneath the fold of cover meant to support her head. There was just a chance— she was reaching into the dark but perhaps by Lyr's favor she could do it.

Resolutely Nosh stretched out on the bed, the zark curling up beside that fold pillow, and closed her eyes, willing herself into the deep relaxation she had managed to reach only a few times under Dreen's training—but which she knew had been one of the priestess's own talents.

Feet relax, legs, hands, arms, body—head—it was difficult. She had to start over twice until she at last felt as if she were suspended in the air, bodiless, calm.

Kryn—she fixed his face in her mind. Kryn?

There was a strange feeling of loss which became freedom. She was no longer in that painted room, no longer even in her body. Kryn . . . !

Stone walls made a corridor before her. There was moisture dripping from those walls, a feeling of . . . underground! This was below the earth surface. Kryn—a door in that wall. It might be sealed yet not against her questing this night.

And though she knew somehow that there was a nearly black pocket beyond the wall, she could also see even as if she read a gem. Kryn, collared, chained to the wall.

Where in this building lay that corridor and cell? She was back in the hallway and speeding in the other direction. Thought-picture—dream—but she was somehow the master of it—could bend this power to her will. Stairs now, ill lit by a flickering lamp set in a niche close to the head of the flight. Another door and now she passed into a wide hallway, a kind of center wall from which many ways were marked by curtained doors.

Which way lay the center of the power she sensed—that! She sped again, unaware of anybody. There was the room in which she had met Markus, and beyond the way upward to her own chamber. Kryn within the earth, and she in a sky-walled room—they were as far apart as they could be planted.

Nosh breathed deeply and opened her eyes upon those glaring paint-streaked walls. Her hand beneath the fold of the cover closed about the bag of crystals. Four she had, and now she was sure that her talent grew with each she had found.

Seek again? But she needed a guide and Kryn could not provide it this time. Markus was the only answer. Resolutely Nosh returned the crystals to the fold beneath her head. Markus—she pictured him in her mind as detailed as she could.

There was again that snap of release. She flashed along the way she had already studied, down the stairs, but not to the room where she had seen him before. No, this pull was from beyond the wall of that small chamber. A warded place even as the one Danus had but here the wards were stronger—and there was a lick of dark across her path.

In . . . she pulled on the full force of her strength, refusing to believe that she could not break this as she had the one the merchant kept to protect his riches.

It was hard but she pierced the ward shell at last and was there, and so was Markus. He sat before a table much like the one Danus had used for the judging of stones, and his fingers pushed gems here and there as if he worked some pattern, yet Nosh had no feeling that he used any power. Rather she picked up a sensation of frustration as might haunt a workman who carried in his mind a picture of what he must do and found that he had not the materials for its success.

She dropped her gaze from the man to the jewels with which he toyed and it was as if she had put light to a fire. There were stones there which held power right enough, but not her power. And in that moment Nosh realized danger and cut her tie with man and room.

Again she lay on her bed. Her hand was twisted up under her head and she was so tightly holding that bag of crystals that the pressure of them bruised her flesh. Not again—she felt the ebb of that strength which had served her. Not tonight.

Instead she willed herself into a sleep which was un-marred by any dreams—or if she dreamed, she did not remember upon awakening. And the morning sun was already striking eye-blinding beams from the wall beside which she lay.

The zark was gone but, as she threw off her covers and sat up, it bobbed back through the window and chit-tered excitedly, jumping up and down on the bed.

When she strove to pet it as she had before, it swiftly backed away and its tail swung out farther into her sight. There was a change in that tail—at its very end now protruded a brilliant red spikelike point. The spike glis-tened as if it were wet.

The zarks of the Ryft had not been so equipped. What . . .

It was a sharp cry, almost a scream, which brought her to the window, gazing down at that roof garden. One wearing the tunic of a maidservant lay facedown, with an older woman bending over her.

A second scream brought a man, and, within a moment, two guards.

"Dead . . . !" The screamer's voice shrilled up enough for Nosh to hear.

The man had rolled the maid over, held fingers to her throat as if seeking a pulse and then he spoke loud enough to drown the noisy sobs of the woman:

"Dead—no. She still lives. Get her below!" That order went to the guards.

The man's head came up—he was looking higher. Nosh instantly pushed back from the window, went to sit again on her bed, to regard the zark with narrowed eyes.

Poison! Had the fears of Danus's household been correct? Yet it was plain that the creature had evaded her touch when it might have been dangerous for her. Nosh held out a finger. That spur had disappeared (withdrawn into the tail, perhaps) and the zark pushed forward, reared up, and caught her finger between its forepaws as if to reassure her.

She scratched its head before she went to wash and dress. Had the changes of fate provided her with a weapon of sorts? Perhaps . . . Her need for a defense made her think of Markus. She was sure that the feeling of frustration she had sensed radiating from him had to do with the gems . . . which meant he would call upon her talent.

Proof that she had guessed rightly came within a moment, as Sahsan opened the door and while still standing in the hall gestured her out.

"Lord Markus wants you."

"I have had no food," Nosh countered, determined to discover just how masterful this armswoman might be.

"Lord Markus wants you." Now she grasped Nosh's shoulder and brought her out in the hall, shoving her forward.

They retraced their way of the previous day—and that she had spied out by night—coming down to the room where she had first met the ruler of this household. But they did not enter there; instead she was shoved along, for Sahsan had not loosened her grip, to another doorway which seemed open but before which her guard brought them to a halt.

A ward here. Was it as easily pierced as Danus's had been? However, she must give no sign that wards were not as binding upon her as all others.

"The girl . . . " Sahsan raised her harsh voice, appearing to address the empty doorway. There was a wavering as if something close to invisible drew aside and she was shoved in, her guard not following.

Markus was there, sipping from a gem-set cup. However, there was something else beyond him that Nosh marked with a single quick glance not betraying herself with any longer look. There, across a side table, lay Bringhope, Kryn's kin-sword.

Quick as she had tried to be Markus had caught her out.

"Yes, the sword—a kin-sword—belonging to an outlaw. Both man and sword are safely bound for now. Come, Talented One, we have some use for you."

He put out one booted foot and shoved forward a stool which faced a narrow board, too small to be named table but which was footed and shaped to fit just at the right height for one seated on the stool.

Once Nosh was down he pulled out of the overlapping front of his robe a bag and tossed it to the top of that narrow board.

"I have heard much of your talent; prove those statements true. Sort these . . . "

He took another sip from the cup as she untied the bag and carefully shifted its contents unto the board. Nosh blinked but she did not gasp. Since she had discovered her talent, she had never been faced with such a rich hoard. Danus's collection was as a beggar's toll when compared to this.

"This is no trial, Lord Markus," she said. "Already you know well the value of what lies here—why ask me to appraise them?"

He was smiling that unpleasant smile. "Stones may have a hidden value—did you not find such a one for Danus? Try these for what they may hold besides their color and cut."

Nosh had already made sure that there was none like that strange black gem which had proclaimed evil as loudly as if it shouted its worth aloud. But were there others like it masquerading under other colors?

"Sun eyes," she said, separating three good-sized and perfectly centered stones to one side. "Snow Gem"— the pale grey with its inner swirl of white was as harmless as the first three. "Sea breath . . . " She had but touched it with the tip of her finger and now jerked her hand away from the green-blue cabochon-cut stone.

Lord Markus leaned forward in his seat. "So—now you have something to tell me, Talented One? What of this Sea breath?"

"Blood," she said starkly, "it is blood-tainted. Ill fortune for him who holds it."

"Continue." He made no comment on what she had said but gestured to the remaining jewels.

"Fire spark . . . " Two of them and nothing to be read by touch. "Tears of mist," another three. Then came the last two. They were not matched—one was a bright clear yellow—faintly tinged with green, so unlike the Sun reds. It was such a stone as she had never seen before and could not name. That which lay beside it was a teardrop-shaped gem, opaque, shading in color from lavender to a peach-orange. It also she did not know.

"These are new to me, lord," she said. "I would say they come from other lands—far lands."

She touched the yellow. It was as if she had released some putrid odor. The thing held within it old danger, rottenness of spirit.

"Evil." Nosh was sure of that though the evil was not that of the stone Danus had shown her. Lord Markus nodded, his smile growing wider.

"And the other?"

It was beautiful to look upon, almost she hesitated to try it lest it be a bait for a trap. But what came from it was something she had never encountered before, a wave of pure sorrow. Tear-shaped it was and tears were locked within it—perhaps to darken the life of the wearer in a different fashion.

"It—it is sorrow engrained. Not evil but such as brings tears with it." She tried to make plain her own feelings.

"Excellent." Once more he leaned back in his chair. "You have proved your worth for my purposes. What you have sorted will become keys—keys to a number of things. Here." He produced another and smaller bag and threw it to her. "Put those which are dangerous by your reckoning in this."

When she had rebagged all the stones he made no move to take back the bags. Instead he shifted in his chair and sat surveying her, so that the awareness of peril awoke within her.

"Such a tool as you are is seldom given to any man," he said. "But it is Markus's luck which has brought you to my hand at the moment when it is most important. There is something strange in Kasgar, something stirring. And when there is a stirring it is a matter of power. He who holds the right weapon then wins his desires. I shall keep you very safe, my Talented One. It may be within a short time you will have an even greater treasure to sort." His smile was now more of a grimace. "Yes—a treasure! You have not been long in Kasgar, have you, girl?"

"No." She had no idea what he was leading up to now.

"The guild of jewel merchants is the strongest of our companies. And that guild is ruled by one I have good reason to wish brought down. For a long time Lathia D'Arcit has been threat to my plans. She has such guards and wards as have never been broken. But . . ." He stopped short and his eyes focused again on Nosh.

Now he reached out and laid hand on the hilt of Bringhope.

"They tell queer tales in the northeast about kin-swords. It is said that no one but the right blood can use such a blade. Seldom do they fall into the hands of any who cannot claim kin—yet here is one. This Kryn, he came into Kasgar with you, he remained behind when his men left with the supplies he bargained for. Was it because of you?" He shot that question at her and she answered with the truth:

"No. He was sent by his lord to bargain for weapons and found that such were forbidden to be sold to out-landers. But—"

"He continued to hope, yes," Markus interrupted her. "He went seeking those he thought were willing to pro-vide what he needed secretly. In fact the very man he sought is under this roof. Unfortunately, we, too, have a need for weapons and have none to spare for rag-taggle armsmen who are outlawed in their own country. In fact,"—he rubbed his chin with his hand and once more it seemed to Nosh he was thinking aloud rather than addressing her—"in fact there is a price on this outlaw's head. So—I have another tool to hand. But that is only a small advantage, what you have to offer is a greater one. And this outlaw Kryn can come to a sorry end—he can die by his own blade—a fitting conclusion to his House."

Nosh found the words she needed. "He is nothing to me, lord. If you seek thus to use him . . . "

"Oh, there are many uses as you will discover, Talented One. And now . . . " He raised his hand and Nosh saw he held a similar object to that with which Danus had dispersed his ward. "Sahsan is waiting for you and she will see you fed. Go now."

She slipped from the stool and went to that door where there was a ripple in the air. Passing through, she joined the armswoman without.

At least Sahsan did not immediately escort her to her room, rather brought her into a side chamber in which there were three long tables, with benches on either side. At one of these were two guards spooning stew out of bowls and drinking thirstily from mugs.

They glanced toward Nosh and her guardian and then away as if they wanted nothing to do with Sahsan, who pointed to one of the benches and, when the girl had seated herself, rapped loudly on the table with her massive fist. Her summons was answered by a spare-bodied, hunch-shouldered man who wore an apron stiff with many drippings and favored both women with a cross-eyed leer.

"Food." Sahsan certainly was not going to serve her charge with the same kind of luxury meal Nosh had enjoyed the night before. However, when the server returned with two earthenware bowls, and mugs, slapping them down and then adding two wooden spoons from his tray, the girl thought that the odor which arose from this humble serving was appetizing.

It appeared that Markus's guards and underlings fared well and she ended up by scraping the bottom of the bowl with the spoon to get the last bite of the thick stew. That which had come in the mug was not to her taste.

A sip told her it was a sourish brew, the like of which was misnamed ale in Kasgar, and she left most of it in the mug.

The two at the other table pushed aside their empty bowls and one of them gave a hearty belch. Nosh measured both in quick glances. They were like any other guards she had seen in house service, save that they were certainly not as smartly turned out as those who served Danus. As they got up they came toward Nosh and Sahsan, the one grinning widely to show crooked teeth with gaps in the jaw to mark those missing.

Coming closer to the two he made a rough sketch of a bow and spoke to Sahsan:

"Easy duty, eh? You want to take an hour off, just give us the hint." He turned a little and surveyed Nosh with a leer. She had no doubt as to what he suggested.

"Lord's hold—keep off!" Sahsan snapped tersely.

However, Nosh's gaze had struck what the fellow wore around his neck, sliding back and forth across his unkempt mail with every movement of his head. One of the red stones! The rathhawk stones!

Was Markus issuing such to his men? But the other of this pair did not wear one, unless he kept it tucked within his shirt. The girl remembered the story about the seller of amulets in the marketplace. What power did these red discs have? Did they bind men as well as birds to the service of some overlord? If so—could Markus be that lord? Yet Kryn had seen one of the hawks so burdened over the mountains and Nosh believed that this ambitious lord of Kasgar certainly had not pushed his rule that far. So—if the red stones were from another source and being sold to such as this guard throughout Kasgar—she drew a quick breath. That opened wide another door—one she was not ready yet, if ever, to explore.

She thought of his words concerning Lathia, whom he

apparently held in dislike—that mutter of plans concerning her. What she had heard of the woman guild master had inclined Nosh to believe that she was not of the same stamp as Markus. And Lathia D'Arcit had influence, powers of her own. Danus had spoken most respectfully of her.

If Nosh and Kryn could win free from Markus, they would still be within the range of that lord's vengeance. But suppose one went to this Lathia with a warning, could enlist her to one's aid? She seized upon that thought with vigor.

"Get!" Sahsan raised her big spoon as if it were a weapon. The two guards laughed, one of them pretending to dodge a blow.

"Hot-tempered little thing, ain't she?" inquired one. "Gets all the good jobs an' is bound to keep 'em. Rest easy while you can, Sahsan, time comin' when you'll have to turn to like the rest of us."

"When that day comes I will," she grated back. As they turned their backs, she pursed her mouth as if to spit, and then drank off the rest of her mug, reaching out her hand for Nosh's, which she also emptied.

Chapter 21

Nosh thought she would be re-turned to her chamber. She had left the zark there, concealed among the bed coverings since she suspected that the creature would once more be in danger if it were sighted. Had its victim on the roof died, or was it a matter of injury only? That the zark had attacked without provocation Nosh would not believe and she had no intention of endangering the small creature.

However, outside that eating hall there was another of those house guards waiting. He jerked a thumb at Sahsan.

"Lord says to give her a look-see in the judgment room," he growled, and turned on his heel while Sahsan nodded to her charge to follow.

What new work Markus had for her Nosh had no idea. But she schooled her expression to one of indifference and followed the heavy-footed guard. Another doorway, this one without wards but with an ordinary barrier of wood, which their guide jerked open and allowed them entrance into a large room.

Nosh stifled a gasp. The hidden crystals were heat-ing—was she about to confront something straight out of the dark power?

When she saw what awaited them she had to hold on to her surface calm with all the strength she could. There was a framework like a doorway. Within that, hanging from his hands, wreckage which had certainly once been a man. She felt revulsion arising in her stomach, warring with the meal she had just eaten.

The guard clumped on to the side of the dangling prisoner, whose head, covered with a mass of sweat-drenched grey-white hair, had fallen forward. Using the tip of his sword, he levered up that head so that the broken and nearly shapeless face could be seen. It was plain that the prisoner had died hard and that his passing was the work of those expert in causing mutilation and pain. Though as much as she could see of that battered face assured Nosh that the dead man was unknown to her.

"Lord Markus," intoned the guard, "says look well at this, girl. Here hangs the proof that he is not to be crossed. This garbage called himself a priest once upon a time, but he was not wise enough when he would not give the Lord what was asked of him. Look and remember, that is what Lord Markus says."

Nosh had taken a step backwards without realizing it, she was so sickened by what she saw. Then she was caught in the iron grip of Sahsan's hold and held fast, unable to escape.

"Lord Markus," the guard was continuing, "says as how he has another prime one to be worked on, as you know. An' he wants you to think about that."

Kryn! They could only mean Kryn. But what did they want to force her to do which would need such an object lesson? Though it made her feel unclean to handle those cursed stones, she did, and would do it to order. But what could be worth this hard dying for Kryn?

"Lord Markus says as how you are supposed to be under some power. Well, this one claimed dealings with that same power an' what has it brought him to?"

"Lyr . . ." she gasped that, not realizing she spoke aloud.

"Some such," the guard laughed. "He pretended to power but when he was taken we catched him as easily as you net a nart at its burrow. No fighting back . . . A fool."

The guard shrugged, withdrew the sword to allow that battered head to fall forward once more.

"Lord Markus said to show you—well, you've seen. Just keep thinkin' about it if you want to get right with Lord Markus."

Sahsan's grip upon Nosh's shoulders swung the girl around and headed her out of the door. In her short life Nosh had seen much of the dark's work. Even now she shuddered away from her farthest and deepest memories, against which she had built a barricade year by year.

That the dead priest had been a priest of Lyr—yes, having seen the deserted shrine in the city she could believe that. And that Markus might well be opposed to all the Hands promised—yes, she could believe that also. But what game he could play with her she had yet to discover—and she might learn that knowledge too late.

Sahsan now pulled her along that familiar route up to her sky-bordered quarters, saw her within and made fast the door behind her—having given Nosh such a shove as nearly sent her careening to the opposite wall.

As that door closed the covers heaved on the bed and the zark was out. It rose to its hind feet and leaped to the floor, running toward that closed door, its tail raised high, and from the tip of that there issued the thornlike appendage she had seen before. It was very clear that the zark looked upon Sahsan as a presumptive enemy to be handled after its own fashion.

For several moments it leaped up and down before the closed door, clearly in a rage. And then it withdrew, slowly, still facing the door, ready to go into action if the woman returned.

Nosh dropped down on the bed and pressed both her hands over the crystals. It had been plain to her as time passed that with the discovery of every new Finger her own small powers expanded. Though it was not night, and she might be interrupted, she was greatly tempted to seek out by projection Kryn's cell.

That ravaged body—it broke in upon her memory no matter how hard she tried to seal that picture away. Now she suddenly recalled that that skeletal frame had lacked feet. Feet—was that what Markus would do to make sure that his prey did not escape?

Kryn—a mixture of fear and rage stirred in her. She closed her eyes and fought for control, for the strength to subdue such emotions—to leave only need—reaching need.

Relax—her body fought against her will. She wanted to be out and about, doing something—anything which would defeat Markus. Relax . . . Nosh fumbled with the bag of crystals, loosed its cord from about her neck, and slipped it up to touch her forehead right above her eyes. She had seen Dreen use her throat crystal so in the past, when the priestess had retreated into one of the trances which were so much a part of her life.

There was a drift of mistlike grey crossing her mind. Nosh pushed through it. Once more she swung free of body but this time she found herself right outside the door Sahsan had so abruptly slammed. The armswoman herself leaned against the wall at the top of the stairs which were the only path out of the room-prison.

So clear was Sahsan to Nosh that she fully expected

the armswoman to sight her in return. But when the girl gathered the strength to will herself forward she appeared to waft by Sahsan as if she had less substance even than a shadow.

Down the stairs, she knew her goal but she was delaying the reaching of it, mastering as best she could the way she must go. There was another guard stationed before that way which led to the cells. However, save for him and Sahsan she saw no one else.

The doors were shut—some of them warded, she sensed as she wafted past. Then she was at the one which closed upon Kryn's cell. Yes, a ward here also. But her thought broke forward as if she put out a hand to tear a curtain and she was again in that dark prison.

Kryn was stretched out on one of the bundles of decaying straw, his arms flung up to cover his eyes. If he only had Dreen's power—if they could meet on this strange plane which was not of this world, and yet in it.

At least he seemed unharmed—there had been no mutilation, no signs that he had been professionally and roughly handled. His arm moved, fell into place at his side. His eyes were open and slowly his head turned in her direction.

Nosh knew a leap of hope. Could he at least sense that he was not entirely alone? She was no adept, this was a hard struggle and—she could hold no longer. This time there was no lengthy passage back to mark the way, the second self of her was snuffed as one might put out a reed dish lamp. She was aware instantly of the bed beneath her, of a patting on her hand where it held the crystals in place. Nosh opened her eyes to see the head of the zark bent so that its lizard nose nearly touched hers. And she could not help but think there was a hint of concern in the creature's wide stare.

*   *   *

Kryn lay looking out into the dim light of the cell—
which came from the two holes no larger than would
allow a man's arm to reach through just below where
ceiling met wall. They had not brought Gudelph back.
Judging by all logic the priest must be dead. Which was
perhaps what any man would have chosen rather than
exist as he had in Markus's hold.

He had thought over the same mental paths until his
head ached. Surely this lord knew that Kryn had been
trying to find him, that he had a purpose. . . .

Not any longer. The purse he had guarded so carefully was gone. Markus had the pay whether or not he
delivered the goods. There was Nosh . . . Markus
wanted the girl. Her cherished talent had brought her
here—and him with her. To what purpose?

Those death stones—sold openly in the marketplace—one worn by a guard here. Kryn was almost certain they were none of Markus's work. Which meant
there was a force beyond Markus, also inimical to the
ones Markus preyed upon. That story he had heard of
the embassy from Valcur . . . He stared down at his
hands. Something stirred here—Danus had known it.
What was abroad in this city?

To be trapped here where he could not learn even
the face of danger . . . ! He had had to learn patience
over the past years—now his shield of it was wearing
very thin. There were too many hints and no answers
save guesses.

Nosh—his thoughts kept swinging back to her. That
thing she had found in the mask above the entrance to
the shrine—he found himself now rubbing one hand
with the other. He had caught that piece of crystal that
the zark had twisted free after he had lent his own
weight to the business. Now there was only a faint ripple
of memory. It had been warm to his touch, had left, for
a very brief moment, a strange tingling in his flesh. A

thing of power—Kryn shook his head in denial. Not for him. . . .

He called upon memory to exile that uneasiness from his mind. In the past he had heard plenty of hidden intrigues between House and House. There were tall tales told of subtle—and sometimes outright hostile moves made by the Lords to advance some ambition or greed.

In the immediate past it had been the Temple—with Valcur as the leader—cutting away at the old rulers of the land and bringing any strong House down. The same game might well be in play here.

Danus's comments on the sudden deaths of people in the hierarchy of command—those amulets on open sale . . . Yes, there could well be a game under way in Kasgar. Kryn rubbed sword-callused hand against hand. This was like being trapped in a bog across which there were hidden roads but to which he had no guide.

Those at Dast must be his first concern—yet here he was trapped like a greedy insect in congealed juice. . . .

He had no way of telling time save that the light from those holes grew more or less. At night there was left the faintest of glows as if a lamp was set close enough to provide that. But he had a feeling that Gudelph had been away too long, that what the priest had hinted at had come—the man of Lyr was dead.

Kryn had made close inspection of his chain. The collar galling his neck could not be loosened, he did not even feel-find any catch in it. The chain he passed through his hands link by link, testing the durability of each with all his strength. That wall ring which was coated with rust was equally strong, though flakes of the rust rubbed away in his fingers. He had been left nothing to use as a tool.

Kryn brought his fists down on his knees in savage blows. To wait tamely here—be subjected perhaps to that horror Gudelph had known—! He refused to believe in the help of any powers—there was none which would answer to any petition from such as he.

What good had Lyr done for Gudelph?

Kryn stared across the narrow cell to that other heap of moldering straw. That hiding place under it—what it held . . . But if it were any power talisman, why had Gudelph remained here? An amulet which promised and did not give—as were all the devices of "gods."

However, he crossed the space to that other bed. The chain allowed him barely enough length to reach a spot from which he could strain out with his arms far enough for his hands to probe that hiding place. Working awkwardly against the choking pressure of the collar, he managed to do as Gudelph and bring out of that pocket the small bundle he had seen the other cradle in his hand.

It was well tied, with even a sealing like gum smeared over it—small—certainly no weapon. Yet the old priest had thought it worth concealing. Kryn weighed it in his hand, pinched it here and there to try and discover what lay within that wrapping of rag sealed over with a hardened substance.

At length he thrust it into the fore of his tunic. And then threw himself once more onto the bed. His body was tense, every nerve and muscle in him called for action. Only that patience he had so vigorously clung to back in the Temple of the One was his barrier against the need to do SOMETHING!

Nosh moved her hands slowly back and forth, stretching the fingers apart, bringing them together again as a fighter might exercise with her chosen weapon. The zark crouched beside her, its bright eyes closed, she thought that it slept. Escape . . . but how?

When? Certainly not by day when she could be easily

sighted. And—not alone! She knew now that she could not leave Kryn here to suffer as had that dead man they had shown her.

By the sky outside her window it was dimming into twilight. Long ago she had tested those bars and found them firm set past any loosening.

To await on Markus's will sapped her own spirit and energy, yet she could see no other path for her now.

There was a small chitter, the zark was awake, reached up with a forepaw to smooth the side of her hand.

"Little one." Nosh caressed that upraised head. "I do not know how deadly is that weapon of yours but perhaps it may be one to serve us both—if I could only make you understand. . . ."

Her half whisper was cut off by a sound from the door. Swiftly she laid a hand on that small scaled body, drew it toward her, and whipped up the edge of her skirt, pushing it as before into that ragged pocket she had made for its transport.

As if it understood perfectly what she wished the creature burrowed into hiding, and she adjusted her belt as best she could so that its small weight would not cause a suspicious sagging.

Again it was the armswoman who gestured her out.

"Come." She was scowling, and Nosh wondered what anger stirred in that hulking body and how it might touch her.

Once more they descended through the house and came to that chamber where in the morning she had sorted the jewels for Markus. And once more the creeper lord sat waiting her, spread before him on the tabletop those gems of ill omen which seemed, when she glanced at them, to pulsate with a dark intensity.

"We have a task waiting," he greeted her with that forbidding smile. "I have had further information con-

cerning your talent—which is greater than it seems. You
read a riddle for Danus which saved him and his caravan. . . . Now you will serve me to an even greater extent. Sit!"

Nosh dropped on the stool. Against her breast, within
her bodice, the fingers were warming—warning. . . . She
did not know what he would have her do but that it was
of the dark she did not doubt.

"Each of these"—he pointed to the gems before
him—"hold power, as you have testified. Very well, if
one is powerful, cannot all be made to act together, thus
increasing such power? And can that power not be
aimed?" He was leaning forward, and the tip of his
tongue followed that last word outward, running across
his lower lip as one who savored some treat to come.

"Lord, I do not know," she held her voice level. That
answer she had received to her dealing with the message
stone was alive in her memory. Perhaps it would do only
good to attract here that same return of blasting energy.

"You do not know," he repeated in a voice which was
hardly more than a purr. "So—now we shall discover.
Unite these stones, Talented One, bind them one to the
other. This night I have work for such a weapon."

Then he stood up. "I have heard also from the chatter
of others, repeating strange tales, that there may be a
backlash from such an experience. If so, it is best that
you do this alone. But you will do it!" He leaned down
like a rathhawk swooping and his fingers bit into her
shoulder. "You were shown this day what happens to
those who do not serve me. . . . " Now his lips appeared
to flatten and show his teeth. . . .

"You will combine this power and you will aim it,"—
from one of the long sleeves of his robe he drew a flat
plaque as wide as his palm, flipping it onto the table
near the gems—"at this one—Lathia!"

She found herself looking at a painted representation

of a woman, not as stylized as those illustrations in Dreen's books, but with an air of life to it as if some essence of the other had been trapped by the painter and so imprisoned.

He turned a little and clicked his ward opener. Sahsan stood in that doorway.

"This one,"—Markus indicated Nosh—"does my work. Make sure that she does so."

How could the armswoman make certain, Nosh wondered. Sahsan had given no indication that she had any talent for sensing the rise of power. But now Markus was setting something else on the table, a small globe within which swirled a greyish mist. He looked again to the girl.

"This is something from afar, Talented One, so perhaps not even known to you. But it will register what you do here. Behold . . . " He rolled it a fraction nearer one of the ominous gems. The swirl within began to change in shade—there was a touch of dull red.

"Lathia—" He gave another of those wakwolf grins. "I want her weakened, made ready for my challenge of her power. This you will do!"

He was gone. Nosh was aware that Sahsan had come to stand behind her, looming over her. And she did not doubt that the armswoman was alert to every move she would make.

But this was madness—she had no learning which would release disaster from these stones. He was crediting her with far more power than she had dreamed of—more than Dreen herself might have raised.

Now—this was the thin chance she had waited for— had unconsciously perhaps summoned by will, if one's will could act upon another's. Under her skirt her knee moved, nudging the zark. At the same time she leaned forward, seeming to study the stones as one might the pieces of a game.

How much would her wishes reach the creature she carried hidden? She could not tell—she could only hope. It had displayed an unusual ease in communication during these past days.

Nosh reached out and took up the picture, holding it in her hand as she felt the zark wriggle from the pocket. She spoke, stringing meaningless words together as she would a chant of invocation. The weight in her skirt was gone.

Then Sahsan staggered back and Nosh turned. The armswoman's skin was a dull gray, her eyes rolled up in her head. And the zark, its weapon waving at tall point, was leaping to cling to Nosh's skirt once again.

Nosh was on her feet. Sahsan had crashed down. The girl froze, waited for any sound from without. That did not come. She turned back and caught up Bringhope—Kryn would not, she knew, leave that behind.

The zark had sheathed its weapon, and had climbed to her shoulder. Dragged a little to one side by the weight of the sword, Nosh walked forward straight through the wards. There was no alarm—apparently Markus felt that they were enough to keep safety.

She crept through the outer rooms—slipped along the wall of the hall beyond. There was another guard, one of the two men who had been at the table earlier. Nosh dodged back into a doorway. She put her hand to her shoulder and the zark clung to it. The creature dropped from her hold to the floor and made such a quick dash forward the eye could hardly follow.

The guard gave a start, raised his hand as if to slap at some portion of his leg, and then, as Sahsan had done, crumpled down.

Nosh darted forward to that door. Wards there, too. . . . She held the sword in both hands and plunged forward, feeling the resistance of the unseen lessen as she broke the barrier to the door of the cell. Her hand slammed down on the simple bar and then she was through, facing Kryn scrambling to his feet and looking at her wide-eyed.

Chapter 22

"WHAT . . ." HE FOUND HIS VOICE BUT she closed on him, looking to the chain which held him. Putting one hand to the slack of the link, she gave a jerk.

"No—the sword!" His hands were both out to grasp the weapon she was holding against her. As he drew the blade free she understood. But Nosh doubted that it was strong enough to break that chain she had just tested.

"Stand here." He motioned to the bed pile. "Hold the chain up to raise the ring, and hold it taut."

She obeyed. He was surveying ring and chain with narrowed eyes and now he raised Bringhope and delivered a forceful downward blow. There was the clang of metal against metal and the chain dropped; Nosh was sent to her knees under the strength of that blow against the links she had tried to hold up and steady. But there was a broken link by the ring and the rest of the chain swung back and free against Kryn as he staggered backward.

"Come!" It was her turn to give orders and the chance they faced now she was not sure was in their favor. She could pass through the wards—but what of Kryn?

251

She could only hope that the gained strength of the Fingers could aid them both.

The cell door was open as she had left it and then they were at the wards. "Your hand . . . !" Nosh grabbed at his wrist as he shifted the sword to a one-handed hold.

Through, she was through, but her arm stretched back and Kryn was left behind. Then as her hold on him tightened and she strove to gather all the strength she could, he swept out with the sword against the unseen barrier. The weapon came up flat against what could not be pierced but Kryn stumbled on, knocked off-balance by that unsuccessful blow. Then the ward gave and they were together in the hall beside the downed guard.

From the side of the armsman the zark flashed and sprang, seizing on the folds of her skirt and climbing as if Nosh were some stone such as those of the valley used for perches. It gained her shoulder again.

Kryn looked down at the man and then to her. His expression turned to one of wariness as he sighted the zark.

"It will not harm us," she told him in haste. But there was another problem now facing them. They were free of their individual prisons, yes. Kryn was tucking the dangling end of the chain still depending from his collar into his belt, so that it would not clang against the walls. But how were they to be free of this house?

Kryn knelt beside the guard. "Not dead," he reported. Then with a turn of his head he directed her attention down the hall. There was another door on the opposite side near to where the stairs ended.

"Is that warded?" he asked.

Nosh ran to it, tested, turned and shook her head, hoping he could see that by the light which was so feeble. He gestured her back.

"Take him there." He was keeping speech to a minimum as if he needed all his strength.

Getting to his feet he hooked hands in the armpits of the limp body and Nosh hurried back to pick up the dragging feet. The man was a hefty burden and she, for one, was breathing hard when they dumped him before one of the doors. Kryn flipped up what seemed to be a simple latch and they were through into a dense dark, drawing the armsman with them.

Kryn did not close the door at once; instead he held it open to draw within what light could penetrate this far. Then he made a quick stride to the left and Nosh saw that he was fumbling with what looked like a travel lantern. There was a small click, a spark enlarged to light in the dark, and then a glow. Instantly Nosh brought the door closed and they both looked around.

This was not another prison cell but rather appeared to be a warehouse or supply chamber of large proportions, for the lantern light did not reach far enough to pick up a wall, only illuminated piles of boxes and chests.

Kryn knelt once more beside the armsman and it was plain that he was striving to free the man of his mail shirt, his knife belt, and whatever other weapons he might carry. The lamplight caught on something else— that spot of red sliding back and forth across the mail Kryn worked to loose.

Nosh saw the Hold Heir tense and she herself jerked back the hand she had put out to aid him. Then Kryn unsheathed the fellow's own knife, inserted it carefully within the hook of the neck cord from which the death stone was suspended, and pulled it free. For a moment he stared down at it, his features grim set, and then he nodded as if in answer to some thought, looking up to Nosh.

"You have the secret of the wards." That was a statement, no question. "Can you take this back to the cell and plant it there?"

"What good will that do?" she countered, unable to guess the reason for such a risk of time.

"It will dust trail for us." He used the metaphor of a scout and she knew what he meant—for she had seen the rearguard men on their trail from the refuge dust over prints to disguise the road. "This is not of Markus," he continued. "There is more than one dark server in Kasgar. . . . "

She caught his meaning at once. If there were any division of purposes and powers, for Markus to find this in place of his prisoner would indeed dust their trail.

Nosh caught up the thong which held the stone and slipped around the edge of a door she opened with the utmost caution. Then she sped down the hall to that other door, once more passed the ward, and opened it to toss the amulet within, where it would lie in plain sight on the stone floor.

She came back to find that Kryn had made good time in his stripping of the armsman, the mail shirt, knife belt, two bootknives all lying plain in the lantern light. He had rolled the man over so that he could pull the limp hands together behind his back and lash the wrists in tight bond. There followed a gag made of a piece of the guard's own undershirt. He had not moved by himself or opened his eyes but still he was not dead, and Nosh began to wonder if the zark's poison simply stunned and did not kill.

Kryn tossed her one of the bootknives and she thrust it in her belt, feeling some reassurance from the very grip of it in her hand. He held up the mail shirt and then put one hand to that metal band about his own throat.

"It was too much to wish from fortune that this one had the key for the unlocking of this. . . . " he said.

A sudden thought out of nowhere crossed Nosh's mind. She held out her hands, flexed the fingers. There was no visible lock on that collar to be seen. And certainly it had not been forged on. Then . . . there was some trick to its fastening—and just perhaps . . .

She made a quick movement which brought her to his side as he still lingered there on his knees. "It can do no harm to try . . ." she said, as much to reassure herself as to have him understand what she might do. Her hands closed about that rusty band, slipped along it while she called upon her talent to read in another fashion than she had ever used it before. Kryn stiffened and held his head up as far as he could to give her room for both sighting and feeling.

There! Right there! Her thumbs came together on the band and pressed while she summoned that inner strength which was a part of reading. Not—not straight—very well, turn a fraction . . . the thumbs moved and there was a click loud enough to resound through the dusk about them. The collar came apart and Kryn's hands were swift to catch it by the trailing chain and drop it to the floor. Then he was pulling on the mail shirt, snapping the latches, reaching for the belt.

Nosh looked down at her hands for a long moment. This was the first time she had tried to use Lyr's talent for anything else than the finding and judging of stones. Perhaps it was very true that with the addition of each Finger to her store the talent was fed, stretched, strengthened.

Yet there was something strange, too. Something she had sensed in that moment when she had solved the invisible lock—as if Kryn also had that which had aided what she would do.

"Put him back there." On his feet once again, Kryn was lifting the shoulders of their captive and heading toward a pile of chests at one end of the room. Nosh hastened once more to aid him and then went back to take up the lantern.

However, another thought crossed her mind. That door through which they had come with their prisoner was of normal width, but as she swung the lantern around, its rays made clear for an instant or two that there were certainly wrapped and boxed things here which outspanned that opening. She had seen Danus's warehouse and that had had another door—one opening directly on the way where carts had been unloaded. If this house, large as it was, followed the general design of Danus's—and she suspected it did—then there might well be another exit, one which would serve them better than to return to the hall and the stairs where there might even be another guard now. She said as much to Kryn and he agreed.

So they struck away from the door through which they had come, threaded a crooked path among the piled-up goods in search of the opposite wall. Suddenly the zark gave one of its chittering cries and leaped to the top of the nearest pile of boxes, racing into the dark. Nosh's hand went to her knife, even as Kryn's dropped to the hilt of his sword.

They paused to listen—but all that sounded was the chittering which Nosh thought she would not have heard if the zark had gone to launch an attack. But they started forward with every sense alert.

Now the lantern did pick up a break in the wall. There was a ramp leading up, wide enough for the transport of the largest things they had seen here. And parked at its foot was a wheeled platform, which certainly must be used for the transport of goods. But, as Nosh swung the lantern out and upward, they saw the zark patting its forepaws against a door which closed that way.

"Locked—or warded?" Kryn wondered.

They could make sure quickly enough. The slope of the ramp was not impeded by any clusters of boxes and they climbed rapidly, joining the zark. Kryn ran his hands across the door. It was smooth of any latch or lock which they could see. Nosh thrust the lantern in his direction and placed her palms flat against the surface, hopefully calling on her talent. It could be that there was a hidden catch even as there had been for Kryn's collar.

She sensed at once that there was a ward, but added to it a second sealing new to her. Catching her lower lip between her teeth, she concentrated on solving that puzzle. Kryn moved closer, his shoulder brushing against hers.

Nosh felt a queer sudden jolt at that contact and then—yes! She had it, indeed a second ward but it was already yielding to her will. She pushed with all the force she could summon to the use of the talent. And under her hands the surface of the door seemed to trem-ble—almost ripple.

Kryn added his strength to hers as if he sensed what was to be done. The barrier slid to one side but what hung in that slit—for she did not try to force it as far as the second ward.

"Take my hand!" she ordered and stepped confi-dently forward, sure that they would meet no resistance now. Again she had to give that extra tug to bring Kryn through, but it was less difficult this time.

They found themselves caught in the coming of night and standing outside the block of Markus's stronghold in an alleyway.

"Return to Danus?" Kryn asked in a low voice.

"We dare not," Nosh returned. "Markus would seek us there. We have one chance—though how good a one I cannot tell until we put it to the test." Her hand had gone to her bodice where she had placed for safekeeping that picture Markus had left with her. All she had was her own speculations but there was no other choice she could see.

"You have been abroad in this city," she said. "Can you guide us to the house of Lathia D'Arcit?"

"Lathia—the head of the gem dealers guild? Why her?"

Keeping it to as few bare words as she could, Nosh detailed Markus's planned attack. "Where else in Kasgar," she ended, "can we hope for any aid? If she will take our warning, then she is, in a fashion, debt bound to us."

"Lathia. . . . " he repeated, but with the tone of one searching for a memory. "Yes . . . but I must find the market and strike out from there. And which way is that?"

Nosh gestured. "We have but two ways—this to the right and that to the left. It must this time be left to fortune. Wait . . . " She stooped and caught up the zark, turning up her skirt to stow the creature away in her pocket. She had no proper cloak; if she were sighted, she would be remembered, if not accosted.

This street seemed very quiet. Nosh was glad of the custom which sent the families in these great houses to their roof gardens for the evening. There had seemed to be, as she had observed during her stay at Danus's, little roving of the streets by the respectable after dark.

"I have no cloak," Nosh said. Kryn had already turned to the right and was striding down the short street at a swift pace. He was frowning as he looked over his shoulder to where she hurried to catch up with him.

"Stick to the side." He jerked his thumb toward the building at their right. "Where there are doorways, take cover until we are sure of what is ahead."

A feeble defense, Nosh thought, but there was certainly nothing else to be offered now. She shivered. Lacking the cloak as a disguise was not all; the night winds were chill and her Kasgar garments were not meant to be worn in the open without covering at such times.

They came to the edge of the next street. Here in niches of the buildings' walls were set lanterns much like the one Nosh now carried. The light those gave tended to gather in pools, with longer stretches of the dark between.

There were people here and Kryn and Nosh remained in the shadow of the short street, Nosh having hurriedly blown out the lantern. They flattened themselves against the side of Markus's fortress and waited. The pair of pedestrians coming their way halted some distance away at the door of a house across the wider way and their voices joined in boisterous good-nights as one went within and the other came on in their direction at a queer wobbling gait.

"Fortune favors us!" Kryn's mutter was a whisper. "Wait!"

The man coming toward them wore the longer robe of a merchant of some substance, such as Danus donned at times of formal gathering. But he was wavering from side to side and Nosh suddenly realized he was drunk. There must have been a guild dinner at which they had dined very well.

Kryn let him pass and then with a leap almost as wide and noiseless as that of the zark he came up behind the man, his arm curling about the fellow's throat so that only a very small choked cry sounded. Holding his captive hard against him, Kryn's other fist—with belt knife grasped by blade—brought the knobbed hilt down in an audible crack against the struggling man's temple. The captive went limp and Kryn let him down to the ground, his hands already busy with the latches of that outer robe, rolling the fellow easily about while he stripped it off. Then he jerked the fallen man closer to the wall in one of the darker patches well between lanterns and was back to Nosh, the robe bundled under one arm.

"Play the guildman—you might pass as the son of a wealthy House. Then we can go openly—House Heir and guard."

He was very right. Nosh shook out the robe and pulled it on. It was too long but she could bundle it up by tucking it under her belt, which she loosened several notches.

Kryn lighted their lantern again and nodded to her to step out boldly. They walked away from their benefactor at a fair pace and turned as quickly as they could into the first cross street. Along the way they passed two other couples of master and armsman—Kryn had been right about the proper procedure—though why the man they had despoiled had been without a guard Nosh could not guess. That they were headed in the right direction was proved a few moments later when they saw brighter lights ahead and heard noises as if a crowd gathered. Though it was past dark, some of the die-hard merchants, determined to squeeze out the last of the day's possible sales, were still at their stalls, apprentices and gearmen calling out wares in voices hoarse from the day's service.

Under Kryn's direction they skirted the open space, keeping to the inner fringes of stalls already closed. As far as Nosh could see no one even gave them more than a passing glance. Then Kryn took another street which was less used, and finally a third, bringing them to the flat wall of another house so large it spanned the entire block between two side streets.

The blankness of that lower story when the shutters of the shop were fastened down was forbidding. Their chance was so small, yet it was the only one. Nosh took the lead, for here she recognized the same general features as were a part of Danus's establishment. With the shop curtain down there remained for entrance only the small door to one side where visitors after business hours could be admitted if wished. She went directly to that, pulling up the too-long sleeves of her robe to free her arm and hand.

There was a code—that, too, she had learned from Danus when she had accompanied him one day to another merchant to verify the gems for sale there. One who came for business did this and this. . . . Bringing out that plaque bearing Lathia's picture, she gave the required number of knocks, rendering them as loud as she could against that door.

There was a snap, and a narrow peephole opened in the door.

"Who comes?" demanded the unseen viewer.

"One with a message of import." Nosh tried to think of something which would convince that door guard. Certainly in Lathia's house those in attendance would be ever on guard.

"The day is over; the Lady holds no speech with unknowns out of the night." And that peephole snapped shut again.

Nosh had been eyeing the door. Lathia was said to have the strongest wards in Kasgar. It might just be that this door was warded so, and not locked and held. She could only try. Sliding the picture back into hiding she set palms against the surface. She could only hope that what had taken them out of Markus's hold would work for them here.

There was a kind of thrumming to be felt—yes, a ward! She concentrated, bending all her will—strength. It was in a way another code, for she could feel the sensation of a snap, and then another and another, as she mastered each of those unseen ties. Fine guards, yes . . . but not against the Hands of Lyr!

The door, with a swish, slid to the right and Kryn was

ready—the heavy blade of Bringhope swung up to hold it so. Nosh stumbled in and he was so close behind her that his body struck hers, sending her farther forward.

"Stand!" There was light aplenty here; they were well able to see that archer, arrow already to cord.

"We come in peace," Nosh found her voice. "We have that which your Lady should know." Sleeves of her borrowed robe swung as she jerked out that plaque with the picture. Turning it so the guard could see it clearly, she continued:

"This was in the hands of Markus this day. Ask your Lady what dealings he would have to hold such."

"Parger!" A second guard loomed into sight behind the archer.

"Take that . . . no, you toss it to him!" he ordered Nosh. She could do none other than obey.

The second guard caught it out of the air as she tossed it and was gone through another door. But the archer remained at the ready. It seemed a very long wait, and the fact that so much depended on so thin a thread wore at Nosh.

It felt as if several night watches had passed before Parger returned.

"She will see these—in the audience hall," he reported.

They moved forward, Parger leading the way, the archer falling in behind as they passed him. Nosh in a side glance saw that Kryn was holding out bare hands well away from any sword or knife.

Skirting what must be the side of the shop, they came on down a short hall and passed through the door at its end. Before them was a wide table and behind it a chair in which sat a woman not wearing the dress of her sex but rather the rich robes of a Master merchant of the highest rank.

She was of middle years and had a majestic form of

good looks. Her hair was dressed high and there was the glint of gem-headed pins holding it so. On the long hands resting on the tablecloth there was a ring on each mid-finger, one flashing a rainbow of coloring, the other the deep gold of the finest of sun eyes. And between those hands lay the plaque.

"You are?" Her voice was that of one who expected answers, correct and quickly.

"I am Alnosha," Nosh answered, not knowing what to add to that.

The woman's gaze was steady on her and after a moment she nodded.

"You have the discerning talent—I have heard. You came with Danus from the north but you disappeared suddenly from his house. . . ."

"I was taken by Markus." At least Lathia was willing to listen.

"Markus!" There was a hint of anger in that. "And you told Amgar that you brought this from there." She gave the picture a push with a forefinger. "What kind of a coil is this?"

"One which was meant to entrap you, Lady. He plans to raid—if he can."

Lathia D'Arcit gave a small sound of contempt. "That one has sought to bring me down for many seasons. What makes him feel that he may do it now? And what would he have of you? That you open wards . . . that is a trick, girl, which will bring you under the wrath of the Council."

"He has collected certain gems," Nosh replied. "They are steeped in black power. He demanded that that power be used against you, and he gave me that"— she pointed to the picture—"as a focus."

Lathia regarded her for a long moment and then she snapped the fingers of one hand. Nosh heard a stir behind her and waited for the hands of the guard to clamp down upon her and then she realized that what they were doing was leaving the room. Drawing a deep breath of relief she felt more secure.

"Alnosha, there has been much rumored about you in Kasgar. Rumor and gossip supply many with occupation. And"—once more her finger moved to tap the edge of the picture—"of such use of black power I have also heard. You say that Markus has stones of the dark—how did he gather such?"

"I think through general trade, Lady. One such came into Danus's hands when I served him. There may be many such in Kasgar. Unknowing, you may hold such yourself."

Lathia's lips tightened. Then she leaned forward a little, one of her hands rising to her throat. The gleam of a chain shone in the light and she plucked out of concealment a crystal. Nosh nearly reeled with the instant answer of what she herself carried. Her hands flew to draw out the bag as the heat of the gems seemed to scorch her flesh. Through the bag itself their burst of life nearly matched that of Lathia's pendant.

The woman arose, her eyes flickering from that bag to Nosh's face and back again. Then her own hands came up, wrist to wrist, palms and fingers back-spread.

"Long awaited, come at last," she said. "Only truth can abide with you; therefore, tell me what I must know."

Chapter 23

"THESE ARE TAINTED." NOSH SAT AT just the same sort of table she had known in Markus's house and before her were sparkling heaps of gems which had been hurriedly sorted. "I do not know, Lady, whether such call to others as the Fingers call,"—she gave a glance to the bag laid beside her and with it that crystal Lathia had worn—"but it is a matter which cannot be overlooked."

She had found five of the dark-stained stones in the collection the guild mistress had had spread before her. Now there was a stir in the shadow behind where she sat, wearily resting her head on one hand, elbow planted on the judging board. Kryn moved forward . . . Lathia had accepted him for what Nosh had declared him to be. But he was scowling, and the head of the guild looked up inquiringly.

"Lady, there is another matter."

"That being?" she asked him.

He spoke of the seller of amulets in the market and ended with:

"This I saw, Lady, some days past. There was one who came from your household—at least she returned to it, for the door she entered is that through which we came. She spoke with this man of dead stones and when she left his stall there was one less amulet. We think that more than the malice of Markus lies heavy in Kasgar . . . " He launched then into a quick report of the rathhawks with their stones, and the fact that one of Markus's guards had worn such.

Lathia who had been pacing up and down the room while Nosh worked, stopped, turned, and stared at Kryn. "Of this you are certain—that one of my household took a death stone?"

"I will swear to it, Lady. I followed her from the market; it was your door she entered."

"Ha!" She went to the door and pressed a stud near it on the wall. Nosh could hear the distant ringing of a bell. Then a maid appeared. She was old and apparently long familiar with Lathia, for she grumbled:

"It is past the middle of the night, Lady. Time for those of goodwill to be safely abed."

"I agree, Varsa. Listen well; these two are honored guests but their presence here is not to be known. You will take them to the sealed corridor and see they are well served. Then return, for I have another task for you."

They followed the maid through silent corridors. Nosh was wearied nearly past the ability to walk. Twice she stumbled and Kryn supported her. She clasped very close to her breast, hoping that their power would buttress her, the bag and that pendant Lathia had given into her hand. Five . . . She had five of the Fingers! Her mind clung to that.

There was another warded door before them but Varsa had the key to that and then they found themselves in a suite of very quiet rooms. The maid disappeared and returned with a tray of cold foods, and Nosh suddenly found herself ravenous while Kryn made eye-widening inroads on his share.

Nosh tumbled onto what seemed the most welcoming bed she had ever known, stuffing the crystals back into hiding before sleep overcame her.

But this was not sleep—it was a demon-haunted nightmare. She stood again in Markus's house before the pitiful body of the priest of Lyr. And the down-bent head this time lifted of its own accord, so the battered face was close to hers. Behind him gathered a dark cloud and she thought that things were a-move in it. She found her voice and screamed!

Hands were on her and she fought that hold until her eyes opened and in a shaft of daylight saw that Kryn held her.

"The priest—the priest of Lyr—they tormented him to his death."

"So it was the truth he foresaw," Kryn said. "He was with me in that cell. When they took him forth he thought that he would not return. He . . ." Suddenly Kryn settled her back on the bed, his hands going to the front of his jerkin. And he brought out that queerly wrapped bundle he had taken out of the hiding place.

"This . . . he told me to take this!"

Nosh held up a hand to wrap around the one in which Kryn held that bundle. There was a surge—an unmistakable answer. Kryn uttered an exclamation and tried to drop the package but she held him fast.

"Open it . . ." she ordered. "Now!"

He had to use the point of his knife to hack at it, attempting to split the sealing which had kept it secure—perhaps a sealing also intended to conceal its powers.

Then there dropped from that grimy roll another shaft of crystal, this smaller than the others, but not to be mistaken.

"Six—one hand and the beginning of another," Nosh crooned as she slipped her fingers along that shaft. Then, on impulse, she caught the hand which still held the covering for that Finger. Twitching away the grimed roll of rag and glue she touched the crystal to Kryn's flesh. He jerked back and away.

"What would you do?" he demanded. "I have no need for powers . . . "

He stood up and walked away from her out of the room. Nosh sighed. Almost she had thought—the priest had trusted him—there had been, she remembered, that surge of power when their shoulders had touched and she had worked to break the door ward. Lyr's influence had traveled far. There was Lathia D'Arcit, who had become a guardian—and the priest—there was that piece in the shrine. How many more lay in Kasgar to be discovered?

However, Kasgar itself had problems, as they discovered later that morning when Lathia joined them in the sequestered travelers' suite in which they had been concealed from the household at large. They had again been fed—cold viands but good and satisfying—and were growing impatient with this seclusion, though both of them were well aware that they must stay close that some of Markus's hidden corps would not rout them out.

What Lathia brought with her changed any vague plans which they might have half-made. With an impatient gesture she summoned them to her as if she feared even the walls of her own supposedly staunchly held house might be growing enemy ears.

"Look you!" Onto the top of a small table she tossed, holding it carefully by the thong on which it was strung, a holed stone. It was a grey shading to pink around that hole.

Nosh almost reached for it and then was suddenly struck by such a pull as made her reach for a chair back and hold on to that tightly, for fear she would be so drawn to that stone that she would have to pick it up, as part of her mind cried out to her to do. Yet that was evil.

Kryn looked down at it as one might thoughtfully survey a new weapon which he was not trained to use. Then he said in a low voice:

"Death stone?" That being more question than identification.

"But those are red!" countered Nosh, having herself now enough under control that she could approach the table, though she held her hands determinedly behind her back so that they might not betray her by reaching, against her will, for that thing.

"This," Lathia said, "was found this morning about the neck of my cousin Indea. And she,"—the guild mistress paused, there was a grim twist to her lips and her eyes were very bleak—"is a babbling idiot, though only last night she retired to her bed a woman of skill and intelligence. Nor is she the only one to be so struck. Kasgar is on the edge of mob violence. There are others stricken down so, from gearmen and guards, even to the second rank of the Council. Death stone? What the wearers of these have had visited upon them is worse than any clean death. It would seem that their minds have been sucked, as one would suck the pulp of a janson fruit through a hole in its skin. What remains is . . .no longer human! And three have died within the hour of their discovery. We do not know yet how deep this evil has gone, how many townsmen and women have been caught in it."

"The amulet seller . . . " Kryn said.

"Has no longer any stall in the market—at the second hour of the sun I sent a guard to see. He was not there. Nor did any of the regular stall owners know of him, from where he came—save he was supposed to have traveled with that foreign embassy the Councilers would not deal with—or where he went."

"Markus . . . " Nosh started to suggest but already both Lathia and Kryn were shaking their heads.

"What you have told me, armsman,"—Lathia nodded to Kryn—"those noxious rocks were known where certainly no arm of Markus could reach. Yes, Markus would play his games here; he is a man of overwhelming ambition and ridden with envy. But this is not a matter of his ability—did you not say you took such a stone from one of his guards and left it behind just to dust your own trail? No, there is a far greater power than Markus's working now in Kasgar, and we can accept that it means ill to all of us.

"Those ill-omened stones you found among my wares,"—now she turned directly to Nosh—"have been subjected to fire and then to grinding. Their dust is buried deep. But these"—she pointed to the death stone—"may be too perilous for any to handle."

Nosh gathered her courage. She faced the guild mistress across the table and put out her right hand, keeping the left tightly curled about the bag of the Fingers. She did not touch the stone, only held her palm flat over it and closed her eyes.

That sense of pull which had struck her at the first showing of it was still there but to a far lesser degree; she could hope that the Fingers fought it to her security. She could pick up no picture—perhaps that was because she did not really hold it, but she knew what had happened. Somewhere someone having more power than she could dream of had used these as a focus and way to draw from those wearing the amulets energy, intelligence, perhaps—in the case of the dead—even the force of their lives. To summon such energy meant that the unknown one was either in fear or preparing for a strike, as the High King might so align his army for the best blow to be delivered.

So the amulets were not only used to relay information—they were deadly weapons in themselves. But perhaps it was far too late to save any of those who had surrendered to the blandishment of the marketplace sender.

"You feel?" Lathia demanded.

"Only the drawing. Some power has sapped those wearing such as these and taken to itself what it has robbed from its pawns."

Lathia sat down suddenly, her eyes on the stone.

"We do not yet know," she said dully, "how many have been stricken. Some of our leaders may be lost to us. Is this some ploy of a new enemy—one we have not suspected? We—some of us—have been aware of Markus. His power has been growing fast in the past year. But he wants no more than the rule of Kasgar—the subtlety of such things as these are not his. Then who . . . ?"

Kryn stirred. His hand had gone to the hilt of Bringhope. "Lady, in the east the worship of a false god has riven from their places those of the blood best able to stand firm against a threat. The High King, who is no warrior by trade, has unleashed his army to march south into a wilderness where there is nothing to repay the loss of men and beast in such a venture.

"Does it not then appear that there is another who seeks in every way to bring down any who can stand against invasion before that invasion begins?"

"Invasion from where?" she countered. "The barbarians of the western plain have never been so subtle as you suggest in preparing for a raid. They are bound to quick raiding, not to outright war where they have to face trained forces. Your High King—does he intend to come over the Heights and take Kasgar—and in this

season, which is the worst he could choose for such assault?

"Your false god's priests have already been within our
walls and gotten a flat answer from us—we do not welcome missionaries of their One here. So who?"

She sat silent a long moment and then put her elbows
on the table and allowed her head to fall into her hands.

"Do we now," she spoke very slowly as if she must
stop to search for each word before she voiced it, "do
we return to the legends?"

"Razkan!" Nosh could not have told why that name
came to her.

"But he must have died long since!" Lathia flared in
return. "It has been four—five—even six lifetimes of a
normal man since he disappeared, leaving the wreck of
a world behind him. You are of Lyr . . . strong was the
power of Lyr but it was shattered in the last days of that
wanton destruction."

"Someone who has discovered the power sources Razkan once drew upon?" hazarded Kryn.

"Perhaps. But . . . " She shook her head. "What would
that one gain by visiting this plague on Kasgar, from the
meddling of the priests of the One, from the urging of
the High King into suicidal war? Is it only destruction
for its own sake?"

Both of Nosh's hands were cupped about the Fingers
now.

"Whoever moves—fears Lyr!" She knew that she was
right. "Lady, I have six of the Fingers now—we need
only four. I do not know what will happen when I have
the full number of them—Dreen did not tell me. But
she was the last full priestess of Lyr and she said my
talent was meant for some great thing."

Lathia raised her head from her hands and looked at
the girl. Then she nodded slowly.

"Yes, that may be one thing to consider. Therefore,

Talented One, the sooner you can get the remaining Fingers the better."

"I cannot go about the city . . . " Nosh began.

"I believe it would do you no good if you could," the guild mistress continued. "My crystal came from my mother and her father was son to a line started by one of the priests who fled the blasted shrine. There were a priest and priestess here in Kasgar, but they were versed only in the scraps of tradition and learning which had been hidden and so saved."

"They are dead," Kryn returned. "Markus saw to that."

"So we suspected, but there was no proof, and none of the Council would move on suspicion alone. Therefore, I would believe, Talented One, you have already reaped all which lie within Kasgar. So you must seek elsewhere, and soon."

"How do we get out of the city?" Kryn asked practically. "Markus will have his creepers out on our trail. He may already know where we are."

Lathia rose. "That can be accomplished. I cannot send you with an escort but I shall provide you with the best gear I can."

Her promise was quickly fulfilled. The elderly maid and one of the guards who had greeted them at the door drew in between them a large hamper. There appeared trail clothing of finely dressed leather with underclothing of first-weave cloth designed to stand up to hard usage. Lathia had been surprisingly accurate with her guess of sizes, for both Nosh and Kryn found it all to fit well. And to Kryn's great satisfaction he was able to put aside the rusty mail he had stripped from Markus's guard for a shirt infinitely better—while there was one of a smaller size ready for Nosh.

They were both trailwise enough to sort through the gear and supplies Lathia made free for their assembling

of two packs. Kryn chose a crestless bowl helm but Nosh
settled for a hood with an attached shoulder cape which
could be pulled well over the face. There was even an
air-holed pouch for the zark, the creature having been
most warily eyed by Lathia and her people. She informed Nosh that indeed the lizard was poisonous but
that its poison produced deep unconsciousness, and
eventual recovery with an aching head as a reminder.

As Kryn tightened the last strap on his pack he looked
to Nosh.

"How now? We can't just walk out of here and make
for the gates."

But Nosh had faith in the guild mistress. "Lathia said
there was a way she can show us. Do you not believe
her?"

Kryn took up the traveler's cloak he was rolling to be
carried on top of his pack—unless they met bad weather
he felt freer without its folds to encumber him.

"We have to," he returned. But it was plain that his
uneasiness was growing. They were served another meal
and ate well, laying up against the time when they
would be reduced to trail rations—though each had a fat
pouch of those to hand also.

It was dark outside the high-placed windows of the
room where they had gathered their gear when, at last,
Lathia came in. She was frowning and it was plain that
something had occurred which she found disturbing.

Nosh's thoughts immediately flew to Markus. But before she could ask any questions the guild mistress drew
from the inner folds of her wide robe sleeve a small roll
which she spread out on the tabletop, held it firmly flat
with her two thumbs to display the lines on it to both
of them.

It was a map with Kasgar plainly marked in the left-
hand lower corner.

"I would advise you to strike north and more west,"

she said as they examined the lines drawn there. "The priests and priestesses of Lyr came over the mountains—that much my own family lore has said. But not all headed south. I would look for what you seek west, or north again. You have what will lead you . . . " She looked questioningly at Nosh.

"Yes. They flare when they are near their kind. Only once"—she glanced at Kryn—"did that not occur but I think it is because he who had it concealed it with something to defuse that light."

"Keep off the caravan road. Yes, it is late in the season, but there are still travelers there. Those who might be moved to track you would expect you to keep to it as a guide. Instead, when you are past the walls, strike directly west for at least a full day's travel before you turn north, and then keep as well as you can to that distance away from the highway as you go."

"When we are past the walls . . . " commented Kryn. "And how do we achieve that, Lady?"

Lathia had let the map curl back into a roll which she left for Kryn to take up and thrust into his belt pouch.

"We of the great houses of the guilds have our own secrets. Kasgar has not always been a place of peace, just as it seems to be losing that peace again now. I must share with you a house secret, but ask also that when I call for closed eyes, you will obey until I say to open them once more."

Both of them nodded. The guild mistress started toward the door and the two, shouldering their packs, followed her eagerly. They went back down a hall and then through a very large chamber centered by a long table along the side of which were tall-backed chairs. Another and wider door here gave upon an open courtyard in the middle of which played a fountain, the lace of falling water causing also a murmur of sound.

Instead of any planting of flowers, or pots of shrubs

as Nosh had seen in the rooftop gardens, here were a number of stones and rocks—but not of the dull common sort one might expect. Each was veined with crystal or ore traces which showed color even in this subdued light, and some had clusters of fire-shooting crystals, taking light from the lamp Lathia carried, which appeared almost as if they grew out of the rocks themselves as leaves might enrobe a tree.

It was a wondrous sight, such as Nosh had never seen since she left the Shrine of Lyr, and she drew a soft breath of astonishment and delight.

Lathia spoke: "Now I must ask blinding of you for a space."

Obediently Nosh closed her eyes and knew that Kryn was also accepting this. There came, after a breath or two of waiting, a queer grating sound. Then Lathia said: "You may look to see your road out."

One of those rocks, nearly the tallest in the collection, had somehow swung about to reveal a dark, irregular hole. Lathia went down on one knee and held her lamp closer so that Nosh plainly saw the beginning of a ladder.

"Down this," the guild woman told them. "Below, there is a road torch with a striker close beside it. Use that for light. The passage does not run straight but there is no other way to confuse you. Go, Talented One, armsman, with the blessing of Lyr, and may success be yours."

"How can we thank you?" Nosh asked almost shyly. That Lathia, nearly a stranger, had been willing to do so much for them now seemed difficult to believe.

"Have you not already repaid anything I can give you with your hands' reading, Sister in Lyr? My house is cleansed of evil, and I am aware of what may be planned against me, if Markus is not yet undone by this new threat. When the Hands reach again, Talented One, think of me."

"I will, oh, I will!" the girl answered breathlessly.

Kryn had already swung over onto the ladder and was descending, and she followed clumsily, aware of the backward pull of her pack. Then she felt her feet touch the ground and there was the grating again and the fresh air of the open was shut off.

The click of a striker was loud in this dark place. Kryn held the spark of fire to ignite the travel torch and Nosh saw that they were standing in a very small hollow from which the ladder climbed, while before them was a dark passage. With Kryn in the lead, his light stretched out a little to show them what lay ahead, they started into that way. The walls were stone and in some places they had to nearly bend double to get by sections where the ceiling dipped down. There were few signs of any usage. Here and there walls dripped with water and there was a blanched white weed growing, to net over the stone.

As Lathia had promised there were no side passages to mislead them. How long had this bolt hole existed? Perhaps it dated back to the foundation of Kasgar as a trading city.

At last there was a gradual upswing of the rock under their feet and Kryn drew back the torch, having no wish to break through into unknown territory with that alight. They had no idea how far they would exit beyond the city walls and how keen-eyed the guards there would be to unusual happenings outside. Since the city was so aroused over the toll the death stones had taken, suspicion might lead to instant perilous reaction to the unexpected.

They came up against what looked like a solid wall of stone. Kryn shone the light across it foot by foot, hunting some sign of a door. Then Nosh thought she understood.

"A ward!" She shouldered by him and set her hands to that rough surface.

Not exactly a ward but a hidden lock, and her fingers found it and probed for the latching within.

"I have it!"

Kryn extinguished the torch and pushed by her to set his strength against the portal and it must have moved, for in the dark Nosh felt the freshness of air, a vast difference from the dead air of the tunnel through which they had come. They climbed up and out into the night and let the door close behind them.

Interlude

THERE WAS LIGHT APLENTY; THE MAN sitting there had to see the results of his labors. Facing him was that telltale mirror. He stared into it as if he could command what he wished to see.

The face he beheld was again free of wrinkles—there was no telltale falling away of flesh. While the hairs showing in a few locks from under the rolled brim of his black cap were no longer white, but again had the hue of dark brown, nor were they so sparse.

His attention dropped from the mirror to the hands which rested on the tabletop. Firm youthful flesh, no enlarged veins, none of the dark spotting of age. So—for the time being he was safe again.

For the time being. His satisfaction was whipped away by a twisted scowl which held a hint in it of that loathed reflection he had viewed before he had begun this night's labors. He had paid for this change—that price was a threat in itself. Almost he dared not reckon how much had been drained from those he had drawn to him unknowing.

His minions had been chosen well, the draught of energy and intelligence he had drunk this night was as rich as the finest wine, and more lasting for savoring.

But . . .

The scowl was black now. The losses—he could no longer ignore the reckoning of those.

There would be a new High King—a drooling idiot could not cling to the high seat. Luckily his heir . . .

The hand, which had been tapping the tabletop as if beginning the scoring of losses, froze. He would not admit he had been a fool. At the time it seemed wise that the heir should also answer to the subtle influence of the stones. So . . . no heir. Well, perhaps he had not been so wrong after all. There would be a period of chaos. With no direct heir a scramble for the high throne would ensue. Unfortunately again, several of the candidates who would be best for his purpose were already eliminated by this night's work.

His shoulders hunched a little as if some unseen burden had come to rest there. Well, neither High King, heir, or those mind-struck lords would have been of use to a man about to molder into aged death. He was in his prime again and there was always a stew into which one could profitably dip in times of chaos. Too many ambitions would flare and not be appeased and one could work easily through the losers while the winner would find the throne a most uncomfortable seat. He thought that, great as his losses were in that direction, he could pull together and reweave his net for the east.

The Voice . . .

His lips shaped a snarl. Now that was indeed a deprivation. This Valcur had been a very worthy tool, being naturally twisted of mind. He had accepted direction from afar without ever realizing that he was but that tool. It was seldom Razkan had ever had such a useful one. If there could have been a way to protect the priest from the indraw . . . that was something to be considered in the future. He was not sure it could be done. Once unleashed, the power was not selective—it homed on those attuned to it. Perhaps there was a way about that difficulty—he would take it under consideration when he had the time.

However, Valcur—*and* his closest associates—they must all be written off. The brooding mage wondered what strange things were happening in the Temple now. Would any of those Valcur had held under his influence and so reduced to slavery be freed? Chaos again.

His right hand became a fist and he brought it down with force on the tabletop.

Those . . . those . . .

His lips worked and there was the blaze of rage near madness in his eyes. To be so faced down—forced into this temporary defeat by such as those!

Before today he could have unleashed, through his chain, death on them. There was no rock big enough to conceal such slimy worms from him! But it had to be summoned all or none. And for the time he could not detach any of what had once been his servants to handle them.

If he could have only found those stupid fragments of crystal himself! But in that much Lyr had defeated him. Even if he looked straight upon one, to his eyes it would have no existence.

He must wait—and waiting did not come easy to him. And—there was this—he had drawn upon all but his last reserves to keep his own life flame burning high. Would it dwindle again? If so . . . Again his fist pounded the table, and then he leaned forward to stare very closely at his reflection.

Youth—what he saw there was strong youth. He might age again, but he would have more years to assume and the process might be longer. Then—when they would return to that place where he could confront them . . . They were nothing—no more than the human animals he had dealt with over and over again—stupid, seeing nothing beyond their own petty concerns. He would have no trouble at that final challenge, and he had time before they would make it. They still had the quest to finish.

Now—the matter of the High King—there was Ingram, the Duke. He was perhaps the best stationed of those to attempt the throne. Ingram . . .

He recalled easily all he knew of the man. A hard fortress of a fellow to be breached, but every man had his weak point—he would also.

Valcur—there was little hope that he could find another as easy to mold and use as the Voice. And with the major priests struck down with their commander . . .The rule of the One had been an excellent idea for getting the country into a choking prison. He grimaced—dwelling on the losses of the past night was getting him nowhere at all.

Most of his newly acquired stolen energy and mental powers must be applied to one thing—the building of the final weapon with which once and for all he would smash Lyr forever.

Chapter 24

AT LEAST THEY WERE OUT OF THE CITY. Kryn gave a half shrug to settle his pack a little easier. But the sooner they got away from even the outskirts of Kasgar, the better it would be.

There were cultivated fields here, where some of the foodstuffs were raised by the Food Dealers' guild, and a wide stretch of pastureland where the caravaners wintered their beasts until the next season for faring off. Kryn thought wistfully of mounts. But to steal those could well bring trackers behind. Though the way to Dast was long, he was willing to slough it afoot and remain uncaught.

The advice the guild mistress had given them was good—to keep from the road was only a matter of sense, so he looked searchingly overhead at the stars for a guide. There was Varge-With-Cloud, the Twin Arrows, the Racer. From his childhood he had known them all well, and the lore of steering a course by them was part of the knowledge of all outland warders such as he had always joined whenever he could.

They were well past the caravan road, lurking along the hedges which marked off fields and pastures. The sooner they were totally out of this settled country the better.

He fell into step with Nosh and pointed, not knowing if she could really see that gesture in this darkness, for the moon had not yet risen fully.

"That way."

He noticed that she cradled against her with one hand that larger bag she had made during the day, in which the crystal Fingers were safely bestowed, each lapped in protective cloth. Did she believe that they would furnish a guide? He had seen too much in the last few days to question anything his unchosen companion might do.

"How far west?" she asked in return.

That presented a puzzle. To steer by the stars one could do by night, still those were not completely accurate guides and he had no wish to strike out into the plains wilderness where the barbarians and the Vors roamed. The sooner he got back to Dast the better, and their only true guide to that was the road.

"We must keep near to the road," he spoke his thought aloud. "The plains can swallow up the unwary."

"You head for Dast?" There was an odd note in her voice.

"Even though I have failed Lord Jarth, he must know of it," he replied.

"You go to Dast with my good wishes, Kryn, for . . ."

She hesitated as if she were lost for words with which to clothe her thoughts.

"We both go to Dast!" he answered firmly. What man would allow a woman, even if she were a priestess, a talented one, whatever they deemed her, venture into the unknown alone?

"I have but six of the Fingers, Kryn. There are four to come. In this I do have an aid, for what I carry,"— she held out the bag a fraction, an only half-seen gesture in the dark—"call upon their kind. When I sense that I must go. If it draws me near to Dast, well enough, but if I am summoned into another path, that one I must take."

He did not allow himself to answer until he had subdued that flash of anger. To let her go roaming by herself at the guidance of some bits of crystal was folly. But there was Jarth waiting for the weapons Kryn had promised and which he could not deliver. The sooner Jarth knew of his failure the better.

The cold season was already breathing down from the Heights. Without the shelter of the caves they had only the rough buildings of the well compound. As for supplies...Unless the hunters had been very lucky, those—in spite of what he had tried to send from Kasgar, and he certainly hoped those had reached the well—would be very lean before spring.

What if one of those greatly feared sleet storms should hit at them when Nosh went hunting crystals in some unknown area? People died within an hour or less if they had no shelter. She would be far better off at Dast, hard as the living would be there, than roaming a winter-shrouded countryside.

There was no use in arguing out the situation until some time when her will would match his. In the meantime, to get as far as possible from the city before dawn and then lie up for most of the day to rest was the task immediately before them.

Kryn had not heard of any predators such as the wak-wolves to be feared here. The city dwellers through generations of guardianship had patrolled and cleared these lands and the fields and pasture stretched much farther west than he would first have deemed possible. Twice they had to avoid herders. Luckily varges were not easily stampeded—their huge bulk, horns, and sharp hooves made them formidable opponents for any except expert archers or a good-sized pack of wakwolves.

The herders riding bonds here were not on duty for the protection of the draft animals but rather to make sure the massive beasts did not drift from their accustomed range. If a varge scented the two who skulked along the hedgerows the beast gave no sign of it.

A large part of the night had passed when they came at last to the end of the fields. They had kept to a steady pace which the outlaws had learned long ago and Nosh had picked up during her time at the refuge. But Kryn knew that they must find some type of shelter and lie up. Though they had had good resting in Lathia's house, still they could not keep to the trail much longer.

There were night sounds, even discounting the moan of the chill wind which had made them unroll their cloaks and go huddled within those shortly after they left the opening from the city. Squeaks arose now and then from the pasture grass, and the zark began to squirm in his prisoning bag. Nosh announced that they must soon let the creature out to go hunting.

At last they came upon an unexpected dip in the surface of the open lands. Whereas grass grew high on the surface circling that, the dip itself was a mat of brush, hard to see in the dark even by the now-present moon except as a mass of shadows. Kryn shed his pack and cloak and slipped down the side of the drop, coming to a stinging halt against a needle-boughed bush which greeted him with such an assault as to bring some forceful words from him.

But he drew his long knife and began hacking at the tough growth, throwing aside the cut boughs. Nosh, seeing what he was doing, quickly joined him in spite of his urging to stay off. There was no arguing with her, he decided sourly. Very well, let her collect her own toll of scratches and rips.

What he suspected proved to be the truth. Once they

had cut their way through the brush hedge they came to a small pool. This was an ancient varge wallow—hollowed by the use of the beasts over a countless number of seasons. When the hot of midsummer came, those were drawn to such small sinkholes where they could lie near-totally plastered with that mud which defeated the attacks of the vicious warm weather flies.

Once no longer in use, such pools would provide moisture for more ambitious growths than the prairie grasses—as it had here. Their knives keeping at a steady swing they cleared out a space by the side of the pool. That they dared to use the water was a question. It could have been standing in the hollow entrapped from the last storm and so befouled enough to be dangerous. Kryn thought it safer that they drink sparingly from the water bottles and Nosh accepted his warning.

They had settled in, nearly shoulder to shoulder, and now he left the girl, for this hollow was far too shadowed now to give him a clear sight. Then he heard the chitter of the zark, which she had apparently freed from its traveling pouch. There was a rustle behind him: the zark was off on the hunt.

There was no room to stretch out at full length unless they would cut more of the brush away, but Kryn re-climbed the slope and came back with a heavy armload of grass he hacked from close by, pushing it down against the ground. It gave them some protection against the roots and they discovered that they could best rest in a jackknife fashion, Nosh fitting herself as well as she could to the curve of his body, drawing both their cloaks over them.

Perhaps the girl was asleep almost as soon as she closed her eyes. He could feel every even breath she drew. But somehow, though fatigue gnawed at him, he could not go so serenely to sleep. He had left above a few small traps intended to sound if their shelter was approached, and somehow he was certain that they need not set sentry. Nosh sighed and moved a little. He felt a strange tingle in his hand where he had put out his arm to draw the cloak down again. Slowly he turned his fingers to explore. The bag—that bag of the Fingers!

Everything which made her so alien to all he believed in was now tied within that bag. That *she* believed implicity in what she was doing—yes, that he accepted. And he could not say either that those who trusted in Lyr were like the priests of the One. But this was not for him. Moving very gently so that he might not awaken her, Kryn pulled back his hand and arm.

What would be the end of her quest? Even if she were able to discover all those Fingers scattered so long ago by the fleeing followers of Lyr, what would she do with them? She had never said. If Dreen had shared more information with Jarth, the commander of the outlaws had not passed it along.

To Kryn now there came an unhappy sense that perhaps this girl, endowed with strange powers as she might be, could meet with disappointment in the end. The longer she believed in what she was doing the harder and deeper that disappointment would be. Yet he also knew that to try and turn her from her path would be useless.

Why should it matter? Her quest had nothing to do with him. Even before the noisome cloud of the worship of the One had overshadowed the land in which he had been born and raised, there had been little enough notice given to gods or powers.

Had it been different before the Dark had riven all the world? Were there indeed beneficent powers known even to those of his blood? He had never heard even the thinnest legend of such. Instead most of the hold kin, except those falling to the One, had had no beliefs in anything more than their own abilities. The hand he had pulled aside from Nosh's bag curved about the hilt of Bringhope. A fighting man believed in his weapons and his skill to use them. That had brought him this far through life.

Again the girl sighed and turned a little in his half hold. He had been considered too young before he had fled his father's degradation, to go wenching in the city with those of his caste. And certainly he had had no close meeting with any female since his outlawry—except Nosh. But to him Nosh had never seemed truly one who could be approached as a man approaches a woman. Even now when she lay against him so close that he heard her breathing . . . no, certain hungers did not rise . . .

Yet he also knew that just as he was bound to Jarth as his lord now, so was he—and he caught at that thought in astonishment—so was he in a manner bound to Nosh. Though to that there was no future—their ways led far apart.

Only, a part of him denied that—and he crushed down that feeble fraction of his thoughts. Perhaps that effort was the key to the slumber he needed, for he did go to sleep.

Kryn was dimly aware sometime later that a small scaly body crawled across his shoulder close enough for those scales to fret his cheek and then he was completely lost to all around him in a sleep so deep that no dreams could reach.

It was the chill which brought him awake at last. He looked up past the ragged brush into a grey sky. Not that of a well-lit day but one which sent an instant touch of fear. There was a wind howling above them across the level land. And as he sat up he could see the massing of clouds in the north. A season storm!

Nosh was gone but a moment later she slid down into the basin. She had her cloak huddled about her though her pack rested still beside his. There was excitement in her face.

"Kryn!" She caught at his arm. "We must go. . . ." Her other hand disappeared under the edge of the cloak and he guessed that it cupped the side of the Finger bag. "There is one—it calls—out there!" She turned a little to indicate the north.

He tried to think. The plains were not his country but since they had come to Dast he had picked up from all who knew that land any information that he could considering its perils. If those clouds foretold such a storm as he believed, then to be caught in it under the open sky might indeed be death. To stay in this wallow which would fill speedily with the floods from above—that would also be impossible.

Shaking off Nosh and refusing to listen to what she was so foolishly saying, Kryn made his own way to the country above. The wind was growing steadily, blowing from the north. To head into that was folly, was . . .

Movement by his side: Nosh was back. Her pack was slung again and she paid no attention to him now but headed straight on into that blast.

Kryn shouted and knew his angry order did not reach her. He hurried down to their camp and gathered up his own pack. It was sheer stupidity to do this but somehow he had to catch Nosh and shake some reason into her.

His return for the pack had given her some headway and she was bending over, hunching her shoulders, the flaps of her hood pulled close, already some lengths away, fighting the force of the wind directly into the path of the storm. Short of somehow tripping her and taking her prisoner he did not see how he was going to stop her. But first he had to catch up.

Kryn had thought he knew the worst Nature could send against his kind. However, this icy blast which seemed to push him back with every half step he took forward was far worse than anything he had faced in the Heights. He felt helpless as one in the hands of some giant being who would continue to crush him back and perhaps down until he was ground into the very earth of this wild, open country.

His eyes teared as he tried to see somewhere—anywhere—any protection. But he must not lose Nosh, and somehow she had lengthened the distance between them so that he had to put extra strength into gaining on her.

She was obviously fighting the storm even as he, yet there was a purpose about her going as if she knew exactly where she went. Kryn cursed Lyr, the Hands, and all to do with this, in a steady singsong under his breath and then had to stop to ease breathing at all.

Just as he drew even with the girl, what he had expected broke upon them. The clouds opened to deluge them with rain—and sleet, which put a coating of ice speedily on their cloaks, made them wince and gasp as it struck their faces. Still he could not get close enough to Nosh to stop her and if he did—to what purpose? There was no possible shelter here. If they were to lie on the ground and cover themselves with both cloaks? He doubted if that would lead to their surviving. The cold would eat into their very bones.

The beaten-down grass underfoot grew slick with the ice, so they slipped and slid. While the grey of the day grew darker and darker. They were staggering now, weaving from one side to another. Yet Nosh pushed on as if there were a torch-bearing guide beckoning to her.

Kryn was breathing in gasps. How could the girl continue this way? It was harder and harder for him. Was it the power of those damned Fingers which kept her on her feet and moving—to where?

Then he realized that he was slipping over ground which was not grassy. The bare soil here had been recently turned as if for the planting of some winter crop. So there was some shelter nearby—there had to be!

Even as he realized that, Nosh slipped and went to her knees. He fought to her side and somehow got her up and moving, one of her arms drawn upward about his shoulder so he could support her.

It was as dark as a moonless night now and they came up against a barrier with force. But the cessation of the wind, kept from them now by this barricade, was such a relief as to give Kryn the needed strength to move along that, feeling a rough stone surface with his nearly numb hand while he drew Nosh with him.

Then he sensed a difference in the surface which he had used for a guide and, with hope he was right, ran his hand up, then down. His fingers hit painfully against a bar and then closed on it, working it out of the hooks which held it. Pushing Nosh ahead, Kryn stumbled into a building, and the screaming winds of the storm were reduced to a rumble.

Swinging around he slammed shut the door he had so fortunately found. Then, having parked his hip against it, he pulled forward what seemed to be a bale of hay to brace that shut. Luckily the door was on the side away from the wind's fury.

From the smells he became aware that they must have taken refuge in a barn. A moment later he heard the lowing of a varge. By all means they must keep away from the beast, which might not take kindly to having its quarters so invaded. He hoped it was stalled but there was no way of telling.

But they needed far more than just a refuge against that wind and sleet; they must have warmth, hot food or drinks, get rid of their soaked clothing. How they were to accomplish that Kryn had no way of telling. He took an unsteady step or two forward, stumbled over a soft mass on the floor, and sprawled across Nosh's inert body. Nor could he summon up the strength to do more than roll a little away so that his weight would not crush the slighter girl.

He must get up, stir around, keep moving. To allow the sleep which seemed to be creeping to hold him to the floor to win would probably lead to death.

There was scraping sound and then to his right a burst of light which set him blinking, blinded for a moment. Finally he cleared vision enough to see a hand holding out a lantern. Whoever held it came on through another door, set the lantern on a tall box, and advanced into its full light.

He was looking at a woman bundled up in the coarse smock and pantaloons he had seen on the farm women in the Kasgar market. Her hair was completely hidden by a cap tied under her chin, and her face was scored with the wrinkles of age. She stared down at the two on the floor and then she spoke:

Her words singsonged in a strange way and were given another accent which was not akin to the city speech but somehow he was able to understand.

"Can you walk?"

He was already trying to pull himself up with the aid of a hay bale, so he did not waste breath answering. Kryn had every intention of walking, no matter how difficult that might be.

The woman wasted no more time in speech but stooped and laced her hands into Nosh's armpits, hoisting the limp weight of the unconscious girl as if she were pitching hay in the harvest field. Kryn lurched closer and was somehow able to steady Nosh on the other side as the woman half pulled, half carried her into a room beyond.

Warmth closed about them and so did light—both from a lamp and from a wide hearth where a roaring fire sent waves of heat out into the room. Flanking this was

a settle and on that the woman deposited Nosh while
Kryn slumped down beside the girl to keep her from
sliding back to the floor.

The woman was gone, back to the stable to reclaim
her lantern. Then she returned, standing before him, her
work-worn hands planted on her hips while she surveyed the two. She beckoned to Kryn. He lowered Nosh
carefully to the settle, though her legs still tended to
trail to the floor, and tottered to his feet, having to catch
at the back of the settle for support.

His hostess had gone to the other side of the large
room and had thrown off the cover of an age-darkened
carved chest, was busy pulling out of it piles of what
looked like folded clothing. She slammed the chest shut
again, dropped one pile on it, added to the top a coarse
length of thick cloth which might serve as a towel and
told him in as few words as possible—as if she spoke so
seldom it was difficult for her to find words:

"Strip, dry yourself, dress—come to the fire. There is
soup."

Few words but enough to cover all which was necessary now, and he did just as he was told. While behind
the settle back the woman busied herself with Nosh and
he finally heard the girl speak. The relief of that was as
warming as would be the soup bubbling in a large kettle
over that blessed fire.

Chapter 25

It was warm and Nosh had thought that she never would be warm again. There was light—and a fire. Someone moved closer to the whirl of the flames to dip from a pot hanging there into a bowl. Then that half-seen person came to her side. Nosh looked up into a wrinkled face in which the eyes were as blazingly alive as the fire.

"It is hot—but drink—eat—as quick as you can."

The bowl was lowered into her own two hands. She looked into its thick contents from which the steam arising made her suddenly weak with an overpowering hunger. The woman was no longer in her range of vision. Nosh felt too weak to even turn her head to follow with her sight.

She had been wrapped in a patched but clean robe which smelt of herbs, a square of quilt pulled over the lower part of her body where she lay on a settle.

Looking down beyond the bowl, she saw something else. On the stones of the hearth was stretched a small scaled body, motionless. Dead . . . ? That carrying bag would have been small protection against the assault of the sleet, and the zarks she had known in the Ryft disliked the cold, which made them sluggish. They had disappeared into their deepest burrows when that had come.

Nosh's eyes filled, she caught her lower lip between her teeth. The bowl shook in her hands and the liquid sloshed from side to side, nearly lapping over. Another had come into the full firelight from around the high back of the settle.

He looked far from the armsman she had always seen. In place of his leathers and mail he wore a coarse smock shirt, much patched, such as any landworker used, but the one who had owned this first had been short of arm, more narrow of shoulder. Kryn's wrists, thickened by swordplay, protruded into the fireshine and the smock gapped open at his chest, just as the leggings below did not reach his bare ankles.

Now he came to her at once. She pointed with one finger, releasing part hold on the bowl to the zark.

"Is—is it dead?"

Kryn dropped to his knees and touched the small body gently. He, too, must realize how much they owed to the creature which had smoothed their way to escape.

"No—it breathes still. The warmth will aid it."

Once more the woman appeared, putting into Kryn's hands a bowl such as the one Nosh held. The girl lifted hers slowly, lest she spill its contents, and set lips to the edge. Hot, yes, but not enough to burn. She sipped and then drank more deeply. The stew was hot and comforting in her throat and that warmth reached her middle.

Out of somewhere—probably the woman had brought it but Nosh in her ravenous hunger was not quite aware of that—appeared a wooden spoon. She had reduced the liquid in the bowl, now she set about filling herself with the more solid contents remaining. But when the spoon scraped at last against the empty container she found the need for sleep so strong that she could not keep her eyes open except by great effort. And her attempts to remember how they came here were mostly defeated.

It was the woman who, with more strength than her supposed years suggested, helped the girl up from the settle and carried more than led her to a dark opening in the far wall where there was a bed place, part of a cupboard. Stretched within that and with the slipped doors shut to a single narrow strip, Nosh fought the needs of her body no longer.

The rage of the storm without was but a murmur of sound which lulled instead of drawing fear. She was only dimly aware later that the zark had found its way also within this place of warmth and soft bedding to curl beside her head on a twist of blanket.

Nosh awoke to a dazed moment of fear. She was imprisoned. Though by her hand was a strip of light. Markus—had he retaken them? Then bits of memory stirred. There had been the call and then the fury of the storm had nearly extinguished that, but enough had remained to lead her here. But where was here?

Warily she sat up, her hand to that lighted crack, and pushed. One of the wooden sides to this strange cell gave way and she could look into the room beyond. There was a fire on the hearth. Yes, she remembered that now, and a pot which had been swung over it. But between her and it stood a table, its top well covered with a number of things, and behind that a woman belabored a round of dough, slapping and punching it with vigor. She seemed entirely intent on her task.

Between the workwoman and the fire was a bundle of coarse blankets in a roll. That stirred even as Nosh sighted it. Kryn struggled up, shaking his head as if to shake out of it some vision or part of dream.

Nosh slid out from her own cocoon of coverings and swung her legs over the edge of the cupboard bed. She was wearing, she discovered, a smock or house robe which fell in voluminous folds. It must have been intended for some much larger woman.

Having dealt firmly with the dough, the woman by the table fitted its well-kneaded substance into a pan which she placed on the blade of a wide wooden shovel. Three steps brought her to the side of the hearth, skirting Kryn. She opened a door in the stone walling of the fireplace and slipped the shovel well within, tipping it with a practiced hand and withdrawing it without the pan.

"Up and about are you?" her harsh voice appeared to greet them both at once.

Nosh slid down from the cupboard, shivering as her bare feet met the stone of the flooring, only too chill this far from the hearth. Her hand had gone to her breast. Yes, the bulk of the Finger bag was still there. Now the zark leaped from the tumble of covers behind her to land on her shoulder as she moved quickly toward the welcome heat of the fire.

While her borrowed clothing was too large, that which covered Kryn was on the small side, straining about his chest and shoulders. He had gathered up the covers of his makeshift bed to let Nosh closer to the heat.

But the girl halted before the woman: "Landwife, we are deep in your debt. Death rode with that storm last night."

The woman had half turned away. She dropped on the edge of a bench and was carving off the twisted skin of a large root with a knife which seemed closer to an armsman's belt dagger than a kitchen tool.

"It is true," Kryn added to Nosh's speech. "We were very close to the end—last night." Was it night or day? The storm darkened so.

Having peeled the root to her satisfaction, the woman was now chopping it into bite-sized pieces to fall one by one into a bowl resting on her knees. She might have been alone in the kitchen.

Now Nosh could see on the other side of the long room (perhaps this whole dwelling consisted only of this one chamber), a rack on which hung clothing she was sure was her own—and Kryn's. And surely the tangle of his mail, surmounted by the length of Bringhope, rested to one side on a box.

"The old customs are followed here." There was a slightly different note in the woman's voice as if at one time, perhaps many seasons past, she had known something besides the language of the field workers. "To the wayfarer at need the door is not barred."

Nosh fingered the bag. She had not been mistaken, there *was* a pull here, the Fingers warmed. But she could not see an answering glint from anywhere in the room, though she turned slowly now, more intent on what she sought than anything else.

"You ride to the hunt with the prairie men?" Now the woman looked to Kryn. "There is no loot here to tempt such as you. But even the winds have brought rumors of the blood and fire you have left behind you. . . . "

"Landwife," he said forcefully. "We are not kin to such. Doubtless they would indeed find *us* prey to their taste."

"It is not the season for caravans." She reached now for another kind of root, a round red one, which she did not peel, but sliced with vigor. "Also this is afar from the route. What manner of wanderers are you, then?"

Nosh came to the other side of the table so she fronted the woman squarely.

"Landwife, I am one who searches, and this Hold Heir travels with me for the present."

A last slash of the knife and the red root was also finished. However, the woman did not now reach for another. Instead she sat very still looking straight into Nosh's eyes.

"One who searches," she repeated. "Searches for what, seeker?"

Nosh took the chance. She loosed the bag and plucked out the top Finger. It blazed even as she was sure it would.

"Landwife, this led me through the storm, drew me, because it sought its fellow. And that fellow lies somewhere here!"

Slowly the woman placed the bowl on the table and placed the knife crosswise on its rim.

Then her two gnarled hands arose, wrists pressing wrist, fingers outstretched and pointing upward. The gesture of those of Lyr.

"Long and long, and long again," she said softly. "But come at last. So the Light rises. Come then, searcher."

She arose abruptly from her bench and Nosh, in spite of bare feet, followed her, Kryn looming behind her. They went through a far door into a stable, this a part of the house as was the custom in the outlands. There was a stall in which a large varge grunted as it fed noisily, and Nosh knew enough of the land ways to recognize that this beast was the herd leader and so cherished as best might be done through bad weather.

"Stay!" The woman held up her hand to stop the other two. "Longnose does not take kindly to strangers—something which has proved of value many times over." She squeezed past the bulk of the varge toward its massive, horned head.

As all herd leaders, the animal wore a bell, and it was into that wooden cup the woman now pushed her hand. A moment later she withdrew her fingers and between them flared the brilliance of a Finger.

The woman chuckled. "A good hiding place, searcher.

There is none but me who could so lay hands on Long-nose."

She led them back into the kitchen. Now there was authority in her again and she pointed to the bench on the far side of the table. The Finger she had laid in the middle of the board on which she was shifting various containers, waiting roots and strings of dried fruit and vegetables to the other end.

"Sit," she commanded. "Eat."

There was a pan steadied on three legs at the edge of the fire and from that she flipped fritters of meal studded with lumps of sweetness which Nosh thought might be bits of the same dried fruit as hung on the cords from the dark ceiling overhead. To wash this down she poured leather jacks of varge milk to which barley water had been added.

Nosh found she was indeed once more famished. However, even as she ate, she eyed the Finger which had been so strangely hidden here.

The woman did not take up her slicing knife again. Instead she seemed for the first time determined to talk. They might have at last discovered the right key to bring her into speech.

"The storm dies. There will not be another for at least three or four days. Where do you travel from here?"

It was Kryn who matched question to question. "How far are we from Dast?"

"Dast! If that is your goal, armsman, you may run into storms again. Look you here . . ."

She pushed aside the bowl and cleared a space before her. "Here you be." Her finger dipped in a thick brown liquid, making a blotch mark on the table top. "And here—Dast . . ."

The matching splotch appeared some distance away.

"In the cold season the raiders do not ride. Or so it has always been. But this season there have been raids.

Here,"—she made a third mark—"there is a village—small, yes, some seven houses. It lies to the north and a little eastward. If you strive to make your march to Dast, you cannot do so easily without the aid of those at PanHigh. The Lady forbid that the raiders have ridden *that* far. The hunters there know well the way to Dast and can show you the shortest trails."

"But—Landwife, it may be that my search lies not in the direction of Dast," Nosh said.

The woman looked from the Finger to Nosh. "Searcher, there are tales—very old tales. When the great shrine of the Lady was plundered and the symbol of Her power seemingly shattered beyond all mending—those of Her close servitors who remained alive took up the Fingers. Perhaps this much of the tale has been told you."

Nosh nodded.

"The dark powers had waxed strong at the defeat of Lyr. It was decided by those who took the Fingers that they must scatter and westward, also afar, that they might not be traced. For this much safety they were granted: That the evil who now searched for what might remain from the defeat could not follow with body, mind or power, the going of the bearers. Nor did those who fled plan any future meeting lest they be betrayed. There was only the guide you know—that Finger calls to Finger when they are close enough. But it is in my mind that you must now venture northward in your search and, since it is an ill season for that, think well before you turn away from Dast."

On impulse Nosh reached out her hand and laid it over the one the woman had been using for the drawing of that crude map. "Who are you?" she asked baldly.

"I am Raganat, searcher. But that name means nothing. It is but worn for this time and this life. However, the blood in me is that of one Lyr loved and brought into safety here—to wait. Peace comes to me for I have fulfilled the task laid upon those of my blood so very long ago. However, searcher, do not set your task above wisdom. This season will be a harsh one. And death rides on the prairie as it never has before. Somewhere, somehow, there is a great stirring of the Dark. Doubtless because of what you have done, and will do. So walk with care. And you, armsman, all things are ordained to come to pass in due time. Through some will we do not understand, you go with the searcher. . . . " she paused, having now turned that very level and searching gaze on Kryn.

"This may not even be to your wish. I can only tell you that never has the Lady stinted on the payment for those who serve her well. It can be that at the end of this journeying lies an answer to your own desires. If Dast awaits you, you will reach it."

Nosh had listened so closely. Before her eyes and ears this Landwife had become another person, in her way as impressive as the Lady Lathia D'Arcit. That the advice she gave was good, the girl could agree. But she also knew that if the call came upon her, she would have no control over it and must answer the summons no matter what peril stood in between.

Kryn had not commented on what Raganat said, and Nosh could guess that he had not found it something he wanted to hear. Why, out of all the men Jarth led, this one had been drawn into the pattern which held her she did not know. His hatred of all kinds of power might even yet be a danger to them both. Yet the Landwife seemed to think that he, also, had in some way been chosen to take this path.

They checked their clothing; there was still dampness and they brought parts closer to the fire. The leather needed to be carefully treated. Kryn settled at last on a stool, rubbing his mail with an oiled cloth Raganat supplied, making sure that no rust could develop from the drenching of the storm.

The zark, having eaten of dried meat until its middle section was visibly distended, stretched once more before the fire, well content to simply bask in the heat.

Nosh, after seeing to her clothing, tried to help their hostess, only to be refused. It would seem that Raganat trusted no one else in her handling of food. While the smell of the baking bread was fragrant through the room, overlying that of the dried herbs hanging from the rafters in a ragged tapestry.

Kryn, having done his best by his mail and his sword, ventured out to return with armloads of firewood from the piles stacked about the outside of the house, a secondary protection against the searching fingers of winter winds. He built up a supply which brought a satisfied mutter from Raganat. Then he went to study the table map before she wiped it away.

It fitted in part with that Lathia had given them, as he saw when he pulled that scrap out of his wallet. Though the guild mistress had made no mention of this village PanHigh. Now he traced the way from that eastward and was pleased to see that it did not stray so far from Dast.

Nosh still had three Fingers left to find but they could not just go trotting off into nowhere hoping to pick up this mysterious drawing of hers. Not with perhaps another storm on its way. He must use all his persuasion—if he possessed such—to talk her into the sensible plan he himself wanted to follow.

They spent a second night in Raganat's house, though this time Nosh insisted until she was obeyed that the old woman occupy her own cupboard bed while she shared the space before the fire with Kryn. For awhile she lay awake watching the slow dance of the flames which, with the coming of night, had shortened their range. The good smell of the bread they had had still warm for supper was comforting.

Tomorrow they must head out into the wilderness again. Raganat had impressed upon them both some landmarks to follow which would bring them to Pan-High. Her story of the scattering of those carrying the Fingers was a little daunting, but Nosh somehow thought that her suggestion to look northward for the remaining ones might be well worth heeding. After all, there had been that one in the bridal crown of Sofina and she came from a northern people.

Sleep came at last. But this night it was not deep and easy. She suddenly found herself in a strange place where she could see only immediately around her—there was a tabletop on which was a globe full of swirling fire that moved faster and brighter as she watched—but the evil in it was like a fog reaching out to engulf her, and she knew that somewhere this did exist and the danger threatened was very great and waiting for her.

It seemed in that dream that she made a great effort and broke away from that place. Then there was a sweep of white fire behind her as if one of the Fingers moved to set up a barrier between her and what abode there, and she felt safe again.

She did not speak of her dream in the morning—it was too vague. Instead she tried to give Raganat thanks for all they owed her. But the woman brushed aside her words and Kryn's.

"What is owed to travelers, it is paid. And may the Hands close about the two of you, closing off all evil and dark."

She did not stand outside the house to watch them off though Nosh looked back to wave. So they headed once more into the open alone—traveling northeast now as well as Kryn could judge. They must watch carefully for the landmarks they had been given, though here in the open he was now somewhat dubious about such guides.

Chapter 26

THERE WAS VERY LITTLE SPEECH BE-
tween them while they plodded on as the day lengthened. They had passed quickly over the few fields about
the landcroft they had left which had been cleared for
planting. Nosh wondered how Raganat had been able to
accomplish so much work and keep this prairie outpost
going. She had not mentioned any other sharing her
home and there were indeed no indications that anyone
did.

Kryn discovered the first of their landmarks, a cairn
built from rough stone which must have been brought
from some distance and which marked the northeast
boundary of that landcroft.

In addition to their packs each carried generous supplies in another bag, which Raganat had pushed on
them, refusing to listen to their protests.

There was a faint gleam of sun and some of the ice
was puddling away from the grass and from a stand of
what Nosh recognized as half-wild berry bushes angling
outward from the cairn. Luckily there was no cutting
wind from the north to be endured today. In fact it
seemed almost unnaturally still, so one could easily hear

the crunch of ice-brittle grass as they tramped.

It was close to nooning when they caught sight of a rise in the land and sighted the first copses of trees venturing out into the plains. A lightning-blasted tree at the fore of that copse was their second guide point and it was under that they shucked off their packs, dragged away the grass, and brought out their provisions—flat cakes of meal which had been fried after baking so that rich juices and fat had soaked in. Even cold these were a feast for travelers. But they were careful with their drink—taking only sips enough to wash down those crumbling cake bites. Raganat had poured out what was left of the water they had carried with them out of Kasgar and substituted an herb drink which she said was better than water in this cold season.

Nosh gave the zark bits of her cake as there was surely nothing the creature could hunt in this frozen land. While for it to stay too long from cover would send it back into the deep torpor she had seen it in after their battle with the storm.

They tightened again the buckling of their trail bags. Kryn half drew Bringhope as if he feared the cold might freeze it into the scabbard, then proceeded to check belt and bootknife also.

Such preparations made, they took the trail once more. But they were not far along, skirting the copse as they had been told to do, when a wandering shift in a slight wind brought a scent which stirred unhappy memory in both of them, if not the same memory.

"Fire!" Nosh put a name to her memory and nearly came to a full stop. But there was more than just the aroma of burned wood in that odor now growing stronger.

Kryn's hand went up as if he were leading a scouting party and Nosh recognized the signal for a cautionary one. From the open beyond the trees they headed right

into what concealment the leafless growth could supply;
having to go at a much slower pace.

Kryn caught a gleam from beneath a low-spreading
bush and his sword was out and ready. When there came
no move he used the blade for a downward stroke and,
as the branches were pushed aside, they saw a slight
body lying facedown. The wrinkles of a mail shirt much
too large had been divided by a terrible blow, which
must have nearly severed the spine.

Nosh put her hand to her mouth to stifle a little cry.
Though the day was cold, the odor of death was thick
here. Kryn, sword still in one hand, took hold of the
shoulder of the corpse and rolled it over.

From a bruised and bloody face sightless eyes of the
same greyish hue as the sky stared upward. The dead
had only been a boy, far from his full growth. Now that
he had been turned Nosh saw, and it sickened her, that
already scavengers had been at work here.

"No raider—he has not the face marks," Kryn observed. "And that mail shirt was never his."

Nosh forced herself to kneel beside the body, take up
one of the cold hands, though inwardly she shuddered
away from that touch, to turn it over. The palm and
fingers were callused, the nails ragged and blackened.

"He worked in the fields," she said as she replaced
that hand gently on the broken body.

Kryn got to his feet, stood looking about him. "The
ground here—it is too hard. I cannot risk sword or knife
to dig. And there are no stones for cover." He remembered that lone grave for Ewen when he had tried to
keep a friend's body from the wakwolves.

Nosh looked up to where he stood. She realized well
the truth of what he said. Yet in her there was revolt
against going on, leaving this boy to the bone-cracking
mercy of wild things.

In the end they had to make that decision and both

of them were grim of face as they went on even more cautiously. The dead boy must have fled from this direction. Yet their way led so and if they swerved from it, they might well court the danger of becoming fully lost in a wide land where, as they had already had proof of, death waited.

The whiff of burning reached them several times. Kryn had waved Nosh into single file behind him and now he hunched down so that the brush formed a curtain. So they came out on the bank of a stream, hardly more than a brook. The mud of each bank was cast with footprints of both mounts and men, remaining intact after the freezing of the sleet. On the other side of the water there was a very distinct trail leading on—to PanHigh they were now both sure.

Nosh followed Kryn's example of keeping as best she could to cover on the bank. They did not try to cross the stream to the other side, but moved along in the tangle, parallel with that trail across the water.

Now the smell of fire was strong and other odors as well—all an open threat. Time and again Kryn halted, the girl behind him, and listened. But there were no sounds save the sighing of the rising wind.

Then the brush thinned. Kryn dropped his pack and went to hands and knees, having mouthed a whispered order for Nosh to remain where she was. He crawled on into that thinning cover and left Nosh to wait, so tense she felt every wind-set motion of a branch about her was a herald to sudden peril.

Kryn reached the edge of what poor cover the last brush offered. He was looking out at murder and desolation.

There were fields, some showing a faint promise of winter-sown crops. However, those before him were churned and beaten back to formless clay. The fields fanned out from what must once have been a village of some sturdy comfort, for the smoke-blacked walls of the buildings were of stone, quarried and set with good workmanship. It could have been a principal garth of his own land.

Whoever had passed here must have been madmen. Every one of the houses had been sacked and burned. There were fire-ravished barns from which came the stench of meat—the animals which had sheltered therein must have been imprisoned to die.

But this monstrous intaking had not been done within hours, or perhaps even days. There were indeed some faint curls of smoke from the larger barns and one or two of the houses; however, those could have smoldered on, even in spite of the storm, if the brands were hidden.

Nothing stirred—except scavengers—black-winged things which, even this far away, he could hear screaming as they fought to fill their bellies. Slowly, still keeping a last bush between him and the open, Kryn stood up.

To cross the open between him and that village was to put himself into full sight. Still there was no other way to inspect that disaster and he had to be sure that there was no living wounded left to suffer out days.

Marching with Jarth's forces had never brought him to such a scene as this. The outlaws had only one enemy, the church and the Templars. And the Templars did not lay and leave waste—they took slaves and they looted. What they left behind they probably fully intended to use for themselves at a later date.

There was no use in waiting—either he was going down there or he wasn't and somehow he could not turn away if help could be given. Kryn made his choice and began to run, dodging from side to side so that if archers did watch, he would have a chance.

He came to a sliding halt beside the first of the buildings. His stomach twisted; bile arose to scorch his throat.

There was a half-burned door, which, by all the marks, had been smashed in before fire was put to it but— nailed fast to that door . . . Kryn retreated before he was aware he moved at all. NO . . . not even the Templers. . . This was devil's work.

With his head averted he tramped on into the small green about which those houses had clustered. And in the green . . . What he saw there made him turn his head and retch until there was nothing left to spew out. They had amused themselves, those devils. He could not believe that what he looked upon now was not some dire nightmare.

Carrion birds rose, squawked, descended again to their feasting, so full of what they would do that they alighted even within sword's distance of him.

Mad—this was the work of madness—it could be nothing else. Somehow Kryn controlled his gagging and was able to raise his voice:

"Is there someone—someone living?" He did not know why he called. Perhaps it was in some way an answer to the horror which had been wrought here—to let the dead know he came in peace and if he could help he would.

His answer was the screaming of the birds and a snarl as a smaller cousin of the eastern wakwolves backed away into hiding in one of the blasted houses. It was the hardest thing, Kryn thought, that he had ever done, but he made himself pass entirely through the wreckage. Only the dead lay there, man, woman—child. The children! He dared not, after the first few times, look squarely at the children.

He had heard much of the depredations of the outland raiders but never had any horror story such as this been told. They would attack, loot, kill if they were opposed—but they did not settle down for a space and torture and maim—as must have happened here.

Nosh! He remembered the girl. Nosh must not see this. They must circle about the village, since their next guide lay a little beyond it. But no—this was place of the dead—and the two of them could offer nothing even in the way of burial.

He trudged across the fields to where he had emerged from the copse and found her there waiting for him.

"The raiders . . . ?" She had looked at his face, drawn a swift breath, and then asked her half question.

Kryn took a moment to try and control both his sickness and the rage which had been born in him. "No raiders such as I have heard of. These—these who were here were devils—of the Black so dark there is no light! They . . . No, I cannot say it and you must not look, Nosh. Such things as lie there are not for the sight of the sane."

Her hands clasped tight at her breast about the Fingers. She was very pale, seeming to shrink somewhat so that she was even smaller—looking almost childlike—child—no! He could not—would not think of children!

"Where did they go—these devils?" she asked in a thin voice.

"By the tracks along the stream in the direction from which we have come—south."

"Raganat!" she cried. "We must warn . . . "

"Not in her direction—more eastward. And it has been—several days since they left. Before the storm, certainly, from the freezing of the tracks."

"But they could circle back," she persisted. "We must go and warn her."

"Nosh." He had resheathed his sword and now he put his hands on her shoulders. "Listen to me—there—is—nothing to be done that we can do. If we are taken . . . " He shuddered and gulped, refusing to allow the sickness to arise again. Nosh—in the hands of such as those who had amused themselves here . . . !

She searched his face. Then she spoke again:

"There is a way, Kryn. Raganat was of the old blood of those who served Lyr. Perhaps, that being so, the power can be used for her. But Kryn, this is a thing I have not tried often and mostly when I had the will of Dreen to push me on. I know you hate and fear all power. But in spite of yourself you have borne power when you brought the priest's Finger out of the cell. You must have been attuned to it a little or we never could have so easily won through the wards. If you had no reserves within you, I would have been sore racked to do that and draw you.

"Now—I ask of you—put aside your fear and hatred for what I carry. If you will back me, maybe I can reach Raganat with a warning. If we cannot return to her in body with such, we must do it otherwise. Would you leave her to be served as you hint these poor village people were?"

He bit his lip. Power—she believed in it—he dared not. Yet—what she said was the truth. If there was a way of warning that woman who had saved both their lives, then they must take it. He let his hands fall from Nosh's shoulders.

"I cannot believe this can be done but—what you wish of me you shall have." And that was a promise he had never thought to make.

They retreated deeper into the copse and squatted down, their packs as barriers behind them. Nosh opened the bag and shook out the Fingers. There was a rich blaze to them as if they welcomed the daylight and the warmth of their coming alive strengthened her in her belief that this might be done.

Carefully she placed the Finger Raganat had given her at the top of that heap, which was now such a handful as she needed the second hand to steady. She closed her hands as best she could about the bundle.

"Close your eyes," she told Kryn. "Draw into your mind Raganat as you see her clearest in memory. When you have done that clasp your hands about my wrists and hold them so."

He obeyed, a part of him still resentful, yet he was willing to recognize the logic of her attempt and, having seen power in action, he could more than half believe that she might be able to do this. Resolutely he built a mental picture of the Landwife as he had seen her across the table in that time when she had spoken freely of the past.

With a frown line growing ever deeper between her brows, Nosh tried to do the same. Yes—that was Raganat—at least as how she had appeared to the girl. Now . . .

The Fingers were warming. Almost in spite of her closed eyelids, she could catch the fire of their awakening. But she held fast to the picture of Raganat instead.

Then—she leashed her will, making of it a spear—or an archer's well-aimed arrow—sending it out with all her force, all she could draw from the crystals—hoping to reach that goal which lay behind them.

There indeed was Raganat. She was seated behind her table. The picture wavered, Nosh pushed, drawing this time not only her own powers but, through the link of flesh against flesh, on Kryn. She saw the woman of a sudden raise her head as if she had been called. It seemed that her eyes probed in search. Again Nosh sent a surge of force—this time weaving into it all possible warning of danger. Raganat in that strange picture which Nosh mind-saw arose from the table. In her hand a blade of knife shone with firelight. The woman stared ahead as if Nosh in truth saw her. Then she slowly nodded three times before the picture tore into ragged shreds and pain lanced through Nosh's head even as she became aware of other pain in her hands. She opened her eyes. Kryn's face, harsh set, his eyes still closed, hung before her.

The strength had gone from her. Her hands were limp and they seemed filled with blazing crystal coals. Then his eyes snapped open, he loosed his wrist hold, allowing her hands to fall into her lap even as his fell nearly as limp against his knees.

"I think . . . " Nosh moistened dry lips with her tongue. "I think—we did it! She—I saw her. . . . " Or was she only hoping that what she had seen had been an answer?

Kryn shifted farther away from her. He was holding up his hands again, studying his palms as if he expected some of that heat from the crystals had left his own flesh seared.

When he looked back at Nosh he was scowling. "What is done, is done. We have wasted time—best be on our way from here." It was apparent that he did not wish to discuss what had just happened and Nosh accepted that.

"There is a landmark beyond the village. . . . " She accordingly changed the subject.

"But beyond that we have none. The eastern path was known only to the dead. We must find cover and a way raiders will not be riding."

He was on his feet and had pushed through the brush to again stand at the edge of the fields above the ravaged village. The stream ran through this right enough but it was too shallow to allow them cover. He did not know why the thought stayed with him that those who had murdered and burned here might return. It was just that the horror of those deaths weighed heavily.

To the west there appeared to be one of those spaces of shallow rolling hills which showed along their slopes some tree growth—not the thick cloaking of a forest but at least cover. He pointed to that.

"It is the best cover," he justified his choice. But inwardly he was uneasy. Having seen the end of PanHigh, he thought of Dast. Had it also fallen to such a raid? Though the enemy would not have found peaceful villagers who knew little of war there. Lord Jarth would have sentries out in spite of a seemingly peaceful country. And Kryn put the skill of the men with whom he had marched so long above raider tactics.

But he had not the least idea of how to reach Dast from here. It lay to the east but he was sure much farther to the north. If they circled west around the village, they would have to turn east again. Their only hope might then be to strike across country to seek the caravan road, keeping to it as a guide. And that might be an act of true folly.

However, for the present they must get yet farther north and the small hills were their only promise of a halfway-sheltered route.

Nosh offered no opposition. She dared not allow herself to surrender to the fatigue that mind-send had put upon her. But Kryn must be suffering also, for he did not set a fast pace and when they had come among the trees of the first hill unchallenged and unseen save for scavengers he halted and suggested they eat. Nosh chewed ravenously at trail bread but she noted that Kryn did not eat much and what he swallowed he did doggedly, as if he found it hard to force every morsel down his throat.

It took them until the fall of dusk to work their way far enough past the village as to be unable to see at least the fields in which it was set. Then Kryn swung a little eastward and they were guided by the murmur of water to where the stream had made a curve to join them.

A fire was out of the question, Nosh knew. However,

again they hacked away some brush, pulled up masses of fallen leaves and branches. One to carpet their hidey-hole, the other to provide it with a hint of walling. It was small: they were shoulder brushing shoulder inside, but to Nosh that was in itself a source of security.

Kryn decreed that they must go sentry in the night and pushed her into the first period of sleep.

She had no dreams—perhaps her efforts with the crystals had burned out of her for the present that facet of power. But she awoke at once as his hand on her shoulder came to rouse her. She sat with her arms looped around her upbent knees as he huddled down. Nosh felt unusually alert as if there *were* something to be heard.

Before the morning dimmed the stars it came—the pull—the need—each time it was stronger. Back to the ravished village? No—rather up into the tall hills beyond. She reached out and shook Kryn awake without any gentleness of touch. His hand went instantly to weapons.

"No!" She had felt rather than seen that reaction. "Nothing comes—but I must go! I am called again."

He tried to catch at her but she was already on her feet and moving, stopping only a few steps away to shoulder the pack she had dragged with her. Kryn might need landmarks to find his goal; she held her guides in her hands.

Chapter 27

Nosh was almost jerked from her feet as hands caught at her back, threatening her balance.

"Fool!" Kryn's voice near her ear was as strong as a curse. "You cannot go running off in this country, not sure of where you must go!"

Nosh struggled to free herself from his hold, which tightened with her struggles instead of releasing her. She twisted her head around to try to meet him eye to eye.

"These know where I must go!" She held up both hands to protect the bundle of the Fingers. "I tell you—there is a call. Did not such bring us safe through the storm? If we obey, we need have no fear." Somehow she was very sure of that.

"First,"—his hold on her still did not loosen—"we shall eat. And we shall not run wildly without keeping watch." He wondered in that moment if he should not have let her see some of the horror of PanHigh—that might have aroused caution. "If you are called—then that call will not fail—or will it?"

Nosh hesitated. Good sense and the need laid upon her by the Fingers were at war. No, she did not believe

319

she would lose that thread of touch which drew her. However, it was hard to control impatience and choke down the last of the cakes Raganat had supplied. She was still chewing on a handful of dried fruit when she shifted out of Kryn's possible reach and got once more to her feet.

At least this time he made no attempt to stop her but shouldered his pack and checked his weapons as he always did before taking the trail. Here the ground was fairly open and, while they had to thread a way among trees, there was no underbrush to battle.

The urge drew her on and she set a steady pace. This part of the northern reaches of the rolling hills was steeper. Here and there boulders, cloaked now in season-killed lichen and moss, protruded. Nosh had been going steadily uphill when Kryn, who had played rear guard—she was aware that from time to time he had struck east a little from the path which seemed so direct to her—caught up shoulder to shoulder.

His arm thrust suddenly out before her again brought her up short and she turned to look at him angrily.

"What . . . "

"We now follow a trail," he informed her tersely. "Look!"

He was right; there were indentations in the ground, a steady number of them, hollowing the way. Kryn went down on one knee and inspected the tracks, running his fingers into some of those pocking holes.

"Ushur," he stated as one who could not be deceived. "And this and this"—his fingers pointed from one mark to another—"are not more than a few days old." He raised his head and turned it from right to left slowly, as one who would mark every twig or bark of tree trunk near that pattern of footprints. Then he was quickly up and reached out to detach from the twigs of a reaching branch a twist of soft hair, cream white, and so clearly visible. Bringing it to his nose, he sniffed, making a face as he did so—to human noses Ushur shearings were never pleasant.

"Days . . ." he commented.

"Perhaps there were survivors from PanHigh," Nosh said eagerly.

She knew from all the talk of Kasgar merchants she had heard that an Ushur flock was wealth for a village of the plains. The beasts did not breed readily and so all such flocks were limited as to size, and most jealously tended and guarded. She began to wonder at the presence of a well-beaten trail so far from the village. Usually a herd was more closely pastured. However, it was also true that the long-legged creatures had a liking for heights and the rougher kind of forage to be found there. They were often wild from birth and hard to tame even though they were bred in old, well-established herds.

Was there another village somewhere ahead? Perhaps it was toward that she was being drawn—she could not deny that such might be true.

"Let us go . . ." Her impatience could no longer be controlled. "Have you sighted any sign of boots—raiders?"

She owed him that much at least. He could read the trails and she would abide by what he read here.

"No—only Ushur. It could be true that they broke pens and fled on their own from PanHigh." But he did not say that as if he actually believed it. However, though his suspicious watch continued as he walked beside her, whenever that narrow trail gave them room he did not try to stop her.

The call remained steady. Nosh could only believe that with the acquiring of each new Finger the radiance of power grew that much stronger, could reach even farther. Now that she found it so she was willing to slacken

pace, to accede now and then to Kryn's demands for a
chance to examine what lay about them. He made her
pause at every open space and cross such glades at a
zigzag run while he stood guard.

There were more signs that this was accepted pasturage for a herd, though there were few scraps of fluff to
be gathered. To harvest all such would be the task of
the flock keeper, for none of the precious stuff must be
wasted.

The hills continued to make steps upward. Though
they could see the uneven blend of them against the
pale sky before them, these were not the Heights of the
east—in ways a more gentle series of rises.

Another twist in the path and before them was a curve
of rough road in which there were deep ruts fast forged.
It was plain even to Nosh, whose trailwise eyes were far
less able to read the land than Kryn, that at one time
there had been a great many heavy loads transported
along here. It slanted slightly toward the west, but they
must have been paralleling it for some time.

At Kryn's signal she settled down behind some brush,
allowing him to make the necessary survey. He was
shortly back to her.

"No recent travel. Yet we're better away from it."

"I cannot lose the call," she said doggedly. "We need
not walk it in the open but my way leads in that direction."

The frown which Nosh had seen him wear since
morning deepened a fraction.

"Beside it, then—out of sight!" His words had the
sharp emphasis of oaths and she knew that he was angry.

She turned and began to pace along the same general
direction of the road. Within a very short time they had
good evidence that that wider way was not in use. A
mighty tree, storm-blasted, had fallen across to block it
effectively.

Even after that they kept to the side trail. There was a sudden surprising lift in the ground on either side of that road as if it had been carved out of the hills.

Here rocky spurs protruded from the earth. The way they followed narrowed until, whether or no, they were forced down into the road itself and so they passed between two jutting spurs of rock and found themselves looking down into a crater where there were rough blocks of stone, cut from the native rock, waiting to be used. A quarry—perhaps that which had supplied the stone to build PanHigh and which might still be called upon to produce materials for repairs.

At the lowest portion of that gouge into the earth there was a dull sheen of what could only be water. As they sighted that there came a rattle of small stones displaced. Kryn swung, weapon ready, toward that sound, only to reel back, his sword falling out of his hand, a wave of blood spurting from just under the rim of his helm.

With a cry Nosh hurled herself forward and dragged him back or he would have hurtled over the edge of the drop. She shook off her pack and stood, astride of his crumpled body, searching for sight of their attacker.

There came a shrill whistle and the sound of more falling stones heralding some movement behind the upper edge of the cliff to her left. Then only silence.

She waited for what seemed the longest moments she could ever remember until she dropped down beside Kryn. His helm had been turned around when he struck the ground as he fell and now hid most of his face. She edged back, striving to pull him with her along the cut of the road, lacking the strength to hoist him up from that well-worn way.

Then, when she was as far from those cliff tops as she could manage to drag him, she got off his helm. At first she thought he was dead. Blood puddled down his neck and over his shoulder.

Her aids for any hurt were in her pack. But first she must loosen his pack, get it off, stand it up as a pitifully poor shelter. Having somehow accomplished this, Nosh wriggled back to where they had stood when that attack had come, trying to make of herself—fruitlessly, logic told her—as small a target as possible.

In so doing she discovered the missile which had brought Kryn down—a rough pebble. When she picked it up she knew how it had been used—a sling! She herself had had such a weapon for hunting back in the Ryft, learning the skill well because the success of her aim meant the difference between food or hunger and the small prey she sought were flashingly quick.

No raider, she believed, would have used this. She tossed the bloodstained stone aside and went for the pack, crawling back and dragging it to where she had left Kryn.

Using a wad of shredded moss from her supplies, she patted away the blood. By some trick—or surprising skill—the slinger had struck below the cheekbone. However, when Kryn's helm was off and she turned his head gently to rest on her knee she discovered much worse. He must, in his fall, have hit full force against some rock, delivering to the back of his head a blow which even the helm could not ward.

Nosh refused to think of the slinger now. It was far more important to her that Kryn's hurts be tended. She feared that all the healcraft she had learned might not serve. The eye above that cheek blow had begun to swell; she could not even be sure that the bone itself was not broken—she could only clean as best she could the torn and bruised skin, spread the wound with healing salve.

Head wounds were always chancy. Though, when she

felt very gingerly at the back of Kryn's head, she could detect no depression. There was a small smear of blood on her fingers when she withdrew them from the examination but not the flow such as spurted from his face.

Having dealt with his wounds as quickly and as efficiently as she could, Nosh sat back on her heels and looked about. It was close to night. There must be shelter. She saw again the gathering of a cloud mass above. Perhaps even another storm. To be caught in the open by such now would surely mean death for the both of them. But where could they go?

The slinger—perhaps the caretaker of the Ushur herd. Both she and Kryn were armed. Such a one could well believe that they were part of a raider party who had trailed hither. The silent attack on them was so explained. But would there come another? Could that lurker, seeing that there were only two of them—that they were not joined by any others—simply disappear as he might have been trying to do from the first?

Well enough to ease the fear of another attack. But that meant nothing as to shelter—warmth. Kryn must have warmth. Nosh was only too well aware in her tending of the injured among Jarth's men that shock of wounds could bring on danger also.

She sat beside Kryn, one arm over her own pack, the materials of her healing still laid out, her other hand to the Fingers. They were warm—warmth! She could not tell if they would act for another—she could only hope. She pulled the cord holding the bag over her head and settled it on Kryn's chest, bringing both of his hands up to lie on it, anchoring it and them so with a strap from his pack. Then she pulled tightly around him his cloak and spread over it hers.

Danger or not they must have a fire—if the storm would allow them such. But first she must make sure that there was no better spot for them to hole up in.

Once more Nosh ventured back to the quarry. There were gashes in the walls—many of them where stones had been hewn out. But none of them were roofed as might be a cave. And the nearest—Nosh stood measuring the distance with her eyes.

She could not possibly carry Kryn. Yet their best chance might be one of those breaks. There was no . . .

A stone struck the rock at her side, sending a flack of splinter flying.

"I kill—you move I kill!" It was a thin shriek, almost like a scream. And it froze Nosh where she was.

More stones fell but these were not intentionally aimed. It was not quite twilight, though the walls of the quarry were filmed with shadows. There was something moving, leaping from one rock point to another with all the skill of the zark. Then that other landed, a loaded sling weighted and ready, to stand staring directly at her.

Nosh stared at the small figure, one skinny arm protruding from bulky wrappings to swing that sling in threat. This was only a child!

Hair which might earlier have been gathered into a braid or knot at the back of the neck now hung in strings about a small face on which dirt was runneled by marks which could only have been the paths of earlier tears, smeared though they now were.

The eyes fastened on Nosh were bright—with something wild about them. So might a cornered animal have looked, and the fierceness of those matched the snarl which showed teeth.

"I will not hurt . . ." Nosh put up her hands, palm out, in the only gesture of peace she knew. In doing so she must have dislodged the traveling bag of the zark—or else her earlier exertions had already done so. For the creature slid out of its padded nest and clawed its way up to squat on the shoulder cape of her hood.

The small stranger blinked, stepped back. Attention

passed from Nosh for a moment to the brilliantly scaled creature whose neck frill expanded in a wide fan as it chittered seemingly in Nosh's ear.

"I—we mean no harm. . . ." Nosh tried communication again. "We are not the raiders. . . ."

If her guess that this lost child feared those who had smashed PanHigh and believed them to be stragglers from that force, then maybe she could get the point across. She must do something and soon—the wind was rising and Kryn had no chance without shelter.

"Ah-ya-law." The child dropped the sling. Its whole body quivered and it fell to its knees both hands over its eyes as if to hide what confronted it—Nosh and the zark.

The girl recognized no words in that wail. But it might be some countryside plea for mercy. Tentatively she took a step forward and then another. The child cowered closer to the ground but did not try to run.

"I am no enemy," Nosh said slowly. "I am one, like you, who must hide from such as the raiders."

Was she getting through? Could the child understand, or understanding, believe? Now she stood beside the huddled body and stooping with infinite care, she touched that head, drawn down as far against the shoulders as the child could contrive.

The whole small body shuddered under her touch and then slowly the head on which her hand rested moved upward. Nosh dared to brush back the bush of hair and look down directly into those eyes . . . not afire now, but bewildered.

"I am Nosh," she said. "This one is a friend." She touched a finger now to the zark and felt its flickering tongue against her flesh. "We would both be your friend. But . . ."

The wind blew a gust against them and she knew

there was little time for exploring a beginning relationship. She must move and quickly.

"There is another of us—he is hurt. There is a storm coming . . . " Surely a child of a farming village must be as weatherwise as she. "I must find a place to shelter. . . . "

Though how, in the Name of Lyr, she was going to get Kryn moved at all she had no idea.

"I be Hanka." The first normal words came out of the stranger. "There be place—down there—Ushur there now."

She pointed to her right turning her body a fraction. Nosh dared to edge past her and look down. Yes, there was even a trail of sorts along there and she caught a whiff of the strong body odor of the animals which she could not see.

However, to get an unconscious man, one with a head wound which might not allow movement, down there! It was as impossible as if she had been ordered to sink the hills about back to the level of the western prairie land.

"My friend is hurt, he cannot walk," she said. "I do not know how . . . "

The child jumped up. For a moment it stared at her as if still in doubt, and then it whistled, a clear call to cut the wind. Nosh moved back toward the entrance into the quarry. Could she possibly hack off brush, make some form of transport she could drag, could roll Kryn onto? She might cause his death by handling, but night and the coming of this second storm would end him anyway. While she could fight for his life she would.

Only when she returned she found Kryn moving inside the cloak she had bound about him. Struggling weakly against the binding.

As she hurried to him he looked up at her. It was not plain he knew her.

"What . . . " His shoulders heaved and in fear that he might undo all she had tried to aid him, Nosh pinned him down still—to hold him so until . . .

Until what? She looked about, at a loss for what to do first. If Kryn was fully conscious, the worst of her fears faded. It might even be possible to shift him without too much danger.

"What do you do?" His voice was louder, more assured and again he tried to free himself, though her strength was still enough to hold him steady.

"There is a storm coming—we must move."

"My hands—fire—hands . . . "

Was he sliding into delirium? She pulled aside the cloaks to look as his writhing grew stronger. His hands were still as they had been bound to hold the Fingers to breast. They looked odd; she could see the dark marks of bones clearly outlined beneath the flesh—all aglow.

Quickly she loosed the bag and drew it to her, then surveyed his palms. No sign of any burn but he gave a sigh of relief. Had the Fingers served him in their own way? Was he conscious now because of power they could exert on his body? Dreen had never spoken of such healing power. But Lyr had healed—the very life of the Ryft had been of Lyr's giving. Perhaps here had also been manifest a fraction of that life.

A clatter brought her head around. Through the end of the road came that bundled-up child walking between two large Ushur—larger than Nosh had believed such creatures ever grew.

Their herder urged them to where Kryn lay. The child had to reach up to lay hand on their shoulders and Nosh found their long necks brought their heads above her own.

"Bashar and Brit." The child's head went from side to side in that naming. "That one,"—now she nodded at Kryn—"can walk between them and hold on."

Nosh heard an exclamation from the man. He was
indeed striving to lever himself up. It was a suggestion
which seemed wildly impossible but what else could
they do?

Nosh took the weight of Bringhope to her own shoulder, slung on the pack. She pushed the zark back into
the traveling bag in spite of its annoyed chittering.
Somehow she got Kryn to his feet. Part of her marveled
at the amount of strength he seemed to have regained—
Lyr's gift—of that she was sure.

Somehow they made that march. The child leading
the way, Kryn swaying and staggering, but managing to
keep his feet, each arm resting on one of the animals,
which made no complaint. Behind came Nosh with both
their packs, though Kryn's she had to drag rather than
attempt to carry.

They took that path and came before the complete
closing in of the dusk, hastened by the storm clouds,
into where there was indeed a shelter built of quarried
rock, roofed with wooden poles which sagged from rot.

There were six more of the Ushur already crowded
within, the rank scent of their damp coats heavy. But
their herder pushed and urged them to one side, making
a place for Kryn to lie down as he wavered to a collapse,
and leaving Nosh to bring in their packs. Outside they
could hear the first spatter of large raindrops on the
rocks.

Chapter 28

To Nosh's surprise there came a flicker of light and she saw small hands replacing a battered lantern on a shelf which the child must have stood on tiptoe to reach. At first the girl was about to protest and then realized that where they were now was too well shielded to worry about any betraying beams without. While the lashing of the ever-increasing force of the storm would surely send lurkers to any cover they could find, even as it had sent them.

Though the lantern light was limited, Nosh could see more of their shelter. The Ushur had been urged on into the back of the hut and a pole dropped as a bar to keep them there as if this were a regular stabling place. Most of the beasts had already knelt and were chewing cuds from their day's grazing.

It seemed that they were not only to have light but that even greater comfort—a fire—for there was an offset in the wall where the child was busy with sticks, arranging with well-learned skill a crisscrossing for the first lighting. From the mass of body wrapping the fire builder then produced a fire snap—an excellent one

331

from the speed with which sparks answered and the fire crackled into life.

Nosh had folded Kryn's long cloak to give greater covering to the stone of their flooring. Now she rolled and lifted as best she could to get him onto that poor excuse for a bed, using part of his pack to pillow his head and being very careful how she moved that.

He was muttering but she thought he was again sinking into unconsciousness and certainly the few words she had been able to understand made no sense. Drawing her own cloak over him, though it was too scant to cover the length of his body, she went back to exploring their packs. Bringhope she had been glad to lay beside its lord and she rubbed her shoulder where the weight of the weapon had chafed even in the short journey they had made.

Meanwhile the small figure nearer the fire had been busy in turn. A long scarf of heavy weave had been unwound and folded aside. Under that appeared a jerkin which had certainly been cut for a much larger body and that was also discarded. Now a slim figure wearing somewhat wrinkled leggings and an oversized shirt squatted down by discarded clothing and looked steadily at Nosh.

That hair which had been an unruly and half-masking curtain outside was being systematically smoothed with a broken-toothed comb produced from a crevice between two of the wall blocks. Now Nosh saw that the herder was a girl, perhaps only a little older than she herself had been at her meeting with Dreen in the Ryft. Behind this child must now lie such horrors as she had walled from her own memory in those days.

"Hanka," she began a little awkwardly, not knowing just how to approach this young stranger. Though the girl now expertly rebraiding her hair, still glancing at Nosh now and then, did not seem as devastated as she might have expected a refugee from PanHigh to be. "Hanka, are you from the village?"

Perhaps there was a second settlement, one the raiders had not erased. Yet Hanka's first fierce cry had suggested that she knew very well armed strangers were to be feared.

The child did not reply. Instead she pulled out of the shadows beyond the fire a bag woven of the long dried prairie grass and began to take out a series of objects she either placed on the hearth or rejected and set to one side. Those on the hearth were plainly food of a most coarse kind—bread of the darkness of that known to the very poorest, then a limp, furred body of a creature hardly larger than a grain rat.

The bag which was the riding place of the zark bounced against Nosh's hip and she opened the confining twist at the top to allow the creature an exit. For a breath or two it sat on Nosh's knee and then it gave a sudden leap into the full light of the fire where it set claws in Hanka's kill, raking fur and skin away from the dead animal's side.

"No!" Nosh grabbed for the lizard, afraid that the child might attack and be stung.

However, Hanka made no move to defend her meager supplies. There was an arousal of interest now showing in her expression, as if she was more intent on what the zark would do than resentful of its stealing the meat of another hunter.

"What be?" Hanka glanced up.

"It is a zark, a rock lizard," Nosh said, glad that at least this proved to be a subject on which Hanka was willing to communicate.

"Zark," repeated the child. She was watching absorbedly as the zark made swift feasting, plainly relishing the fresh meat it had not tasted for some time and which Nosh was sure its nature craved.

Having seen Hanka bring out provisions, Nosh without any more questions produced her own, as well as some from Kryn's supplies. They had used the last of Raganat's cakes but there were small blocks of dried fruit and meat, well preserved and pounded together into a firm whole before being cut down into bite size. There were also dried roots, which Nosh proceeded to push into the heart of the small fire with the end of a stick, leaving them to roast.

"You..." Hanka, having carefully inspected this array, sat back a little to address Nosh. "Why you come upper pastures. This be storm time—bad for them who don't know it."

For the first time since Kryn had gone down Nosh was jolted back to the matter of the quest. On impulse she brought out the bag of Fingers. There was the upblaze—bright enough to outshine both fire and lantern. She expected some sign of fear from the child. Instead Hanka looked at the bag with that light shining through its sides. Then she pointed with a grimy, nail broken finger.

"What be that?"

Nosh only hesitated for a moment. What harm could there be in showing this child something which she could never have even imagined existed? She drew out the Fingers with care and laid them in a line on the floor just before her knee. They flashed into joyous fire and the warmth they gave off could be felt even though she no longer held them.

"Ahhhhhh!" Perhaps there was a trace of awe in that, but there was something else, Nosh was sure, a surprise—a surprise which was close to delight.

Hanka was on her feet and within two steps she had reached that pole which kept the now drowsing animals from intruding on their own section of the shelter. She reached along the wall there past the barrier and brought

into the light a herder's staff, one which had been worn
by long carrying into a slick grey length. At the very top
of that there blazed an answer to the display before
Nosh.

Once more the child hunkered down by the fire, extending the brilliant spark-laden end of the staff in
Nosh's direction. The girl could see it well, but she already knew that she had found what had drawn her
here. The Finger had been pocketed into the wood and
kept safe there by a timeworn hooping.

"Lyr . . . "

Nosh was startled. How could this waif of a herder
know of the Fingers? She did not try to take the rod
from Hanka; there was a feeling in her, as always, that
this must be offered freely.

"The Hands . . . " She held out her own hands in the
traditional way she had been greeted before. Hanka
nodded vigorously and then poked the rod at Nosh more
energetically. Nosh took that for the permission she had
been waiting for.

She drew her belt knife and, with care, dug at the
hoop—Hanka holding the staff very steady as she
worked. Then the crystal length was free and tinkled
down before Nosh could catch it, landing without harm
on its fellows. While greater heat blazed forth from that
collection.

From behind sounded a moan. Nosh turned. Kryn had
thrown off the top cloak cover. Trembling hands were
going toward his head. Then his eyes opened. Though
he was looking straight at her, Nosh was somehow sure
he did not see her.

"Lyr . . . " Just as Hanka had said that word earlier he
repeated it. Then his hands dropped to his side, but true
sight came back to him and he looked at Nosh with
recognition.

"Power . . . " he said slowly, not with the resentful

accent he had always given to that word. "Power—living power!"

"For the light." She edged about a fraction more to show that flaming line of Fingers.

He turned his head. His eyes closed and then opened. When he spoke again his voice was stronger. "You have won to your goal then, Nosh."

"To this goal," she returned and then spoke to Hanka. "Thanks be to you, little sister. . . ."

"Eylyn said keep safe, wait, one would come. It be promised. Joss keep safe—and then Yankyn. . . . There be dreams." Suddenly her face twisted as if she would cry and then it smoothed again. "Yankyn tell me—be ready—take the small herd to the hills and do not come back. Watch for men—devil men—wear shining coats like you—him,"—she pointed to Kryn. "Have bad paint on faces—no paint on yours.

"Five days ago Yankyn come very early, tried to tell others there be death. They say not season for raiders. He said he would go see—but he give this"—she slipped the staff back and forth through her hold—"to Hanka. I be with Yankyn as helper. Ushur—they like me. So I whistle up Ushur belonging to Yankyn's house and they answer as always though it be early, early— and we come to this place which Yankyn made for storm time in the hills.

"I leave Ushur here in pen and go to lookout tree, climb . . . see . . . see fire . . . big fire and men from far away ride. So I come back—but Ushur must eat—there be no grass packed here. I take them to cup valley where I put this pole for, while it be with them they do not stray far. Then I come back and watch. No one from village . . . In time only you."

"Yankyn was your brother?" asked Nosh gently.

Hanka shook her head. "I be no kin. Woman come village long time ago. Not say who she was or from where she came, I be baby then—she carry in basket on her back. She very sick, die. I be left one kin house, then another, and another. The village people, they say I might be bad luck. So none keep me long. Yankyn— he son of chief family but he found me with Ushur and know they like me. Ushur not like everyone. Sometimes hard to handle if one they do not like tries to herd. So he take me."

"And it was Yankyn who told you about this." Nosh touched the Finger she had taken from the rod.

"He tell me as secret. People laugh—old thing—no meaning anymore. But he tell me—he believed and so he was right!"

She was silent again, running the staff back and forth in that loose hold, her face half-turned from Nosh and away from the crystals, watching, instead, the fire.

"Yankyn say," she began again with an almost sly, swift glance at Nosh, "I handle this." She thumped the rod against her knee. "When we away from village on herd he give to me. Show me different things. Ushur fall among rocks, hurt and bleeding. Rub heal salve with this and Ushur quick well again—no scar to show. In storm, hold this and there is light to see. But people in village do not know—they think only old, old staff, pass from one herder to another—maybe kind of luck thing. Now I know that this be so. For Yankyn said one would come and the herder who had staff then would come to great good luck. So, Lady, you have found me and I found you. And I think that this be a lucky thing."

Nosh nodded slowly. There was something different in this encounter than there had been in her other discoveries. There had been the skeleton in the wood—a delivery from the chances of long ago death, the ornament in Sofina's bridal crown (and looking back it was odd considering the dislike in which the merchant's wife held her that she had allowed that to pass to Nosh at all).

Then the deserted shrine and the aid of the zark and Kryn to bring her what she would have. Kryn's imprisonment with the murdered priest, and then the fact that they had called upon Lathia for help because there was no other way and she yielded them not only a means of escape but also another of the Fingers. Afterward the storm and Raganat, then here. She could not help but believe that indeed fortune was favoring her. But . . .

This meeting . . . Nosh kept thinking back now to that kinless beggar child she had been and whom Dreen had taken and shaped to what she had become. Here was another child like her in a tragic beginning, wanted by no one—save this Yankyn, who seemed to have seen something worth cherishing in her. Even when Kryn regained his full strength, they could not possibly push on leaving Hanka alone in this wilderness.

The raiders out of season—they might well ride back this way. And the Ushur would be bait for any large predator in these hills. No—when they went, they must take Hanka with them, even if it meant a side search for somewhere she could stay. Dast—above all Kryn wanted to return to Dast.

A camp of the outlawed men was hardly the place in which to leave an orphaned child. But in a camp ruled by Lord Jarth, Hanka would certainly be guarded as best they could. Perhaps Kryn was right, they must head east when they could, try to strike the caravan trail and find their way back to Dast. And do so soon, before the heavy storms be followed by the worse weather of winter.

"Eat now." Hanka had turned back to the provisions before the fire. It was true the smell suggested that the tubers Nosh had provided were well roasted and she used another stick to roll them out, tapping each in turn to loosen the charred outer peel.

The zark was stretched before the fire, having tidily pushed the remnants of its own eating to the far side. Its belly down, its forepaws crossing under its chin, its great eyes nearly closed, it lay at ease.

Nosh used her belt knife to cut and scrape the soft interior of one of the tubers onto a flat piece of wood Hanka had brought out of another hiding place in the walls and then went to Kryn. She touched his forehead, taking care to avoid that bloody bruise down one side of his face. His eye on that side was swollen shut but the other came open.

"What..." There was more strength in that word then there had been previously in his voice.

"Lie still," she commanded, even as she had when she had served with Healer Layon among Jarth's injured men. "Eat...."

She shifted the support of his pack behind him but, when she saw that his hands shook as they reached for the bark plate, she drew that back and set about feeding him bite by bite with the morsels balanced on the point of her knife. To her surprise he made no protest.

But she noticed that chewing was hard for him and she guessed that he was in pain from that jaw hit. He tried only one of the meat-and-fruit chunks and then shook his head. However, he drank thirstily from the bottled drink Raganat had pressed upon them.

When he had done it was plain that he had roused into a need to understand what had happened, and Nosh told him swiftly.

"I remember," he said slowly. "There were beasts...."

"They are back there," Nosh nodded toward the other end of the small building. "And this is their herder—Hanka."

Nosh crooked a finger and the girl edged forward into Kryn's line of sight.

"From PanHigh?" he asked.

"Yes. They had a warning—a dream—but the dreamer was not given credit by the others. He went to hunt his proof and did not return." She thought suddenly of that youthful body they had found in the wood, the first warning of what lay ahead—had that been Yankyn?

Now she continued with what Hanka had told her and reached out her hand so that the girl could slide into it the staff now bare of what it had held all these years.

"Thus the call was a true one," Nosh ended. "There need to be found but two more. . . ."

Kryn gave a sigh and settled his head deeper on the improvised pillow. "Please, Talented One, do not begin another hunt—not yet!" To her surprise a smile curved his lips bringing a twitch of pain to follow when that movement lifted the lips on the injured side of his face.

"No, not yet." She had rebagged the Fingers and no longer tried to hang it about her neck. In fact it had become too bulky to be carried so. Instead she dared Kryn's reaction and rested that bundle beside his head, not touching him but close. She expected protest.

He did not try to move his head, but rolled his good eye in that direction.

"I am learning," Nosh told him, "that there is more to the Power of Lyr than Dreen ever told me. Hanka has seen it help injured Ushurs. And . . ." She sat silent for a moment, her hand cupped upon the top of the bag. "I left it with you when I went to find help. You were already in wound shock, which healers fear. . . ."

He blinked. "You have such belief?" There was something almost wistful in his voice.

"I have such a belief," she replied soberly, "that I ask you this night to allow these to remain here. I will swear—by blood if you wish—that they will do you no harm and that perhaps they will work for the good, even of such a determined unbeliever!" Now her tone lightened and she smiled.

"Oh, go and eat, Talented One." Again his own half smile quirked. "Leave your treasures where you will; I shall not deny you that."

Hanka had already withdrawn into the midst of the Ushurs in their own portion. When Nosh held the lantern high in search of her she saw that the child was between the warm, thick-fleeced bodies of two of the beasts, her head pillowed on the forequarters of one. It was plain that she had sheltered and slept so before.

Nosh put out the lantern, fearing that they might run out of oil. And added some long-burning pieces of gnarled root lengths to the fire. Then she lay down beside Kryn, her cloak wrapped about her, the bag of Fingers agleam between them. A moment later she felt the zark nudge its way into the folds of her cloak. Nosh closed her eyes with a sigh and heard the fury of the storm without. Perhaps the herders had made a weathertight shelter of this abandoned quarry building, and none of the rain or wind could reach within.

Chapter 29

KRYN WAS AWAKENED BY A FEARSOME noise sending him jerking upward, still half-entangled with the cloak about him. Then a thrust of pain in his head added to his grogginess and he fell back. The noise continued to trumpet, feeding the pain bursting in his skull as if it would break the very bones apart and he groaned, fighting his hands free to hold to his head. There was an addition to the pain as his left hand touched his cheek.

"Suuuueeewww! Suuueeww!" Now a shrill young voice was added to the clamor.

Kryn discovered that he could not open one eye but that the other was staring up into a gloom which suggested that he was under cover of some kind. But the pain fed by that clamor made it hard to call upon any memory.

"It is the Ushurs." Nosh's thin face came into sight over him. "They want out to the pasturage. If I aid— can you move out of the way?"

One part of his bemused mind thought *Ushurs?* but enough of the rest responded so that with Nosh beside him and lending her strength to what little he seemed to have Kryn was able to turn his body, moving closer to what appeared to be a very rough wall.

"Suuuueewee, Bashar!" piped that shrill voice. A huge four-legged form moved through the gloom, something much smaller scrambling along beside it. However, that was just the first of the line of beasts to pass. Whiffs of their rank body odor made him gag a little. Then they were all gone and the space around him was clear enough to see a small fire. But there was another source of light and that not far from his limp hand. He looked at it a long moment sluggishly and recognized it. Then as if a barrier forced to let all memory out Kryn knew where he was at last.

"They go to graze?" he said. "But what . . . "

Nosh, having watched him closely for a short time, was now raiding their supply bags. "Hanka tells me that the Ushur have a sentry system of their own. She takes them now to a small valley near here where they can graze. But the provender there will not last for long and we shall have to find other pasturage. . . . "

Kryn had recovered enough to catch out of those last words some with an unexpected meaning. "*We* have to find pasturage. Why, what are these beasts to us. The child, yes, she must go with us. . . . "

"To Dast, yes; Hanka must not be left here. But she will not leave her beasts behind—no herder would. And can you say that those who are at Dast will not welcome such wealth on the hoof? Not for meat—but for what the fleeces will bring come spring shearing. At Dast there will be caravans and traders coming along to deal with."

"Dast!" The importance of that word as spoken by her caught him. "But—then you *will* go to Dast?"

She gave a small smile. "If we can find the road, armsman. To simply travel eastward in hope is not quite enough. But I am willing to head for Dast—unless"—

she faced him squarely—"the call comes again."

"May fortune forbid!" he said in answer to that, and now she laughed outright.

"Alas, Kryn, you have indeed been led down strange roads since you agreed, oh, how reluctantly, to show me a certain shrine in Kasgar. But now I lend my will to yours and say Dast. However, not until you are able to walk a steady pace again."

The storm, which had lasted nearly a day and only cleared just before evening of the one after they had reached the shelter, seemed now to have driven even the clouds from the sky.

Outside the door of the shelter—which was a crazy-shaped erection cobbled out of knobby saplings and smeared with clay—the sun was shining brightly even though it was on its downward path. There was a softness in the air, which provided a welcome freshness after the smell of the animals, one which made one think of spring rather than winter.

Sometimes there were remissions of the cold northern blasts which happened this way, and it would seem they were being blessed by one.

Kryn, finding the ache in his head lessened somewhat after Nosh had renewed the dressings, passing, he noted, the salved wadding over the Finger bag before she bandaged them in place, was sitting up facing the door which the girl propped open. He had found Bring-hope and was inspecting the blade, fingerbreadth by fingerbreadth. Its grey surface showed no nick or scratch but he would have felt the better for a chance to give it a good honing in some well-equipped arms room.

Having finished busying herself with the repacking of various small boxes, Nosh came to sit cross-legged beside him. She had taken off the hood which so often shadowed her face and drew in deep breaths of the clean air.

"How far is the caravan road, I wonder?"

Kryn slid Bringhope back in its sheath. "There is no way of telling—we have no merchant's trail measure. I only know it lies to the east and we will cross it sooner or later if we head in that direction."

Though his headache faded away, and, in the three days which followed, he assayed walking (stumbling on the first tries), Kryn himself had to admit that he was not yet ready to take a trail through unknown territory which might present greater risks than they could yet imagine.

He spent time in the early evenings after Hanka had brought back her flock questioning the child about the surrounding territory. However, her knowledge was limited since where they now sheltered was a sanctuary discovered two seasons ago by Yankyn—one to be used only in a time of great need.

Nosh and Hanka for the time being must serve as his eyes and ears. The younger girl brought Nosh back to that tree from which she had sighted the death of PanHigh. A prolonged inspection of that distant blot on the landscape assured them that there had been no return of anyone—raider or possible refugee.

Impatience ate at Kryn. It was his old fault and he knew and recognized it for what it was. He would accomplish nothing if he pried them out of this shelter and went unto the unknown when he could not do a full day's trailing without ending in shaking weakness.

On the fifth morning after he had awakened here Hanka did not have the Ushurs out with the coming of light, though the animals were stirring in their section of the building and their ear-shattering cries grew ever stronger. The herd girl crouched beside Nosh and spoke into the older girl's ear. Nosh appeared to be considering some point and then she nodded.

Now she came to Kryn. "The pasturage is used up;

the Ushurs must be taken elsewhere to graze. Hanka will lead them—I have told her eastward—though that is strange country for them and her. We must follow with the gear, for it may be that they will seek so far they cannot return by nightfall."

Kryn met that news with a grimace. This was like jumping from a height with one's eyes tightly closed and, only too likely, rocks waiting below. Yet he had known that it would come sooner or later. At least he could keep his feet now and most of their supplies had been so depleted that he would be able to shoulder a pack. Though he noted that when Nosh (after the animals and Hanka had left) sorted their own belongings into two piles, hers was the larger.

At his instant protest she shook her head.

"You bear Bringhope, and do not try to tell me that this is not a major weight, for I bore it myself to this place. In the Ryft I learned early the bearing of burdens—and—you must be free for defending us if there is need. Since we have no archers . . ." She showed him a piece of skin, slipped a stone into the wider center portion of it, and gave it a testing twirl. "In the Ryft I used such many times over, it is a skill which returns upon practice. You cannot deny its effectiveness . . ."

His hand went to the still painful bruise on his face. "That I cannot."

They had eaten well that morning in preparation for the setting forth and Nosh had provided Hanka with a portion to carry with her. Now she gave a last look about this place. Bare and abandoned as it had been, it had given them refuge, and she sighed a little at leaving.

They came out on the old quarry road, able here in the width of the trace to walk side by side. The ruts were crumbled and overtraveled by the Ushur and certainly the trail left by Hanka and her herd was an easy one to follow. By mid morning they had caught up to the herd itself. The hoofprints they had followed turned out of the quarry road just as the sun appeared well up in the sky, pointing through a break in the brush wall.

A short time after they had made that turn they came again into an opening which was knee-high in autumn-dried grass and there the Ushur were grazing avidly while a dark blot perched half up the slope unwound thin arms to beckon them on.

"They slow us too much." Kryn stared resentfully at the beasts tearing the dried grass from its roots with rasping tongues. "We cannot limit our pace to theirs and hope to reach Dast before the real cold strikes. If they must graze their way . . . "

"They must," Nosh returned. "If you are so pushed to reach Dast—strike for it by yourself in the morning, armsman." She was tired, not so much from the tramping she had done this day but with the battle within her. What Kryn stated was the truth—the beasts were a drag upon them, perhaps a near-impossible one. But—there was Hanka. And when she looked at the small girl she saw always beside her that other child wayfarer who had been taken out of the road of death by the Grace of Lyr. No, she could not leave Hanka and she knew that the herd child would not be separated from her beasts.

Kryn got up and walked a little away. Every line of his lean body was a warning of his own frustration. Perhaps what she had suggested in her weariness would be the best answer after all. Let him go on to Dast—he could always there raise his companions and backtrail to find Hanka and her—once he got there.

She was about to enlarge upon that suggestion when he returned. His battered face was grim. "Lady,"—his voice had taken on the formal note of the high blood kin—"I am sworn to Lord Jarth. So far I have failed him. But also he was in some way bound to your Priestess Dreen. He would well have furthered any work she asked of him. Therefore—in this matter I am answered. We stay together and hope that the north winds will hold off yet a while." He said no more but turned a little aside and sat staring out over the small valley. However, Nosh was sure that he saw neither the beasts nor that field, but that, for this moment, his gaze was truly turned inward.

She made a business of picking over some of a fall of gravel, searching out stones which would fit in her sling. To think of what might lie before them—weighing this disaster against that—would win them nothing. They must face each moment as it came.

They spent the night at the edge of the pasture. There was no chance of building a fire. But Nosh drew Hanka under the edge of her own cloak and between their two bodies and Kryn she put out again the bag of crystals, which were once more aglow. She knew that he intended to go on sentry even though Hanka had assured them both that the Ushur would give instant warning of any intruder.

The Ushur must have awakened before dawn as, when Kryn opened his eyes (he had lapsed into slumber at last, and found himself, as he jerked awake, to have his outflung hand nearly touching the crystal bag) he could hear the tearing of grass.

Hanka rolled away from Nosh and sat up in the limited grey light. She cocked her head a little to one side as if the crackling of that chewing had a meaning for her. Then she looked to Kryn.

"Bashar knows. They will trail today, armsman. The Ushur are not, as other beasts, unknowing."

By the time they themselves had eaten sparingly of what they had left the sunrise painted the sky ahead and then Hanka gave that shrill cry. The tallest of the grazing beasts raised its head, grunted and began to move, its fellows somewhat reluctantly following.

Near sunset they had covered a goodly distance for any so hampered, Kryn believed. The Ushurs had taken to grabbing mouthfuls of any grass they passed, chewing as they plodded on. Hanka kept her place beside the leader of the herd, her small arm stretched up to loop across the creature's shoulder.

They did not find another meadow that night but they were on the edge of open land again and here the Ushur fed with a wariness unusual to Kryn's knowledge, for they did not push out into the open as would varges or mounts, rather slipped along the edge of cover, feeding in hurried mouthfuls. It was almost, he thought, as if Hanka had in some measure managed to communicate to her charges the need for constant movement and wariness.

When they established their own halting place the Ushur came drifting back, kneeling, blowing, chewing their cuds, closing in like a wall of dirty and twig-entangled fleece about the travelers.

Kryn could not play sentry for the night—not and travel again tomorrow. He had lagged this afternoon. So he must accept Hanka's reassurance about the herd—that they would stand watch.

For three days they worked their way along, heading northeast, reluctant to venture into the open. For their good fortune the weather continued to hold. The lead Ushur found a spring at which not only the herd but they drank and were able to fill their water bottles again. Hanka brought down three grass hens with her sling skill and Nosh matched her by securing a small lorshog they had routed out of a clay wallow beyond the spring. It was lean and spare compared to the domesticated sort but it made excellent eating.

Twice Nosh noted herbs which she uprooted, making them chew the tart leaves. Their hunger was never truly satisfied but they had enough to keep going. At each halt Nosh loosed the zark, which had its own hunting plans and brought back grubs it had dug out of the loose soil of the open—perhaps it more than the other of its traveling companions went well fed.

At last Kryn decided they could no longer drift north. They must find the caravan road. That they might also find trouble along it could not be denied. But once with that for a guide they could be sure of coming to Dast.

So they struck out across the open. At least the land was not entirely flat, but, like that around PanHigh, it lay in long low rolls and they kept from ridgetops as much as they could.

From time to time Kryn scouted ahead—his impatience could not always be controlled—but when at last he came through a low gap and saw before him the unmistakable scarring of the land which was the road he sought, he felt a fraction of his self-assumed burden lift.

Now they were able to keep to a better pace. Even the Ushur seemed imbued with the idea that they must keep going and returned to their habit of feeding as they moved. How far they still might be from Dast, Kryn had no way of judging, but he constantly watched ahead for the rise of those buildings he had helped to repair at a time which now seemed long past.

At least, from this section of the road, he could see those dark humps against the sky which marked the Heights—the beginning of the border of his own homeland.

Somehow it was more and more difficult to remember the keep of Qunion. His boyhood there was a long-ago thing which had little connection with the here and now. When he tried to picture faces around the feast board in the great hall they had a tendency to waver and fade. He was the only free man of the kin left. And he was part sworn to a would-be priestess, a waif child, and a herd of Ushur. For the first time in days he smiled at the thought. At least smiling no longer triggered pain from the bruise and he could see as well out of one eye as the other.

Yes, there was something about the sight of the Heights which seemed to bring strength. Surely they could not be far. . . . And at that moment his gaze fell from the promise of the distant rises to something else— Dast! Surely that was Dast! In spite of the herd, in spite of everything, there was Dast!

On impulse he threw back his head and sounded the flute-bird call which was used by the scouts in open country. If he knew Jarth, there were those out to sweep goodly distances beyond Dast. It might be very good sense to let any such know that their own strange company were friends.

There was no answer; no one arose out of hiding to wave them on, and Kryn felt, first disappointment, and then the rise of fear. He would never forget PanHigh and what he had looked upon there. Had Dast, too, been overwhelmed by some such band of madmen?

His hand went up in a signal for a halt as he found himself sniffing the air for those throat-tightening stenches which the wind had carried from the village. No . . . no scent. How long would it take that to die away?

Then he was aware of a tug at his belt, demanding attention. He looked down into Hanka's sun-browned face.

"Bashar does not scent. There is no one ahead."

He blinked, hardly understanding. When he did his fear was bitter in his mouth. Dast—fallen . . .

"They are dead. . . ." he said more to himself than to Hanka or to Nosh who had moved up on his other side.

"No dead." Hanka's voice somehow pierced that cloud of fear-born rage which now walled him in. "No one."

How could the beast know? That was stupid—to listen to such a fancy from a child. There was only one way of learning—he must go on. But alone—Nosh—the child—if Dast had been served like the village, he did not want them to see.

"Stay!" He barked that as such an imperative order that even the lead Ushur seemed to understand, for it turned its head in his direction, watching him with its large brown eyes.

Kryn shook off his pack and cloak. If there were any lurking there to finish off travelers, he must have already been sighted. So—he drew Bringhope. The sun of late afternoon caught the grey length of the blade, seemed almost to awaken sparks from the metal. And, sword ready, Kryn strode forward at a swift pace to make sure of the death of Dast.

The comrades would have made their last stand within those walls, which had only been partly started when he had left and now were more than shoulder-high, connecting the six huts one to another. There had even been a gate mounted since he left, and that swung open. He came up to it as if he walked through a nightmare—where were the bodies?

He was now within that gate, staring from one to another of the huts. Doors were closed but not burned away. There were no horrors to be faced.

"Tuver?" He raised that shout. "Hasper!" The names seemed to echo back to him. Somehow he got to the nearest hut, pushed at the door. It swung open under his hand. In the dim light he could see the bunks they had constructed. However, all were bare—no blankets, no dressed hide coverings.

He raced now across the small open space about the well, heading toward the hut where he had last spoken with Jarth. Again emptiness, stripped. They were gone . . . but somehow, he was sure, by their own will and in order. There had been no fighting here.

Completely bemused by the mystery Kryn went back to the gate and out so he knew he could be seen by those who were only an irregular blot down the length of the road. They were certainly closer than he had left them, but that did not matter now. As if Bringhope was a battle signal flag Kryn raised it over his head and waved them on.

He did not wait to see them enter, he was too driven by his need to know what happened here. Jarth—certainly he should begin with that one of the houses which had served as their headquarters. Again he crossed the well surround to enter. There was a table, rudely assembled from the wreckage of one of Danus's wagons. And on it . . .

Kryn, for the first time in his life, dropped his sword to the ground and forgot that he had held it as he pushed up to the table and stared down at a square of hide folded several times over and pinned to the wood underneath by a weapon he knew—had last seen in Jarth's own belt—a weapon perhaps meant to identify him who had left it here past all question. Kryn pulled out the dagger and flipped open the skin, dust sifting from it.

Chapter 30

THE USHUR WERE MILLING ABOUT IN
the open about the well and some were hanging their
heads over the edge of the well curb crying out their
demands. Nosh dropped the packs she had brought
along by a wall far away from the tramping animals.

"Lady—they be thirsty!" Hanka bore down upon her.

The well windlass was indeed a stiff one to be turned,
even when one was strong. And where was Kryn? He
had disappeared from sight before they entered the sagging gate. However, Hanka's importunities were not to
be denied. The older girl went to the worn handles and
began to turn, her efforts raising a greater clamor from
the animals.

A brimming bucket reached the brim of the well and
Hanka darted in, to turn its contents into the dusty
trough made to water caravan beasts. It took three buck-
ets to satisfy the small herder and her charges and by
that time, Kryn did appear from the building which had
been Lord Jarth's, in his hand a roll of writing skin.

"Where are they?" Nosh asked. The desertion of
what had seemed an excellent winter post was a mystery
to her. There certainly had not been any attack here—

there were no signs of such. Yet all those she had known for weeks of over mountain travel and in the refuge before that were gone as if they had never been.

"Lord Jarth . . ." Kryn held the roll up at its opened length and she could see it was printed with symbols but those she could sight the best were strange to her, not the formal old writing of the books Dreen had so treasured.

"Lord Jarth has used trail code," Kryn began again. "This is the message he left:

"The Dark threatens us in new ways. There have been five rathhawks brought down and all wore amulets which we destroyed. A band of Kolossians from the high north hills say that raiders have wiped out two of their villages in sudden attacks, their coming somehow hidden by a power even the Kolossians could not sense until too late.

"Our supplies are limited. Of those bought in Kasgar only two of the carrier beasts reached us. Hansel was wounded by an arrow out of the night. Also there are dreams—and those have so assaulted even such unbelievers as Tuver as to make them fear sleep and deny themselves rest.

"We have no true Dreamer but each man who dreams flees some great Dark in his sleep. This may be a device to twist us out of Dast as one twists a pond limpet from its shell. But then again—it may be a warning.

"Here we have few mounts and those the worser beasts Danus offered us. We cannot try to reach Kasgar now. But for seasons the Heights have sheltered us and to those we would return. The dangers there we understand; what strange things may come upon us here we cannot guess.

"We leave scout trail markings. If you live to reach here, Hold Heir Kryn, follow us—for it is my true belief that this is the best choice we can make."

"Dreams and rathhawks." Nosh shivered. "They were Dark beset here. And they are men better used to the highlands. Perhaps the Dark omens misfired— warning instead to save or they might have been swept away by such as took PanHigh, were the raiders' band large enough."

Kryn refolded the message and pushed it under his belt.

"Lord Jarth is not one to be frightened by shadows." He stated that defiantly, as if in answer to some argument he would not admit. "Surely this was strong dreaming. . . . But,"—hands on hips he now looked about him—"those houses I have looked into are swept bare. They took with them all supplies. And their arms. . . ." He bit his lip and turned his head a little from her.

Nosh answered him swiftly. "What could you, a lone stranger, have done to secure him those in Kasgar where the guild lords seemed enmeshed in some intrigue? Were we not caught in the fringes of such ourselves and through no mistakes of our own? Lord Jarth must have learned from the men who returned that there was this difficulty."

Kryn was staring now at the ground, stirring the dust of the square with the much-worn toe of his trail boot. She could guess something of his feeling of failure. But now he must be pushed on into action which would keep him from dwelling on that—she was sure Jarth had not counted failure on his part at all.

"We follow them." Not a question but a statement. She reached for the clay cup which hung from the windlass and dipped out of the last bucket the last of the water there. "Drink," she ordered now. "You have eaten road dust long enough to be one with these snorters, even as Hanka and I are."

She used her elbow to make an Ushur, busy gulping water, give her more room.

Kryn drank. Once he had handed back the cup he looked to Jarth's headquarters. "Perhaps..." He did not finish but strode purposefully toward the door through which he had so shortly come. Nosh followed him to see that he gave a determined shove to the heavy table, sending it a half length away from where it had stood.

He was down on his knees now, running his fingers across the splintering, ancient wood of the flooring. With an exclamation he pulled Jarth's dagger out of his belt and set it to a place his fingers now pressed, and bore weight upon it. Three of the planks, creaking and cracking, were slowly forced up and Kryn speedily grabbed into the cavity below. He brought out what could only be a bow well wrapped, below it was a quiver of arrows, and then there were three bags, plump near to bursting. Sitting back on his heel Kryn surveyed this treasure.

"Rolf's work." He had freed the bow from its wrapping and caressed it with his fingers. "None better in the company." He laid the bow beside him and tossed Jarth's knife into the air, catching it skillfully. "And I wondered why he sacrificed you for a pointer!"

"A bow, arrows." Nosh nodded but now she was more interested in the bags. "What else?"

He untied the cord of the largest and shook out an array of small tools. There was a hone stone to reedge a blade, two needles for leather work, a snap-spark with a new in-stone. Below those, a roll of well-cured skin for the mending of trail boots and clothing if need be.

The other two bags were as useful. One Nosh seized upon as soon as the scents from it arose at its opening. This was Layon's, surely, well selected and beyond price. The other held a packet of gritty salt and a roll of smoked laster meat. Small provender but when taken from what must be the company's own shrunken supplies a gift beyond measure. It was plain that Lord Jarth had had confidence in Kryn. Enough that he not only expected the eventual arrival of his subordinate but also that the Hold Heir would follow the trail he promised would be set.

As Kryn reexamined all the finds for the second time, Nosh became aware of a small hand touching her shoulder, and she looked up at Hanka.

"This be a shadow place," the child said slowly, glancing back at the door as if she feared that she might be overheard. "We do not stay?"

"We do not," Kryn answered decisively. "There will be a trail set, cunningly as only Jarth's scouts can contrive. Soon we shall take it. But . . ." Suddenly a look of uncertainty crossed his face as he regarded Hanka. "We shall be heading into the Heights. Those are no ranges for beasts such as yours. There is forage in the land hereabouts, loose your herd leader and they will survive—take them up and . . ."

Hanka crossed in front of Nosh to face him, a red tinge rising beneath the brown of her dusty cheeks. She planted her small, callused hands on her hips, her lower lip pushed out a fraction and then she said:

"What know you of Ushurs, armsman? How many have you herded and tended? Where I go Bashar goes, and the rest follow. There may be little forage up there"—she jerked her head in what might be the general direction of the lowering Heights—"but when there be lean times they live on their back fat. How else can they winter? Also they can find food when you think there is none. You go, the Lady goes, Hanka goes, and so the Ushurs."

So set she was on that, that nothing Kryn could add in the way of protest might prevail. Nosh thought she knew what was raising his anger and feeding his frustra-

tion. A scout could skim the countryside unseen, but
what effective scout ever took a concealed trail with a
woman, a child, and eight large beasts in his wake? Almost she could have smiled but she did not—she was
sure that what seemed to her to have a measure of hu-
mor would mean the opposite to Kryn.

Even though they were agreed to set out on the trail,
there were preparations to be made. Nosh took the too-
large and shapeless outer garments Hanka had been
wearing, and, with her knife, cut them closer in size to
the small girl's wiry body. All scraps were carefully saved
and Hanka, herself, produced a rough bag of tufts of
Ushur wool gathered from bushes where the herd had
wandered.

Kryn made repairs on their own boots and now he
cobbled some for Hanka, using smooth bark for the
outer parts and lining that with the fleece bits, anchoring
it all with odd pieces of leather from the store Jarth had
left.

They overhauled also what they had in their packs,
Nosh making a special place for the supplies left by
Layon together with those she already carried. Hanka
came to her when she was sorting out those and squatted
down to watch. Nosh found herself telling the little girl
the use of each she handled even as Dreen had done
for her long ago—or it seemed long ago.

At the suggestion of Hanka they checked the hooves
of each Ushur, a liberty the animals certainly would not
have allowed had not their herder soothed them into it.
And from her ointments Nosh spared one which Hanka
vigorously rubbed along the hocks of two of the younger
beasts where there were signs of some bruising.

Hanka took the Ushur to pasture each day, setting up
her herder's staff, around which, almost as if they were
penned, the beasts grazed, while she used her sling to
good purpose, returning each time with something for

the pot—as well as meat which could be smoked for
their journey. Kryn warned her against the rathhawks,
ordering her to be at watch for them at all times. However, the sky remained bare of any such spies. Perhaps
with the leaving of the band Dast was no longer considered worth spying upon.

Nosh turned her old skill to account and wove, with
the toughest and longest grasses Hanka could bring her,
bags which could be slung over the backs of the Ushur,
so that the animals might carry with them some of their
own fodder for times when there might be none about
the trail.

The three of them worked from dawn to twilight and
then slumped about the fireplace in Jarth's house, which
they had chosen for their shelter. Nosh rubbed some of
her cream into fingers cramped and cut during her labor.
While Kryn went over his weapons each night as if he
feared rust had sprung upon them during the day.

Last of all Nosh, from the first night they spent under
that roof, performed what came to be a short ritual. She
spread out a small grass mat on the hearth (the band had
left a supply of wood behind them) in front of the
flames. On this she laid the Fingers in the proper order
by which they would be fitted to the hands. Only two
to find and then . . . the knowledge had grown on her,
perhaps dream-borne and strengthened each night—she
would return to the Ryft. Though there was danger waiting—looming like the deepest of shadows—from which
her thoughts flinched now but in the end must be faced.

She left the crystals so, there in the open, for the night
and she was careful to place herself in sleep so that her
head was close to them. What strength might be so
drawn from Lyr by that she did not know, only that this
was a thing she must do. Kryn watched her each night,
but he rolled in his hide blankets apart. This troubled
her faintly. She had begun to believe that the Hold Heir

had lost his dislike for power. Now it seemed to be rising once more in him.

They spent a ten-day at Dast, preparing in every way they could to face the eastern wilderness. In all those days they might have been alone in a deserted world except for the animals and a few birds, none of them a rathhawk threat.

Also, mercifully, they had been free of storms. However, each day brought colder winds. Ice formed at night in the water trough so that it must be broken in the morning before the Ushur could drink. So far there had been no snow, and Nosh was trailwise enough to know that they must be on their way before that arrived.

Thus she knew relief when on the eve of that tenth day Kryn spoke of starting their trek in the morning. So they arose in the grey light of the dawn, moving in the same order as they had when coming—Kryn to the fore, Nosh a step or so behind—then Hanka, her hand resting on Bashar's shoulder, her staff swinging free in the other hand. Each of the beasts carried somewhat unwieldy burdens of grass-filled bags, but they made no complaint when they were so loaded.

The small party thrust overland from Dast toward the Heights that loomed ever darker and higher as they went. The sun spear topped those and then was like a lantern signaling them on into the beginning of the woodlands. Kryn quickened his pace but Nosh held with the rest. He was seeking the signs for their trail, she knew—and she only hoped that it would be such a one as the Ushur could travel.

But the band had had varges and a few mounts Danus had left as well as the ones from Kasgar. Varges alone, unwieldy as they were in body, could easily leave a trail which could be picked up at once by anyone with scouting knowledge. Had the band separated into two sections for traveling?

She looked about her as she went, trying to see if she could remember any of this way from their labored journey to Dast before. Then she had traveled with the wounded and walked, ready to help with any stretcher slung between varges which might be in danger.

They camped that night in woodland not far from a spring at which the Ushur could be watered. The animals nosed about under the loom of the trees, and Bashar suddenly hooted, alerting not only Hanka but the other two humans, drawing his herd swiftly to him.

His long neck was bent as his yellow teeth caught and stripped a mass of fungi from the trunk of a long-fallen tree. Nosh's protest was drowned in a crow of delight from Hanka.

"Bashar be a good hunter! Rufwell...Rufwell!" With her staff she knocked loose the crinkle-edged growths, tossing them to the crowding animals, who caught them avidly even out of the air. Hanka made sure that all had received a share of the bounty, rapping one pushing yearling male over the nose when he strove to shove a small sister away from the feast.

Nosh found a fragment she raised to her nose and then in violent reflex action hurled from her. Such a stench she could not believe could be connected with any possible food.

"Not for us." Hanka had ceased her efforts to harvest the last of that weird crop. "But for Ushur—yes—oh, yes. Yankyn always bought it dried from winter market. I have never seen it growing before."

Now she turned as if to start out away from them in hunt for more. Nosh caught at her.

"Not in the dark," the older girl said firmly. "If this thing is like others of its species, it grows on rotted wood and in the dark you cannot hunt for such."

Hanka looked mutinous for a moment and then shrugged. Kryn had placed their packs against that same downed tree, erecting a frail barrier, and they settled within that small suggestion of shelter, hearing the Ushur chewing cud and beginning to lie down for the night about them. Kryn made no move to build a fire and Nosh accepted his trail wisdom that they should do without. At least gathered thus closely together they could keep warm after a fashion. While she did not spread out the crystals in show, she put down the bag of them as she might have lit the missing fire in their midst.

In the morning the weather changed at last. There was a heavy fog-mist through which they must go at a near-crawling pace so that Kryn would lose none of the signs which had been left. Certainly the varges had not come this way, but it was the path Jarth had marked.

The fog thickened. Nosh was striving to catch sight of Kryn, who had vanished into it, when her whole body jerked as if a blow had landed on the right side of her head, spinning her off-balance. So intense was that call she could not have denied it unless she had been bound to one of the trees about them.

She threw herself in that direction, paying no attention to a shouted question from Hanka, uncaring. All which moved her was need. That need she had felt before but this time so intensified that it swallowed up her thinking mind. Something—some small part of her still not so leashed—kept her from crashing directly into trees, but she was bruised and battered as she wavered from one to the next, unheeding of any barriers.

Twice she slipped in the leaf mold and fought once more to her feet, her hands held out before her now as if she were blind and sought a way she could not see.

Nosh was dimly aware of some noise behind but that had no meaning for her now, gripped as she was by this consuming need to find. . . .

The mist wreathed heavy here. Tall trees were only

half-seen even as she was near enough to brush against their rough bark. Underfoot the thick mulch of leaves was as slippery as a glare of ice. Nosh began to whimper as she went. Never before had it been so hard to answer this call.

"Lyr—oh, Lyr!" Her call for help came out in a panting which distorted the words. "Lyr—why . . ."

Out of the mist ahead arose a dark wall and under her feet the very ground gave way, so that she fell forward. One of her outstretched hands struck on a sharp point which pierced the flesh, and then her head slammed into a nest of roots embedded in mucky earth.

But that which had drawn her here was not yet finished with her. She must somehow pull herself up, past that heavy mass of dank-smelling earth and interwoven roots. Her hand blazed pain as she made it close about the thickest of those protruding roots. With the aid of that she dragged herself up, tears of pain cutting through the smears of mud and leaf mold on her cheeks.

Somehow, she was never sure just how she was able to accomplish it, Nosh dragged herself up and over that obstruction to discover that she now straddled the trunk of a fallen tree, a giant of its kind. Her nails cut into the soggy bark to give her aid as she pulled herself along that trunk.

Then—before her a familiar blaze cut through the mist.

"Lyr!" She mouthed that name and fought along the last space of trunk between that beacon and her outstretched hand.

It had been well hidden either by accident or design, so wedged-in that bark had near completely grown over it before the death of the tree. Nosh steadied herself on the trunk. With her bloody right hand she drew her dagger out of her belt sheath, and, holding hard with her left hand to this slippery perch—made doubly so by the condensation of the mist on the decaying bark—she stabbed at the spongy wood around that flame of light. Then it was free and she dared loosen her hold on the trunk to snatch it to safety as she resheathed her knife.

However, those movements had made her lose her precarious balance and she slid to the left, falling from the trunk to the forest floor with enough force as to drive the breath out of her. Nosh lay there on her side, weighted down by her pack, holding the Finger in a death-tight grip, sobbing with reaction.

So Kryn found her. He tore off her pack and held her against him as he knelt beside the tree.

With a childlike smile Nosh held out her hand. "See?" she asked softly.

His hold on her tightened. "Stupid . . . lack brain— you might have been lost—fallen—killed here! All for a piece of glass! Never—never must you go racing off so again!" The hot anger in his voice was biting.

"It was the call. . . ." she tried to explain. "So strong—so very strong! I could not stand against it—not even long enough to say where I must go."

"Well, you have it. Can you stand? We are far from the trail." He was brusque and harsh, dropping his hold on her to get to his feet and reach down and jerk her up beside him.

There was a crashing not too far away. Kryn bit off a hot word. "Those doubled-damned beasts have followed us. And one of them is likely to break a leg in this mess."

Chapter 31

LUCKILY KRYN PROVED TO BE A FALSE prophet; none of the Ushurs suffered hurt from their climbing up into the full grip of the forest slopes. Without speaking to Nosh, Kryn approached the leader of the herd and secured the girl's pack on top of the grass load it already carried.

Nosh watched the beasts mill around by the long length of the dead tree, bending their necks so they could sniff at the decaying bark, apparently on the hunt for the fungi they esteemed so highly. She felt odd, as if somehow there was more than just the now-tattered mist between her and the rest. One more—only one and then—what would be demanded of her?

She was woefully tired and it was hard to get to her feet. Kryn, having made sure there had been no hurt of any of the Ushur, came to her side at last.

"There is the track that they used for the varges—I came upon it just as you left the trail. Perhaps it would be better now for us to follow that."

His words meant little or nothing. They could take any trail that he pleased to set them on. But—both of her hands gripped the bag of Fingers, softly glowing—

but if the call came again, she must take the path that chose, whether Kryn cared or not.

They came back along the way the Finger had drawn her and found a cut marked heavily with hoofprints; Kryn estimated that the freshest of the tracks was nearly a ten-day old. But varge pace was limited. They would find only perhaps a trio of herders with the ponderous beasts; the rest of the band would have followed the upper way at a much swifter pace.

Unfortunately the varges also needed pasturage and what little there had been was cropped to the very roots. At sunrise of the second day Hanka made her protest.

"There be no graze—even the patches where it once was are smaller and farther apart. The Ushur must take another trail." She spoke with authority, slamming the butt of her herd goad into the ground to add emphasis.

Kryn frowned. To trail the animals off again, seek to find that other marked way—it would lose time and perhaps even at the worst lose them, too. He had no true knowledge of this side of the Heights. But Hanka was speaking the truth. If they wasted the grass loads to feed her herd on this level, what would they have left when the road—such as it was—climbed into bare rock and perhaps even the first of the snowfalls?

Nosh resumed her pack on the second day. That odd feeling of being apart still clung, though not so obtrusively. As Kryn now she looked upslope and wondered where above that other trail might lie. The Ushur were surefooted beasts; they had proved that earlier, and perhaps would be as able to walk the same narrow way there as the men who had gone before.

So they changed course and left the well-marked trail behind them, climbing with Kryn not only in the lead but vanishing now and then on a circular ranging ahead to pick up any lead he could.

Nosh found herself stumbling more often. The bag of

Fingers was now so large that she must cradle it in the crook of her arm. She was aware not only of an ever-present glow but thought, though she did not say so aloud, that the crystals gave off a low hum, like the contented purr of a tothcat well fed and stretched before a warm fire. She waited—how long would it be before that other call came? The one which would again take over her mind and body to race in answer?

Kryn found his trace before nightfall. They made their comfortless camp near that half-hidden mark. Nosh had dropped down as they halted, too tired to loose her pack for the moment. She thought suddenly of the comforts of Danus's house—the only time she had known such living. Of the warm water for washing. Not the plunging of one's hands and face in some cold spring rill, rather the washing of one's whole aching body. Of soft soap to be gathered up by the handful and used without stint. Of fresh clothes to be worn.

They had washed and rough-dried what they could at Dast before they had left but now her clothing clung, clammy with her own sweat, to her itching skin. She scrubbed her hand across her face and felt loosened dirt roll at the touch.

Nosh wondered why cleanliness had suddenly come to haunt her. In the Ryft their water had been very scarce, drawn—for the river was suspect—from a rock pool, and she had never thought of that as being a deprivation. Surely her weeks with Danus had not weakened her so much.

Wearily she went to sleep that night, Hanka curled against her under the same cloak, her last thought one of longing to be done with this eternal traveling, free in a world which would welcome and not sternly forbid.

That this new thought of hers was shared she learned the next day when Kryn stood holding his helm in one hand. He had not been able to wear it until they had left Dast well behind because of his head wound. Now he lifted his face up to the wind which tugged at the fringe of hair plastered to his begrimed forehead.

"It would be good to find a stream large enough to bathe in," he commented. "But those do not lie in the Heights. Well, one takes what Fortune hands and there is no use to speak against it. We have been favored in many ways."

The packs of dried grass on the Ushurs' backs were being emptied one by one, while the creatures grew gaunt under their shaggy fleece. Yet none of them strayed afar. They might bellow a protest at the morning's setting out but still they followed Bashar faithfully even as he followed Hanka.

Nosh cut off a portion of her own cloak and used it to cobble the boots they had improvised for Hanka. The best faring of their company now appeared to be the zark, who rode at ease, sometimes on Nosh's shoulder clinging to the pack, and sometimes even leaping to Bashar's, the Ushur making no protest.

But when it grew chill with the wind, the lizard sought the inner part of its bag again, perhaps passing into a hibernation-like sleep.

It was on the fifth day after they had left the varge road—though Nosh found it difficult now to keep track of any one day, each was so like the next—that Bashar suddenly lifted his head to the farthest extent of his long neck and blatted forth a sound which Nosh had never heard any of the beasts voice before. He pressed forward, lowered his head to butt at Hanka, not pushing her ahead but to the left.

The little girl obeyed that rough command and swung away from the direction in which they had been traveling. Kryn was too far ahead to stop her, and Nosh, slowed all morning by that feeling of otherness which wore on her more and more, made no attempt to. Instead, as if she were one of the herd, she followed along, hearing the cry of "Stop" from Kryn but paying no heed.

Bashar apparently knew where he would go and he was not about to be kept from his goal. While in Nosh grew a feeling—not the wide open call which had sent her plunging into the unknown before—but one that this was right and meant to be. Kryn caught up with her and tried to pass to get to Hanka and Bashar, but she roused to greater effort than she had made for several days and caught at him, setting her weight to slow him down.

"Let go!" He raised his hand as if to push her away.

Nosh numbly shook her head. His eyes narrowed. "Have those blasted crystals gotten to you again? Or to these beasts?"

"We go . . . it is meant. . . . " Yet this was not the pull she had waited for. A trick of the dark? She looked to the crystals. They were blazing through the bag. No— she did not think that a shadow illusion had trailed across her mind.

Kryn was staring at her, but he had not shaken her hold away and now he matched steps with her.

"You feel—too!" That was no question she spoke, rather an assertion.

He scowled. "I do not know what I feel, what tricks you are playing, Talented One. But yes, I feel something—ahead."

"And it is not of the Dark." She was also sure about that.

He looked from her to the beasts pushing along about them, their rocking gait ever increasing and then his attention came back to her.

"I understand nothing. . . . "

The gloom of the trees ahead was broken by rays of open sunlight and Nosh realized that their travel in these woods had always been shielded from that—they had been too sheltered by the towering trees. Bashar and Hanka, the girl clinging now to his shoulder fleece, broke out into the sun and Nosh and Kryn followed.

Nosh drew a deep breath of wonderment. These were the first days of the cold season and they were in the Heights. Yet they came into a warmth like that of midsummer. Here grass grew tall and green and was bejeweled by gems of flowers.

It was a valley shaped almost like a bowl. The rocky sides of it, save at this place where they had entered, were free of any of the luxury of the growth that floored it.

Yet that rock was not dull grey as in the Ryft—the curtain of a place of death. Rather it was broken in irregular patches with sparks of fire, as many in color as the flowers below. These caught the sun and sent forth its rays again—seemingly in rainbows of light.

The bowl valley was centered with a lake. Across the surface of that were spirals and drifting clouds of mist which almost appeared to take on a faint sheen of true rainbow. Nosh dropped where she stood, content for the moment to simply sit and look upon this glory.

Down to the water of that lake padded the Ushurs, not quite so fast now that they seemed to reach that which they sought. Bashar waded out into the water, dragging Hanka with him. Then he shook himself vigorously and the little girl was sitting down with wavelets lapping at her chin.

"It—it be warm!" Her thin little cry reached Nosh but she could not rouse herself as yet to go on. The strangeness of what Hanka reported was all a part of the Power which rested here. A mountain lake needs must be as chill as the winds which ruffled it. Here were warm winds and summer sun. . . .

Kryn had left her, striding along beside the last of the Ushurs, a strange look on his face as if he were a man who had strayed by chance into an illusion woven by a mage. Yet Nosh was certain this was no illusion.

At the side of that lake Kryn dropped his pack. Deliberately he was also ridding himself of sword, of belt, then of mail shirt, of dark worn leggings, near-holed boots, dropping each discard as if he had no mind for it again. Hanka had stood up, the water rising to her middle. Now she waded back a little to the shore and pulled and tugged at her garments until she was a small, lean body bare to wind and water. Then joyously she splashed back to where Kryn was wading steadily forward, his own body as bare as hers, that strange look still holding.

Nosh arose to her feet and went down the slope toward the water. She was warm—she was hot—she was tired of the smell of too-well-worn clothing. The Ushurs had ventured even farther out so they were hidden from sight now and then by that drifting mist.

Her pack and hooded cloak she dropped before she set aside with more care the zark's bag and that with the Fingers. But the rest covering her she tore at with impatient fingers.

"In—come in!" Hanka urged her. Kryn had reached a point where the water lapped at his shoulder. Hanka was plunging up and down between them and now she was splashing toward the shore. Without thought Nosh stepped out of her last grimy, body-clinging garment, and then Hanka's hand reached hers, dragging her forward.

"Come!"

Water which felt as warm and caressing as the finest materials Danus had had to show rose about her. Hanka dragged her on, the water rising higher and higher. Nosh blundered through a tendril of mist and realized it must be steam born in this miracle of a lake.

"Yes—come!" Kryn had ducked down under the water and then arose again, his dark hair plastered to his head, a strand of it hiding most of the scar on his cheek. He flung wide both of his arms. Looking upon him Nosh realized for the first time just how young he was. He looked like a boy who had taken absence from all responsibilities for the day.

She moved on, Hanka paddling ahead now. The bottom under her feet had the smoothness of sand. There was no gravel such as she would expect to find here. Then Kryn's hand caught hers.

"Under with you!"

She laughed and tried to resist. He stumbled back and went under, coming up sputtering and spitting water. Then he dipped again and rose again, one hand high, holding in it a brilliant flash of pure light.

"Stepped on it. . . . " His voice died away and he was staring at what he held. "But . . . I am . . . you are the searcher!" he said to Nosh, almost in accusation.

"Lyr chooses, and this is her own domain!" she said slowly, and knew that what she said was true. Somewhere, in another place and time, a pattern had taken a new turn; and what would come of this they could not yet tell. But it was designed to serve the purpose of Power.

More of that man shell he had been forced into so early was cracking. When he looked from her to what he held and then back again, Nosh could see there was here someone different from the Kryn she knew—but— not less dear!

She gasped at the way that thought had ended. This was new and strange and must be studied over privately before she answered to any quick impulse.

"I am no priest!"

That was a sharp protest.

"Not only priests served Lyr." Again she found words which came from somewhere. "*She* had her armsmen, also. Many of them died in the Dark Days."

He waded to her side, holding out the Finger. "Where do you go, what do you do now?" he asked slowly.

"That too will be shown to us. Kryn,"—she did not accept the Finger he held out, not yet, instead she placed her hand on his shoulder—"Kryn, learn for yourself—as I did. It will be shown to you also."

He waded past her to the shore and placed the Finger on the bag holding its fellows. Instantly there resounded over the water a sweet, heart-raising melody such as might be wrung from crystal wind-swayed against crystal.

The Ushurs ceased their honking cries as that music echoed back from the bowl walls. Nosh found tears on her cheeks. She wanted to sing as the crystals but such a talent was not given her.

Kryn stood looking down at the bag and the last gem rod he had laid across it. She could not see his face now but his whole body was tense, as if he faced some trial of strength. Then he turned abruptly and went back to his discarded gear. From its scabbard he drew Bringhope and he held it high into the bright sun of this strange pocket valley.

No, she could not be mistaken. Along the cold grey of that blade there was a sparking of light, as if in its forbidding substance there were also crystals deep-buried. Kryn must have seen so also, for he gave a hoarse cry and went to his knees, the sword dipping into the earth as he let his arm fall, chance setting the blade fast there so it stood upright. Kryn's hands closed about the steel beneath the pommel, his head bowed until the knob on the hilt touched the skin above and between his eyes.

The music of the crystals had died away. Kryn continued to kneel, his eyes closed from what Nosh saw as she waded ashore. How she understood she did not know, but Kryn was shaking away the last of the old shell, becoming a new one who would never be a stranger.

At last he raised his hands from their achingly tight grip. He ran his fingers down the blade as one touches something long known and highly cherished.

"No longer kin blade," he said in a low voice which also harbored a break.

"No less for that," Nosh said as softly. She wanted to touch those slightly bowed shoulders, give comfort for what he must feel as a loss.

He did not turn his head but she knew that when he spoke it was to her.

"Your Lady of Power has me. For what that may gain her...." There was a trace of his old anger in that.

"Wait and see, armsman pledged. The Lady is a good Lord."

To her surprise he laughed. "Well, all the heroics are not going to do me out of one pleasure. Hanka is making better use of time than we...."

He gestured to the lake. The little girl was in the shallows, apparently far more intent on using handsful of the soft sand to scrub herself clean than on what her elders were doing.

Nosh echoed his laugh. She felt light and free of spirit, more so than she ever had in her life before. Stepping back into the lake she knelt in shoulder-high water and began to echo Hanka's firm use of the sand. It was not long before she heard Kryn likewise splashing nearby.

The Ushurs finally had their fill of the water and were lumbering ashore, to fall upon the grass, making up for the lean days behind them.

Nosh washed her hair in many dippings, combing the wet strands with her fingers. It had been growing and was now well below shoulder line. She tried to dry it by tossing the sodden locks in the air, then fell to combing it with the wooden comb Lathia had put in her pack.

What was the guild mistress doing now? What happened in Kasgar when that blight struck those who had meddled with the Dark? Suddenly some of her childish pleasure in being clean, in being warm, was troubled. The Dark did not give up easily. What would face Lyr's chosen now?

Having washed their bodies, they turned to their clothing and spread that out under the sun. It was afternoon now but there was no need to move on this night. Nosh was reluctant to leave the bowl. She need not be ready ever again for that pull to take her as it would.

Hanka, refusing to put on her damp clothing, burrowed into the grass and brought out handsful of small sweet berries, which lay like sun eyes against her flesh. They savored these and for the while sat in contented silence, glad to live only for the moment about them. This renewing—for Nosh thought of it as such—might be needed later on. But she would not think of that now.

They ate also of their rations and, at twilight, bedded down in the grass beside the lake, the Ushurs peaceful at a little distance. Hanka went early to sleep but for a space Nosh looked to the stars overhead. It had been a long time since she had lain thus able to see them shine like faraway crystals. She did not know whether Kryn slept, but at last her eyes closed.

She was in the shrine of Lyr, facing again that pedestal on which were the wrists of the broken hands. Over those swayed menacingly that dark globe, now shot with sullen fires which appeared to swell and swirl against the outer limits of the ill-omened thing as if they would burst forth and put an end to all of the Light.

As the dream held her there Nosh knew what was to

be done as if Dreen herself stood patiently instructing her, as the priestess had so many times in the past. If—if only Dreen would be there to meet her!

Always the globe appeared to bulge the larger. Did its skin really thin with every surge of the light so that it would break—now? No, its power would not be summoned until she stood here in truth. Now there was another stirring, as against the crystal-studded wall of the cave, a hunched shadow twisted this way and that, like a wakwolf sniffing for prey. Still it did not turn in her direction and Nosh knew that for the moment she could not be detected.

So vivid was her dream that when she awoke she found her hands moving even as she had been instructed, though what they held now was only the lightsome air of the valley. But the drive was back—she had that to do which must be done and time was running out.

Even as she sat up she saw Kryn busy putting together his pack.

"We go to the Ryft," she said.

"You have dreamed? Well, so have I. Yes, it is your death valley for us, Nosh. But what of her?" He looked to Hanka.

"We could leave her here. . . ." Surely the child and her animals would be safe in this happy place.

"You need us. . . ." Hanka appeared out of nowhere to stand stolidly before Nosh, her hands on her hips in her usual pose when making a point. "We also go."

"Did you dream?" Nosh was surprised.

Hanka smiled. "Maybe." She had a teasing note in her voice. "Just wait and see."

Chapter 32

THE DULL GREY, DEAD WORLD OF THE
Ryft stretched before them. As usual, though it was full
day, the clouds curtained out the sun and a sullen wind
whistled among the pinnacles of rock which guarded the
way from the west. Strangely enough, it had been the
Ushur who had scouted out that road. On the third day
after they had headed east from that place of renewal
Bashar had shouldered his way to the fore, trumpeted a
call which rounded up his followers.

Nosh had seen no traces of any pathway. Kryn had
been wary, unwilling to allow a beast to choose for them.
Still, some of the bemusement they had felt in the bowl
still held, enough that he only grumbled and did not try
to force them in another direction.

They came indeed to that shallow river which Nosh
remembered of old. It was here that she and Dreen had
met with Jarth and his men. Across that stream they
traveled on into a land which grew ever more stark and
forbidding. Where life failed . . .

Not all life! From where it rode on Bashar's bag of
grass harvested in the valley, the zark reared high, its
forepaws reaching for the neck column of its mount.

Now its throat swelled, its frill arose in ever growing color, and it shrilled forth a sound quite unlike its usual click-clocking.

There was movement among the rocks and Nosh, from her former experience at seeing the ability of the creatures to hide in plain sight because their skins were the color of Ryft walls, detected more of his kind—or else of a cousinage to him, since none of these sported the brilliant scales he wore. They scuttled among the rocks and continued to parallel the march of the party, clicking among themselves sometimes in almost frantic choruses.

Now the travelers had come near the end of the trail. The Ushurs, far more surefooted than one might judge, had found passage up slopes Nosh on her own would have hesitated to dare. And so at last they stood—the Ryft wide before them.

Nosh made a slow survey and then was sure she was right. . . . "To the north."

Once more the old drive closed about her, shrilling somewhere inside her head—hurry—hurry. . . . She scrambled down to take the lead, Kryn close behind, and, like a string, the Ushurs and Hanka following.

Perhaps it was memory, perhaps it was something else which set Nosh weaving a way among the upstanding rocks. Could she actually remember the trail Dreen had taken? Whether or not she did, she was certain this path was going to take her where she would go.

As they neared the hidden way to the shrine she unloosed her pack and set it down against a tower of stone. Kryn followed her lead. Hanka turned toward the Ushurs. Her herd staff waved out. Bashar sounded an answer and when the three went on the animals remained behind, gathered into a close knot as with their teeth they tore at the nets of grass on each other's backs. While the zark leaped to a rock top and there performed one of its frantic dances as the dull-colored others which had followed it closed in.

This way—and this—and this. . . . With each step she took Nosh was certain that she was right. The grey of the day was fast darkening into night. But time was short—that she knew. They must move now.

As she found the entrance Dreen had taken them through she began to be aware that the bag of Fingers which she held tight to her breast was humming, humming and throbbing as if each of those spears of crystal had a strange alien life of its own.

There was no need for any torch or lantern here, the crystals' glory shone before her, and when they turned at last into the shrine all those gems embedded in the walls came to life, their glitter seeming to project rainbows into the air, even as the mists of the bowl had done.

However, that light was not supreme. Above the pedestal hung the globe. Now it did resemble a bag heavy with some foul liquid, while the dried-blood colors which coiled within its walls were in a mad race.

Remembrance of her dream drew Nosh's eyes beyond that whirl of foulness to where the misshapen shadow had crouched. Yes, there was indeed a splotch of thicker dark there, and it appeared to waver and weave as if it strove to reach the pedestal and what hung above it.

Kryn moved before her, blade bared in his hold. Along those well-honed edges ran the myriad tiny sparks which they had seen first appear in the bowl. He was ready for attack; perhaps in *his* dream there had been instructions also.

Nosh gave to him in that moment her full trust. She knew what she had to do and she could not be turned from it by shadows. There was a tug at her sleeve; Hanka stood beside her, her small face intent, her gaze fastened on the blazing bag of the Fingers. She kept that hold on Nosh, moving step by step forward with the older girl.

She must not think of what she had done, turned her back on Kryn and what was fighting its way to life in the shadow. This was *Her* battlefield.

Hanka held out her two hands and Nosh, as if Dreen stood by her shoulder telling her that this was what must be done, put into that hold the bag. It fell open as she gave a jerk to the restraining cord.

Nosh reached in and took up the first Finger. She must strain up on tiptoe to place it where it had once been based. But as crystal touched crystal it adhered instantly as if there had never been a break.

There was whiff of such foulness as made her cough. The bag was surely looming closer, dipping far-ther.... Nosh fitted the second Finger to the waiting Hand. Now there was a distant howling, a sound which echoed in the head, and she knew, without turning to see, that the skulking shadow was drawing to it sub-stance from some evil place.

She forced herself to ignore what might be gaining a true form behind her. Trust—she could only trust Kryn and keep to what must be done. Again foulness like smoke bit at her lungs so she breathed shallowly, pant-ing.

Weight—weight seemed to be closing down upon her as if the bag above could project its heaviness toward her hands and arms. It was harder and harder to reach so ... Forget—put out of mind anything but what she did here. Another Finger in place—a full Hand!

There was a deafening roar of rage which might have issued directly from the bag. The thing was dipping far now, plainly threatening, striving to elongate itself to touch her hands as she worked. For a third time that vile stench was puffed into her face and she stood coughing, her eyes streaming.

Even the Fingers, which had blazed so high, were losing their glow now—seemed but broken shards of crystal without meaning. Before her eyes the Hands whirled dizzily, grew large until they might encircle her, and then shrank to a size her watering eyes could hardly distinguish. Surely she could not fit these large slivers to such tiny stumps.

Nosh's hands shook but she made contact and another Finger raised toward the bulging bag. But something—perhaps that bag—was drawing her strength out of her. She must race against time—for given time, that would have her helpless.

Another Finger. No angry bellow this time—no—rather a cold wave of ice-rage—of rage beyond the experience of any true human. And the very menace of it was like slave chains bound about her arms.

She had forgotten Kryn—she could only hold one thought in her pounding head—that she must do this—and this—and this. She was gasping for breath, the pressure against her was like a giant hand crushing her in. Nosh planted the last Finger in place.

She reeled back as that bag-globe broke. A red, viscous flow poured from it downward toward the Hands. From above that, also centered in the globe, shot something else—a wave of black flame—if flame could be black.

Nosh sank to the rough floor of wide-strewn crystals. Darkness was gathering in. It might be that one strip of the wall gem glow was quenched, and then another and another. . . .

She felt a small body crouched shivering beside her. Hanka. Dull memory supplied that. But she did not look down or try to soothe the fear she felt fan from that body.

Stiffly Nosh turned her head to follow that line of

black flame. That it went to feed the shadow she knew without being told.

The shadow was thickening, filling out, producing a body which took on solid being. Nosh watched that growth from shadow to man. She was so spent she could not have raised hand in any defense.

But there was another waiting. Even though the crystals about them were losing their life-lights, there was a line of fire traced in the gathering murk, outlining a blade. She could no longer see clearly the man who held it, who stood fast to confront what came out of the very depths of evil power.

That Black One stood completely revealed to them now—and he was smiling gently as one smiles at children who have done something stupid and must now face punishment.

There was a strangeness still about him—a kind of wavering when one looked at him closely. At times he appeared shrunken, aged beyond telling, and then he steadied and was once more a man of middle life, strong and vigorous.

"Fools, such young fools. . . . " His voice was soft, almost caressing. "Yet I am in your debt. You have returned into my control that which was lost—far spread—concealed by minor mage trick from my finding. You have brought what I most desire. Behold now what will become of the Hands!"

Nosh, under the pressure of that strong will, looked up to the pedestal. That viscid substance she had seen flow from the bag was still poised, not yet dripping, across the Hands. But they were dim—blighted.

Her gaze swung back to the Dark One. He was raising a hand, negligently as one would to brush aside a fly.

In that moment Kryn moved. Bringhope blazed brighter and it swung in a circle, not at the man who was set upon his magic, but on something else, that only half-visible cord which united that appearance with the globe. Down cut a blade which was now afire with green and blue, and the gold of open sunlight.

Before the man could change the aim of his spell the blade sliced through that cord.

There was a flash from the pedestal. Upward speared clean white fire from the tip of each Finger. The viscid mass was gone, the fair light was returning.

"Noooooo...." The man born from shadow was moving his hands in frenzied gestures. Even as he did so the flesh shrank under the skin, he somehow drew in upon himself. From a man of middle years he aged before their eyes to an ancient whose toothless mouth still spewed forth useless black curses. Then that hairless head fell forward on a bony chest and the whole of him crumpled to the rock. Within the huddle of a silken, rune-patterned robe there was only the push of bones, until those also vanished from sight into ashes.

But from the Hands of Lyr there struck upward flames which grew and reached, and in place of the foulness there was a taste of spring-warmed air. And those Finger flames sought out an upwards roof chanel which had once been theirs and rose swiftly up and out—up and out.

Kryn's hand on her brought Nosh out of the exultation that sight had wrought in her. Under his urging she got to her feet. Hanka, still holding to her, was brought up with her.

But Kryn's sword lay across the foot of the pedestal and up and down the blade ran lights which might have been small stars taken from the sky. He made no move to take it up again.

"Yes." Nosh's exhaustion was forgotten, she was again under a spell which must be obeyed. "Let us out—out into Lyr's land."

Thus they went and the clouds overhead were breaking apart, so that for the first time in seasons beyond reckoning the sun shone full upon the land. Hanka loosed her hold on Nosh now and ran forward. To her came the Ushur. She twisted her staff free from the bindings of Bashar's burden and again she ran, the beasts trumpeting as if they paraded for victory behind her. Then she reached a patch of free ground away from the stone pinnacles and there she used all her small strength to stab the butt of the rod into that waiting soil.

Along its length there was a shimmering. There uncurled from the trunk twigs which grew into branches, branches putting out buds. This was not the season of cold and death but of renewal and life.

Then, as if they were summoned, the three of them climbed to a tall look-out rock above the old highway. Above there was the rich warmth of the sun.

Below, the grey dark soil showed the beginning of a green carpet. Beyond, the sluggish river moved with a cleansing current.

Even as they watched in awe, tips of new saplings burst from charred stumps in the long-since ravaged orchards and woodlands.

Breezes brought fragrance now. There were flower gems opening brightly in the new-risen grass—showing even as they had in the growth of the bowl.

The Ushurs threw up their heads and galloped, chasing one another as if they were again kids. There came a clicking and a small rainbow form leaped through the air, caught hold on Nosh's tunic, and then scrambled into the crook of her arm. On the rocks below, the zarks that had answered the call of this one climbed and performed their graceful leaps of spring mating.

Following came another sound—a thud of shod hooves, a creak of wheels, the snorting of varges at a steady pull. Nosh turned her head, and her sight seemed to become lengthened so she could see every detail of those travelers, though they were still only on the border of the Ryft.

A clumsy farm wagon, old, battered, pulled by two varges, gaunt animals, that now flung up their heads to sniff the air and then increased their lumber to a near trot. Their heads wavered from side to side as if they wished to be free of their yoke to taste of the spring green.

By the side of the team strode a girl on the border of womanhood, varge prod in hand. But her head also turned wonderingly right and left. Behind her skipped another, still half child.

In the cart was a woman cushioned as best could be done by unwieldy bundles. She cherished against her a baby lately born.

While behind came four men. Their bony mounts, no better off than the half-starved varges, were showing as much eagerness as the draft animals for this miraculous forage. Two of the men trudged by the sides of their near-floundered steeds, the others rode. Alike in pattern they were, with weathered faces, eyes which bore shadows of unhappy dreams. Now they stared about them in almost childish awe.

Nosh raised her right hand. Radiance leaped from her fingers—flew arrow straight toward the travelers.

"The Ryft lives!" she cried, and that truly, for there were tears on her cheeks, "hither comes the needed seeding—the new heritage will begin."

"And what of you?" Kryn asked quietly, a small, strange note in his voice.

That far-sight which had served her so magically for an instant or two faded. She could no longer see those travelers clearly but they were coming on.

"Lyr is to be served." She answered Kryn's question almost absently.

Hands which were hard, nearly flesh-bruising with their grip, closed about her upper arms as he drew her back into a half embrace.

"Priestess, is that then your choice?"

Her own hands moved swiftly up to close tightly, near demandingly as his had done over his flesh and bone.

"Lyr welcomes closeness—love—of mind and body. She would have fruitfulness for all. There is nothing to harm here now. This is no Temple. And as once I told you, even of old, Lyr had her armsmen and they were as dear to her as her priests and priestesses."

His grip on her changed, she loosed hers and allowed herself to be turned to face him. Again her power-blessed hands moved up, setting palms to his gaunt cheeks. It was she who drew his head down so that their lips met—first in awkward tentativeness, and then in the same glowing warmth as filled the land and sky.

It was said in later seasons that in the outer world chaos began to yield to order, dark to light, for Raskan no longer meddled in the affairs of men. The Light of Lyr spread outward from the Ryft, touched a woman here, a man there, even a child, so that those so called had much to give and gave it gladly.

Lord Jarth, who had risen to the High King's throne, rode south one season to stand in the Shrine below those Living Hands. He bowed his head and gave thanks and from that time forward his House prospered and his many feats were long remembered.

He wore when he returned home a cloak woven so finely of Ushur fleece that it seemed to have the quality of the rarest western silks. It was plain of any decoration or broidery and was but fastened at the throat with a faceted ball of crystal which some said glowed in the dark. Plain though it was, he made it his robe of state and wore it for the rest of his long life.

But that was all of the outer world. The Ryft had its own children and those were highly beloved and gifted by Lyr.